EVERYTHING YOU DREAM IS *Real*

AF075312

Also by Lisa de Nikolits

The Hungry Mirror
West of Wawa
A Glittering Chaos
The Witchdoctor's Bones
Between the Cracks She Fell
The Nearly Girl
No Fury Like That
Rotten Peaches
The Occult Persuasion and the Anarchist's Solution
The Rage Room

Praise for Everything You Dream Is Real

"What I love about reading Lisa de Nikolits's books is that every time I start one, I never know what I'm going to get! Each new book is a totally different, quirky, fun, wild ride and I love that. The hilarity mixed with the darkness makes for such a weird, delicious combination! Seriously, there is not a dull moment!"

—**WENDY BARROWS**, Wall-to-Wall Books

"Witty and elegant, dorky and weird: *Everything You Dream Is Real* is a fantastically riveting book, loaded with strange delights, scary caprices, and an infinity of comic turns and twists."

—**LYNN CROSBIE**, author of *Chicken* and *Where Did You Sleep Last Night*

"This is one rollicking ride! In her stunning follow up to *The Rage Room*, Lisa de Nikolits punches the gas right from the starting line and never stops, taking us through a mind-bending series of twists and turns that will leave you breathless."

—**RICHARD EHISEN**, The Open Mic

"In this wonderfully weird sequel to *The Rage Room*, an ensemble cast of quirky characters create havoc inside the head of time-travelling anti-hero Sharps. Sexy and funny, *Everything You Dream Is Real* combines futuristic adventures with irreverent romance to create an entertaining, high-energy read."

—**TERRI FAVRO**, *The Sisters Sputnik*

"Lisa de Nikolits's uniquely subversive, quirky approach to writing about complex topics is entertainment at its finest. A zany excursion with vivid characters, *Everything You Dream Is Real* manages to balance absurdity with profound insight, leaving me with much to contemplate even as I'm still laughing."

—**DARCIA HELLE**, Quiet Fury Books

"A strange story that is oddly satisfying and thoroughly entertaining … I liked that there were many twists; it helped with the suspense. My favourite part of the book was the author's writing style. It felt like your best friend was telling you a story in a uniquely funny way."

—IOANNA KORMOULI, Nana's Book Reviews

"*Everything You Dream is Real* encompasses a whirling world. This is kaleidoscopic, cerebral and turbulent storytelling, interspersed with wry, dry humour and incorporating time travel-unravel, with diverse transitioning, transfixing situations, and beguiling entrapments… deceptions and pell-mell displacements, driven by decidedly volatile, fickle, and dodgy doctrines, zig-zag plunges, and frantic fragmentation. There is a sly warring against any remaining individual intactness with flickers and flashes of insightfulness, alongside dizzying addictions, driving exhilaration and desperation… and some tender healing within hellishness. We observe corrupt and dodgy dynamics galore… people being modified and 'oddified'! Amidst pulverizing toxic policies of authoritarianism… a venomous and, in large part, squalid and crushing lifestyle, triggering outbreaks of valiant stances and plucky stalwart unity. Some powerful and enduring relationships occur, alongside others less stable and made frail with stirrings of disdain, baldly brazen behaviour, and outlandish craziness of 'sexploitations'… purely ravaged and depraved copulations, a tightly controlled community, wheeling amidst uncertainty and unpredictability, degrading manipulation and subjugation, wherein schemes of mutiny are whispered and hatched against numbing political pulverizing… grotesque and blatant distortion and fear-fuelled by seamy and sordid surveillance. These are fraught times, driven by power, greed, and exploitation, with shrewd and lewd undercurrents, yet outwardly showcased to be a community thriving and free. This juggling of ongoing egotism and immense uncertainty is however threaded through with a somewhat fragile, yet sustained undercurrent careening towards hope of escape… of liberation and cohesion… and inclusion… to forging a complete community."

—SHIRLEY MCDANIEL, Artist, Art Explorations

"Lisa de Nikolits's *Everything You Dream Is Real* is aptly named: this novel reads like a delirious hallucination, but one with unmistakable immediacy. Come for the sci-fi and action-adventure; stay for the love story that lurks just below the surface."

—MARK SAMPSON, *All the Animals on Earth*, *The Slip*, and *Sad Peninsula*

"Anything can happen; you just have to dream it. *Everything You Dream Is Real* is a story that will hook you with butterfly wings but with these dreams, watch where you're going. You could wake to a whole other world."

—ELAINE SAPP, Elaine Loves to Read

"An original, adventurous, and vital writer, Lisa de Nikolits holds up a cracked, kaleidoscopic mirror to our times. *Everything You Dream Is Real* thrusts readers into an extraordinary, disturbing future and takes them on a raucous, high-stakes, one-of-a-kind journey filled with hope, revenge, love, and tentacles."

—DANIEL SCOTT TYSDAL, *Wave Forms and Doom Scrolls*

"A riot of imagination. Most authors trot out the same tropes, but Lisa de Nikolits takes you on a triumphantly bizarre roller coaster of a novel where mass murder can be solved by time travel, 1980s pop culture rules, and sometimes love can survive dystopia. Read *Everything You Dream Is Real* and challenge your perception!"

—MELISSA YI, author of *Wolf Ice*

EVERYTHING YOU DREAM IS *Real*

A NOVEL BY LISA DE NIKOLITS

INANNA poetry & fiction
Toronto, Ontario, Canada
www.inanna.ca

Copyright © 2023 Lisa de Nikolits

Except for the use of short passages for review purposes, no part of this book may be reproduced, in part or in whole, or transmitted in any form or by any means, electronically or mechanically, including photocopying, recording, or any information or storage retrieval system, without prior permission in writing from the publisher or a licence from the Canadian Copyright Collective Agency (Access Copyright).

We gratefully acknowledge the support of the Canada Council for the Arts and the Ontario Arts Council for our publishing program. We also acknowledge the financial support of the Government of Canada.

Cover design: Lisa de Nikolits
Cover art: Vecteezy.com

Everything You Dream Is Real is a work of fiction. All names, characters, businesses, places, events and incidents in this book are either the product of the author's imagination or used in a fictitious manner.

All trademarks and copyrights mentioned within the work are included for literary effect only and are the property of their respective owners.

Library and Archives Canada Cataloguing in Publication

Title: Everything you dream is real / a novel by Lisa de Nikolits.
Names: De Nikolits, Lisa, author.
Series: Inanna poetry & fiction series.
Description: Series statement: Inanna poetry & fiction series
Identifiers: Canadiana (print) 20220399921 | Canadiana (ebook) 2022039993X | ISBN 9781771339308 (softcover) | ISBN 9781771339315 (HTML) | ISBN 9781771339322 (PDF)
Classification: LCC PS8607.E63 E94 2022 | DDC C813/.6—dc23

Printed and bound in Canada

Inanna Publications and Education Inc.
210 Founders College, York University
4700 Keele Street, Toronto, Ontario, Canada M3J 1P3
Telephone: (416) 736-5356 Fax: (416) 736-5765
Email: inanna.publications@inanna.ca Website: www.inanna.ca

To Bradford Dunlop.
And Luciana Ricciutelli.

Sharps.

I'M UNDERGROUND. I'm in a cave. A coffin? Am I dead? I can't feel my body. Is this how babies feel in the womb? Maybe I'm tumbling and turning in some comforting fluid so soft and fine that I can't tell where I end and it begins. Are my eyes open? It's so dark I can't tell the difference.

I blink a few times to test the situation. When my eyes are closed, an aurora borealis floats across my vision, but when I open them I can't see a thing. Time to engage the cerebral cortex and figure this shit out.

Let's start with the easy stuff. Who am I? I know I'm a guy. And I know I fucked up royally, but I can't remember what I did. A sick feeling fills what must be my gut. I'd like to rub my belly and reassure myself: hey buddy, it can't be that bad. *Yeah, you keep telling yourself that.* Even without intel, I know my failure was epic. And it was public. Add a couple of doses of shame, guilt, anger, fear, and regret, and you've got me in a nutshell. I was the anger guy. Famous for being the ultimate anger machine. Or should I say, infamous?

I'm immediately exhausted. I don't want to know the details of what I did. I want to go back to sleep or whatever it was I was doing before I started thinking. But no, it's too late for that. I'm awake and it's back to self-interrogation. Who am I? I can't even remember my name.

Static fills my ears, like a needle scratching a gramophone. Gramophone? Since when did I parley with the likes of gramophones? Maybe I'm a nineteenth-century lord of the manor, resplendent in knickerbockers, playing croquet and drinking tea with my pinky aloft. I don't think so.

Ah shit, it's probably just my old friend tinnitus doing the fandango in my ear. If it is tinnitus, then I've got a body. Which means I can't be dead.

I entertain myself by blinking slowly and morphing the scenery from a black void to bright lights, like a big city, albeit muted and blurry. Since it's the only game in town, I'll ride this horse 'til he falls over. He? I'm being chauvinistic. The horse could be a she. A she-horse. There must be a better word for that. I hear a tinkly laugh: "*She-horse? Oh sweetie, you're such a fool, try mare!*"

That would be my wife giving me her two cents. Shapeless as I am, I straighten up. Good news, I've got a wife! *Wham*, another punch knocks the wind out of my gut. Yep, I've got a wife, but I can sense right off the bat that she's a nasty piece of work. I can't remember the details, but I can see that evil, disembodied Cheshire cat grin as she waves at me, "*Cheerio, cheerio, baby.*" I catch a quick glimpse of her in my mind's eye—a big, buxom blonde. I was married to Marilyn Monroe?

Shit. These memory fragments are pissing me off. It's like I'm waking up from a dream that slips away as fast as I try to grab hold of it.

The noise scrapes across my nerve endings. *Ugh! Make it stop!* I search for my voice, to utter a cry of help, but a sock is stuffed down my throat.

A strobe light blasts my eyeballs and fills the room. Hallelujah maranatha, I've got a body! I can see it! My legs stretch out in front of me. Cool, trendy sneakers, fella. Red with black soles. I'm trendy! This eases the your-wife-hates-you acid roil in my gut, and I tremble slightly with happiness.

But hold that thought, because the next thing I know, a taser flambés my spinal fluid and the lights go out. Holy shit. I'm kinda regretting rejoining my body. Who the fuck tasered me? God? The devil? Either way, I'm in big shit. Surely God wouldn't taser me if He (or She, I remind myself) was about to let me into the good old sweet hereafter?

I sit up in the darkness. I feel a wall against my back. It wasn't there before, or maybe I hadn't noticed it.

"God?" I squeak, but a tiny meow is the best I can manage. *Great.* God has reincarnated me as a cat. I meow again just to see if I can. The light flashes, and glittering pain swashbuckles through my body. I pass out.

Twenty-four hours earlier

It's time to kick some ass. I'm going to get my man. The others would shit a brick if they knew, and who can blame them. Saving him is completely fucked up. He screwed up royally, and I paid the highest price. I should hate him more than anyone, but I crave him so much my whole body hurts. *Sticks and stones will break your bones, but love will break your heart.* Truth is, my love for him is the only thing keeping me from going crazy in this stupid, broken world.

Admittedly, he fell in love with my avatar, not me. And admittedly, we were only together for a few months, but man, I fell for him, hook, line, and sinker. And sink I did when he ditched the real me. I should hate him for that, but I don't. I'm obsessed with him, and I just want to go back to what we had. Is that too much to ask? It was the happiest time of our lives.

Sure, my plan isn't exactly a walk in the park, but I've got a couple of shiny aces up my sleeve. Firstly, because of his situation, I can control what he can and can't remember. Numero deux, I've got the key that will lock him to me forever. One bun in the oven, baking as we speak. I pat my flat belly and say a quick thank you to the kangaroo-pouch mama I hired to carry the fetus.

I can't have a baby because the idea of another person growing inside of me makes me want to puke. Talk about weird alien shit. Plus, I've got to keep it a secret from the others. They'd have puppies if they knew what I was up to.

I had to bust a gut to get the moolah to pay the surrogate, but it will pay off big time.

It was kinda weird how I met her—Anise, the surrogate. It was like god—in whom I do not believe—decided to throw me a bone.

I was hanging out in my fav dive bar, intent on scoring nefarious substances, when along came this supermodel. She sat down next to me. One thing led to another, in other words, and I spilled the beans of my sad and sorry life. How I'd lost my man, *yadda yadda*, and how maybe if I'd had his kid, we'd still be together. Shit like that.

"Well," said the spider to the fly, "I can help you. I can carry your baby for you. It'll just cost you a premium."

"I'll make it worth your while," I immediately replied. I've got deep-dive access to the government coffers since I'm officially part of the postwar administration. I don't owe the others diddly squat because they banished the love of my life to waste away in lost time without so much as telling me.

I get momentarily distracted, thinking about Anise. She's so fricking hot. Of all the bars to walk into, she walked into mine. I got a kind of flirty vibe off her, too. That must have been my mind playing tricks on me because no way would a super hot babe be interested in me. When she rested her hand on my leg, it sent tingles up my spine. But I'm Sharps's girl all the way. Loyal to a fault.

Eleven long years. That's how long I've been planning his rescue.

That said, I find myself in a pinch. Eleven years and I'm not as ready as I should be. Procrastination is my middle name, but still, it's crazy how time flies.

My plan was to have our baby birthed and drooling with cuteness by the time I sprang him from the joint, aka the Mainframe. Sharps would fall in love with the kiddie and ergo me, but what with the government's unexpected plan to shut down the Mainframe due to a looming digital insurrection, I had to bring the schedule forward. Honestly, there are always rumours of an insurrection. Blah blah blah. My problem is that Anise is only four months pregnant.

I'm not proud of sperm-burgling Sharps's spunk. I made him use condoms and the minute we were done, I "cleaned up" by banking his splooge in the lab. The furtive act of irrational greed dampened my post-coital glow, but I wanted a piece of him for myself in case he left me or died while time travelling.

Eleven years. After we hoisted the victory flag, I kinda lost my mind for a while. Add to that the stresses of the postwar world. World domination did not work out as planned. This was one of the few facts we could all agree on.

At the top of the bad surprise list was nature's retaliation for years of abuse. We were at war with lattices of wild ivy, as thick as your forearm. We were under constant attack by deadly butterflies. Speaking of which, one crazy fucker just speedballed headfirst onto my drag racer's windshield.

Talk about kamikaze. The vicious little creature was the size of a fist, decked out in yellow, green, and blue, and had wings so lush they looked like angel feathers. I swear it snarled at me before it died, baring vampire teeth. One of the weirdest postwar mutations was the morphing of the luscious black and orange Monarch butterfly into a multicoloured, almost furry, parrot-like creature. We still called them Monarchs—a nostalgic nod to the past—but these rainbow fuzzballs were nothing like their beatific predecessors. The mutation was our fault. We tried to give nature a helping hand in our many secret labs, where we nurtured forbidden forests outside the city perimeter. Our rebel cause worked earnestly to foster the growth of plants and animals, but in a misguided attempt to speed up floral and faunal regeneration, the underground labs unknowingly developed lethal insects and deadly plants.

As soon as the war was over, we released our genetically engineered projects back into the wild, with horrifying results. I guess the joke was on us.

We'd also been experimenting with fusing human and animal DNA. Our fearless leader OctoOne was the primary flagbearer of that initiative.

I pull over to the side of the road, grab a pair of tongs from the back of my racer, and throw the furry beast into a canister. I lick my lips, looking forward to harvesting its narcotic feast when the mission is over.

I brush my hands on my pants, just in case. Goddamn, but those butterflies are deadly. Kind of ironic how panic-stricken we were pre-war when we thought the fricking things would become extinct. Who knew our efforts to protect them in the lab would turn them into vicious mutants with a paralyzing, leprous sting?

I settle back into my made-for-my-ass-by-me bucket seat and pull out onto the strip. Being on the open road feels fricking amazing.

"Yeah baby!" I scream out into the wasteland. I then look around, sobered by the hostile surroundings. Talk about barren.

Time to get my head outta my ass and lay down some miles.

I race down the pink-paved plastic asphalt road lined with rusty red dirt on either side. There's a cobalt cloudless sky overhead. Pretty as a picture, and deadly as a rattlesnake. I glance at my gallon-jars of water riding shotgun. I've got no idea how long this rescue operation will take, and I sincerely hope that dying of dehydration isn't in the cards.

How I love my sweet ride. She's steampunk, vintage-style, a throwback to the first drag racers back in the days of the cavemen. Okay, maybe not to the days of cavemen, but to the 1950s at least. Lady Luck, I call her. She's got a manual gear shift, and she hits three hundred clicks when I'm on the open road and gunning it. Like now. She sports one windshield wiper, which means I gotta lean out at full tilt and drag the wiper across the plexiglass. Since we've been drought-stricken for over a decade, I only use it now and then to clear bugs.

I put my foot down harder, and my lady shakes her buns with giddy delight. Thank god we've still got endless miles of perfect plastic roads beyond the city limits. The plants leave them be because there's nothing to be had.

The temperature gauge on my dashboard ticks to an alarmingly high notch, and my heart kicks into overdrive. *C'mon honey*, I beg the car, *mama needs you to stay steady*. I ease off the gas slightly.

I pass through a former central business district, eyeing the ruins from my cockpit. Incongruously cheerful plastic mansions and skyscrapers are cobwebbed with thick lacy green veins. *Green Halloween*, I call it. No one goes inside those buildings. You have to hack your way through the fibrous veiny cords, and all you get for your efforts are more plants and creepy-crawlies. No thank you. The vines don't care about being pretty; there's nary a flower in sight, and they use all their energy to tangle themselves into ropes.

A quick temperature check tells me that my girl's okay, and the needle drops back down. I'll take good news where I can.

I ponder the machete work ahead of me. I'll have to clear the thick net of green vines on the outer walls of my love's prison, then fight my way down to the underground console that houses the central computer. I'm armed with my blade and a flame-thrower. I'll burn the shit off if I have to. Once inside, I can only hope that the Mainframe computer will be intact and that the code will still work. *What if the electricity fails, as it so often does?* I shake my head. No negative thoughts. I'll cross that bridge when I get to it. There's got to be a generator somewhere. Our head scientist, Sting Ray Barb, is too savvy to be caught with her dungarees down. Plus, I shouldn't forget the most important get-out-of-jail-free card: the reintegration pod. Without it, there'd be no way to get my guy out.

I bite my lip. The logistics of navigating the reintegration pod scare me shitless. Let's face it, computers aren't my bailiwick.

No siree Bob. Back in the day, before my meltdown, I was the General. Fearless in battle, wielder of axes, Xena Warrior Princess. That was me.

Surely there'll be a manual, *How to Download Your Ex-Lover from Cyberspace 101* or some such? But no dummy am I: I've been touted as a shrewd military strategist and a savvy politician. I can recite *The Art of War* by heart, but I've got no regard for computers.

I chew a nail and decide not to think about it. *Be in the moment, girl!* I focus on the red earth flying past my window while the pale pink paved road curves ahead of me. *Life is good! Life is peaceful!*

Until my walkie talkie cackles like an evil witch.

"EmoOne, are you there? Come in EmoOne, can you hear me?"

Goddamn. I hoped I'd gotten away clean and slipped under the radar. But no, of course not. Mother just can't let me go.

"EmoOne here," I reluctantly answer the call. I'd dubbed myself EmoOne as a joke, riffing off the name of our legendary phantom leader, OctoOne. We'd all heard the stories of how she infused herself with octopus DNA and now sported several arms like Durga, the Hindu goddess. She lives in the shadowy darkness, seeing no one but her inner circle. Mother's got a backstage pass to the leader's sewing circle. So do my former friends, now my marginally congenial colleagues, all of whom are upper-echelon government ministers. I'm an outsider, kept on retainer because they owe me big time for my role in the war.

"Nellie," Mother drops protocol. "Where are you? What are you doing?"

It fricking annoys me when she calls me Nellie and she knows it. My name is Noelle but after they imprisoned Sharps, her son and my ex-lover, she started calling me Nellie. She forgives me my foibles because she knows how much I love him, and god knows she loved him too, despite the fact that he tried to kill her.

I'm forced to remember things I'd rather forget. Actually he *did* kill her, but time travel, our trusty friend, fixed things, and she lived happily ever after. Maybe not entirely happily, but she did live. Were it not for time travel and the ability to undo his heinous crimes, Sharps would have been one of the most notorious serial killers of our century. Which is ironic because all he really wanted to do was have a family and be a stand-up guy.

After I fell apart, Mother took me under her wing, whether I liked it or not. I was definitely on the side of *or not*. I wanted to crawl under a rock and be left alone to die, but Mother was like an old basset hound, rounding me up and licking my face with her big wet tongue.

She pumped me full of meds, propped me up, and got our resident in-house genius scientist, Sting Ray Barb, to give me a clean psych evaluation. Mother insisted I was the best person to head up the Health and Wellness portfolio because of my personal experience with postwar grief. The others were happy to shunt us both off into remote corners of irrelevant governance, because really, who cared about Health and Wellness or Education when there was money to be made and power to be brokered elsewhere?

"Nellie? Can you hear me? What's going on?"

Talk about annoying.

"I'm good. Taking some time to go on a blast," I say, being purposefully vague. "Heading out for a couple of days. I know I should have said something but you're so overprotective. I need some time to clear my head."

"Nellie," Mother says, and I can hear equal parts love and frustration in her voice. "I've been worried about you lately. You've been more distracted than usual, and I know why. Dear, I know you're struggling with, how shall I say this, chemical dependency issues."

I blow out a sigh of relief. Ha ha, she thinks I'm out chasing Monarch pollen. Yep, dastardly though the butterflies are, they have a hidden benefit. The dust harvested from a sac behind their tiny butts sends you tripping beyond your wildest dreams. A highly imaginative doctor, clearly having nothing better to do with her time, went rooting around in the butterfly's anus and discovered that tiny amounts of the dust made for a fantastic anaesthetic. Unfortunately, it's also wildly addictive. Dust quickly made its way from makeshift surgeries and shanty hospitals to being the street drug du jour. I fell prey to its terrible charm, but I thought I'd hidden it well.

I need to end this conversation asap.

"I'm fine Mother. Nothing to worry about. I've got water. I've got butterfly ammo, and Lady Luck is fully charged. Give me a couple of days, and I promise I'll be back, right as rain, you'll see. I deserve a blast and I won't be long."

"Blasts are time-out trips for kids who don't know what to do with their lives." Mother is disapproving. "You're not a kid. You're the Executive Assistant of Health and Wellness. People rely on you."

I give a snort. Rely on me, *pshaw*.

"I'm entitled to take a break," I defend myself. "We invented blasts for emotional well-being. Haven't you ever wanted to go on one?"

I expect Mother to say, *no, of course not*, but there's silence. It occurs to me that maybe she's tired of her life, tired of teaching thankless kids and being limited to ancient '80s and '90s VHS cassettes as resource material. God knows I couldn't stand having to watch *Pretty in Pink* or *The Breakfast Club* year in and year out. And this is no doubt made worse by the fact that Mother was a genuine intellectual who hung onto secret stashes of illegal print for as long as she could.

Hard copy books were destroyed during the digitized age of Materialism and, *oops*, we lost the e-books when we shut down the Mainframe and all things digital were declared illegal. We were "going back to the land," resetting the Earth. It was a shame about the loss of all that reading matter, but shit happens.

Luckily, some fanatic stashed hundreds of VHS cassettes in his storage lockers, along with several VCRs and several fifty-five-inch TV screens. Mother quickly realized their worth. "Schooling" now involves watching *St. Elmo's Fire* or *Sixteen Candles* and handing in essays analyzing the literary theory and sociological issues behind such gems. Sting Ray Barb, Mother's BFF, drew up a math and science curriculum, and kids who showed an aptitude for biology were trained in first aid and midwifery.

Mother headed up the Education department, and she did her best. She was aided by another warehouse stash—a cache of stationery and school supplies. You'd have thought Mother had discovered the crown jewels when we found enough Post-it Notes to line the Milky Way.

I know Mother deplored the schooling system, and, to make matters worse, the video cassettes were coming to the end of their poor, sad, Mylar-ed little lives. I've got no idea what we'll do when they kick the bucket. I couldn't care less, either. If you ask me, postwar life is pointless. Life expectancy is short, and our time on this godforsaken planet is limited. Blasts are the one opportunity kids get to run wild before they're shackled by reality, at which time most kids become butt-heads. Because really, where else can you get your kicks?

A part of me wants to fess up and tell her that being the Executive Assistant of Health and Wellness was what had gotten me into the Monarch dust in the first place. I was responsible for trying to help the addicts, and I stupidly ended up testing the shit just to see what made it so irresistible. Admittedly, it wasn't my wisest move. I told myself I was doing due diligence, but who was I kidding?

"Mama bear," I say. "I'm fine. I gotta run, and you need to chill. H&Dub doesn't need me. It's running like clockwork with you at the helm. I've got to take care of a few issues, bond with nature, such as it is, and clear my head."

"Nature's a bitch," Mother says, bluntly. "I hope it's not butt dust you're after, Nellie. Come home, honey, let me take care of you."

She sounds so kind that I nearly do a U-ey right then and there. I seriously consider flying into her big old kind arms, but I can't do it. I've come this far. My eyes spill over with tears, messing up my goggles. I pull over to the side of the road.

"Mother," I say, choked up. "Thank you. I mean it. But I've got to go."

"But honey," Mother says urgently, "are you equipped for a blast? Blasts take planning and supplies."

She's asking if I have Monarch-resistant tents and camping equipment. I do not.

"It's more like a mini blast, Mother," I say. "Just a couple of days. I've got enough ammo to down a flock of butty-flies, don't you worry."

"Watch out for the ampu-gangs," Mother says. "And for god's sake, do *not* get bitten by a butterfly."

Monarch bites lead to gangrene. Amputation is the only cure. The world is filled with wandering ampu-gangsters who fill you with dust and cut off your offending limb. Of course, you get addicted to the dust, but in a happy coincidence, the ampu-gangsters double as dealers, so you go to work for them to get your next fix.

Ampus. Not the kind of party I've got in mind. I gotta concentrate. I scan the horizon for wounded, limping people covered in oozing, blood-stained bandages, hooked on dust and willing to kill for their next fix. The coast is clear, for now.

But enough shooting the breeze with feel-good banter and trips down memory lane.

"Mama bear," I say, "don't worry, kk? I know the drill. Listen, I gotta go. Seriously. I'll keep you updated at some point. Don't fret your pretty little head about nothing. Ciao for now. Roger, over and out."

I press the disconnect button before she can say anything else. I switch off the two-way radio and toss it into the back of Lady Luck. Time to put the pedal to the metal. It won't take them long to put two and two together about where I'm headed, once they figure out that I overheard the Board talking. My window of opportunity is short.

Nothing will stand in the way of me rescuing Sharps. It's now or never.

But things don't go according to plan. Why would they?

***

It takes me a lot longer to reach the Mainframe storage facility than I had figured. I'm glad I've got spare gas in the trunk, or I'd be stranded on the way back.

Darkness has fallen when I arrive in the deserted parking lot. I decide to spend the night in Lady Luck because god knows who or what is out there, lurking in the darkness, waiting to feast on me. Plus, it's hardly a good idea to start hacking at what I can hardly see.

Lady Luck's not exactly a five-star abode, and I lie awake all night, freaked out of my skull, convinced I'm going to be attacked.

At least I thought I lay awake all night. I must have slept because I wake up with crusty eyes and my limbs twisted into an ungodly pretzel. Note to self: *next time, bring a camper van.*

Dawn is breaking, and the world is silent as I hoist my axe. "*And no birds sing.*" I hear Mother's much-lamented refrain. It was a poem she loved, about some guy palely loitering near a hedge. Well, she's right, there's nary a singing bird, but there is a shitload of hedge. Hedge that I have to hack through. It's not exactly a quiet affair, attacking eleven years of ivy.

I hope the noise won't attract any ampu-gangs or butterflies, but I can't worry about that.

I attack the foliage like a crazy woman, grunting and groaning, smashing and hauling axe.

By the time I clear the door, my hands are wrecked and torn, and I'm out of breath. Holy shit. I gotta add some jumping jacks to my breakfast routine.

I eye the keycode, which still looks in good shape. Will it work? I take a deep breath and punch in the numbers, fully expecting the door to remain shut.

But it slides open, startling me. I hadn't figured how creepy it would be going into the dome-shaped lodge all alone. Inside, the decor is cubism meets minimalism. A pelt of furry dust covers every boxy desk and Atelier de Troupe–style chair. The auto-lights flicker on as I walk down the corridor to the elevator. My heart is hopping around in my chest like a big, fat, slimy bullfrog, and I feel sick. In my rush to get to Sharps, I haven't eaten anything except a kale and almond bar.

I catch sight of myself in one of the mirrored windows, and I stop dead. Oh man, do I ever look bad. Hedgehog hair and a furry coat of vine leaves and sawdust, superglued with sweat. All of which settles one issue: I'll have to present my avatar self, Janaelle. There's no way Sharps will look at the real me and think "*Oh honey, yes I* do *love you, I somehow just forgot.*"

I'm sad. I'd wanted to reach out to him as Noelle, but that hadn't exactly gone well before, had it?

My mind flashes back to that terrible day: the day after the female army won the war and defeated the Materialists. It should have been a day of joy and victory, but it was a day of heartbreak for me. Mother had pointed me out to him, and I read her lips. "*The woman you knew as Janaelle was an avatar. That's who she really is. Her name is Noelle, and she loves you.*"

I watched his face fall. With it went all my dreams.

It was hard to take. After everything we'd been through together? My heart shattered into a thousand pieces, but I grinned at him like I didn't give a shit. I stood my ground and gave him a mock salute. After they sent him away, I tried to kill myself, but Mother saved me. Took me under her wing, like the daughter she'd never had.

I stare back at the mess of a woman in the mirrored glass.

"Avatar program it is then," I say out loud, my voice echoing in the empty building. I clap my hand to my mouth. *Shut the fuck up!*

The elevator hums down to the server floor, and I pray that the power won't go down during my mission. The place is as chilly as a nun's tit, keeping the hardware in good shape. The AC must have been running all these years, even while the Mainframe slept like a baby. I exit the elevator and notice that the reintegration pod isn't where it used to be. Which is a fricking nightmare, but not something I can afford to focus on now. I have to find Sharps. If his data has disintegrated, then the reintegration pod is a moot point anyway.

    I inch ahead down the corridor. Framed pictures of green cacti on pink backgrounds line the walls at regular intervals. I'm starting to feel dizzy with the stress of it all. *Breathe. Power on.*

    I'm in the bowels of a ship. A spaceship. I reach the doors to the Mainframe and push through. There's a creepy low humming noise, kinda like a steady, guttural *om*, and little lights flash and flicker like alien fireflies. I'm so cold I'm covered in goosebumps. So much for couture keeping me warm. I'm fashion forward and fucking freezing to death.

    The main console is housed in a small, glassed-in cubicle overlooking acres of hard drives. Teeth chattering, I power up the Mainframe, having watched Sting Ray Barb do it a bunch of times. I call up the avatar software and log in as Janaelle. I find the rage room software and log in using Sharps's ID. I was the one who activated his time travel jumps all those years ago, and I've never forgotten his access codes.

    I can see him! He's there, in a rage room, lying on the floor. His mouth is moving. He's talking. Why can't I hear anything? The audio must be muted. *Unmute asap!* But I get the audio selection wrong and end up selecting feline instead of anthropoid, blaming my ineptitude on my icy, shaking fingers. Who the frick needs feline audio anyway? Now I've got sound and I can hear Sharps meowing, but it won't let me change the audio. I'll have to reboot the Mainframe.

    I restart and the activation bar drags itself slowly across the screen. There's nothing to do but wait.

I'm so cold I contemplate jogging on the spot to warm up, but, to my great joy, I spot a sequinned parka thrown over a chair in the corner.

Warmth! My happiness is tempered when I realize that the jacket probably belonged to Ava, leader of the female army and my sworn enemy. She was the one responsible for banishing Sharps. She's a condescending, power-hungry bitch who saw me as a broken old veteran with nothing left to offer.

Still, desperate times and all that. I pull it on. Faux-Chanel. It even smells like Ava after all these years—citrusy and sharp.

I study the screen. Ah! The computer lives! No, wait, it doesn't. The menu bar stops. Freaking hell.

An unexpected error has occurred. Please try again later.

Oh shit. I reboot again, gnawing at my fingers. No, I curse the screen, I do not wish to report the issue. I just hope no one else in the world noticed me diddling around with billions of dollars of sleeping hardware.

Okay, here we go again. The bar creeps along the screen. It looks like it'll work this time. I bury my teeth into my knuckles. *C'mon, muthertrucker.* Work, for the love of god.

And yeppers! There's Sharps. In the rage room. Crashed out on the floor. I peer at the screen. Why isn't he moving? Did the reboots kill him? Holy shit. Come on, Sharps, *move*, for god's sake.

And he does. He raises his head. Hallelujah! Sharps is alive and well, virtually at least. I've woken him up from his digital slumber, and it's time to finally reunite.

And it pretty much goes to hell in a handbasket from there.

Sharps.

WHEN I COME TO, a large yellow fish swims past my nose. I try to scream, but I meow instead. I duck. Holy shit. Holy fish. The fish doubles back and burps, releasing a stream of rainbow-tinted bubbles. I scrabble backwards, but more fish come at me. Striped red and yellow fish, blue fish, and jellyfish. All shapes and sizes and all swimming back and forth in neat lines, gurgling. I freeze. Is this a nightmare? It has to be. I'm Aquaman, paralyzed in a black aquarium with a gaggle of burping fish.

Wait. This is familiar. *After Dark*. That vintage screensaver. My BFF loves it. Great, I've got friends! Well, one friend, as far as I can remember. What's his name? Jonesy? Something like that. Oh shit. I'd pissed him off, too.

The fish waggle back and forth. A seahorse trots past and I try to grab it, but it shatters, cheerfully reassembles, and prances off.

I resign myself to watching the fish. It's actually kinda relaxing.

The lights flash on. The fish are gone. Of course they are, doofus, they need to be in the dark. Three white fluorescent lightsabres are barnacled to a filthy, grey speckled ceiling. I'm in an office? Can I go blind from staring at lights? Best not to test the theory.

I'm alone in a concrete room with a two-way black mirrored window. Six inches of broken plastic toys litter the floor. Smashed TVs and old boom boxes look like someone kicked the shit out of them. Man, there's enough vintage crap in here to fill a football field. Heaven is a garbage bin full of broken crap?

Have I been thrown out with the trash? I look down. I'm holding a sledgehammer. I should get up and smash the glass and have at it with whoever's on the other side, but my limbs are ketamined and I can't move.

The static grates again, and the lights flicker. The fish reappear in the darkness. The light flashes on, and they vanish.

"Sharps? Over here."

The voice blasts out of nowhere and scares the bejesus out of me. If I could have jumped out of my skin, I would have. *Oops, mustn't blaspheme, wifey doesn't like that.*

"Sharps?" The voice is annoyed, and I look around. I can't see or do anything.

"Meow?" I manage. The cat thing hasn't gone away after all.

"Frick," the voice mutters. "Wrong audio installed. One sec, bear with me."

The static is like sandpaper on my raw nerves, and the voice chatters on, muttering inaudibly. The blackness returns and with it, the fish. Giant red fish, jellybean green fish, blobby grey jellyfish, and jaunty little seahorses. Bubbles float past my nose, and I meow just for fun, to see how long I can hold a note. I'm about to try a purr when I get the shit tasered out of me again, and I lose consciousness.

* * *

I wake with a hangover as heavy as a ten-ton truck. What the fuck? The concrete is cold and rough under my cheek. I'm drooling. Disgusting. I wipe my cheek on my sleeve and raise myself up in the darkness. I can move, a new development. I look around for my aquatic buddies, but they're gone.

My head is killing me. I rub my temples, and my good cheer is gone. I'm tired of getting zapped and toyed with.

"Sharps?" The voice speaks and the fluorescent lights flash on.

"Yeah?" I reply. I sound surly even to myself, but at least I'm not auditioning for some kitty cat musical anymore.

"Oh thank god. You can talk. You're you!"

"I am? Who the hell are you? While you're at it, fill me in on who I am, too. Why am I in a room full of crap?"

The voice laughs, and it's a beautiful sound: wind chimes, summer breezes, and church bells. I sit up straighter.

"Come to the window," the voice says.

I clamber to my feet. Oh god. My head's going to explode. I go over to the black glass, but I can't see anything.

"You there?" I ask, "or is this a blind date where you see me, and I can't see diddly squat?"

"Oops-a-daisy, my bad." The room on the other side of the window floods with light, revealing a woman so stunning I forget about my pounding head. I gasp out loud. She's got long, dark, wavy hair and enormous dark brown eyes with impossibly long lashes. What a mouth! Full, sensual, and red-lipped. High cheekbones and flawless skin.

She laughs again and I feel like an idiot for staring. I flush red.

"I wasn't expecting one of Charlie's Angels," I quip, trying to make up for my lack of cool. "Maybe you can fill me in on what's going on here?"

"You don't remember anything?"

"Nope. Just some vague feelings that I screwed up royally on a thousand levels."

"That you did." The woman is cheerful. "But everyone deserves a fifth chance. You're right, let's start at the beginning. I'm Janaelle. You might not remember me, but we're deeply in love."

I burst out laughing. "No way. You're an Everest above my pay grade."

"No, we're in love," she insists. "I'll explain everything but first I've got to get you out of the rage room."

"The rage room?"

"The room you're in. It was a place you went to, back in the old days, to work off your anger issues. Only we used you to create fuel for our world when we were running out of energy."

"Yeah sure, that explains everything. Correction, no, actually it doesn't. What the fuck do you mean?"

"We, and by that, I mean a bunch of revolutionaries who succeeded in taking over the world, harvested rage room subjects and engaged them as subjects in a time travel experiment that generated a bunch of energy. Forget about solar power, forget about wind: we used anger. You were the best subject out there. You were the only guy in history who managed multiple jumps. You're so damn special, no one can figure out your magic. However, you also did some pretty bad shit when you were on your various trips, and that's why you're stuck in a virtual rage room. My bosses, the new heads of state, put you there. You're in a virtual prison. It's super complicated, and that's all I've got for you right now because we're in a time-pressured situation. You're stored on a server called the Mainframe that's going to be unplugged in a few weeks. I'll explain everything as soon as I get you out."

The Mainframe rings a bell. "The global, satellite-controlled server that connects all our virtual interactions via a pathway called the Crystal Lattice." My hand shoots behind my ear. "We're all microchipped, with software hidden in our teeth, if I remember correctly."

Funny how I can remember all that shit, but I don't know this woman from Adam.

She looks sour because she's probably thinking exactly the same thing: *He remembers that and not me?* But that's me, always managing to say exactly the wrong thing at the wrong time.

"You got it. The Global Accord shut it down, but now there's a call to go one step further and destroy the Crystal Lattice, which is housed in the Mainframe. Our Mainframe. Our army, headed up by our hacker genius OctoOne, and aided by Jazza, Sting Ray Barb, and Ava, shut down the rest of the world's access. All that remains of the great and powerful world wide web is housed in this bunker. The concern is that it's too dangerous to have one holding tank with all the world's data in it, and they're calling for it to be destroyed. The Mainframe used to control the weather, which if you ask me, wasn't a bad thing. We may need it again."

"Because?"

She sighs, like I'm wasting her time. "After we unplugged the satellite weather control systems, there were floods. Like Noah's ark floods. They exacerbated the growth of mutated insects and spawned the growth of ivy that's strangling the shit out of humanity. It's like Mother Nature had been biding her time and man, was she ever ready to sucker punch us for the wrongs we'd dealt her." She chuckles. "I was such a self-righteous fanatic. Shut down the satellites, let Mother Nature rule! After the rains, came the drought. No more lakes. No more water."

"How do you survive?"

"Do you remember Sting Ray Barb, Ava, or Jazza?"

I shake my head. "The names sound vaguely familiar."

"They're the brains behind most of our postwar survival techniques."

"It's annoying as shit to not be able to remember stuff." I rub my head as if that will help jog my memory. "If I'm just data, why does my head hurt so goddamn badly?"

"I'm guessing it's because of the reboots," she says. "There might be a background calibration in progress. We'd better make this quick." I want to ask her what she means, but she's moved on to explaining their water systems.

"We harvest water on condensation farms, big warehouses where the temperatures are yanked up and down while we milk the fog."

The lights flicker, and this time we both flinch.

"The power could go down at any moment. I've gotta get outta here," she says. "I'll be back, and we'll get you out. I promise."

"No! Don't go!" I'm panic-stricken.

"I have to. I'm sorry. I won't leave you here, don't worry."

"When exactly will you be back?"

"I don't know. I'll have to ask for help, which won't be easy. I'll be blunt, you don't have a lot of friends out there. Actually, you don't have any friends except for me. But don't worry, I'll rescue you. The problem is that my bosses moved the reintegration pod to lord knows where and you can't get out without it. But oh my god! It's so amazing to see you!" She beams at me, and I feel uneasy. My knightess in shining armour is an escaped psych patient.

"Are you some kind of crazy dream?" I ask. I'm not really asking her if she's a dream but if she's nuts, and she laughs.

"Only if everything you dream is real. This is very real in one sense but maybe not in the exact way you think it is."

Great. My life is a hallucination, but only maybe sort of? And I'm stored on a server? This chick is nuts. I've got to find a way to ground her, and I change tack.

"Can I ask you something?"

"Anything!"

"You're wearing Christian Dior. And Chanel. Not exactly what I'd have expected from the cavalry. You got all dressed up to see me?" I grin, and her face closes. Bad joke, obviously.

"Everyone dresses like this," she says shortly. "Your Materialistic world is to blame. When our army gear fell apart, we had to raid the fashion warehouses. We've got enough couture to clothe the nation for the next hundred years. Fucking Materialism!" She spits the words at me, and I flinch, even though I'm behind the glass.

"*My* Materialistic world?" I'm confused. "It was my fault?" She really *is* nuts, this woman. Into me one minute, mad as a rattlesnake the next.

"You were a main player, marketing and selling shit. You were a company man up the yingyang. Thanks to you and your kind, there was no nature!" She's yelling. "Everything was made of plastic. We lived in virtual reality, only coming out to buy shit you made us believe we couldn't live without." She pauses to take a deep breath. "But whatever, the past is the past, I've gotta go and find a way to save your ass."

Clearly, she and I hadn't shared the same politics or philosophies. And yet, she wants to save me? But never mind the whys and wherefores, I've got to keep on her good side to get the heck out of Dodge.

"Are you going to taser me again?" I ask, trembling at the thought. She blows me a kiss.

"Of course not! No more force quits or reboots for now. I'll activate sleep mode. You just hang out on the Mainframe, and before you know it, I'll be back. Don't you worry your pretty little head about a thing!" Her good cheer is back.

Wait. Sleep mode?

"So I'm going to be stuck here in this manky room, twiddling my thumbs?" I'm trying to delay her departure.

She looks perplexed. "I'm not sure what will happen," she admits. "But don't worry, I'll be back as soon as I can, to save you! Fear not!" And with that, she disappears, and with her goes the light. I'm left in total darkness, but at least it doesn't hurt this time.

Noelle.

I POWER DOWN THE MAINFRAME and sink to my haunches. That did not go well at all. I want to wallow in self pity, but I've got to get back to Lady Luck and head home.

I rush out into the parking lot. I gas up my ride and spin out of there, burning rubber.

I drive recklessly, faster than Lady Luck should fly. I slam my fist against the steering wheel. Why didn't he remember Janaelle? Sure, I hadn't wanted him to remember that he didn't love the real me, Noelle, but he should have been delighted to see Janaelle. He had loved her. He'd cried when he thought he wouldn't see her again. He'd been prepared to give up everything for her. And now there was nothing.

Hot tears sting my eyes, and I sniff hard, sucking my heartache down into my belly. I'll fix things by reworking his data. The next time I go back, I'll reboot the Mainframe and download a different version of his memories.

But I can't do it alone. I'm left with no choice. I've got to ask the others for help. The Fab Five, as I sarcastically dubbed them. Ava, Jazza, Mother, Sting Ray Barb, and that blonde bitch Shasta. Shasta makes my hackles rise. She came to our attention when she piggy-backed a time travel jump with Sharps, and they got stuck in lost time together. There was a crazy story about how Celeste, Sharps's wife, had been part of a church community sex cult and she'd forced Shasta to have sex with her. Shasta wanted to go back to confront her. It wasn't like Sharps was on team Shasta because he felt bad for what his wife had done. He did feel bad, but he liked Shasta in the way I wished he'd like me.

After we got Shasta and Sharps out of lost time, Ava and company jumped on the bandwagon and fell in love with Shasta. When I fell apart, they conveniently promoted her.

Shasta caused all kinds of trouble riding along with Sharps, but she also gave us loads of data and proved that Sharps was even more special than we'd thought. Not only could this guy survive multiple time travel jumps that killed everyone else, he also had the power to take a passenger. Sharps is our last resort because he can reset time. The Fab Five will help me because they understand his value.

But when he gets out into the real world, there's no way you'll be able to be Janaelle, an unwelcome voice in my head chirps. *Add to that, eleven years have passed. He'll saunter back into the world nary a day older, and here you'll be, showing every hour of wear and tear. Never mind not being the woman he loved in the first place.*

"Maybe there's a way I can manipulate his data even further," I muse out loud. "Parse out everything except his love for Janaelle. Make him unconcerned with appearance. It might turn him into a bonehead, but he'll be a loving bonehead—a good husband to me and a great dad to our unborn child. He loves children. It'll be the clincher."

But rewriting the code to that level means I'll need mega help. Jazza could do it. Or Sting Ray Barb. Ava would be the best from a tech point of view, but I can't even get an audience with the Whispering Queen these days. That's what Sharps called her back in the day, and he was right. Who the heck could hear what she was saying? Jazza's a stay-at-home daddy to his and Ava's three kids, and maybe extended pat leave fried his brain and he can't even do tech anymore.

Not to mention the fact that none of them have the time of day for me.

Oh, Sharps. How I wish we'd never met. I was focused on the war, but when they brought him in, I fell off a cliff. Talk about drop-dead gorgeous.

I take a deep breath and rub my eyes hard. My whole life is such a fucking disaster.

I reach into a deep pocket and take out my stash of butt dust. I'm aching for a hit that will send me to never-never land where I'll feel no pain, but I've got to get home first. Besides, I'm worn out, and butt dust is soporific. I tuck away the vial and reach for a tiny vial. Nix. A savvy new-world equivalent of speed, cocaine, and methamphetamine. It lives up to its name and nixes out everything you've ever worried about, or were ever likely to worry about again. I try to use it sparingly, but I need chemical help now. I've driven god knows how many miles, hacked through a freaking jungle, and had a heartbreaking one-on-one with my guy. Anybody would need a pick-me-up. I snort a shot. Wowza! Yeah baby! Instant superwoman!

Good thing my senses are heightened because a blood-stained amputee hobbles into the middle of the road, and I swerve around him in the nick of time. I give the finger to the crowd who joins him and swarms after me, their growls an orchestra of horror even over the din of Lady Luck's super horsepower.

I tell myself to count today as a win. I wasn't even sure if Sharps would still be in the system, data intact. He could easily have been corrupted or deleted. But he's still there! I punch a fist in the air. Onwards and upwards!

Sharps.

WHO IN GOD'S NAME WAS THAT WOMAN? Or, what in god's name was that woman? And where did she go? She was nuts, whoever she was. I stare at the blackened mirror. There's nothing except my own reflection. The lights dim, and I'm left in darkness. Great. Here we go again. I wait for the fish to come floating by, and thank god they do, because they shed some light on the situation. Ha ha! I'm the master of puns. Sharps, you crack yourself up. In the eerie aquarium luminescence, I watch the room change. It peels apart, as if I'm standing inside an unfolding cardboard box. It's cool to watch the blackness expand, but it's also immeasurably weird. I swing back to the mirror, but it's gone, and there's nothing but the surrounding darkness. And yet there are the fish: jellyfish, red fish, blue fish, one fish, two fish. Seahorses bob past me, burping as they go.

I look down. The seabed is swirling around my ankles. I move, and the pixelated renderings break up and reintegrate. I kick the sand-coloured Jell-o and realize it's no more than a digital mirage.

This is what that woman meant when she said my dream was real. It seems like a dream, but I'm coexisting uncomfortably with software I can't control. I'm living on the Mainframe. I'm data, stuck in a machine and I need the reintegration pod to get me out. I tell myself that none of this is possible, but I know it's true. I'm connected to and stuck inside a computer.

I search my brain for fragments of information the way you search your mouth for a tiny seed lodged between two teeth. If I'm inside this computer, there has to be a way to access the hard drive. There has to be more than just the fish.

I decide to start walking. It doesn't make a difference which direction I choose, so I put one foot in front of the other and wade through the seabed. It becomes a game of sorts, punching fish and watching them dissolve in a spray of pixels.

Then wait, what? I slam into something, and my kneecaps, virtual or not, howl in pain. This thing doesn't dissolve. Amazing! I take a step back and crouch down. It's a large metal trash can, a vintage Apple Mac relic from back in the day, when my best friend and I goofed around. What was his name, my best friend, that Jonesy fellow? My brain hurts, so I stop trying to figure it out, but what I do know is that this bulging trash can contains data. Data that can potentially get me out of this hell hole. But how can I access it? Is it as simple as double-clicking on it? Double knocking? *Knock knock, who's there? The rest of your life?* Ha ha. I reach out and tap it twice. Nothing happens, but at least it doesn't disintegrate. I circle the thing, tapping it from all sides in case there's a secret access area. I try to pry off the lid, but it's stuck fast. I yell at it, hoping that might help, but the trash can remains impervious, a locked treasure trove of information.

Exasperated, I sit down on the seabed floor and the muck parts politely. *Come on Sharps.* You've got to access whatever's in the trash can.

And that's when I find the seed stuck between my teeth. I know how to open the trash can! I just need to think about it in the right way. As I recall, we are all connected to the computer by chip implants. Granted, I don't have a body, so I don't have access to the chip in my physical brain, but I'm part of the Mainframe. In theory I can access all the files that my chip held. But wait— doesn't that mean I have access to *all* the files in the Mainframe? I'm pretty sure it does! I just need to find a way in. And the way in is with my mind.

Something else occurs to me. I'm wandering around in darkness with a screensaver for company. That means the computer is asleep, but not shut down, just like that woman said. I must find a way to wake it up.

I reach into my brain almost meditatively. *Come on Sharps, you can do it.* A small, blue light flickers in the corner of my eye. Progress! I feel ridiculously excited. I close my eyes and zone in on the blue light. *Access trash can.*

Whatever I'm doing, it works. A soft humming noise sounds, a joyful symphony. The computer's waking up! Yes, the woman set it to sleep mode but I, with the power of my thoughts, using my connection via the data in my brain, am activating it! I feel inordinately proud of myself. Ha! The woman hadn't bet on the Sharpsmeister being at the wheel! I'm captain of my own ship! *Access trash can.* Never mind the trash can, the whole world floods with white light, and the fish vanish.

I look around and see a bunch of neatly arranged rectangles glued onto a wall, stretching up as far as the eye can see. I spin around. I'm surrounded by skyscraper walls, all covered with folders jutting out like thousands of tiny balconies. The boxes are pale blue with a slight drop shadow, and oh my god, there are so many of them. I study the names of the ones closest to me. *QuinquagintaSeptemMiliaSescentiTriciensCXII*. Is that Latin? They couldn't have found a more user-friendly naming convention?

I crane my head back and notice a pattern forming. There's a beach scene behind the folders. There's something achingly familiar about the palm trees and the setting sun. And then it hits me. It's the screensaver wallpaper from the life I'd left behind long ago, when I had my own avatar and pretty much lived on my computer. Holy shit! I'm on a desktop. The beach and palm trees are wallpaper, one of my favs, peaceful and inviting, and— yes! There's the hammock, with the frozen waves rolling in, and sunlight glinting off the white caps.

The fact that it's my old wallpaper tells me something. This cyber reality is mine. This may be a cyber dream, but it's *my* cyber dream. Otherwise the wallpaper would be random or have a company logo. This is my reality, and my entire life is in one of those folders. I just need to find the right one. It's like being lost in a metropolis, looking for the tiny room I once called home. I've got no idea how to begin.

I walk over to a folder and reach for it, but it remains stubbornly shut. *Sharps*, I chastise myself, *think about it! Don't be tactile, be mental!* That cracks me up too. *Ha ha, Sharps, you were always mental.*

I sit back down and focus on one of the folders. I do the same thing I did to activate the computer. I focus on it with my mind. The folder snaps open and reveals a long list of files.

I scroll through them at high speed. Oh shit. There are so many of them. How can I sort through them? I force the files to slow down, so I can read the names.

None of them are relevant to me. Plant Guard rotas, pay schedules, tax forms, orders for scented paint, data from weather-controlling satellites, rain and snow schedules.

I've fallen into the black hole of government archives. I've got to get out of here before I die of boredom. It is full of City bylaws, comfort centre allocations, statistics, ledgers, and monetary policies.

Oh. My. God. Make it go away. I shut my eyes and will the folder to close. When I open my eyes, the folder has complied. I look at the wall again. Those insane Latin essays for names. Ridiculous.

There must be a search engine. Keyword search! But what's the word? *Sharps!* I'll search myself. *Control F.* Lovely, up comes the tiny magnifying glass icon and the menu bar. I type in *Sharps*. Is that enough? I don't know my last name. My search reveals a bunch of stuff about vintage rifles and how to safely dispose of used needles but nothing on me.

I smack my hand on my forehead, which is when I notice a tattoo on the inside of my wrist. *Janaelle!* Note to self, when you get back into your real body, tattoo all the information you might ever need on yourself.

I type in *Sharps, Janaelle*.

Yep, there I am! Man, there are a lot of files about me. And they're black flagged. What do black flags even mean? It can't be good.

I start at the top and explore my life chronologically, one file at a time.

Sharps Barkley, adopted son of Mariangela and Dustin Barkley, employee at Integratron, father of Baxter Hunter Williamson the Fifth Barkley and Sophie Marigold Tracy Barkley. Disappeared when he was forty-four, suicide assumed due to impending investigation into corporate theft and fraud at Integratron. Frequenter of rage rooms. Diagnosed with mood disorders and violent anger.

I have a mother named Mariangela? And who in their right mind lumbers their son with that many ridiculous names? I deserve to be in hell for that reason alone. But fraud and theft? That doesn't sound like me, nor does suicide.

There has to be more. I apply new keywords. *Husband, father, fraud, Integratron*. Nothing. Wait, I'm the anger guy. I key in *rage, anger, fury*, and, oh dear god, am I ever sorry I opened up that can of worms. I find all the information I never wanted in a file titled *Subject Forty-nine*. My doings were documented by a gang called The Eden Collective, who meticulously logged my every failure—of which there were many.

Pandora's Box has got nothing on this clusterfuck disaster of a life. Turns out I'm a natural-born killer, although there's nothing natural or right about me. I killed my children to save them from finding out I was a fraud, a nobody. I had tried to con myself into believing I killed them to save them from the meaninglessness of life, but I killed them so they wouldn't despise me. To my credit, I signed up for a time travel experiment to try to undo my evil actions, and I did save my children; however, in my own inimitable way, every time I went back, I made things worse. At one point I threw my boss, Ava, down a flight of stairs, and I drove Jazza, my BFF, to take his own life. Both of those actions were undone by me going back in time, but the fallout was sprawling and chaotic. No wonder they locked me up. There's no way I'm getting out of here, regardless of what that crazy woman thinks.

I close the file. I don't want to think about what I've seen, but I also can't just sit around waiting for that weird woman to come back. I lie down and fold my hands behind my head. A thought crosses my mind. Maybe I'm not alone in cyberspace? I'm Subject Forty-nine, the forty-ninth guinea pig. The other forty-eight must be in here with me!

I search *Subject Forty-eight*, but nothing comes up. *Shit.* Wait! Keyword *rage room*. My jaw drops. There are hundreds of thousands of files. I narrow the search to *rage room subjects*.

This reduces the number of files but there are still way too many for me to process.

I'm stymied.

I try *time travel, rage room subjects*. Bingo! Five files appear. But whoa. Only five out of forty-eight?

I select the five files and double click to activate, a move I will live to regret the rest of my life. Holy mother of soda crackers. The floor falls out from under me, and the room spins with a kaleidoscope of colours and images. I'm flung onto a roller coaster of pixels and glass shards and I smash into screaming, broken faces, with a soundtrack of tortured howls. The exploding fireworks and stained-glass puzzle pieces finally reassemble, and when they do, I'm surrounded by four accusing men and one woman, hands on her hips. If this is a popularity contest, I'm not going to win any prizes.

"What's the story, morning glory?" A tall, thin man chuckles, and a geyser of ice chips shoots up my anus.

"Sing a song of sixpence, a pocket full of rye," another voice chimes in. I swing around to face a chubby fellow wearing a top hat and a double-breasted black frock suit with a long swallow tail. He looks confused.

"Hey good lookin', whatcha got cooking?" A third man in full western riding regalia tips a big black Stetson.

"The dish ran away with the spoon?" The only woman in the room adds her contribution, but her gaze is empty.

"A pocket full o' posies, we all fall down," a fourth man speaks up, and I stare at him, fascinated. He's a stunning young David Bowie. He's got wolf eyes, pale blue, and one pupil is twice the size of the other. Sensual red lips, dark, thinly arched eyebrows, and clean planes that cut his face like alabaster.

"*Sanctus, Sanctus, Sanctus. Dominus Deus Sabaoth,*" a fifth man says. I force my gaze away from Bowie and wish I hadn't. The new man is pockmarked and potato-faced and about as appealing as a floating ball of mangy black hair in a swimming pool. He makes a slicing action across his throat. We all shrink back, although back is a misnomer since there isn't anywhere to go except infinity.

The man closes his eyes. He waves his hands like a symphony conductor. "Silence!" he yells, although none of us were talking. He screams incomprehensibly, and his waving crescendos until I'm sure he's having a heart attack.

He pounds his chest like a gorilla. "Yeah baby," he screeches. "Zuub, genius, baby, you've still got it! You're the man!"

Oh shit. I'm so fucked. What have I done, activating this psycho?

He reads my expression and dials it down a notch. "I fixed the comms, you a-hole. Be grateful you're finished parleying via nursery rhymes and song lyrics. I'm the intergalactic Grandmaster to end all Grandmasters, and you can start by thanking me on bended knee!"

Okay, so he hadn't dialled down anything. That was wishful thinking on my part.

"Who are you people, and why am I here with you?" The woman speaks softly. She's young, about thirty, statuesque and wide. She reminds me of someone, but I can't remember who.

"We're pharmers," Bowie says. "Not with an *F*. As in pharmaceuticals. I'm Jinx, by the way. Who are you?"

I'm about to reply when the lights flicker and die. We stand in the kelpy darkness, and the fish come bobbing along, cheerful and implacable as always.

"I gotta get us hooked up to the emergency generator, stat," Mr. Potato Face bellows. "Zip the pie holes, and let me have at her!"

"What Zuub means," the well-dressed, portly gentleman explains, "is stop talking nineteen to the dozen, and let the man do his work."

We fall in line. The cowboy snarls silently and points his revolvers at a belly dancing group of grey jellyfish, but he doesn't fire. We stand still for a timeless time. I must have nodded off because I'm awoken by a strobe light stabbing my eyeballs. As one, we drop to the ground, howling.

"Too high!" Zuub yells. "Drop illumination to forty percent!"

I cradle my head in my arms, fetal position, until I hear a laugh. I look up and the portly fellow in the dress suit extends a hand.

"Come on lambkin," he says kindly as he hauls me to my feet. To my chagrin, the only person on the floor was me. The light is benevolent now, kind and warm, and I blink, wishing I could *command-undo* my panic attack.

"Is the generator working?" I ask. "Are we safe?"

Zuub shrugs. "Who knows? I've done what I can for now."

"So, you guys were pharmers," I say. "Hard core."

"The pharms were prisons," Jinx explains to the woman. "Maximum security out in the back end of nowhere. We manufactured pharmaceuticals. Pills for everything, and all from our factories."

I'm curious. "But if you guys didn't have anything to do with the rage rooms, how did you get into time travel?"

"Bad luck and off-the-chart anger psychometrics. The pièce de résistance was a badass prison riot that landed us in very hot water."

Jinx giggles and looks nostalgic. "Fifty men dead. It was a hoot, but every wild night has its hangover, and we were ordered to become fuel for the time-travel fire."

"Fuel! You time travelled to create energy!" The woman marvels. "It worked! It's all coming back to me. Incredible! I was the first person to time travel. I died trying. Or I ended up here."

"Oh. My. God," I say. "Shut the front door. I remember now. You're Jazza's mother! Jazza is, or rather was, my BFF. But you're so young!"

Next thing, the woman is in my face, her nose an inch from mine. And I'd thought Zuub was scary.

"Of course I'm young, you idiot. I wasn't even twenty-six when I died. You don't age in cyberspace!" She bares her teeth at me, and I do a backbend. Good thing she hadn't asked me to guess her age. In my experience, women do not respond well to being aged up. "You know my boy? How is he? Where is he? How do you know him? Does he know what happened to me? Is he safe?"

I wish I could help her, but I don't have the answers.

"He thinks you're dead," Zuub offers. "And it will come as a shock when Noelle tells him there's a good chance you're holed up here with pretty boy. She won't want to tell him that, but she'll need help with the reintegration pod. And he won't do it for Sharps. He doesn't like you," he turns to me, "but he loves his mother."

"Who's Noelle?" I ask, confused at every turn.

"The woman who came to see you," Zuub says. "God, you're stupid. We've been stuck in data archives forever, but after one tiny nanosecond of post-activation we all know what's what, whereas you're like Mr. Snail."

"How do you know all this? How do we get out?" The woman swings her attention to Zuub.

"We wait," Zuub says. "Snail's lady pal is hotfooting it back to call the calvary. Meanwhile, we must sit tight. Play with our imaginary friends. How do I know what I know? Some of it's speculation based on my understanding of human nature, and some of it's what I picked up before they shut down the Mainframe after the war."

"Why did that woman tell me her name was Janaelle?" I ask, and Zuub shakes his head.

"I'm not wasting my time telling that very long, very boring story. You'll find out eventually."

I want to throttle him until he spills the beans, but I know there isn't anything I can do.

"Can we please stop with the riddles?" the woman asks. "Come on fellows. Let's play nice."

She calms the bad boys down, and they nod. She knows how to wrangle these misfits, and I'm glad she's on my side. Wait, is she on my side? I hope so.

The cowboy holsters his guns. "Cool bananas," he says. "Let's loop the beatnik in." He grins and sinks crossed-legged to the ground. One by one, like tired whack-a-moles, we follow suit.

"Who will go first?" the woman asks.

"Keep it short," Zuub says. "I've got very low boredom threshold." He burps and a clown fish swims out of his mouth.

"How did you do that?" I ask, and he waves me to silence.

"I'll go first," he says. "That way I can address the myriad of issues you lot have."

"Myriad." The portly man corrects him. "It's not myriad *of*. It's just myriad."

"Whatever." Zuub smiles. "Just remember that I'm the brains you will need when the calvary comes back. I can hardwire, hack, and yack with the best of them. I've got the power!"

"I'm Zayne," the cowboy says. "Fastest reflexes in the galaxy." Zayne tips his black cowboy hat, points at me and blows on the tip of his finger, a smoking gun.

"I'm Dorland," the British gentleman says. "I'm known as Mr. Manners. I take it very seriously when people are rude."

"Believe me, he means it." Zuub turns to the woman. "Lady, who are you? I can find intel on anyone, but nada on you."

"That's because I'm ground zero," the woman replies. "I was the very first time-travel jumper. They had no idea if it would work, and I volunteered. Of course, I thought I'd get back. I wasn't planning on dying."

"You pissed your son off big time by leaving him," I tell her, and she flinches.

"I can imagine. I can't blame him. I'm Beverley Jean Sigafoose, but you can call me Verlee. What's the plan? For us to sit around and wait to be rescued?"

"I'm not sitting anywhere." Zuub waves an imaginary wand.

The room scatters, and I scream. I'm hunkered down next to a giant-sized black horse. It looks like a statue, but it snaps at me, missing me by inches with its big yellow teeth. I turn to run and bump into another statue, and I look up in terror. What is that? It looks familiar but I can't place it. The Eiffel Tower? No, it's the Queen, and she grins a ghastly smile.

"Look down, pretty boy." I can hear Zuub but I can't see him or the others.

Chequered tiles light up the floor in black and white and, as the pieces move, the squares flash lime green.

"Chess? We're playing chess? Where are you guys?" I crouch down and try to hide behind a pawn, but it darts at me, fanning out dragon-spiked wings. I leap from square to square, narrowly avoiding being crushed and yelping in terror.

"Don't you like games?" Zayne materializes in front of me, and I realise why these guys were at the pharm. They're all crazy.

"Everything you dream is real, boy!" Jinx yells at me. "If you can dream it, you can be it!"

"He's right, loser!" Zuub adds his cheery support. "You've got the power to create any world you want to. Grow an imagination!" And with that, he vanishes.

"I've got my eye on a Wyoming ranch," Zayne grins. "And a bright bay mare." He too vanishes.

"I'm retiring to Chillingham Castle in Northumberland," Dorland says. "Visit the blood-soaked dungeons and drink sherry. Cheers, old chap!"

"What are you going to do?" I ask Verlee, and she closes her eyes. She stands *en pointe* and twirls, ballerina style. When she comes three-sixty, we're standing in a flower-filled meadow with deer and colourful birds, with a babbling brook running alongside us and snow-covered mountains in the distance.

I turn back to see if any of the others are still with us, but I'm on my own with Verlee. What world can I possibly create? I don't deserve the family I loved. I don't deserve anything. I sigh and sit down to watch Verlee.

Noelle.

Who can I enlist to help me? Mother's my best bet. After all, Sharps is her son. Plus, there were all the problems we were having with that creepy little shit Baxter, her grandson and Sharps's firstborn. Surely Mother will be in favour of having the kid's father show up to participate in the parenting? Baxter is fucked up because of Sharps, so it makes sense that Sharps should be the one to fix it. And once I convince Mother, she can convince her geriatric but brainiac buddy, Sting Ray Barb, to pitch in too. Sting Ray Barb invented the reintegration pod so she's crucial to the operation, but she won't do anything without the go-ahead from Ava. And Ava hates Sharps and vice versa.

I retrace the history in my mind. Ava set up Sharps so it looked like he had embezzled funds, and Sharps was so ashamed that he murdered his family that perfect Christmas Eve. And let's not forget that Sharps also tried to kill Ava by pushing her down seventeen flights of stairs, but Ava miraculously lived. So yeah, things weren't great between them.

I dodge another crowd of amputees and curse when a Monarch hits my windshield. I can't take the chance of stopping the racer to retrieve it. Can't risk being mauled to death and eaten by the bloody hordes.

I've lost my train of thought, and I bite my thumbnail. Right. Bad blood between Ava and Sharps. And then there's Jazza. He was Sharps's best friend and the brains behind all their crazily lucrative materialistic inventions, but Sharps managed to screw it up big time and nearly got Jazza killed.

Yep, Mother's my best bet.

I finally turn into my driveway and pull up outside my shack. It too is assembled from bits and pieces of long-dead robots and found pieces of plastics. A lot of people still live in their creepy vine-covered McMansions, but I prefer to live in the forest. I'm pretty darn proud of my humble abode.

I get out of the racer and stretch. I've been gone a week. I lean into the back and grab my now-empty water cans, the two-way radio, and the canister with the dead butterfly. Normally I'd be distracted by the lure of the butt dust, but I'm too anxious about my dilemma. I've got to figure this out, and I've got to do it sober.

I head straight for the outhouse. Because of the vines, flushing toilets are a rare luxury, and vintage outhouses are the norm. I'm dying to take a shit and figure out my next move. I'm still carrying the two-way radio, and I set it down on the ground while I pull down my pants. Frickin' couture dungarees are a bitch to unhook and unzip. Talk about rhinestone bonanza on the fabric. I undo all the snaps, sit down, and pull a few non-poisonous leaves within arm's reach.

But the anticipated evacuation doesn't happen. My bowels are clenched from the long ride and the stress of it all, and I flick the walkie talkie on just for something to do.

"EmoOne!" God, it doesn't take Mother three seconds to call me. "Pick up, Noelle, pick up now."

Noelle? What had happened to Nellie? She must be mad at me. "Yeah Mama bear, I's here," I drawl. "Wassup?"

"Are you high? Oh for god's sake, Noelle."

"Sober as a church mouse judge. You sound royally pissed off, Mama bear," I say. "What's the story?"

"Where are you?"

"Home. Just got back. I told you I'd be in touch when I was ready."

"You need to get your ass into the office, asap," she says.

"I'm taking a shit," I reply, and I sound whiny.

"Noelle. Get here now. We will all be assembled and waiting. And I do mean all of us. OctoOne will be here! You told me you'd be gone for a few days, and I believed you. It's been a week. OctoOne is not happy!" She hisses the last part. I shoot upright, my dungarees a knot around my ankles.

"Wha?" my voice trembles.

"See what I mean?"

"I'll be there in two shakes of a lamb's tail," I say, and I scramble back into my clothes.

"I'd be a shade speedier than that if I were you," Mother says, and the line goes dead.

I run to my racer and jump in. Holy shit. OctoOne. I practically fly to the office, which is close to Sky The Tower. Sky The Tower was home to Integratron, the corporation that employed Sharps, Ava, and Jazza. Home to two hundred pink and blue plastic floors, filled with scads of eager beavers all helping the company make money by selling shit to people with shit for brains.

After the war, we housed the government HQ in the forest, to be at one with nature, but the early rains turned the whole enterprise into a gooey gluey nightmare. We quickly admitted defeat and slunk back to the roomy offices of our former enemies. The skyscraper had died a sorry death and was nothing more than a creepy shrine to the ivy vines, so we appropriated the Sheds, igloo-shaped huts at the base.

I pull into the office compound and run towards the main Shed. Wait. I stop and snort a shot of nix. Yeah, that's better. I straighten up and march into the boardroom, my expression stony. Show no fear. Don't speak until you are spoken to. I've got this.

The boardroom is dark. I reach for the light, but a voice stops me.

"No light." The voice is musical, like wind chimes, if wind chimes were the ironically whimsical laugh of an evil clown. I peer around. I can't see anything except for a pale green glowing shape. Are there blackout blinds on the windows?

"Sit down," the voice says, and I hesitate. How am I supposed to find a chair?

"On the floor," the voice tells me, and I do as she says. This must be the infamous OctoOne, who I've never met in person. Do you call an octopi-infused person a person? I'd hate to get my terminology wrong. Are the others here? I can't see them in the dark. I look over at the green blobby shape, and my vision adjusts—I see a few waving arms and bobbing tentacles. OctoOne, our batshit crazy leader. The rumours are true!

Using gene sequencing tools, OctoOne infused octopus DNA into her own, resulting in a truly fucked-up hot mess. We all know the story. She chose the octopus because they could regrow limbs and organs and they were poisonous, which was great for self-defence. The suction cups on her tentacles came in handy, and she liked that some scientists thought octopi were aliens because of their unique genomes, which were almost as large as a human's. Octopi can adapt to environments, out-think their enemies, strategize, hide, and even flatten themselves.

It's rumoured that she nibbles at her own fingertips, or tentacle tips, when she's stressed, and she's developed an addiction for flesh. She allegedly lives off amputee body parts delivered by her minions. She's not someone to mess with.

A negative side effect of the octopi infusion is her constant need for hydration. Given that water is a scarce commodity, she's vulnerable, which must piss her off royally. She hadn't anticipated the postwar drought. None of us had. She lives in a tank, but she's come out to meet me. It must be important.

I hear a weird hissing sound and feel the cool spray of water. Her guards are hydrating her.

"Find a chair and get the fuck off the floor," a voice whispers. Ava, of course.

I feel my way over to the table and haul myself into a chair.

"Shasta, darling, will you take notes?" OctoOne asks. I stop myself from snarling, but a smart-ass comment escapes before I can help myself.

"Yes, Shasta, darling, take notes like a good little girl," I mimic mockingly. Next thing I know, a thick rubber hose whips around my neck, crushing my bones and cutting off my air. I slam my fists on the table and claw at my throat, but the slippery wet tentacle tightens around my neck. OctoOne is killing me. My last thought is that I truly don't know when to shut the fuck up and that I'll die for my sins, but then I'm not so much released as flung across the room.

"Conduct yourself with more respect," OctoOne says with her wind-chimey voice, and I manage to grunt in acquiescence while rubbing at my throat. My eyes have adjusted to the light, and I can see the Fab Five at the table. Not showing much warm or fuzzy love, might I add.

"We have so much in common," OctoOne says, and I've got no idea what she's talking about.

"Show me your legs," she commands.

Ah. We are both body adjusters. I get it. I stagger to my feet, still reeling from the chokehold. I get out of my troublesome couture with as much dignity as I can muster, and I stand naked. I'm proud of my body. I'm not tall, but I'm strong and hard with big solid breasts, washboard abs, a magnificent black bush, and two gorgeous titanium legs that fit snugly into my hips. I am beautiful. I run my hands down my legs.

"You were one of the first to bio-adapt," OctoOne says admiringly. "Which is why I will let you live, for now, anyway. You chose lifeless mechanics, and I selected superior nature. But you are here because you have intel that we don't."

I fold my arms and glare at her. Lifeless mechanics?

"Get dressed, dear," Mother sounds tired.

I grab my clothes and pull them back on.

"So where were we?" OctoOne asks. "Ah. Right. You were going to tell us how Sharps Barkley is doing."

I'm a second away from retorting that I've got no idea what she's talking about when another tentacle slams the table in front of me, and the room shakes.

"Have you learned nothing from me?" she roars. The whole room fills with the bioluminescence of her anger. She literally lights up when she yells, and the air glows. If it weren't so terrifying, it would be kind of cool.

"I was just—," I say, and another tentacle grabs me by the throat again and shakes me like a rag doll. To my chagrin, I poop my pants. Great. The stench fills the room.

"Oh, very nice," Ava whispers sarcastically.

"Nellie, just tell us what we need to know." Mother is weary.

"I will, I swear. No more messing around." My voice shakes, and I shift in my chair. Man, shitting yourself is really uncomfortable. "Can I maybe get a change of clothing and get cleaned up first?"

"No." OctoOne is implacable. "Get on with it. I'm dehydrating here. You've taken far too long already. Describe the trip from start to finish, leave out nothing. I will stop you if I have questions."

And did she ever have questions. About everything I did. Everything I said. Everything he said. Everything I observed. About the drive there. The drive back. Four hours later, I was shattered, crying shamelessly and still covered in shit. I had nothing left.

"We need to take a small break, and we shall reconvene," OctoOne says. She waves a tentacle at me. "I need a tank dip, and you need to go and get cleaned up. Ava will go with you to make sure you don't do something stupid."

"Great," Ava and I mutter in unison, and then we glare at each other.

I follow Ava to the outdoor shower, and she hands me a bar of soap. Ugh. Soapweed yucca. I much prefer Buffaloberry. I jump under the shower and scrub like crazy.

"Done," I say. I stand naked in front of Ava. "Any clothes on hand or do I stay *au naturale*?"

"You are such a fuckup," she hisses at me. "If it were up to me—"

"You'd what?" My nose is inches away from hers. "You'd what, sweet pea?" I lean in and kiss her lightly on the lips, slipping my tongue into her mouth. She slaps me across the face. I laugh.

"Girls, please stop," Mother says. "You exhaust me. We are supposed to be the bastions of intelligence and world order, and look at you two, bickering like toddlers. Why do I have to constantly remind you both that we're on the same side?" She's got a point. Besides, I'm going to need Ava's help. I give her a grin, and she looks over her shoulder as if my smile was meant for someone else.

Mother hands me a pile of clothes.

"Pink dungarees?" I'm aghast. "With shoulder pads? You know I draw the line at *diamantés*."

"Noelle!" Mother yells at me, and I jump.

"Fine." I give in. "Can I get some food? Dying here."

Mother herds us back to a different, larger shed. This one has an armed guard at the entrance, a Brittle Star. OctoOne coded her battalions with oceanic designations: brittle stars, helmet heads, pajama sharks, and the like. We are the Bombay Ducks, named after a lizard fish. I'd thought that the title was childish, to say the least. I'd fought for us to be the coffinfish or dragonfish, but OctoOne had overruled me.

Thankfully, the names got shortened over time, and we were simply known as the Bombers. Brittle Stars, just called Stars, were armed and dangerous. I swallow the bile that shoots into my throat. It's time to get my shit together.

OctoOne is floating happily in a tank and seems more serene. The room is atmospherically lit with a few scattered candles, and at least this time I can see what's going on. I think back to the desert I've just driven through, and I calculate how long OctoOne would last out there, splayed out on the unforgiving gravel like a fleshy dying balloon, leached to death by the brutal sun.

"Don't think I can't kill you from here." She smiles at me, and I shut down my daydreaming. "Nice outfit," she says. "Let's continue."

To my great joy, large bowls of sweet potato stew are distributed, and I fall on mine with enthusiasm. Of course, one bowl just whets my appetite, and I nod when Ava pushes hers towards me. I'm surprised by the unexpected gesture, but who cares, hunger trumps. I hadn't realized how much my epic journey had taken out of me.

"Why did you move the reintegration pod?" OctoOne turns her wrath on Sting Ray Barb. OctoOne is floating like a mermaid, and she's much younger than I imagined. Her pale long hair floats alongside her limbs. She's buck naked and looks like a beautiful multi-limbed sea horse.

"Hey, rockstar, stop staring." OctoOne snaps her tentacles at me, and the sound carries through the glass.

I flush.

"Why did you move the reintegration pod?" OctoOne repeats. Sting Ray Barb sighs but remains silent. It's been a while since I've seen Sting Ray Barb, and she's aged. She looks like strung-out rabbit jerky, and she wasn't exactly a spry young chick when we started out. How old is she? Ninety? Her dreadlocks proved too high maintenance for the new world, and she'd lopped them off. Her thick glasses are wired together in the centre, and she's skinny as a pencil, her coffee-coloured skin dotted with dime-sized age spots. She might be the Executive Assistant of Science and Technology, but she looks ready to kick the bucket. I hope we've got a backup plan.

"I moved it," Jazza pipes up.

"He speaks," I comment, mopping up the last of my stew with a piece of flatbread.

"I do when I have something to say," he retorts. "It was me who moved it, not Sting Ray. I didn't want Sharps to get out. I figured it was more likely he'd get out if he was housed in the same location as the pod."

"But it weighs a ton." Mother is perplexed. "Not to mention that it's as fragile as all heck. When did you do that? And how?"

Jazza shrugs. He's attractive in a somewhat misshapen way, and I can see why Ava is attracted to him. She catches me looking at him, and I shrug.

"I've got friends," Jazza says. "They helped."

"He's so hot," I mouth at Ava. She folds her arms and glares at me.

"I cannot believe you lot actually worked together to bring about the coup," OctoOne comments, making a throat-slicing motion with a tentacle and glaring at me. "I'm glad I only dealt with Ava, or I'd have fired you all, or had you killed. Focus, please. Jasper, where is the pod? Cut to the chase."

"In the bunker under Shed Fifty-nine."

"And how the hell will we get it out of there?" Sting Ray Barb yells.

"Same way he got it in," Ava replies evenly. "But here's my question. Why do you want that sorry loser out at all?"

I thought I'd have to coerce them into helping me, but here's OctoOne leading the charge. Interesting.

"Can't say." Octo is vague. "Or rather, I won't. Jasper, here's something that should give you a small nudge of incentive. If we get him out, there's a very good chance we'll get your mother out, too."

A look of fear and wonder crosses Jazza's face, and he jumps to his feet.

"Of course! She's there too!" He slaps his forehead. "Why didn't I think of that before? Duh!"

"It's the slimmest of possibilities. Her data might have corrupted long ago," Ava reminds him, and he shoots her a look that makes me wonder if all's well in paradise.

"And it equally may not have," he replies evenly. "I'll action the pod relocation asap."

"All of you Bombay Ducks go along for the ride," OctoOne says. "No stupid bickering, you got that? Noelle, contain yourself and do the heavy lifting. Ava, do not provoke Noelle. Your job is to work on the code. Have every contingency plan ready. Mother, you keep a lid on the whole shooting match and keep me informed. Intel comes only from you. I can't bear listening to all of you chattering like starlings at a feeder. Sting Ray Barb and Jasper, you focus on the technology and make sure the pod works. Shasta stays with me. All clear?"

"All clear," we echo, and she waves a few tentacles at us.

"Why are you still here?"

We scatter.

Sharps.

I'M WATCHING VERLEE DANCE. She's swooning in the arms of her new partner, one leg held high above her head, her pink ballet shoe aimed at the ceiling lights.

I've got no idea how long we've been here, but we've worked our way through *Cinderella, Coppélia, Don Quixote, Giselle, La Bayadère, La Sylphide, The Nutcracker, Romeo and Juliet, Sleeping Beauty,* and *Swan Lake.*

I'm bored out of my mind. I've tried with all my might to fabricate my own world, but to no avail. I have no fabulous fantasies. I have no great escape or dream that I long for.

Zuub unexpectedly appears at my side, and I scream.

"Haven't exactly grown a pair since we last parted," he observes. "Wow." He looks over at Verlee. "Look at her go. Who knew? Very luscious."

Zayne and Jinx are next to arrive. The band's back together.

"We're blowing this pop stand," Zuub announces. "In breaking news, Noelle is en route and she's bringing the cavalry."

"And you know this how?" I ask.

"Verlee's lad, Jazza, tried to access the Mainframe. He failed but his better half, Ava, got in."

"Ava? Oh shit." I wring my hands. "My goose is not only cooked, it's fried."

"From frying pans to fires for you," Zuub agrees. "It would have been curtains for us, but I've written a code, Trojan Horse style, that will get us all out."

"Malware disguised as software." Verlee is impressed. "But we're data. How do you do that with data?"

"Because I'm a legend! Have no fear, my sweet innocent little dear, we will live happily ever after in the real world! Tell you what," he suggests, "how about we watch a movie while we wait?"

He waves his hand, and suddenly we're in a theatre for five with massive black lounging chairs and side orders of popcorn, Cokes, and candy.

"Sure," Jinx says, "whatever. Better than sitting around and waiting to die."

"Townes Van Zandt!" Zayne nods. "Yeah baby. Great song. Let's have at her."

"FYI," Zuub says, and he smiles at me, flashing his broken teeth, "the world we're returning to is fixated on the '80s and '90s. Another boring story, but the storage lockers of an old cult were all that remained when the world as you knew it ended. Therefore, we're going to bring ourselves up to speed, and number one on our list is the panty-wetting *Dirty Dancing*. Just up your alley, darling." He leers at Verlee, and she shrinks closer to me.

Yeah, like I'm anyone's protector. Besides, I've got my own problems. I'm trying to get my balls out of my throat.

Ava. Oh my god. Fucking Ava. She's coming for me. There's no escape.

***

"She's here," Zuub yells. "Huddle, huddle."

We grab each other and hold tight.

"Do *not* let go!" Zuub yells again. "And you, dingbat," he pokes me, "be convincing and don't tell her about us."

I wonder what would happen if I did. What if I shouted, "*Hey, Janaelle, there's a bunch of lunatics in here? Get me and Jazza's mom out and leave the rest of the loonies behind, please and thank you!*"

It won't work. Besides, Zuub has superpowers. Knowing him, he's written a code to mute me or a virus that will corrupt all our files if I turn against him. *The application is shutting down due to a fatal system error, files corrupt, zero percent of retrieval.*

So I hang onto Verlee, and pray for the best.

It seems like we're stuck together forever, an uneasy barnacle, and even the others begin to complain.

"It's taking longer than I thought. We could have watched *Flashdance* again," Zuub admits.

"Or *The Breakfast Club,*" Dorland says.

"You guys. I'd take *Mannequin*," Zayne says. "Andrew McCarthy was the best of the Brat Pack, if you ask me."

"No way. Demi Moore rules," Verlee says, sounding annoyed anyone would think otherwise.

"You guys are such romantics," I say. "*The Lost Boys* is the best."

"Jason Patric was such a loser," Zayne says. "Good thing you're our golden key because otherwise you'd be no damn use at all."

Great.

"Why is it taking so long?" Verlee asks.

"It's proving trickier than they thought, setting up the reintegration pod. Sting Ray Barb, resident genius, although I hate to admit it, is here and working on it with Ava and Jazza. They're arguing about the code. Jason Patric's dingbat girlfriend, Noelle, is also here. She isn't actually doing anything, but she's here."

"Besides a fascination with bad movies from the '80s," Verlee says, "I wonder what the world's like now."

"It was pretty shitty when I left it, which was right after they won the war and unplugged everything," I said. "It was raining cats and dogs, and I do mean that literally, although there were rats and raccoons too. Mud everywhere. Filth. A group called The Eden Collective decided to reboot and give nature the chance to make a comeback. Sayonara to our lovely clean plastic world. However, according to Janaelle, or Noelle, there's a been a drought. I thought you guys knew everything?"

"How? We were here for about five years before they pulled the plug, trapped in cyberspace after we jumped, but just like you we went to sleep when the Mainframe was powered down."

"At least we didn't die," Verlee said. "Thank god for the chips in our heads and the Crystal Lattice, or that would have been the end of us. Let's just hope they can reintegrate us successfully." She looks confused. "Zuub, you and the others had a level of consciousness here in cyberspace before the shutdown, but I've got nothing. Why is that?"

Zuub shrugs. "Maybe it had to do with the time travel technology they developed after you? Bear in mind, there were forty-nine subjects—actually, fifty if you count Shasta, that girl who jumped with Sharps—and only the five of us survived. I can't tell you why we did and others didn't."

"Shasta's in here too?" I'm delighted. "Wait, she isn't, or I'd know. Did her data corrupt?"

"She got out," Zuub says shortly. "She wasn't a real time traveller. She hitched a ride with you, which in itself was remarkable. I hate to say it, but there is something impressive going on with you. Not that anyone would ever be able to tell, given your moronic utterances."

Why does everyone hate me so much? Still, thoughts of Shasta are lovely! I remember her now. She and I were waiting to jump forward in time, and we were shooting the breeze. *Her face is so close to mine and her hair smells like strawberries. She's eating a glazed donut and a tiny piece of it sticks to the side of her mouth. I want to reach over and wipe it off.*

"Dingbat!" Zuub yells at me and I snap back. "Here, boy!"

"Stupid moron finally finds his happy place," Dorland snarls. "He's our ticket out. Keep him focused."

"Don't pull that shit again," Zuub says. He wedges himself in between me and Verlee, and his fingernails dig into my arm.

"Ow," I try to free my arm, but his iron claw grip is relentless and deep.

"Hang on guys, here it comes!" Zuub shouts. The light flickers, breaks up, and reassembles. Static flashes back and forth, and there's a sound like an old cassette tape rewinding. I swear I hear boom box buttons clacking: stop, start, record, click, snap, click, snap. And then, nothing.

***

"He's conscious!"

I'm glad they think so. As far as I can tell, I'm faceplanted at the bottom of a well, and my nostrils are filled with clay. My eyelids are glued shut with concrete and sandpaper. I manage to slightly open one eye. A bright light lances my cornea, and I can't make out any kind of detail. Faces come into focus one at a time, like a magnifying glass is being passed back and forth. The motion blur makes me want to throw up, and I slam my eye back shut. I hear shouting, but I still can't move. I'm a million pieces of shattered ice, and every shard burns like the blazes.

"Give him heat," a voice adds, and I'm flooded with warmth. I relax into the glow.

"Heart rate is steady, pulse normal. Heat is good."

"Where's my mother?" It's Jazza. Verlee's son and my former BFF. "I thought we were getting my mother out too. She's the only reason I agreed to help get him out in the first place."

"I don't know," Sting Ray Barb admits. "Something went wrong. We need to activate him and see what he remembers. Find out if he can shed any light on the situation. The data's screwed. There's nothing left as far as I can tell, which is weird. There should be something left. I've tried the backup hard drives too, and there isn't a trace."

"Is he brain damaged?" a worried voice asks. It's a voice I recognize. The woman who came to visit me. "What if he never comes to? It's been over two weeks."

"He'll pull through." Oh. My. God. That's my mother. I'd know her voice anywhere. Great. Just great.

"He's the world's biggest dickhead. Dickheads never die." This is Ava, of course. My scrotum clenches.

"Come on guys, give him a break. He does have a few good points." Jazza's defence of me is as exciting as lukewarm coffee. "Sure, I would have left him in there were it not for my mother, but he does have a good side. You guys didn't know him like I did."

"He killed you," Ava reminds him.

"Actually, that was Shasta," Jazza says. "Sharps tried to save me." I did? Bully for me.

"Sharps meant well," Jazza says. "He always meant well. Things just got out of control."

Ava snorts. "Understatement of the day."

"He was the only time traveller to survive multiple jumps. I admire him for his stamina." This is from Sting Ray Barb, head time travel technician. Nice to know she holds me in some regard.

"He's a great man!" Noelle cries. "He always felt judged by you guys, and for good reason. He was never good enough for any of you, and he knew you felt that way."

Hmmm. Maybe there's something to this woman after all.

"None of this excuses him killing his family," Mother says. Everyone falls silent for a moment.

"He tried to fix it," Noelle offers a rebuttal. "He risked his own life repeatedly, to try to undo what he had done."

"Yeah, and then he screwed things up so royally it was hilarious," Ava says. "And let's not forget he killed me too. Pushed me down a flight of stairs." At least she's stopped whispering and I can hear her clearly. Not that I want to.

"He had good reason," Noelle snarls. "You were going to publicly frame him for embezzling funds! You pinned everything on him. He couldn't live with the shame of it. You were the one who put all of this in motion."

She's so right! I open my mouth to agree with her, but nothing comes out. My tongue is glued to the top of my mouth.

"Chicken or egg, blah blah blah," Ava says. "The scorpion and the frog. We all know the story. We find ways to succumb to our nature. He was a pawn to his darkest desires."

"Pawns are extremely important pieces in the game," I hear a voice chirp, and it isn't coming from way up high. It's coming from inside my head. What the heck? This is a new kind of weird.

"Dingbat? Are you awake? Ha ha, I know you are. Time to get with the program, baby boy. Things haven't turned out quite as I had planned and…"

But then I hear "Let him sleep," from Mother, who is far away. "I'm sure all of us looming above him doesn't help."

"I'm staying." Noelle is stubborn. "I want to be the first person he sees when he wakes."

"Sure, whatever." Ava. "Not like you're needed anywhere else. You sit here and hold his hand. Just remember, he never loved you, and it's not like he's going to wake up and say 'hey honey, I'm home.'"

"Why do you have to be such a bitch, Ava?" Noelle sounds close to tears, and I really feel for her. I too have been on the receiving end of Ava's wrath, and it isn't fun.

"Leave her be," Mother says.

"Zuub?" This from a panicked Jinx. "Why are we stuck in the dark? Why aren't we out in the real world?"

"Calm down, laddie," Zuub says, but I can hear he's freaked out too. "We'll sort this out. I need some intel. Just breathe."

"I hate it when people tell me to breathe," Jinx hisses. "It never helps anything."

Where are they? I can't figure it out. And why can't Mother and the others hear them?

"His vitals are showing increased activity," Sting Ray Barb says, and I hear the others rushing over to wherever she's standing. "Look. Massive spike in neural activity in the brain."

"It's going wild," Ava marvels. "Maybe he's having a stroke?"

"He's not having a stroke. Stop trying to fuck with Noelle," Sting Ray Barb snaps. "Noelle, he's fine. There's an inexplicable spike of neural activity coming from multiple sources. Baffling, yes."

"If you don't shut up, I won't be able to figure this out," Zuub says, and Jinx falls silent.

Oh my god. They're inside my head. But surely that isn't possible? I manage to unglue my tongue and work up some saliva. Who knew saliva could feel so good? I lose myself in the happiness of my own spit but am interrupted when the voices start up again.

"Let's take a count," Zuub says. "Who else is here? Verlee?"

"Yeppers."

"Dorland?"

"Present and accounted for."

"Zayne?"

"You got me, babe."

Meanwhile, Noelle is crooning in my ear.

"Honey, we're going to have a baby! Isn't that exciting? The others don't know, so don't say anything, but isn't it wonderful? We're going to be a real family! You've got to come back, honey. Come on, you can do it."

"Open your eyes," Zuub hisses at me. "Open your fucking eyes, boy."

I do, and the whole world screams. Noelle screams with joy while Zayne, Verlee, Jinx, Dorland, Zuub, and I scream in horror. To make matters worse, the only scream Noelle hears is mine while I've got a symphony of terror ringing in my head.

"Shut up," I yell. "Shut up, shut up!"

Noelle thinks I'm talking to her, and she pushes away from the bed with a look of hurt and fear. She holds her hands out like I'm a mental patient. "Sharps, baby, it's okay. It's me. I know I look older, but it's been eleven years."

The others rush over to me. Yep, it's been eleven long years all right. Sting Ray Barb looks like a bald cadaver, Mother looks surprisingly good, and Jazza has acquired a certain middle-aged handsomeness. Ava looks like she hasn't aged a day. Of course not, the bitch. Wait, who is that gorgeous blonde? Something about her is familiar. Oh my god! Shasta! All grown up. She was what, twenty-one when we jumped? She had a dickhead boyfriend who I think I killed by mistake. I push that memory away and do the math. She's thirty-two. Maybe I've got a chance with her? My chest is flooded with joy, and I'm suddenly glad to be back.

"Sharps?" A crowd of voices is yelling my name and I close my eyes. Is there a way to talk to one group without the others hearing? I duck under the blanket, whimpering.

"Sharps, it's me Zuub. I got the others to pipe down. Can you hear me buddy?"

"Yes. You guys," I whisper, "you're in my head, right?"

They shout affirmations at the same time, and I clap my hands to my ears. "Noooooo!" I cry. "One at a time! Only Zuub, only Zuub!"

"I told you," Zuub yells, which doesn't help.

"Sharps?" It's Noelle. "What do you mean honey? What's a shoob? What can I get you?"

"We're stuck in here!" Jinx is going nuts. "I'm claustrophobic! How could this happen? Oh Zuub, you idiot! You moron!"

They all chime in with clamours of the same nature. I wish I had a mute button, but there's nothing I can do.

I scream "shut up, shut up" as loudly as I can, until they finally fall silent. "ONLY ZUUB!" I yell. "He got us into this mess, he will get us out. So, only Zuub!"

"He keeps shouting shoob," Noelle says, "he's hysterical."

"Yeah, that much is clear," Ava. "He's totally lost it. Might be time to pull the plug on this loser once and for all."

I hear a scream, and I pull the blanket away. Noelle is attacking Ava. She's got her on the floor and is giving her a good old pounding. Jazza's trying to haul her off, but he's failing. Man, Noelle packs a good punch. I remind myself to stay on her good side.

A referee's whistle blows, piercing the room. Everyone freezes.

"Time out," Shasta says. "Get off her, Noelle, or I'll have you thrown into the penalty box for a couple of days."

Noelle gets to her feet, and Jazza helps Ava up. Ava's face looks like a pulverized tomato. She ices Noelle with a stare, and Noelle grins and shadow boxes.

"Better yet," Shasta says, "I'll have you both thrown into the box together. Leave you to sort things out. Noelle, Ava might have lost this round, but my money's on her. You willing to give it a go?"

Noelle looks sulky but slightly fearful.

"These people are crazy," Jinx whispers.

"And to think we were the ones sent away," Dorland pipes up.

"Moving on," Shasta says. "OctoOne wants a report on Sharps asap, and all we've got so far is a mess. How are his numbers doing?" She turns to Sting Ray Barb, who looks confused. "The same. Spiking all over."

"I can explain." I sit up in bed, and Shasta comes up close to me.

"Explain what?" she asks.

Dear god, she's beautiful. My eyes must have widened, and I feel a wave of hatred coming from the far side of the room. I turn, and Noelle tasers me with a look that sears my soul. I wither back onto my pillow. She's still in love with me, and she's just watched me melt like an ice cream sundae on a patch of hot asphalt.

But who can blame me? Flawless skin, tumbling golden locks, lips like cherries, eyes like sapphires, and the breath of an angel. Is she going to kiss me? She's going to kiss me! She's that close. I lean into her, my lips pursed like a teenage boy. She slaps my face, and I recoil.

"Stop jerking us around," she says. "This is taking too long."

"There are people inside my head with me," I manage to stutter. The others flinch like the cute puppy just peed on the sofa.

"Knew he'd be messed up," Ava mutters. "Loser."

"There are," I insist. "I found a bunch of files and I activated them. Other jumpers. They were supposed to get out too, but now they're in my head."

"It could happen," Jazza admits.

"Not possible," Sting Ray Barb snaps. "I designed the reintegration pod, and it delivers one carrier per download."

"Time travel was designed for single users," Shasta points out, "but there I was, piggybacking with Sharps, and we both survived."

She remembers the quality time we shared! We'd bonded. We did have a thing! Well, a kind of thing. She'd slapped me pretty hard, so maybe she wasn't feeling the love in quite the same way I was.

"It would explain the multiple neural spikes," Ava says, and Sting Ray Barb grunts in agreement.

"A lot of your science hasn't exactly been on the mark," Ava says, and Mother spins around.

"Ava, stop being so tiresome. We wouldn't be here were it not for Barb. We wouldn't have won the war."

"We would too," Ava argues. "You guys constantly act like time travel was the key to our success. It wasn't. OctoOne took control of the Universal Mainframe, and our armies did the rest. I'm so tired of hearing about time travel. I'm so tired of this guy even being part of the conversation. Why do we even need him? I don't get it."

"We need him," Shasta says, her voice like ice, "because he's the only one who survived multiple jumps. OctoOne needs time travel to survive. The world is dying. We've got to go back and activate the weather satellites so it will rain. We got an extension to the Mainframe shut down so we could send Sharps back, but he seems pretty messed up."

"OctoOne is dying?" Ava sounds jubilant. "Not like she's done such a stellar job. I say let the great old lady of the sea admit she made a serious faux pas when she cloned the wrong animal species into her DNA and let us get on with running this world. Do you know how much precious water we waste on her? Tons. Per day. I am talking *per day*. Water that our civilians need. She gets a tank while your average Josephine gets a bathing bowl a week. One bowl! And what exactly does OctoOne contribute? Nothing."

There's a stunned silence. The door bursts open, and a bunch of naval-clad ninjas rush in, armed to the gills. Halloween? There are white sharks on their epaulettes, and they're wearing jaunty white navy caps.

They grab Ava and drag her off before she can utter a syllable.

"What the fuck?" I'm chilled to the marrow.

"SSBs. Super Shark Brigade." Jazza sounds tired. "Ava's been saying shit like that for a while. I'm surprised it took this long for them to haul her off." He sinks into a chair and rubs his face in his hands. "What a mess."

"Will they kill her?" I try, unsuccessfully, to keep the hopeful tone from my voice. I never liked that bitch.

He shakes his head. "She's too valuable. But they will make her life extremely uncomfortable. Let's put it that way."

"They've taken your children to a youth commune," Shasta says, and Jazza looks at her in horror.

He springs to his feet and rushes over to her. "My kids are *mine*! What the fuck?"

"They're safe." Shasta is calm. "You know I'd never hurt children. I love children more than anything. I even love your warped offspring, Baxter," she says, turning towards me.

"Bax is warped?" I ask. "Warped like how? Because of me?"

"I want them back!" Jazza howls. He rushes towards the door, but another Shark officer arrives and blocks his way.

"Jazza," Shasta says, "we need to navigate our way through this. When we get to the other side, you'll get your kids back and life will go on. Until then, they're an incentive to help you focus. No distractions."

"Oh. My. God. You're holding my kids hostage. Beyond disgusting."

"That's a really negative way of seeing it," Shasta says. "We like to think that we're taking care of them so you can focus on your job. Get through this and everything will be fine."

"Which commune are they at?" Jazza asks, and Shasta shakes her head.

"Of course I can't tell you that."

"What if Ava hadn't given you cause to arrest her?" Mother asks.

"We would have taken her anyway," Shasta says. "As Jazza said, she's been spouting treason for a while. But enough chit chat, we need to get this sorted out."

"I'm not time travelling again," I pipe up. My voice sounds like the rusty edge of an old saw-blade. "You can't make me. You can't. It hurts. Stick me in cyberspace again, I don't care. I'm not doing it. I'm not."

"YOU ARE SO!" the voices in my head yell at me.

"Hey guys," I point out to the voices in my head, "you guys died doing it. It's not like you'd live. Only I would."

"He's got a point," Jinx agrees.

Meanwhile, Shasta's telling me I will most certainly time travel, Sting Ray Barb's muttering about a spike in my heart rate, and Jazza's hitting the wall with his massive fists.

"I won't help," he yells. "I'm sick of all of this. I'll rescue my kids and Ava will find a way out, she always does. I don't even care about her anymore. I'm sick of all of it. *Take your meds and be a good boy Jazza, do whatever I say Jazza, don't parent like that Jazza.*' Nag, nag, nag. I'm not sorry she's gone. Throw me into a Shark pool. I don't care. I know you'll take care of the kids, Shasta, I can trust you with that at least. And I'm such a fuckup, maybe they're better off without me."

"Someone's having a pity party," Sting Ray Barb observes, bald eagle style. "I thought you had bigger cojones than that, big guy. You're just having a bad day. Things will work out."

"Yeah? Like life's been peachy so far. Nope, count me out."

None of us know what to say.

"Wait!" It's Verlee to me. "Sharps, let me speak to my son."

"But how will you speak to him?" I ask. "The only voice he hears is mine."

"Just repeat what I tell you, okay?"

"Zuub?" I ask.

"See what I mean?" Noelle cries. "Shoob, he keeps saying shoob. Honey, is Shoob one of the men in your head?"

"Go for it, buddy," Zuub says to me. "I got nothing else."

I pull the pillow over my face and whisper urgently. "Verlee! Feed me my lines."

"JayJay, Mommypop's here," she instantly replies.

I feel like an idiot, but I remove the pillow and repeat what she's said. "JayJay, Mommypop's here."

Nothing. Jazza looks as if he hasn't heard. If he has, he doesn't care.

"JayJay, Mommypop's here," I say again, a touch louder.

"Maybe we should tranquilize him," Sting Ray Barb suggests. "Help him relax."

"No!" Zuub yells. "Who knows what might happen. No tranqs."

"No tranqs!" I yell at the same time. "JayJay, Mommypop's here. Come on Jazza, listen to me!"

Jazza turns to me with a quizzical expression, but he doesn't say anything.

I sit up and throw off the blanket. The others turn to look at me, mouths agape. "Mommypop's here JayJay," I repeat, "Mommypop's here." Still nothing, although Jazza's expression is increasingly perplexed. It's as if he's trying to reach back in time to the land of lost-and-found memories.

"Verlee," I mutter, "I need more."

This gets Sting Ray Barb's attention, and she sticks her face close to mine. "Verlee? Did you say Verlee? Jazza, she *is* in there! It's a miracle! Well, I'm a scientist, I don't believe in miracles, but she did jump although the data survival odds weren't great."

Jazza's face thaws slightly.

"She's here." I tap my head. "Along with four others."

"Who are they?" Sting Ray Barb asks.

"Don't tell her!" Zuub hisses. "We're escaped prisoners, they won't want us in the real world."

"Your problem, not mine," I shout, and Sting Ray Barb looks confused.

"They're convicts," I yell, and I jump off the bed. Bad idea. I crash to the floor. Right, I need a bit of time to readjust to real time. "Verlee's in my head with four convicts, and they won't shut up."

"Fascinating." Sting Ray Barb comes over and points a light in my eyes. I flinch.

"Mommypop?" This is from Jazza. "Mommypop, is that you? Talk to me."

"Tell JayJay I love him, and I'm sorry I left him. I really thought our time travel would work, and that I'd be back." Verlee starts sobbing, and such is the force of her love and sorrow that I start sobbing too.

"I'm sorry JayJay," I cry, "I love you. I really thought it would work, and that I'd be back. I've missed you so much, buddy." Okay, so that last part was me—Verlee wouldn't have called him buddy. But I had missed him, and when he grabs me and hugs me, I hug him as me, not as Verlee, although she's squealing with joy inside my head.

"There are no words to describe this hell," Jinx mutters. "Focus people, for god's sake, focus. We've got to get out of here."

"Get them out of me," I say as soon as Jazza releases me and wipes his eyes.

"We're going to try." Sting Ray Barb looks at Jazza. "Are you onboard, boy?" This sounds odd, since Jazza's in his mid-forties.

"To tell you the truth, I'm not sure how to do it," Sting Ray Barb admits, wiping her glasses clean with a cloth.

This makes the five people in my head scream full throttle, which in turn makes me scream. This doesn't go down well with the others.

"Calm down, Sharps," Shasta admonishes me, and I turn to her.

"You can't hear them," I yell. "All of them, screaming at me. You'd scream too. They're very fucking vocal in here. It's hard to take."

"We need to download their data back onto the Mainframe server and then send them to the reintegration pod one at a time," Jazza says.

"No way," Zuub immediately objects. "They won't print us out. They'll print out you and Verlee, and that will be that."

"Zuub says you won't print them out," I relay.

"What the fuck!" Zuub yells at me. "Don't say my name! I'm not exactly Mr. Popularity!"

"Sorry, sorry, just shut up, okay?"

"Jazza's right. It's the only way to do it," Sting Ray Barb replies. "Tell the convicts not to worry. We need them. The rest of the pharmers have all gone to ground, taking a bunch of chemistry and science with them. We believe they've formed a new militia, headed up by some cult maniac fellow. A lot has changed since you were gone, Sharps. Tell the others we do need them."

"You hear that?" I ask the crowd in my head. I hear murmurs of affirmation.

"But how do we download the data out of Sharps?" Mother is perplexed.

"Easy," Jazza replies. "Well, kind of easy. As long as the Mainframe is up and running, Sharps is still connected to it via the chip that got him out in the first place. We'll redownload him, give him a brain scour, separate the files, and Bob's your uncle."

"A scour?" I'm horrified. "Jazza never recovered from his."

"What's a scour?" Mother asks.

"It's akin to rebuilding a desktop and reinstalling software and data," Sting Ray Barb explains. "Generally used to defragment data, run diagnostics, clean up issues on the hardware, logic board, memory, and wireless components. And very handy for file and data management."

"Yeah, I remember when they did it to Jazza," I protest. "It was not pretty."

"Why did they scour Jazza?" Verlee shouts inside my head, but I ignore her.

"Why?" she yells again.

"Oh for fuck's sake, he was fucking Ava, and the board of directors wanted Ava's freedom manifesto, which he'd read. He wouldn't hand it over, so they scoured him to get it."

There's silence and confused looks from the crowd around my bed. "Verlee wanted to know why he was scoured," I explain.

"I'm fine, Mom," Jazza says. "I have to take meds, and I suffer from mood swings, depression, anxiety, panic attacks, and insomnia. I'm bipolar and have post-traumatic stress syndrome, but it's better than being dead."

"Is it?" I ask. "Really?"

"Of course it is," Mother comes over and strokes my hair. "Don't worry son. You need to come back for Baxter and Sophie. Granted, I was taken aback when I heard about the plan to free you, but it was Bax who changed my mind. He insisted we had to get you out. He wants to work through his issues with you. You disappeared when he was five, and he's very traumatized by that. You've got to come back and face the music."

"Does he hate me?" The crowd in my head must find this fascinating because there are no chirps from them.

"I wouldn't use the word hate. It's probably just teenage hormones." Mother looks uneasy. "Poor boy's had a rough life because of you. Celeste wasn't exactly mother of the year, and when she died of alcohol poisoning, he and Sophie were left orphans. I took them in, and Shasta helped me a lot. Bax needs you."

"I hate to be the bearer of bad news," Shasta says, "but I think it's more than hormones. I think he's got sociopathic tendencies that we may or may not be able to work with."

I stare at her. "A sociopath? Who died and made you Dr. Seuss?"

"You're thinking of Dr. Spock. Dr. Seuss was a children's book author," Shasta says. "I've studied Bax for years."

I bury my face in the pillow. There is no escaping the hell that is my life.

"Perhaps you can schedule this parenting session for another time?" Dorland asks. "Pretty please with cherries on the top, whipped cream, and spiced rum? We need to move on."

The others agree, and even Verlee sounds impatient.

"Fine." I sulk. "Whatever."

"I was classified as a sociopath when I was nine," Jinx mutters. "Subcategory callous-unemotional. It really hurt my feelings."

I hear Zayne give a creepy chuckle. Apart from participating in the group screaming, he's been silent. "Me too, only my subcat was attention deficit hyperactivity disorder, narcissism, and a marked lack of empathy."

"I was a manipulative liar, aggressive, and hostile," Zuub says.

"I'm glad you guys weren't this forthcoming when I asked before," Verlee tells them, and I silently agree with her. There are a bunch of fruitcakes locked inside my skull. Oops. I hope they can't read my thoughts.

"Good thing the others can't hear you," I say out loud, and Mother looks at me.

"Shut up, you idiot," Jinx says. "Ask them if there is anything they can do to knock us out until our day of freedom. Being stuck inside you is killing me."

I relay the question to Sting Ray Barb who cocks her head to one side.

"We'll have to induce a medical coma for the scour anyway," she says. "And we can do it sooner rather than later, while Jazza sets up the pod."

"You want the coma now, guys?" I ask the fruitcakes. It's kind of insulting how quickly they all agree.

"No offence, but you're tedious," Jinx says. "I'd rather be unconscious than listen to you."

"Why don't you like me?" I ask, feeling genuinely hurt.

"Sharps, I love you," Mother says. "I always have. I wish you knew that."

"Not you," I tell her. "But thank you anyway. The guys in my head hate me."

"You're pretty unlikeable at times," Shasta says, "but that's a discussion for another day. Consensus on the early coma, please."

"Unanimous. Knock us out."

"But will my mother be safe?" Jazza interrupts.

Sting Ray Barb nods. "The danger will be the brain scour. There's a chance Sharps will die, and it will be tickets for him and all of them."

A rollercoaster scream erupts from the gang. I join in, and Mother and company leap back.

"Great!" I shout. "Imminent death. Thanks a lot!"

"Yeah, thanks for sugar coating it, bitch," Jinx yells. I flinch.

"Onboard passengers are not reassured," I say. "So, it's like see you on the other side, maybe?"

"Affirmative," Sting Ray Barb says. "That or live with each other 'til the end of time. I just thought it best you know, in case you have any final words of wisdom."

"Tell my kids I'm sorry I did what I did," I immediately say.

"Tell Jasper I'm sorry too," Verlee says, and I relay the message. The others remain mute.

"We're ready," I tell Sting Ray Barb, and I shoot a look at Shasta. I'm hoping she'll say something nice, like "*I hope you make it*," but she's making notes on a clipboard. Noelle glares at me, and Mother rubs my feet.

"I'm inserting the anaesthetic into the IV," Sting Ray Barb says. "Good luck."

"Wait!" I yell. "Jazza!"

He looks at me. "Will you take care of us?" I implore. "I trust you. Will you get us out?"

"My mother's in there," he says quietly. "So, you can bet your bottom dollar I will."

And with that, the darkness enfolds me in a warm blanket.

***

Jazza is good to his word. The next time I wake up, I'm in a hospital bed, trussed up like a turkey and wired from head to toe. I gingerly sit up.

Four beds surround me. I can't tell who's who because their heads are covered in bandages. I try to touch my head, but my hands are bound by IV tubes. I try to speak, but my jaw is wired shut. That's unexpected. I look around for a help button, but there's nothing. And I'm strapped to the bed. It's hard not to panic. I try to look on the bright side. One wannabe prima ballerina and a bunch of psycho convicts are out of my head. That makes for a good start. Besides, I know these guys, Jazza and the rest. They'll show up when they feel like it. They'll show up when the data tells them it's time to. I must lie back and chill.

The room gives no clues. Windowless and white, with tubed lights on the ceiling that make a slight buzzing sound. White beds, white blankets. White bandaged people. I should probably be freaked out, but I bet they've got me drugged to the gills. I wriggle my toes and am relieved to see them working. Then I remember what Mother had told me. Ugh. My son wants to talk to me about what went down. Great. Something to look forward to.

My teenage sociopathic son blames me for all his screwups. I wonder if there's a way to explain to him how much I loved him when he was a baby. How obsessed I was with his every bowel movement, his every utterance? How I wanted, more than anything, to be a hero to him?

The perfect family man. That was all I wanted to be. I married Celeste thinking if we could fake it, we'd make it.

Memories of my struggles at work make me break out in a sweat. I had tried to fix things. I tried to get out of the marketing grind, but there were no other jobs. And then Ava set me up, making it look like I'd embezzled funds, so she could have money to fund the resistance.

I couldn't let Bax see me shamed like that. He was so trusting. I couldn't be a failure in his eyes.

I remember that Christmas Eve so well. Picture perfect, it was. Celeste sure did put on a great Christmas. And, in that perfection, I realized I had to kill us all. Celeste was a bad woman. I couldn't leave the kids with her. We all had to go, as a family. Except that when it came to me, I lost my nerve. A coward to the end.

My addiction to the rage rooms connected me to the time travel bandits, aka Noelle's crowd, and I jumped because I was sorry for what I did. I wanted to make things right. Time travel is the most selfless act there is. It hurts like a bitch and fucks you up big time. I hope I'll be able to apologize to Bax, tell him I was sorry that I disappeared. I never meant to let him down. It was the last thing I wanted to do.

To my left, I hear a groan. I turn, and whoever it is starts thrashing about, pulling at cords and tubes without much success. They start squealing like a stuck pig. This wakes up the others, and they join in. Great. So much for a few peaceful moments to reflect on my life. There's always some eager beaver showing up to ruin the party.

Sting Ray Barb, Mother, Jazza, and Noelle rush in along with a group of Super Sharks.

"I'm going to sedate them," Sting Ray Barb says tersely, and I watch her do the rounds, leaving me for last.

"Glad you made it back," Sting Ray Barb says. And then my world goes black again.

***

When I wake, Mother's reading a book, glasses perched on her nose. We are in a different room.

"Sleeping Beauty awakes," she says cheerfully.

"What happened?" I'm groggy, and she hands me a glass of water.

"There was trouble in paradise. There was an attack, and we had to move you to another location. An asset was kidnapped."

"Warm and fuzzy as always, Mother." I drink the glass of water gratefully. "Glad I'm not still tied down. Which asset?"

"Jinx. The kidnappers tried to take you too. Feel free to leave the bed if you'd like to use the washroom, but be careful when standing. You may experience bouts of dizziness and nausea." Mother sounds like a robot and I grab her hand.

"Are you real?" I ask and she laughs.

"Oh Sharps. Get dressed."

I survey my wardrobe. "Louis Vuitton sweatpants and hoodie. Gucci sneakers. Really Mother, you shouldn't have."

"I didn't. Remnants from the days of Materialism," she says. "There's no escaping it. It's all we have. You left us with warehouses up the yingyang."

"How long have I been in the real world?"

"It took us a month to get you out of the Mainframe after Noelle first made contact with you. Then we had to wait a week to do the scour. It took longer to set things up than we had hoped. And now you've been back for nearly two weeks."

"One long party," I yawn. "Or not. So, my sociopathic son hates me?" I cut to the chase.

"He's just confused. You'd be too. It will all work out in time."

I yawn again. "I'm so tired. My body hurts. My head's killing me. It's like I can still feel you guys extracting the others. I'm glad they're gone. Having a bunch of voices in my head is a trip I'd like to never repeat. Bunch of lunatics. What about the post-scour effects? Jazza was never the same."

"We've sorted out a lot since he had the procedure. Try not to worry. We'll take it day by day."

"Where are the others?"

"Verlee's with Jazza, helping him look after the kids. The rest of the convicts are locked up under Shasta's supervision."

"Who took Jinx?"

"The leader of the militia, a shadowy figure. Calls himself Alpha Plus. Clearly no ego there. We just call him AP. God knows why he wanted Jinx. What is concerning is the size of AP's army. All the pharm workers are apparently in his thrall. We tried to track Jinx's chip and discovered that AP has commandeered the Mainframe. Whoever his hackers are, they're better than Ava, Jazza, and Sting Ray Barb."

"AP moved the hardware?"

Mother laughs. "Nope. He changed the password and installed new firewalls. He must have impressive computer systems and tech support, I will say that."

The chip. My fingertips explore behind my ear. Yep, there it is, a tiny nodule under the skin. "Can he access us via the chips?"

"Not yet," Mother says. "He hasn't activated the satellites. In order to do that, he'd need buy-in from all the world leaders, and that's not going to happen. In an unexpected turn of events, Ava's our head honcho. OctoOne lost control, but, in all fairness, none of us thought AP had the power to infiltrate us."

I'm shaken to my core. "The last time I saw Ava, she was being dragged away for treason, and Shasta was calling the shots."

"Shasta and Jazza sprang her after AP's attack. Ava's got OctoOne in custody, swimming around in her tank. Ava was right. OctoOne miscalculated when she chose the genome she did. She's a liability."

"Why didn't Ava kill her?"

Mother looks at me like I'm an idiot, an expression I'm familiar with. "She's got classified intel we need. And a thousand other reasons."

"And Shasta and Ava are buddies now? I thought Shasta had her taken away."

"That was OctoOne. As for Ava and Shasta, savvy politicians are what they are. Even Noelle will work with Ava when push comes to shove. At least for now. AP's a real threat. It's time to bond, not fragment with internal bickering. Shasta's not interested in being the queen bee, she just wants world peace. Ava's more territorial and likes the visual optics of being top dog."

"Did Shasta ask about me?" I ask hopefully, and Mother smiles. "As a matter of fact, she did."

My heart runs in circles like a cocker spaniel at the beach. "What did she say?"

"Don't get too excited, she just asked how you were doing."

But it's enough. I want to do cartwheels.

"What now?" I ask. "Is Ava going to use OctoOne's army to attack AP?" I'm proud of the way I've mastered the new-world lingo.

"Unfortunately, our army is largely depleted. We were too busy dealing with the water crisis, the killer butterflies, the alien vines, and the drug pandemic to pay attention to domestic terrorism."

"Man. What a mess. Killer butterflies? Harsh." My head throbs like a heavy metal base guitar with a faulty amp. It's hard to concentrate on or even care about what she's saying. "Mother, can I have some painkillers?"

She checks the time. "It must have stopped again," she says, winding a small antique wristwatch that she's always worn. "Now I don't know when last you had meds."

"I won't die of an overdose, but I am dying of pain."

"You always had a low pain threshold," Mother says. She unscrews the lid of a small glass pill bottle. "Dissolve this on your tongue. It's a powerful opioid."

The tiny tablet melts like chalky sherbet, and I instantly feel better. "Wow. Yeah. Thank you."

"Good. Back to the problem at hand. I have every confidence that Ava will get things under control. She just needs a bit of time to rally the troops and get reorganized, which is why she needed the men who were in your head. They're key to helping us overthrow AP. He's won the battle but not the war. In my opinion, the butterflies pose a worse threat because there's no antidote to their bites and they're getting more aggressive. We need to find a vaccine, or we'll all be wiped out in short order. Sting Ray Barb is working on it."

She looks at me. "Don't you want to know about your kids?"

I'm immediately ashamed. "I was getting to that," I say defensively. "Give a guy a moment, sheesh."

"I hate to say it," Mother says, "but I agree with Shasta. Baxter has issues. And don't put the blame on yourself. I feel like he was born restless."

Restless? I remember an intense, quiet child, more timid than restless.

"Sophie's a quiet girl, docile and easily swayed," Mother continues. "Thirteen years old and stunning, blonde with enormous green eyes and perfect teeth, while Bax has got long, dark, floppy hair and dark brown eyes. Did you ever notice that his one eye wanders?"

I shake my head.

"Maybe it came later. He also has a bad case of myopia, which would have been an easy surgical fix back in the day but isn't an option now. Sting Ray Barb made him a pair of glasses, but he wouldn't wear them. Said they weren't cool." Mother chuckles. "Does know his mind, that boy. Barb came back with a pair of steampunk goggles that look more like a gas mask from a war, and the boy's never without them."

"Sounds like quite the character." Not quite the son I had imagined, that's for sure.

"He is that," Mother agrees. "He's a handsome boy and smart as a whip."

"Is he like me?" What I mean is, does he have my anger? And Mother understands.

"Yes Sharps, he is like you in that way."

I turn my face to the wall. I had no right having kids. At least it sounds like Sophie worked out okay. But Bax. Mother's wrong, I do need to put the blame on myself. There's no one else to blame. Maybe I sensed he was headed for a troubled life, and I wanted to spare him? *Bullshit*. You don't spare your kids by killing them.

Not for the first time in my life, I wish I was dead. What use am I to anyone?

"I sense the onset of a pity party," Mother comments. "Instead of wishing you could avoid a problem or smash it to smithereens, you could try facing it head on, Sharps."

Blah blah blah. Once again, Mother makes me feel completely spineless. I don't reply.

"How about a sandwich?" she asks brightly.

"A sandwich would be nice," I mutter, and she smiles.

"Hey Mother," I ask, "is Shasta seeing anybody?" I give a giant yawn.

Mother sighs. "Oh, Sharps. Have a nap while I get your snack. The more you can rest, the sooner you will heal."

I lie back and fall asleep before she leaves the room.

Noelle.

I HEARD HIM. I was listening outside the door and managed to get the heck out of there seconds before Mother left the room.

What a bastard. Not even five minutes out of the reintegration pod and he's asking about Shasta. Makes me want to kill her, or him, or both of them. He hasn't even asked about me or our child.

I gnaw my fingers and taste blood around my cuticles. *What to do, what to do?*

I decide to check in with Anise, who's close to six months pregnant. It's not like I'm doing anything of use. Ava and the brains trust are figuring out the vaccine. Ha, unbeknownst to Sharps, they're studying his DNA to see if it holds some superhero antidote to the butterflies. As if time travel and poisonous butterflies are connected. It's the main reason they went to so much trouble to bring him back. That and the fact that Jazza wanted his mommy.

Whatever. But Sharps is *mine*. He belongs to me, Shasta or not. I sacrificed everything for him, and I'm not ready to roll over and admit defeat. I've been dreaming about our life together for too long, imagining it down to the tiniest detail. I'm going to make it real, by hook or by crook.

I run over to Lady Luck and fire her up. Time to get this show on the road.

Of course, my plans go awry in a way that I could never anticipate but in a way that actually works out for the best. Maybe god does give a shit about me after all.

Mother.

I'M DRENCHED IN SWEAT. Pain. There's pain everywhere. Why am I being jolted like this? It's so hot.

I blink, but my eyes are full of sand. My head is throbbing, and I can't think straight. I try to recall the last thing I did, but there's nothing. Come on, *think, think*. I try to swallow, but there's a slimy wet sock or sponge in my mouth.

Blink. Blink. Clear your eyes. More jolting.

I reach up to take the thing out of my mouth, but my hands are bound in my lap. I look down and make out plastic ties. A remnant from the old days.

I hear a muffled sound behind me, and I swing around as much as I can. It's Baxter, moaning balefully. And there's Sophie, with wide and frightened eyes.

And then I remember what happened. I went to make a sandwich for Sharps. I was in the small kitchenette across from his room when I felt a sharp prick on the back of my neck. I remember reaching up and thinking that somehow a Monarch had gotten inside and stung me, but blackness overcame me and here I am.

And Baxter and Sophie are here too! I face the obvious conclusion. AP has taken us. It must be him. We've been kidnapped. I wonder how long we've been gone. How long will it be before they notice we've been taken? A few days at least. People might assume I'm with Sharps, but surely Shasta will check in on the kids and raise the alarm?

I turn back to Sophie and try to give her a reassuring nod. I crane my head forward to see who's driving, but all I can make out through the smoky glass are two shadows.

I stop fighting the restraints and try to gather my thoughts. I take a deep breath. I need to trust that Ava, Shasta, and Sting Ray Barb will come and get us. What if AP kills us before they've got the chance to rescue us?

My thoughts are spinning while I try to figure out what happened, what it means, and what to do.

Baxter is still moaning behind me while Sophie is characteristically quiet. I chastise myself for being grateful that Baxter is gagged because I need to think and his histrionics don't help.

I look out the tinted window. We're in the middle of nowhere. Desert, red sand, burning sun, and stunted trees. A few rocks here and there.

We drive for what seems like hours. I twist my wrist to see my watch, but it's stopped. The sun is high in the sky. Have we been travelling throughout the night? There's no way to tell.

It's hard to think straight while being jolted like this. But I realize one thing. As bizarre as this situation is, it's nice to have a respite from my life. It's nice to have a time out from the infighting. A time out from managing volatile Noelle and from worrying about Sting Ray Barb's health. A time out from Ava's paranoia because of Shasta's increasing political power. Although, for now at least, Ava's got what she wanted, and they're co-operating.

I'm tired of all of it. I wish I'd never become involved with the resistance, at least not to the degree I have. I could be living a relatively normal life like the rest of the population, growing alfalfa, carrots, onions, pears, cherries, or grapes; tending to goats; and working on making the hemp clothing that's slowly replacing the godawful faux couture. Monitoring my water allowance and protecting my family from the Monarchs and ampus would be my biggest concerns. Actually, come to think of it, there isn't a lot of peace to be had there either. Maybe my life hasn't been too bad, but there is still something freeing about leaving it all behind. I tell myself I could be facing torture or imprisonment, but I can't summon the energy to be distressed. The road evens out, and the motion of the bus becomes soothing. I look behind me, and Sophie and Baxter have both fallen asleep.

Suddenly, in the middle of nowhere, we pull over. A wave of fear sloshes into my belly, replacing my calm acceptance. I swallow hard, taking slime from the cloth in my mouth with me. Nausea rises to my throat, and I gag, twisting this way and that. After everything I've been through, I'm going to choke on my own vomit. I kick around, bashing the floor with my heels. Darkness closes in. Suddenly, there's sweet relief. The gag is pulled away, and clean, clear air fills my lungs. But I still can't stop choking. Tears stream down my face. I'm lifted and carried outside. The hot sun feels like a solace, a baptism of sorts. I try to blink, but it's too bright. I'm propped up against the side of the bus, and I bury my head in my arms. I stop heaving. I'm not going to die, not yet anyway.

"Hey gorgeous," a man's voice says, "take a drink. Swish and spit." A gentle hand cups the back of my head. I take a gulp of water and rinse out my mouth.

"Y'all right, darlin', y'all right. Now drink." I take a large swallow. I'm startled by the coolness and purity of the water. It tastes different than our harvested fog. I reach for more water, and once again, I revel in how delicious it is.

I shade my eyes with my hand, look up at my captor, and fall head over heels in love.

Ha! Foolish nonsense! I've got sunstroke, no doubt about it. I've been alone too long, and I'm a closet romantic, loving a mix of happy ever-afters with heart-rending endings. And I'm staring up at a sixty-year-old, shaggy haired Warren Beatty.

My breath catches in my throat. Maybe my foolish dreams haven't been so foolish after all.

My mind flashes back to my secret VHS stash. *An Officer and a Gentleman*, *Nine and a Half Weeks*, *Splendor in the Grass*, *Bonnie and Clyde*, and *Love Story*. I particularly loved *Harold and Maude*, as it gave me hope. I'm a way off from Maude's seventy-nine, but maybe there's still hope for a splash of romance in my life.

The object of my attraction has a wild thatch of bright grey-blond hair. His skin tone speaks to a lifetime of sun-loving, and his eyes are sky blue, with perfectly crinkled edges. His fashion sense needs some work. His shirt is a psychedelic clash of yellow and blue seahorses on red starbursts, and his shorts are lime green. But at least it's not couture.

Incongruously, he's wearing thick, black-framed designer glasses. Perhaps this is what makes me trust him. He sits down next to me, and my whole body fires to attention.

I look away and take another drink of water. I tell myself I'm being crazy and irrational, but all I can think is, *I can't wait to see what happens next.*

"Axel Pattersen at your service." He peers at me, as if examining every pore on my face. I'm uncomfortable, aroused, and disturbed.

"Axel Pattersen," I repeat. "You're Alpha Plus."

We've only heard about him. I had no idea he was this handsome. I need to gather myself, take control of the situation.

He laughs, a braying honk that makes me rethink my attraction to him, but when he scoots even closer my nerve endings do the Watusi. I shake my head, dismayed by my reactions. I must be on guard. The man is a cult leader. Cult leaders are notoriously charismatic. I will not fall prey to his charm.

"Just Axel is fine, darlin'," he says. "Drink more water."

"Where are the children?" I spring to my feet, which is a mistake. I would have fallen over were it not for Axel's princely catch.

"Round the other side of the bus," he says. "Have no fear, Axel is near."

"What do you want from me?"

"Nada, nary a thing. I'm your magic genie, darlin'. I want to make you happy. You may not have realized it, but you've been very unhappy for a very long time. You wanted to change your life. And you tried by being part of the coup, but it didn't work, did it, sweetheart? You thought you failed, but it wasn't you. You deserve so much better, and now here I am. I'm the answer to all your prayers, even if you think you never prayed. You don't know who you are in this world, but I do. I can show you the way."

You don't know who you are. Hadn't I been regretting my life's choices only moments earlier?

I close my eyes and lean back against the side of the bus. How could this man know that I've been obsessed with the meaning of my life lately? That I often lie in bed at night, wondering, *who am I? Have I done anything that I wanted to? Why didn't I love more?*

Axel pulls an old-fashioned stopwatch out of his pocket and flicks it on.

"This is your life, darlin'," he says. "Tick tock, tick tock. I'm offering you a new start. Let me take you where you are needed. I can't explain everything right now, but I'm asking you to trust me. Those you left behind will be fine. The children are here with you. Be a snake, darlin', shed your tired old skin. Come to the garden of Eden with me. I know how tired you are, with all of it. The government, the new administration, all of it. Let me take you and the children to a place of love and peace."

"You're not making any sense," I protest. "There's nowhere to go. I'd know if there was. You're a cult leader. I won't be brainwashed by you, I won't."

But what if he's Clyde to my Bonnie, and we're destined to be together? Yeah, look how well that ended up.

He brays again, and I flinch.

"It's not brainwashing when it's common sense. I've got a civilization up north, an hour or so from here. We live with like-minded people who want to make the world a better place. It's not a cult. It's a better way of living than what you lot were offering. We live in total privacy. Once you're on the compound, you don't leave. Unless, of course, you want to. *You can check out anytime you like, and you can always leave!* " He sings "Hotel California" and grins.

"The song says you can never leave," I whisper, and he chuckles.

"I write my own lyrics in life, darlin'. That's who I am. Now here, there's no one to bug you. You can talk to people or stick to yourself. Up to you. You'll look after the children. Oh, and we need help in the kitchen. You'll report to the head cook, a very lovely woman. You'll love her. It's simple fare, don't worry. Grilled cheese, tomato soup, stuff like that. Now, tick tock, tick tock. It's time to decide. Are you in, or are you out?"

Axel brushes the hair off my sweaty forehead, and I'm embarrassed that I'm so hot and bothered. His touch is gentle and kind, and hot tears well up in my eyes and bounce down my cheeks. I can't remember the last time I cried.

"Darlin'," he says softly, "if you come with us, you wouldn't have to be *this* anymore."

I understand what he means. This is my opportunity to shake off all my baggage. Maybe this will be no more than my nine and a half weeks of adventure, but surely I'm entitled to it?

"If not, I'll turn the bus around and take you and the kids home. But the boy, he needs help. I'm right, right?"

How does he know? He's right. Baxter is headed for trouble. But what about Sharps? He's just come back. He'll need me and the kids. The thought of Sharps makes me want to run even further away. And Noelle. She's exhausting. They're all exhausting.

"I can't cook," I say faintly.

"No worries, darlin'. Simple fare. Worry not. You're in?"

Then it occurs to me. This is a blast! My own personal blast. Not only do I deserve a blast, but I've also been craving a blast.

I straighten my shoulders.

"Fine," I say. "I'm in."

"All right! Kiddie winkles, Jinxie boy, come on back, we're going home!"

Jinx, Baxter, and Sophie walk into view, with Sophie holding Jinx's hand.

My heart sinks. Since the moment he stepped out of the reintegration pod, I've been equally enthralled and terrified by him. He's close to seven feet tall, slender, pale, and exotic. He was the one we were all watching, and his kidnapping only added to his allure.

Sophie runs up to me and throws her arms around me. "Nana," she whispers, "I've met Prince Charming!"

She beams at Jinx with adoration, and I sigh. We're two peas in a pod. My granddaughter's crushing on an escaped convict while I'm crushing on an aging heavy-metal rocker.

"How did they get you out?" I ask Jinx. "We had you in a fortress."

He winks at me. "Axel's got the power. Hey, no offence, but your boy, Sharps, the lights are on, but no one's home. Man, was I ever glad to be out of his vacuous skull."

Baxter rushes at Jinx and punches him in the calf. Jinx just laughs and picks him up. Baxter dangles, struggling like a demented beetle.

"Put me down," he yells. He reaches up and scratches Jinx's face, drawing blood.

Jinx retaliates by throwing the boy to the ground and howling.

"Ah, come on y'all," Axel complains. "Now look what you've done, Jinxie. You broke the boy's arm."

"Don't care," Jinx screams, holding his face. "He destroyed my face. I'll be scarred. I'm going to kill the little shit."

"You won't touch a hair on his head," Axel says and, to my surprise, Jinx freezes. Sophie rushes over to Baxter, but he pushes her away. Baxter isn't crying, he's laughing and holding his twisted arm with a look of satisfaction. I know that look. Baxter's won. He's broken Jinx's self-control, and his broken arm is the spoils of war.

"This is going to delay us," Axel scowls. "I'll have to attend to the boy." He throws a shotgun at Jinx. "Keep an eye on the flutterbyes. They'll be here soon. Not sure why they've taken so long."

"I can't concentrate," Jinx howls. "My beauty is destroyed."

Axel sighs and walks up to the distraught drama queen. "Sonny boy," he says gently, "fixing broken beauty is what I do. You know that. I'll fix you better than you were before. But," his voice is stern, "we need the flutterbyes for drugs. You know that too. So, stop being such a diva and aim right." Axel squints up at the sky. "Where are they? They should be here. I'll get some bait. Kiddie winkles and Mariangela, you get on the bus."

Mariangela? How did he know my name?

"Who's Mariangela?" Sophie asks.

Baxter laughs derisively. "Mariangela. What a weird name."

"You're a nasty little thing, aren't you?" Axel asks Baxter conversationally. "I'd leave you to the birds and the bees and the forces of nature, but we need you. Can't say that you're exactly making friends and influencing people with your attitude."

He reaches into the back of the bus. "Y'all! For god's sake! Get back on the bus!" We do as he says and watch from the window as Axel throws a bloodied carcass into the desert brush.

"What is that?" Sophie asks in a small voice.

"Don't look," I say. I draw Sophie close.

"Here they come." Baxter sounds delighted.

"Jinx will get killed out there," I say to Axel, who has climbed onboard and is taking a medical kit down from the storage area.

"He'll be fine."

A murmuration of butterflies descends on Jinx in a cloud of blue, yellow, green, and red. Sophie and I, and even Baxter, are riveted as Jinx takes aim time after time. I hadn't noticed before, but when his shotgun runs dry Jinx flips open his coat and uses his revolvers wild west style.

Before the dust settles, the butterflies are dead. A lake of colour lies on the desert ground.

"Load them up," Axel yells. "Put the gloves and gas mask on first. Be careful of the dust. Do not inhale."

"As far as I recall," I say, "he wasn't the one who could shoot like that. The good shooter was the other guy, Zayne." We studied the files during the brain scour, and I knew every detail about the convicts.

"An astute observation. Well done, Mariangela!" Axel claps his hands. "Jinx is now—thanks to me—extremely talented. When he was inside your son, I was poised like an eagle for the perfect moment to make my move. I had access to the Mainframe, as you now know. When you lot performed the brain scour to separate the bunch of them, I pitter-pattered inside and collated data on all those bad boys. Okay, well, maybe it wasn't me exactly. I've got a guy. And what a guy. I couldn't do it. Don't get me wrong, I'm a genius in so many ways, darlin'," he winks at me, and I flush beetroot, "but this guy's a master chef, mixing and matching and getting the batter just right. Jinx can now do what all of them could. Ha, joke's on them. Wait 'til they try to use their formerly unique skills. It'll be hilarious. They're as impotent as a duck's waddle."

I feel a frisson of terror. This man, or his minion, has achieved the unthinkable.

"What about Verlee?" I ask, and Axel shrugs.

"Don't care. I let her out as is. She's got nothing of interest to me. By the way, Jinx was wrong about your boy Sharps. He's got a lot to offer, he just doesn't know it yet."

"What does he have?"

Baxter laughs. "He disappears! Leaves us alone with a drunk mother. That's his superpower."

"We don't know why he left," Sophie defends Sharps.

"Be quiet and hold still, boy. You're going to feel a small pinch."

Baxter gives a piercing scream as Axel grabs his arm and straightens it. Axel brays with laughter. "See what happens when you mess with Jinxie? Leave our treasure alone, do you hear me?"

"You did that very well," I note. "Are you a paramedic?"

"Darlin', I'm a bona fide physician. Dr. Pattersen at your service. I'm world famous." He flashes a wild grin at me, his big white teeth wolf-like. "You will be most impressed when you see my work. I'll fix the boy's eyes too; we'll get rid of the gas mask. But for now, we must get this show on the road."

I'm not sure I want Baxter fixed. I prefer not seeing the hate in his eyes.

He leans out the window and yells, "Boyo, pick up the pace."

Jinx looks up and scowls. "There are a lot of them. Filthy, disgusting creatures."

He finally finishes loading the dead butterflies and climbs onboard the bus. "Hi-ho, the derry-o, the farmer in the dell. Where's the cleanser?"

Axel nods towards a gallon jug, and Jinx liberally douses himself. The smell of raw alcohol fills the bus, and Baxter sniffs in delight.

Sophie can't stop staring at Jinx. There's something fundamentally damaged and raw about Jinx, with his porcelain skin marred by Baxter's fingernails and his pale blue eyes with those odd pupils. He's a whippet python, and the air ripples like a heat mirage when he moves.

Axel brays, and I drag my gaze to him. That laugh. So unfortunate.

"You want compelling and charismatic?" Axel asks. "You mentioned cult? There's the perfect leader. World domination is heading our way, darlin'! I've got big plans for him."

"What if he doesn't want to do what you want?" I ask.

"He's got no choice. I made him. I designed him, he's mine! I know him like the inside of my mouth."

He sticks his tongue out at me, and I can't help but wonder what else he can do with it.

He seems to know what I'm thinking, and he comes close to me. Once again my body flames to attention. He leans down and whispers in my ear, his breath tickling my skin.

"Mary, my girl, we'll have some fun you and me. But," he shouts, "it's time to get this show on the road and get back to the compound. Enough wild frolicking for one day."

He climbs into the front seat and fires up the bus. Jinx lies down in the aisle, and Sophie gazes at him in adoration.

"Are you excited for our new adventure, Mary-Ann-gelo?" Baxter asks. I turn to him.

"The name," I say, "is Mariangela. Say it properly or don't say it at all. No more Nana or Mother. I am Mariangela."

Baxter isn't used to me being sharp with him. "Can I change my name too?"

I shrug. "Up to you."

Something has changed inside me. I'm free. Baxter and his issues aren't my problem anymore. Axel is here. Dr. Pattersen. We're heading for a new life. I intend to leave the baggage of the past behind, and a lot of that baggage was Baxter and his issues. I am Mariangela again, and anything is possible.

Mariangela.

I TRY TO GET COMFORTABLE ON THE BUS. The air sears me, frying my skin. I'm desperately thirsty, but Jinx is still asleep in the aisle and Axel is hunched over the steering wheel, way up front. The bus is noisy as all hell, and it's shake, rattle, and roll as we barrel forward on increasingly hostile terrain. Axel said he had a place an hour north, but it feels like we've been travelling for days. The smooth road deteriorated into corrugations the likes of which I had no idea even existed.

Axel swings the bus into a small, boulder-lined road that narrows abruptly. We're in a ravine with tall canyons on either side. It feels like we're in a valley of blood and pain, with nothing around us but death.

"A few hours to go," Axel yells over the loudspeaker. I sigh. A few more hours?

"I'm so thirsty," Sophie whispers to me, and Jinx springs to his feet.

"Why didn't you say so?" He looks close to tears. He digs into a bag and hands her a canteen. "Drink as much as you like. You must be so hungry too." He reaches for a bag of rations and lets her choose from a bunch of kale and almond bars.

"Yo bro, me too." Baxter holds out his unbroken hand, and Jinx ignores him.

"You can have some of mine," Sophie says. She's about to hand her food over to Baxter when Jinx shoots in between them.

"Only if he asks nicely," he grins, his incisor teeth sharp. "Come on, Baxie boy, ask nicely. Please Uncle Jinxie, can I have some food and water, pretty please?"

"Fuck you," Baxter says.

Jinx shrugs. "Whatever."

He hands me a bottle of water and a kale and almond bar, and I gratefully chug the water and swallow the bar in three bites. Baxter glares at me, and I look away. It feels so good to not bow down to Baxter. I hadn't realized how much I had feared him.

"Go sleepy time, little princess," Jinx says to Sophie, stroking her hair. She closes her eyes in bliss. How old is Jinx, anyway? Should I worry about this? Is he a pedophile? Is that why he was in prison? He catches my glance and hisses at me. "Don't be disgusting, old woman. Get your mind out the gutter."

How had he known what I was thinking?

"It was written all over your face," he says. "Now you go to sleep, too."

I instantly fall asleep, only realizing I've done so when I wake in darkness. The bus has stopped. "Welcome to your new home, darlin'," I hear Axel say. I shake myself awake.

Is this the Pearly Gates? It certainly looks like it. No wait, it looks more like the entrance to Elvis's Graceland. Two Grecian pillars support a large blue triangle arch. "The Fountain of Youth" is gracefully scrawled across it in a scripted font, and the neon lights glow against the black night.

We drive under the arch and through the grounds. We are, inexplicably, in a hotel resort. We pull up outside the main entrance of a wedding cake–styled hotel with a massive marble fountain in the centre of the circular driveway. Is that a replica of the Trevi Fountain? It certainly looks like it. "Dad was a big fan of Rome," Axel says. "But I'll explain later. Do you like it?"

What's not to like? I stop and admire Oceanus with his rock-hard abs and magnificent biceps. Is it possible that this is the real Trevi Fountain? A ridiculous thought!

The sheer opulence of the exquisitely carved marble overwhelms me, but, more than that, the water looks like sheer heaven. So much water! I want to dive into the fountain and wash myself clean of eleven years of hard living.

"There's lots of running water inside," Axel guides me into the lobby.

"But how?" I'm speechless. We've been living off drifts of fog while these guys were skinny dipping in an oasis I had no idea even existed.

"There's an underwater spring no one's ever been able to explain. Don't worry, we don't squander our fortune on fountains, we've got reservoirs of the stuff. Mummy Earth's been very good to us," he beams.

"And yet you couldn't share?" I'm stupefied.

"With the enemy? Course not, darlin'. I'll forgive you that stupid question because I know you're tired. I've got something to show you. Come with me." He leads me to an elevator and up to the rooftop.

Night has fallen, and I hear the cry of unfamiliar animals. The sky is dark blue velvet, not quite black. The stars are a map of bright diamonds, and the moon is a thin sliver of white.

"This is amazing!" I look around at the resort. The hotel is huge, two stories of whitewashed cubiform buildings with blue topped domes.

"My father also loved Santorini in Greece," Axel explains. "It's all tied into the fountain of youth, yeah?"

"Stunning. Did you build this empire?" I ask. He chuckles. To my relief, he's stopped braying when he laughs.

"I wish I was the architect of such magnificence. Nope, my grandmother owned it, her mother before her, and my Mumsy before me. But my father made a lot of changes. It's a bit of a designer's buffet. Daddy loved Europe, while Mumsy and Granny loved old Britannia. I loved Sinatra's Vegas, and we've all added signature touches along the way. As they say, the more the merrier. We've got a whole compound, very impressive if I say so myself. I'll give you a tour of the various buildings in a few days when you're more rested. They're all connected via underground tunnels because at one point we were all convinced nuclear war was inevitable and thought we'd be stuck down under."

"Will I meet your mother?"

A strange expression crosses his face. "Unlikely." He slumps but soon straightens up. "Enough of that! What do you think of my setup, darlin'? Impressive, no?"

"It's beautiful." The place looks like a blue and white neon wedding cake.

"Where do you get all this electricity from?"

He cocks his head to one side and looks disapproving. "You're very nosy. If I hadn't invited you here myself, I'd think you were a spy." He smiles and I want to remind him that he'd not so much invited me as brought me against my will. That said, he gave me the chance to back out, and I threw it away.

"And not a vine in sight," I marvel. "How is that even possible?"

"Just one of my many secrets, darlin'."

I clap my hand to my mouth. "Oh, my lord. Where are the children?" I've completely forgotten about them, and I chastise myself.

"Jinxie's taken them inside for hot milk and cookies," Axel says. "You worry a lot, woman, you know that? You need to laugh more."

"There hasn't exactly been a lot to laugh about for the past few decades."

"Yes, but that life's behind you. Are you hungry?"

"I could eat a bear."

"That may be a tiny bit tricky to come by, but I'll make sure your hunger is assuaged. In fact, I'll make sure all your needs are assuaged."

He pulls me close, and I feel giddy. How long's it been since I've been held? I lean into him, and the tension fades from my body. "I can hear birds singing," I murmur. "This is crazy. We're in the desert."

"It's good place to be," Axel whispers, "you'll see, you'll be—" He jerks back suddenly and scratches his head.

Dear god, don't tell me the man has lice.

"Enough loitering." He looks nonplussed, stops scratching, and grabs my arm. "Come on, girl, I want to get you settled in. As much as I'd love to just hang out with you, I've got work to do."

He leads me through the front door and into a lobby area.

"Anise?" Axel yells. There's no reply. Whoa. We've gone from Santorini to the wild west, with a handy dose of lumberjack thrown in for good measure. The lobby walls are studded with fieldstones, and a wagon wheel chandelier hangs low, illuminating a stuffed polar bear. A raccoon perches on the countertop, his tail circling a silver bell. Axel rings the bell and thumps on it repeatedly until I think I'll scream.

"Cool your jets. I'm here," a voice from the corner growls in a low, affected fashionista baritone.

The person uncoils herself from the leather sofa, and my jaw drops. Talk about stunning. Six feet of Miss Universe perfection. Tanned skin, cat-shaped amber eyes, and long, long legs. A pissed-off expression at having been disturbed. And a big pot belly. She's at least five or six months pregnant.

"Why didn't you say so?" Axel is grumpy.

"Wanted to see how quickly I could wind you up, grandad."

Axel glares at her, clearly unimpressed by the ageist crack.

The girl pulls on her cigarette. The cherry glows like an evil eye, and the smoke curls around her face. She stares at me. "That her?"

"Should you be smoking?" I ask before I can stop myself.

"Cures my asthma."

"Where do you get cigarettes?"

The girl snorts in reply.

"Full of questions, this one." Axel pats me on the back. "Darlin', I keep telling you, this is the land of plenty. Unlike your sad little town that misguidedly thought it was the be all and end all. I hate to break your heart, but you lot were a pinprick on the map of civilization. It was sweet to watch, but you were the anomaly."

"We were?" I'm so tired that I'm starting to feel ill. It's too much to take in. We lived our lives so earnestly, and yes, we thought ours was the only way. This is a shock.

Axel turns to Anise. "Yeah, it's her. How many other women do you see with me? Come on, Anise, get with the program. I'm too tired to have my chain yanked right now."

Jinx emerges from the shadows, and I jump. Anise slings an arm around him and licks his face, jaw to forehead. He doesn't move a muscle, and Anise giggles.

"Let's go through to the dining room." Axel sounds exhausted.

He shepherds me to an old-fashioned diner with red leatherette banquette seats and silver-edged Formica tables. The place is vast and mirrored, with pale blue walls and black and white checkered floors. A bar runs to the one side of the cavernous room, and the reflections and shadows make dizzy. I moan, and my knees buckle. Axel catches me by the elbow and steadies me.

But wait. "Where are Baxter and Sophie? I thought they were having milk and cookies?"

"Gone beddy-byes."

I stop short. "I want to say goodnight to them."

Axel pulls me along in a way that brokers no argument and eases me into a seat.

"They're fine," Jinx says to me reassuringly, the light glinting off his sharp incisors. "You worry too much. Relax, Mary-Ann-gelo." He's mocking me just like Baxter did, but I'm too tired to say anything.

"I'm so tired," I moan. "Can't I just go to bed?"

"Nope. Can't sleep well on an empty stomach. Just one of Mumsy's rules." Axel holds me upright and puts his arm around me. It would have been romantic if I was sixteen and naive.

"Listen, you've been a brave girl, don't fall apart now. Take a breath."

I put my head in my hands. "Sensory overload," I mumble. "This diner's like a time-warped carnival attraction."

"It is special." Jinx grins at me as he slides into the booth. His teeth are like snake fangs. He's so pretty, yet he can look so evil.

Anise scoots close to him, wraps herself around him, and smiles at me. "Cookie, what's the matter? Hey, you want me to show you your kitchen?" She moves away from Jinx and snuggles up to me. She lights a cigarette, blowing out the match just seconds before it burns her fingers.

"Give her a chance to get settled, Anise," Axel chimes in. "And I'll have a beer, thank you very much. You want a drink, my lady?"

I shake my head. "I don't drink," I say.

"Righty ho. Oh look, here comes the food! Told you I'd feed you!"

Which is when the Barbie doll shows up, bearing a laden tray.

"Axel! Baby! Where've you been? Oh, is that her?" The woman looks excited to see me.

She puts the food on the table. I glance down. Steaks. Not my style.

The woman smells oddly chemical, and it takes me a while to figure out why. It's the bleached bitterness of hair dye, depilatory creams, deodorant, hairspray, and fake tan. A throwback smell I haven't encountered in years, and it occurs to me I could have lived happily without ever smelling it again.

Her body is a ship's prow with enormous breasts. Her waist is tiny, and her buttocks are smooth round apples.

"Hi! I'm Fiona! I'm Axel's fiancée, isn't that so, baby?"

Fiancée? And here I thought Axel was interested in me. My whole world deflates like a used party favour.

Fiona cracks a smile. Horsey teeth and a fat beaver-butt pout. Her jaw, cheekbones, and eyes are an architecture of implants and surgeries. Her nails are crimson, manicured talons. She's a beauty queen on display, and all she needs is a crown and sash.

"Fee's my finest work." Axel gets up and runs his hands over her appreciatively. "Fee, show Mariangela, the full show."

Fiona sheds her clothes with the practiced moves of a woman familiar with being watched. Axel nods. "Do a spinorama, sweetie. Show off the artwork."

Naked as a jaybird, Fiona spins and I stare. An open-zipper tattoo runs in a V-shape from her collarbones to her pubic bone.

"Now turn around," Axel says. Fiona does as he says. She bends down and straightens up, her ass facing me. The zipper runs through the crack of her butt and back up her spine. The tattooed pull tab is at the base of her neck.

"Wow," I say, and Axel nods.

"Fiona is what all my clients aspire to."

Fiona gathers her clothes but shows no sign of putting them back on. "Look at my engagement ring," she beams. I'm amazed her hand can hold the weight of the bauble. "Eight carat emerald-cut stone with a diamond pear-shaped halo ring. It's modelled on the Chalk Emerald owned by the Maharani of Baroda, India. For all we know, it's that ring!"

"The Chalk Emerald is nearly thirty-eight carats," Axel corrects her. "And the setting's different."

I turn to Axel. "I didn't know you had a girlfriend."

"You didn't ask, sweetheart." He is gentle. "You've had quite the day. I know this is a lot to take in. I'll explain everything in good time."

What an idiot I am. I got caught up in the moment. I wanted to escape being myself, and now, here I am, the same old fool, just far from home.

I want my old life back. I want to see Noelle. I miss Sting Ray Barb and Jazza. I threw them all away without so much as a backward glance. What kind of feminist am I anyway, thinking that a ride into the sunset with a handsome man will save me from my drab life? I guess I still believe in fairy tales. Tears, hot and somehow reassuring, fill my eyes and flow down my cheeks.

"She's crying." Fiona scoots in close to me, still naked as the day she was born. "Oh honey. Don't be sad. I understand. You're old and wrinkly, but Axel will fix you just like he fixed me. Sure, it hurt, but you get to rest up and you sleep a lot of the time."

She crushes me in a chokehold. Her version of a hug, I guess. "I don't care about that," I sob. "I want to go back to my old life." Her chemically fragranced breasts do make for comfortable pillows, and I burrow in just a bit.

Axel pats me on the shoulder. "I know you're feeling out of sorts, but you'll be happy here, you'll see. I can work my magic on you too if you like. Although to be honest, I like you just the way you are."

"What?" Fiona is outraged, and she pulls away from me and jumps up. "Why would you say that? I'm the ideal, you've always said so."

"And you are, sweetie. You're my showroom masterpiece, but Mariangela is a natural beauty."

Fiona glares at me. "Think you're special?" She spits the words at me. "Very nice Axel, very fucking nice." She marches off, naked apart from six inches of pink stilettoes.

My heart, however, is lighter. He likes *me*! He thinks I'm beautiful just the way I am. Somehow, that makes everything better.

"If you're not going to eat that, I will." Anise spears my rack of whatever it is. "Mmmm, nice and bloody, just like I like it."

"I'm a vegetarian," I say faintly.

"But sweetheart," Axel says, "you asked for bear! Be careful what you wish for."

"I was being metaphorical." I decide that I've had about as much weirdness as one brain can take. "Axel, how long were we on the road? I feel like I've got jet lag."

"You've only been gone less than a day, sweetheart. The ride here takes seven hours. We lost two with Baxter and Jinx mucking about. We stopped one other time, but you were fast asleep."

Kidnapped and drugged, I want to say. "I'm so tired. I have to go to sleep."

"Your wish is my command," he says. He runs a finger up the inside of my wrist, and I nearly melt. I hope he won't stop touching me, but he goes back to his steak. I've got no idea how he can be so repulsive and yet so attractive. At my age, surely I don't have any hormones left? Am I attracted to his power?

"Campers," Axel says, gnawing on a large bone, "mind your manners. Give our new guest a round of applause for being here."

Anise puts her cigarette in her mouth and squints through the smoke. She nods at Jinx, and they both obediently clap and shout "hip-hip hooray!"

"You do realize that's an antisemitic chant, don't you? You can say hooray but not hip-hip," I admonish them.

"Look at her, history lessons at midnight. What a trooper. Time to get Mariangela all tucked in for the night. Lots to learn tomorrow. Well, you lot turn in anyway. I've got war strategies to plan. Anise, will you show Mary to her room?"

I don't like being called Mary. I make a note to tell him in the morning that I'm done with derivatives in the same way I'm done with being Mother or Nana.

Anise slides out of the booth with her hands on her hips. I'm eye-level with her tiny cropped white leatherette shorts. Her belly's a tanned, smooth balloon, and her belly button's a perfect outie. She swings the fringes of her bra in circles and gives me a twisted half smile as I scramble to my feet.

"Goodnight, darlin'!" Axel says. "See you at brekkie. Get some shut-eye."

Anise doesn't speak as she flounces down a floral carpeted hallway and into the kitchen. She stops outside a small cubby hole next to the pantry.

"Don't I get a hotel room?" I ask. My voice is shaking, which annoys me, and Anise shakes her head.

"Reserved for the guests. You need to be near the kitchen anyway. You're going to be Fiona's assistant, isn't that exciting? Now, go in and don't leave the room until we come and get you."

"What if I need the washroom?"

Anise points down the hall. "Second on the left. There are jammies on the bed for you. Toothbrush, face cloth. Fiona made a care package for you. She's so excited you're here. If you don't have what you need, you can ask her tomorrow. She put some clothes in the cupboard for you."

I peer into the room. I turn to ask Anise where the children are, but she's vanished.

I go into my room and close the door. A white pallet bed is set close to the floor. The coverlet is a bright coral floral, and there's a puffy red pillow. The room is windowless. A bedside lamp glows yellow on a white table and an electric radio alarm clock shines bright. It's close to 2 a.m. I take off my shoes and wriggle my toes in the blessed carpet pile. I feel like I'm hallucinating. Axel has a fiancée? I just can't get over that. And this incredible place. I'd been so sure that our world with OctoOne was the only viable choice, but I'd clearly been mistaken.

I lie down for a moment, but then I realize I must find Baxter and Sophie. I can't sleep until I know they are okay.

I open the door and rush straight into the arms of Jinx. More like into his waist, given his height. He doesn't have an ounce of body fat, and I slam into his washboard abs.

"Oof!" The wind is knocked out of me.

"Oh darlin'," he says in a chilling parody of Axel, "you're supposed to stay in your room! Come on, honeybunny!"

"I just want to see Bax and Sophie," I whisper. He puts his hands around my waist and picks me up so I'm eye-level with him. I'm not a small woman, but he dangles me like I'm a small stuffed toy.

"Not so good at following the rules, are you?" He smells of ozone and wet earth. Yet again he reminds me of a pale python or a boa constrictor.

"Look at you, squirming like a good little worm." He flashes sharp incisors. My bladder lets go just a tiny bit. I know he knows what happened, and he laughs as if it's the funniest thing. "Oh, Mary-Ann-gelo, relax! We all have issues. I myself was a bed wetter of note until I was what, twelve, thirteen? Oh, the glory days! So never you mind."

"What are you doing, Jinx?"

It's Anise, and I've never been so glad to see anyone in my life.

"She had an accident," Jinx says musingly. "On her way to try to find the children." He's still holding me aloft, and my legs are swinging.

"Oh, Jinxie boy," Anise purrs, "come on, put her down. AP wants her safe and sound."

"Yeah," Jinx says reluctantly. "You're right. Okay Mama bear, down you go."

Mama bear? That's what Noelle calls me.

"Let's get you cleaned up," Anise says. "Don't you worry about Jinx here, he's just a big old softie!"

Not exactly how I'd describe him. My panties bear the stamp of my shame. Just when I don't think things can get any worse, my heart starts doing cartwheels in my chest. I clutch my left breast and fall to the floor. That's it. I'm going to die.

"Ah, look Jinxie, you nearly killed Fee Fee's new assistant, and it's only her first night. Come on, honey, open wide." She shoves her fingers in my mouth and I feel a small tablet dissolve on my tongue. I instantly feel better. Did she just give me butt dust?

"Bye, Jinxie," Anise sings, and he slinks into the shadows.

Anise disappears into my room and re-emerges with a pile of clothing and a stack of white towels.

"Come on, I'll take you to the washroom." She hauls me to my feet.

Anise has switched from cigarettes to chewing gum. She snaps the pink mash loudly, blowing bubbles, one of which bursts on her face. She laughs her deep laugh.

I wonder where she got the bubblegum, but I'm too tired to talk. I strip down and turn on the shower. So good. So hot. All of it was worth it for this. To get clean. To get warm. I'd gotten so used to lukewarm basin-baths, to running a sponge over my body and in between my legs. This is nirvana.

I turn to ask Anise if there's a limit to the shower time, but she's vanished.

I dry myself and scurry back to my room. The drugs are wearing off, and I'm shaking. I search the room for clues as to who these people are, but I don't learn a thing.

Shower aside, what have I done by coming here? It's all a terrible mistake. I'll gather the children in the morning and tell Axel we want to leave. He said we could, and I'll insist on it.

I climb under the covers and rest my head on the pillow. It smells of fabric softener, as does the comforter, and the mattress is ridiculously comfortable.

There's something about being clean and warm and tucked up in bed that soothes my soul.

What if I'm dreaming all of this? What if I've had a psychotic break and none of this is real? This must be a fantasy of some kind. I'm convinced I'll be awake all night worrying about my mental health and trying to find the bridge between dreams and reality, but the next thing I know, Anise is shaking me.

"You slept all morning," she sings, and I sit up, groggy. It takes me a few moments to remember where I am and what happened.

"Get out of your jammies, it's time for me to show you around. Man, is Fee ever mad! She expected help with brekkie!"

I get changed and wonder what on earth is going to happen next. The first thing I have to do is find the children.

***

I follow Anise, marveling at her outfit. It matches her previous day's apparel, only today's version is black leatherette.

She leads me into a windowless banquet hall with a small linoleum stage at one end. Floor-to-ceiling mirrors reflect the parquet dance floor, and a giant disco ball waits in the wings. A mustard-coloured wooden bar runs along one side of the cavernous room, and the place is lit up with green and orange lily-shaped lamps.

A lunch buffet is set up at the far end of the hall across from the dance floor. The wall above the table is lined with enormous oil paintings of self-important big game hunters. The moustached men are resplendent in khaki gear with their hands on hips and their elbows jaunty with victory, posing with their trophies. So that's where all the polar bears went. An elaborate centrepiece gold frame showcases an emaciated dowager crone. She's snow white, an albino warrior off the Serengeti, only she's rocking a '50s beehive.

"That's Mumsy." Anise points to the woman. "Say one trashy word about Mumsy and Axel will cut your throat and watch you bleed out."

That's reassuring. "Thank you for the heads-up," I reply.

What amazes me is how crowded the place is. Where did all these people come from?

Anise grabs a black coffee, and I examine the array of meat dishes. Anise is right. Fiona does need help with the menu.

"I can't eat any of this," I say. "Surely you have normal food?"

"If by normal, you mean not chockablock with red blood corpuscles, yeah, we do. It's just that Fiona's a big fan of the Carnivore Diet. She says it is the best thing for anti-aging. Axel's been selling the clients on high protein food, saying it'll promote super-fast healing. They eat it up, ha."

"Never mind the food. I want to see the children," I insist. Just then Axel shows up, beaming. He's wearing a white medical coat and has a stethoscope around his neck.

"Dr. Pattersen at your service! Did you sleep well?"

"I slept way more than I meant to. Axel, I need to see the children."

"Of course you do, darlin'. Please don't fret. Walk this way. Well, not exactly this way—old joke, but it cracks me up every time. Follow me."

He leads me through a maze of corridors, passing dozens of neatly numbered doors. Axel moves fast, and I trot to keep up. I look over my shoulder, but Anise is nowhere to be seen.

And then we are outside, surrounded by red desert and tall palm trees. A rowdy crowd is gathered on what looks to be a cricket pitch, albeit it on sand.

"Where on earth did all these people come from? And where are the children?" I ask.

"You're so impatient! This way, my lady. Your chariot awaits. As for the people, we have a decent population of close to a million, and we're growing every day. That excludes the spa guests."

One million people. Where do they all live and sleep and eat and work? And what do they do to make a living? I decide to park my questions until I've seen the children. I must keep Axel focused.

He guides me into a large garage filled with golf carts.

"Not as fast as your average Ferrari, but they get us from A to B. Climb aboard!"

I get into the golf cart. "I didn't know these even existed anymore."

"You just didn't know where to look."

We drive across a track and field schoolyard. "There's the convent," Axel points proudly. I gasp. "That's incredible!"

"Mumsy all the way!"

The school is a multi-levelled Victorian asylum in a Gothic Revival style and is embellished with Châteauesque adornments. As we approach the grand entrance, I see a military parade of Virgin Mary statues with outstretched arms lining the way. The statues are six feet tall, and I lose count of them as we near the school steps. The army of the Blessed Virgin?

"Welcome to the Aqueduct of Grace," Axel says. "This school has stood the test of time since 1998. Isn't it amazing? We did not succumb to the evils of virtual reality to educate our children. We kept the faith in bricks, mortar, chalk, and religion. Not to mention the strict policy of spare the rod and spoil the child."

I don't agree with his educational methodology, but I keep my opinions to myself and segue to safer ground. "Why does 1998 feel like it was three centuries ago, when really it's been only sixty-eight years?"

"Look at you! Adding and subtracting like a genius!" Axel grins, and I blush. I also keep mum about the fact that I was born in 1998.

Inside, the school smells of lemon furniture polish and orange-scented floor wax. The stained-glass windows throw rainbows across the gleaming floor. "It's so peaceful," I marvel. Then I hear a piercing scream, and, to my horror, I recognize the voice.

I rush towards a classroom to my left and fling the door open. The room is empty except for Baxter and a penguin-suited nun. The woman is towering over Baxter, and she's slapping a wooden ruler on the palm of her hand.

"Fuck you!" Baxter yells at the nun. She lashes out at his unbroken hand.

"Stop that right now!" I shout. I run over to Baxter, and he pulls me into a one-armed hug. That he's hugging me is more shocking than the situation. I try not to crush his sling, but he leans into me.

"Nana, she's hurting me, make her stop."

I glare at the nun. "Don't worry Baxie, I'll take you away. Come on, we're leaving."

"Um, darlin'," Axel pipes up. "You're not going anywhere."

I keep Baxter close. "You said we could leave whenever we wanted to!"

"Yeah." He looks earnest. "That was me managing the situation. Keeping you calm, darlin'. And it worked! Look, you're here, and everything's great!"

"We're prisoners!" I make for the door, but Axel stands in my way.

"Mary," he says gently. "Don't make this harder than it has to be. Come on, darlin', you know what's what, you always did. Let Sister Colmcille take care of Baxter. The boy needs help. You know that as well as anybody."

"No, Nana, don't leave me," Baxter howls. All the while the penguin looks on impassively, her nose beaky and cruel and her deep-set eyes cold.

"I'll take you to Sophie," Axel says. "And you'll get a better sense of how this all works. Baxter boy, you stay here with the good sister. A word to the wise, the sooner you learn the ropes, the sooner things will improve for you."

The nun clasps her hands together, and she and Axel face one other and bow. "Namaste in the name of the Holy Trinity," they both say, and they make the sign of the cross.

Baxter and I exchange a look. For once in our lives, we're in agreement.

"Baxie, I'll come back," I say. "Can I, Axel? Can I at least visit him?"

"Of course you can!" Axel is jovial. "This isn't a prison! I'll show you where the schedule log is kept, and you can schedule a mutually agreeable time."

He leads me away, and I hear Sister Colmcille telling Baxter to sit down. For once in his life, the boy does the sensible thing and listens to her.

"Axel, can I ask you something?" My heart is pounding and, given that I've just learned we are indeed prisoners, I am taking a risk.

"You and your questions!" He's cheerful, but there's an undercurrent of ice. "Sure, darlin'. Knock yourself out."

"Can you not call me Mary?" His face freezes, and I rush to make amends. "It's just that I love being called Mariangela. It's been so long since I even heard the name. Truth be told, I hated it for years, but these days, I feel like I've earned it. It's got heft, you know. And I'm a woman of heft, so it's fitting."

I'm babbling nervously. He takes me by the shoulders and gazes into my eyes. "Darlin'," he says softly. "Your wish is my command. You are Mariangela and nothing less. Thank you for your honesty. You're the first person to ever tell me what they really want. That's what a real relationship is." He leans in and his forehead touches mine. He smells of cedar and soap and his hands are warm and strong. "And you're fucking gorgeous, so how can I possibly say no? Mariangela it is!"

I want to stand there forever, leaning into him. I feel conflicted by my desire. But he grabs me by the hand and pulls me along while he hums Ave Maria.

The corridor is filled with sunbeams and rays of light. The sound of a choir floats softly on the air and, barring Baxter and the evil nun, there's a sense of sanctity and order. We pass a science lab, complete with Bunsen burners, test tubes, and microscopes. Students earnestly chew their pencils, and I recognize the equations scribbled on the blackboard. Axel's right! This isn't so bad! Baxter and Sophie will get a great education. And god knows Baxter needs discipline and guidance.

Axel opens a classroom door and breaks my reverie. "Sophie, say hello to your Nana!" Twenty or so little girls look up. They're dressed in matching pale blue pinafores with neat little white ankle socks and black patent leather Mary Janes. They're poring over mathematics books and wrestling with protractors and slides. "Learning the good old-fashioned way." Axel is proud. "No computers. Look at them drawing their isosceles triangles! Adorable!"

"We're in a different universe," I say. "Or have we time-travelled, and I just didn't notice?"

"Nope. Same time, same place, same country, darlin'! This was all Mumsy's idea." Axel's eyes mist over. "What a woman. No one like her on the planet, present company included, darlin', if you'll pardon me."

"She's alive?" I squeak.

He stops dead. "Of course she is. Why wouldn't she be?"

"I don't know, I just assumed. Or thought you'd said."

"You know what they say about assuming darlin', makes an ass out of you and me! Excuse me, Sister Berkman, can we have Sophie for a moment?"

The nun beams at us. "Sure! What a darling little girl! Sophie, you've got visitors."

Sophie looks up from her book, but she seems distracted, as if she doesn't recognize me for a moment. She gathers herself, leaps up, and smiles. "Nana! I'm so good at math! Sister Berkman says so!"

I run over to her and hug her. "Sophie! My angel! Are you okay?"

She seems confused by the question. "Nana, I love it here! Look, real books! Much nicer than having you show us math on scraps of paper at home! Books are just like you said, they smell lovely! I'm top of the class!"

I'm glad that my lessons, rudimentary as they were, did actually teach her the fundamentals.

"I share a room with Jeanette. Hey, Jeanette, say hi to my Nana!"

A button-nosed girl with thick bangs looks up and waves.

"And Jinx is teaching me to play chess, he says it's the foundation for all of life's strategies and—"

So much for my happiness. I interrupt her. "Jinx is here?" I swing around, looking for him.

"Not right now. He said he'll visit me later."

"Tick tock, Mariangela," Axel says. "Time for us to get a move on. But now you know the kiddies are in good hands, and all is well. Say ta-ta for now." Hearing him say my full name doesn't sound quite as kind as when he'd called me Mary, and I wish I hadn't said anything.

"I'll be back as soon as I can," I reassure Sophie.

She shrugs slightly, and then realizes she's hurt my feelings. "Sorry Nana! I'm so happy here! We get puddings after supper and we sing songs in chapel and I've got friends and it's warm and cozy and there's so much water!"

I can't argue with any of that. "I'm very glad you're happy, Sophie. I love you."

"Love you too, Nana," she says, but she's back at her desk, and her reply is remote.

I'm subdued as we walk out of the school.

We get back to the golf cart. "I can't believe this has been here all this time," I say, more to break the silence than out of any real interest.

"Yeah," Axel says. Neither of us speak again on the ride back. He looks uneasy as we pull up at the main entrance and walk inside. I have a horrible feeling of foreboding, which is instantly compounded when he opens his mouth.

"Darlin', it's time for me to explain your role in the scheme of things." He pushes his black-framed glasses up his nose, and my heart sinks. What now?

***

I follow Axel down a whitewashed hallway and up a magnificent glass spiral staircase. He courteously opens a set of double doors and gestures for me to go first.

"This is where the brains trust does all the planning!" he jokes. "Welcome to my office, be it ever so humble."

It's far from humble. The glass-walled boardroom stretches across the hotel rooftop, flanked on either side by blue triangled arches, each resplendent with an enormous gold bell.

A treacherous canyon carves the earth on the left, with an equally deep canyon to the right, and miles of desert stretch in front of us. There's no road in sight, no way out. My eyes adjust, and I make out a city and a large church spire in the distance.

"Spectacular view, isn't it?" Axel is proud, and I nod.

"What's that?" I point to the city.

"All shall be revealed and explained, my darlin' girl. Give me one moment to get set up."

I've lost my bearings. "Where's the school?" I ask.

"Behind us, darlin'." He rummages in a filing cabinet, and I look around. Axel certainly does love an isosceles. A large crystal triangle rests on inverted silver triangles. Sharp corners everywhere. He likes white, too. Fluffy white shag carpet, white lounging chairs with leather triangle backs.

"All righty then, ready when you are!" He pulls up two chairs side by side. Wait, is that a slide projector?

Axel presses a button, and blackout blinds drop like silent ninjas. He presses another button, and a white screen unfolds in front of us. The whole thing feels weirdly intimate.

"In the beginning," Axel says, "God created the heavens and the earth. The earth was formless and void, and darkness was over the surface of the deep. But the Spirit of God was hovering over the surface of the waters, and thus we created a Garden of Eden."

I hope the rest of the narrative will make more sense than that.

Axel quickly clicks through a few slides: the hotel in its heyday, surrounded by sloping green lawns and tree-covered hills. Several high-tiered fountains dot the landscape, and a blue swimming pool makes my mouth water. Oh, to be submerged in cool water, caressed by silky serenity.

I force myself to concentrate on what Axel is saying.

"The Fountain of Youth was founded by my father in 1996. He was a mere twenty-six years of age but was already a plastic surgeon of note."

A slide of a handsome man in pale green scrubs comes up, and I do a double take. What the heck? I'm looking at a stethoscoped George Clooney avatar, a throwback to a show that later became an online rerun classic. I lean forward to protest, but Axel clicks to the next slide.

"He called the place the Fountain of Youth because of the eternal wellspring that feeds our endless supply of H-two-Oh."

He clicks to a slide of a babbling brook flowing between tall trees in a sunlit glade. Wherever it was, it bore no relation to our barren countryside.

"My father was loved by Hollywood stars," he continues. "He created a getaway for them, a place of rejuvenation and rebirth."

A slide of Joan Collins pops up. I open my mouth to ask if Joan Collins actually stayed at the hotel, but Axel quickly clicks onto a slide showing a buffet of sliced fruit and almonds. This is followed by a row of bedridden mummies in a windowless room.

"Patients were treated to a personalized nutritional regimen of fruit and nuts while his great hands sculpted them back to their youthful beauty. He was an astonishing success. And then the electronic, digital, and virtual world began its slow encroachment into our lives. All of which you know, so I shall not bore you. But notice Exhibit A, the modest modem, which made groaning noises as it connected. And there is the fax machine. My father loved them! He said that the screech of the fax as it churned out the miracle of long-distance communication was just a marvel! And let's not forget, said the spider to the fly, the world wide web! Considered at first by many, myself included, to be a fad. But the internet slithered its evil and inexorable way into our lives, taking all that was good with it."

"You were a supporter of the regime that banned it?" My heart is hopeful. If he was a supporter, then we're on the same side after all!

He sighs and turns to me. "Mariangela," he asks quietly, "will you please let me tell this story my way? Would that be alright? Could you do me that courtesy?"

"Yes Axel, I'm sorry." I slide my hands under my thighs, as if that will help me curb my tongue. "But I've changed my mind. Call me Mary."

He grins. "Woman, thy name is indecision, but sure. To continue, I was born in 2000. My twin was born three minutes later. Life was good, but Mumsy could see that the world was headed in a bad way. Steve Jobs, the Antichrist, has a lot to answer for." We stare at a black and white picture of a very young hirsute Steve sitting in the lotus position, cuddling a Macintosh.

Meanwhile, I'm quickly calculating Axel's age. He's sixty-six. I'm older than he is, but perhaps it doesn't matter? Wait, am I seriously thinking about him and me? There's Fiona—his fiancée—to consider. And Baxter and Sophie are my responsibility.

Axel continues. "Mumsy made a lot of powerful friends because of my father. Things were booming here at the Fountain, but Mumsy knew she had to prepare for a dark future."

He clicks through dozens of slides, moving from the earliest Apple computers to BlackBerrys, iPads, iPods, iMacs, and Google glasses. He finally stops at an image of the brain chip we all had implanted in 2055. The one that connected us to the Mainframe.

"But we did not succumb!" Axel yells, and I jump in my seat. "No sirree bob! Mumsy turned the Fountain into a city. She stockpiled all manner of supplies. She added a wing to the school."

Axel clicks through a few slides to find one of the school. "There you go! And there's Mumsy!" The pale, beehived octogenarian is flanked by a platoon of inscrutable penguins. And yes, there's the school, looking much the same as it does now.

"Mumsy went to a convent in Ireland, you see, and was at her happiest with the nuns."

Mumsy doesn't look super happy to me, but I stay silent.

"Rose gardens, bleach, chalk dust, and floor polish," Axel muses. "Nothing makes Mumsy happier." His face falls. "Well, never mind. Moving on."

He clicks on the next slide. "Mumsy began to build the neighbouring Fountain City. She started with the cathedral."

A cathedral? How far away is that church spire?

I look over in the direction of the spire. Axel must know what I'm thinking. "Mumsy bought all the land as far as the eye can see and farther! We practically own a country!"

"And she built the army barracks," he adds, as an afterthought.

I shoot up in my seat. "What?"

"Yes, the army barracks. We knew what you lot were up to." He turns to me and chuckles kindly. "I admired your ambition. A small band of revolutionaries led by a woman infused with octopus DNA. Ten out of ten for creativity."

I sink down in my chair and watch a series of slides flash across the screen. Ava, Jazza, OctoOne, Sting Ray Barb, Shasta, Noelle, and myself. I'm startled by how young I was when all that started. And of course, there's my boy, Sharps.

"You thought you'd succeed because of your world-famous time travel. It is one of the reasons you're here, but we'll get to that later."

Never mind later, I want to know now. I start to say something, but Axel yawns. "Being in the dark for so long makes me sleepy."

"You followed in your father's footsteps and became a surgeon?" I need to get as much intel as I can.

"Yeah. Blah blah blah, sins of the father etcetera." He leans in close, and I stay where I am, hoping he'll come closer. He does, and his breath smells like cinnamon. "Mary," he whispers, "you make me hotter than July. You know that? This was strictly business, but I'm aching for you. Crazy, huh?"

I don't want to admit it to him, but my groin is hot and tight. What am I, a teenager? This is ridiculous. And I'm glad to be his Mary again.

"Mmmm" is all I can manage.

"You feel it too?" He strokes my face, and I grab him with both hands and kiss him. We slide off the chairs and onto the floor. "Oh Mary," he whispers, "what are you doing to me, girl?"

I pull his clothes off, getting as close to his skin as I can. I wrap my arms around him. Skin. Oh my god. Skin. Sheer heaven. I'd been dying of thirst, and I'd had no idea.

He guides my hand to his erection.

"My word. You are well endowed. That's a bit intimidating to be honest."

He laughs. "Yeah, he's a big boy. Don't you worry darlin', we'll take it as slow as you like."

It turns out that I'm not in the mood for slow. The feel of that gorgeous prong in my hand gets all my juices flowing. I climb astride him and guide him inside me. Dear god. Who knew this pleasure still existed? Fireworks explode behind my eyeballs. I rock us to pleasure, enjoying every second.

"Wow." I finally roll off him. "I wasn't expecting that."

"A least we don't have to worry about teenage pregnancy. Which reminds me," he says casually, "did I mention that your son is here? Feisty fellow."

"Sharps? What do you mean, he's here?" I shoot up, aware that I'm leaving puddles on the shag rug. "Where? Why didn't you say so before?" My good mood has flown out the window.

He lies back and tucks one arm under his head, his elbow out.

"I forgot," he says sheepishly. "I was getting to it. It was all part of orientation, and then we got distracted. I looked up and remembered." He gestures to the screen, where a slide of Sharps's face looms, contorted in puzzlement and confusion. Oh my god, how off-putting. I turn my face away.

"That's pretty much his standard expression unless he's angry. He's here? Axel, do you have any Kleenex? I hate to be blunt, but that was a generous ejaculation."

"I had a lot pent up." He hands me his undershirt. "It's been a while for me, too. Use this."

"So you and the Barbie doll don't…?"

"Not for a few years. I mean Fee's gorgeous of course, but she's a bit abrasive. You can't change a person's voice, and you've heard her, she's very shrill. And I'd never tell her this, but she smells very chemical."

"But you're engaged?"

"I proposed about the same time we stopped having sex. I felt bad for not desiring her in one way, so I led her to believe I desired her in another. I blamed the physical side on me. I genuinely thought I was done with desire."

"But surely you've got access to all kinds of, um, arousing medications?"

"Not my style, sweetheart. The lad springs to action or he doesn't. And he stopped. Fee was happy to lay claim to the giant emerald ring and the status of queen bee. She let me carry on sculpting her, and she does a great job as the iconic face and body of the Fountain. I don't think she cares about me as long as she can keep that ring. She seems increasingly happy to escape into the kitchen and cook, but she's going to have to offer more than the Carnivore Diet or people will start revolting."

"I can help her vary the menu." I'm seeing Fiona in a whole different light and I feel positively magnanimous towards her.

"Axel, I need to see Sharps." Then again, do I really need to see him? My heart sinks at the thought. Sharps is so exhausting.

"Sure darlin'. Let's just enjoy this peace for a while."

"When did you take him?"

"The same day we took you. It was a piece of cake. That stupid Starfish Brigade, or whatever they're called. Such useless soldiers! What a joke!"

"Yeah. The naming conventions got way more complicated than we had planned. This carpet is really comfortable. Let's just stay here for a while."

I settle down next to him. He's fast asleep, and his arm is flung over me. I stroke his hair and am shocked to see pinpricks of blood on his scalp. Hair implants? But he's got great hair. I examine his head more closely and see more blood spots along his hairline. And on his hands and arms. What on earth is going on?

Sharps.

I'M DROWNING AND ANTS ARE BURROWING UNDER MY SKIN. Their tiny piranha fangs are razor sharp, and I swat and claw at myself, screaming.

"Sharps! Wake up!" Someone is shaking me. I lash out and must have struck something or someone because I hear a yelp. Then I'm doused in a wave of cold water, and my eyes shoot open.

"Thank god," she says. "I thought you were never going to wake up."

"Shasta? Why are you here?" I look around. "Where *is* here? Where are we?"

"We're locked up. You don't remember anything?"

"I don't. Well, yes, I do. I remember being scoured and separated from those maniacs. Don't ask me how I remember that, but I do. That procedure really, really, really hurt. I remember waking up in a hospital room. Mother was there, and she was mildly nice to me. She even went to make me a sandwich."

"A jakelope sandwich. Jakelopes are a kind of deer rabbit, like an antelope mixed with a rabbit. Quite tasty really. I told her I'd wait with you while she made it."

"You wanted to see me?" I feel ridiculously happy about that.

"Ava sent me."

"Oh." Goodbye happiness. My t-shirt is sodden. She really drenched me.

"She wanted to know what each of the convicts' special skills were."

"She could have asked them herself. I know for a fact that Ava doesn't lack for interrogation skills."

"She tried, without success. None of them would say anything. In my opinion, they didn't have any skills and were remarkably stupid. Of course, their main man, Jinx, had disappeared. But they got me before I got to you. And the next thing I knew, I woke up here, with you." She rubs her neck. "I thought I'd been bitten by some kind of insect or something, but before I could think about it, I passed out."

"I was probably napping when they got me," I admit. "Story of my life." I look around. "Oh shit. They made us time travel, didn't they? We're in the 1950s."

"More like the 1960s," Shasta says, and she's right. There's an onslaught of ivy and mustard paisley wallpaper to the left, and a lime green wall to the right. A third wall is covered with floor-to-ceiling books, and the fourth wall is home to an enormous baroque mirror. I try to rearrange my expression from perplexed to calm and in control. I also really need a shave and some hair gel. And a couple of headache meds would be nice because someone buried an axe in my skull. I check the mirror just to make sure there isn't an axe lodged at the base of my neck.

"Do you know who took us?" I ask.

"It doesn't take a genius to figure it out. AP's militia. My guess is they wanted you for the same reasons Ava does, but I don't know why they took me."

"You're OctoOne's right-hand man. You've got all the intel."

"Right-hand woman. Maybe. But OctoOne has been disabled by Ava, albeit it temporarily."

"Why does everyone want me?" I don't get it. "Man, my head hurts."

Shasta gets up. "The bathroom cabinet is stocked. I'm sure I can find you something."

"How long have you been awake?"

She shrugs. "I'm not sure. I found a windup clock, so I started keeping track. But I don't know what time of day or night it really is. We're in a windowless apartment. One bedroom, one bathroom, and one living room. One very tiny kitchenette stocked with canned food. Spam, ravioli, rice pudding, assorted vegetables, tuna fish, soup, macaroni and cheese—"

"Do they have sell-by dates?"

She nods. "2020."

"The year the first pandemic hit! No wonder they were stocking up. Toilet paper?"

"Enough to create a king-size bed, should we not wish to share the one in the bedroom."

My heart rate pops up a notch. She'd entertained the thought of us in the same bed, even if the notion was to keep us apart.

"I guess this was a pandemic bunker," I say. I spot a stack of vinyl records in the corner. "We can have a dance party while we while away the hours." I desperately start humming "Stayin' Alive." I'm really trying to deflect my thoughts because my skin is shrinking like Saran wrap under a hair dryer. We're locked in a windowless apartment. We are most probably underground. Reality bites. An oil slick of cold sweat covers me and puddles in my lower back.

"I'm claustrophobic," I howl, and I bury my head in my arms. My heart's going to explode, and I can't breathe. I'm going to die, smothered by terror and madness.

"Sharps? Sharps? Open your mouth." Shasta fumbles with my arms. "Keep your eyes shut and open your mouth."

I manage to do as she says. Another chalky pill dissolves on my tongue, and just like that, the terror lifts. I am free.

"Thank god." I'm filled with relief. "I didn't even hear you go to the bathroom."

"That's because you had a total meltdown. Sharps, this isn't like you. We've been in worse situations, you and me. Don't you remember? I was the one who relied on you."

"I remember every single moment with you," I instantly reply. I don't care if I sound like a pathetic moron. "You piggybacked time travel with me. We got stuck in lost time. Those were the best days of my life."

She laughs, a lovely sound, and I smile.

"It was a terrible time, and you know it. But we had some fun. Remember when I wanted to stop for takeout? You were so mad at me, and then you ate most of the food!"

"Yeah, I remember that. I remember before that too, when you were hanging out with that loser, Knox. No idea what you saw in the guy."

"He was sweet and harmless. And then you killed him."

I sigh. "I did. Of all the people I killed, he's the one I regret the least. No wait, maybe that award goes to Ava."

"Except that they all lived in the end." Shasta is sitting cross-legged in front of me.

I'd rather not dwell on my past transgressions. I look around. This place is such a hoot. Now that I'm appropriately drugged, I can appreciate the décor. Orange bean bags slouch on the floor. Empty macrame baskets hang listlessly from the ceiling. The floor is an incongruous mix of Persian carpets and red shag rugs. I'm lying on a brown corduroy sofa, and Shasta is sitting on a Moroccan love seat. Aqua footstools and a few lava lamps make the place complete. But the true beauty in the room is Shasta. The freckles on her nose are just adorable.

"In reality," she reminds me, "you didn't kill anybody."

"Hmmm. Kinda, but not really. Never mind that, let me get the math straight. I've been gone for eleven years. You were twenty-one and I was forty-four. Now you're thirty-two and I'm forty-four. How nice is that? Although that said, you look exactly the same."

She smiled. "I do not. It's been a tough eleven years."

"It was a tough eleven years because you missed me?" I'm hopeful.

"Nice try, but no. It wasn't because I missed you. Well, okay, I did sort of miss you a bit. I knew they had downloaded you, and I wondered if you'd ever come back."

"I wasn't even conscious. If it wasn't for Noelle, I'd still be there."

"Yeah, wingnut Noelle. To make matters worse, she's a junkie. And she's still obsessed with you. You broke her heart, yet she still wants you back."

"She wasn't real! She was an avatar the whole time she was with me, and I didn't know it!" I'm indignant. "That's not on me. I thought she was a hot general called Janaelle in a game called *Alterna Inferma*. Look," I shove up my sleeve and show her my tattoo, "I'm branded for life by a video game, all because of her. She lied to me from day one. The only thing real about her are her steel legs. Her fake legs are her most honest feature. I'm the one who should be angry, except that I couldn't care less about her.

"I'm worried about how long we'll be here," I add. "I really do have a thing about being locked up. I didn't freak out when I was on the desktop, but that's because I knew it went on for infinity."

"The desktop? You're rambling. Don't worry, there's a very large stash of feel-good meds. Why is it wherever I go there are truckloads of drugs?"

"Yeah, as I recall, you used to like nose candy."

She shakes her head. "I've been sober since we got stuck in lost time. But don't worry, I'll look after you."

I beam at her, and she shakes her head and smiles. "Such a doofus." She gets up. "Let me show you the ins and outs of our rather strange abode. As you can see, there are a lot of books, which I know you love. Kinda weird, these little paper boxes full of words. So quaint."

I had forgotten how young she was. No books in her world.

"So, Mr. Talks-Like-A-Dictionary," she continued, "you'll never be bored. I might try one myself, escape into a good romance."

"I can give you a good romance." I raise one eyebrow, hoping it looks sexy, but she giggles.

"You look constipated."

"Not exactly what I was going for." I wander over to the wall of books. "Look at all these books! One thing's for sure, I'm not reading any books about time travel!"

"We do need to figure out how to get out of here," she reminds me.

"True enough. But this is nice. Give me a moment to just chill, okay? I couldn't have planned to land in a more idyllic place. A corduroy sofa and a library. Just give me a few minutes?"

She sighs and wanders off. Whatever. I'm going to enjoy myself while I can. Oh my god, Charles Bukowski! I've died and gone to heaven!

Noelle.

"You're the fucking enemy!" I yell at Anise. "You totally used me!"

She shrugs. "Sweetie, it's all for the best. You'll see. Calm down."

"Calm down! I am calm! This *is* calm!" I turn to march to the other side of the room and quickly regret my move since it's a fair distance. I make it halfway and turn back.

"Why did it take you so long to come and get me? Some fucking neanderthal grabbed me at the gate and locked me in a makeup room. Like what the fuck? How long was I in there?"

"Sweetie, it was only two days. You're lucky he didn't kill you. That's Robbie. Be nice. I know he took good care of you. I would have come and got you sooner, but things have been going to shit here like you wouldn't believe. I came as soon as I could. Besides, Robbie took care of you, right?"

I know what she means. "Yeah. He gave me food and butt dust and a pot to shit in. But I was locked up and I'm not happy about it. I still don't get why you had to wait so long to come and spring me?"

"I had to wait until AP took Mariangela on a guided tour. He watches me like a hawk. But he's losing it, he's got this weird alien shit going on and—"

I hold her face in my hands. "Anise, you're babbling. Who is Mariangela? Do I even care?"

"Mariangela is the woman you call Mother," she says, and I stare at her.

"Her name is Mariangela? How bizarre. I never knew that."

"Robbie took care of your car. I'm telling you, he's a good guy."

"Whatever. What the fuck is this place, anyway?" We're in an underground dance hall with an acre of rose-patterned carpeting and a parquet dance floor. A wooden stage is draped with long red velvet curtains. Round dinner tables with high-backed, creamy satin chairs and red sashes await ghostly guests. Crystal bud vases are replete with plastic pink carnations. The lighting is warm, dim, and cozy—Vegas lounge-style. Anise hits a switch, and white neon floods the place. I shrink back, preferring the dim.

"NellNell, please take a seat."

"NellNell? No one calls me NellNell. Don't pretend like you know me. You don't know fuck."

I'm steaming mad. I'm also craving a hit of butt dust and nix, but of course I can't say that.

Anise lights a cigarette. "I'll take one of those," I say rudely and hold out my hand.

"You don't smoke," Anise says, and I mimic her shrug, knowing I look desperate. I'm jonesing for a hit so badly I'm shaking.

"Sit down and do what you have to," Anise says, and I look at her. "I mean it," she says. "You feel pretty ill right now, right? C'mon baby, we can't have this little fella's mama out of shape."

I sink into the nearest chair. "I know you're holding, but you won't admit it," she says. "I'm going to check out something on the stage. And when I come back, you'll be better, yeah?"

I look at her with relief and wave my hand. "Off with you then."

She smiles like a cat, blinks, and glides away, her leather tassels swinging and her butt tiny. From behind, I can't even tell she's pregnant. But when she turns around, whoa mama, she's pretty huge. And she's only six months? She's still got a way to go. But before those thoughts have time to register in my brain, I've taken a hit of butt dust and follow it up with a snort of nix. Hot joy shoots through my body. Thank god.

The stage lights flash, and Anise appears in the centre spotlight. She's so damn amazing. I feel amazing. Life is amazing. I'll take her to task later for having left me locked up for so long, but right now I just want to enjoy my high. The thing with butt dust is that that the high never lessens. It always hits with purity and flows like mercury through my blood. Everything in the universe makes perfect sense, and the stars spangle and sparkle as they turn.

Never mind high, I'm know I'm lucky to be alive. I successfully navigated the most vicious journey known to man or woman, crossing terrain that killed Lady Luck. She died at the entrance to the hotel compound, and I patted her gently as she heaved her final gasping breath.

I'm scheming my escape even while I float on butt dust. I figure that Anise will give me a ride out of this hellhole, she has to. I still owe her for the baby, and I know she wants the moolah.

I was lucky I even saw what was going down. I'd overheard Sharps whining about Shasta to Mother—did she like him, had she asked about him, yadda yadda yadda. I stormed out, planning on summoning Anise to the dive bar on the edge of town. I had my walkie talkie in hand when I saw a bunch of men I'd never seen before move into the hospital, all macho soldier style, crouching low and holding rifles.

I put in a call to Jazza, but the little shit didn't pick up. He never does when I call him. I tried Ava next, but same thing. Silence. Fuckers. They never took me seriously. I was about to call Sting Ray Barb, my last hope, when I saw Mother being carried out and loaded onto a bus.

I hopped into Lady Luck and followed the bus. It was tough keeping out of sight and still keeping track of them. There were times I was convinced I'd lost them and I was sure I'd die alone in that godforsaken wasteland, devoured by butterflies and amputees.

I hadn't packed for the trip either, so all I had was a small canister of water, one kale and almond bar, and a pocket full of drugs. At least Lady Luck was gassed up.

It was dark when we arrived, and I congratulated myself on having made it. I had just enough time to notice how huge the whole fucking compound was. Like, who knew it could be so big? And then three seconds later, steroid-boy nabbed me and threw me in a hole.

I'm still shaken up from my whole ordeal—the trip and being locked up—and I still can't believe Anise is one of AP's generals! Like WTF!

She, oblivious to my inner fury, grabs a mic and bows. Great. Clearly we've got time for karaoke. She snaps her fingers and "Venus" by Shocking Blue blasts through the speakers. Anise tosses her head, and her eyes flash wide. She throws herself into the song and blows me away.

When she's done, I walk up to the stage, put my fingers to my lips, and wolf whistle. Her smile melts away my anger like it never existed. God, she's gorgeous.

"Encore," I yell.

"Any requests?" She juts one hip forward, supermodel style.

"Yeah, 'Bang a Gong (Get It On).'"

"Ooooh, sexy! Sure!" She beckons me onto the stage with her.

Maybe it's the drugs or the crazy ballroom with the rose-patterned carpet, but my brain's exploding with feel-good lava and my vajayjay is hot and full. I clamber up and walk over to Anise. I lean into the mic and sing along with her. Pretty soon our hips are grinding. Okay, our bellies are gently swaying together. She licks her lips and flicks her hair back, and soon we aren't singing at all. We're kissing. What the fuck! Her tongue is sweet and full and insistent in my mouth. She pulls me down to the floor, and her tongue is sweet and full and insistent in my vajayjay. I hold her head and come over and over again. Then I take my turn, and I don't think I do too badly. At least I hope I don't, since it's my first kick at the lesbo rodeo.

"That okay?" I ask hesitantly afterwards.

Anise grabs my hand. "Are you kidding? I came like a dozen times."

I want to ask her about her vagina, but it seems rude. I lie back in silence.

"Yeah," she says after a while, like she can read my thoughts. "I'm special. Down there, I mean." She laughs. "It's my superpower, ha ha."

"It's beautiful," I say reverently. Everything is beautiful. I feel like I've died and gone to heaven. I never want to come down. But of course, like a deflated balloon, down I come, and not too long after.

Anise lights a cigarette and watches me as I lean up on one elbow.

"I don't think it's good for you to be smoking," I tell her, and she shrugs.

"I don't think it's good for you to be a junkie. But I'll tell you what, cupcake, I'm gonna do you a favour. I'm gonna help you get clean. Get you nice and sober."

The thought terrifies me. "Why on earth would I do that?" I spring to my feet. "I've got this under control." But I know I'm lying. I turn away from her. The backstage is full of shit—props, tutus, backdrops of Paris, an underwater sea scene, and a fairytale forest with three enormous trees, magic mushrooms with red caps and white polka dots, green grass, and a blue sky. This place is so nuts.

I turn back to her. "If you give up smoking."

She looks annoyed. "Why? It's not like you care about this fetus. You only want it to snare your lover boy."

"It seems that I care less about him than I thought." I look at her pointedly. "I don't just drop my panties for anyone. Or was that just a roll in the hay for you? Tell me the truth, or I'll fucking kill you, fetus or not."

"Babe, I've been flirting with you since we met. I've never worked so hard to seduce anyone in my life. You were so oblivious."

"And now that you've landed me, you'll add a notch on your belt and move on?" My heart is pounding. I'd been so focused on Sharps, but he was nothing more than an illusion or, rather, a delusion. My reality is standing in front of me, belly at full prow, hands on her impossibly tiny hips.

"In case you haven't noticed, I don't wear belts. Not now, not ever."

"I beg your pardon?"

She laughs. "'I beg your pardon'. Haven't heard anyone say that in forever." She spins around and starts singing "(I Never Promised You A) Rose Garden," but I hold up my hand and interrupt her.

I look at her. "In spite of your protestations that you're into me, you've got some explaining to do. You and AP. You are high up in the enemy's army. A small but very pertinent fact you neglected to mention when we met."

"Yeah. You're going to hate me."

"I'm pretty sure I'm not going to like what I hear, but spit it out."

"Remember how we met?"

I wrinkle my brow. "Yeah, in our dive bar. I went to score, and you arrived and got me drunk. Next thing I know, I was telling you all my guy problems. You said the best way to catch my guy was to get pregnant. It was like you were reading my mind. I said I can't carry a baby since the thought grosses me out. You conveniently and immediately said you'd carry the baby if I paid you. And you were so fucking stunning and perfect and it all made sense in the moment. And your timing was right, and I knew I could get the money, so I said yes."

"Whoa. You said all that without taking a breath. Impressive." Her honey and green eyes are imploring me to forgive her. She smells like musk and vanilla, and the only thing I want to do is kiss her again, but I must hear this.

"And the real reason you did it was because...?"

"My uncle, Axel Pattersen, aka AP, aka the head of the militia and the leader of the Fountain of Youth, set it all up. He knew you'd saved Sharps's sperm. He knew you could access the Mainframe. He knew how much you were into Sharps and that you'd buy into the plan to spring him since it's what you've been wanting forever. And since you were saving his sperm, logically, a baby was on the cards as an option. AP is the savviest strategist in the world. He's not really my uncle. He adopted Robbie and me when we were kids."

"How the fuck did AP know about me, the sperm, and the rest?"

"He's got spies everywhere, including in your lab. He knew you had a problem with butt dust, which made you vulnerable. He sent me to the dive bar to lure you in, and it all went according to plan."

"But if he wanted Sharps, why didn't he access the Mainframe and spring him himself? Why go through all this trouble and get you pregnant? And why send me in?"

"You had the access code. The one thing he didn't have and couldn't get. He could hack the Mainframe once you were in, but he needed you to restart it and get it up and running. And he didn't know where the reintegration pod was. Also, he wanted me to get pregnant. He wanted Sharps's baby because of the DNA. Everybody is fixated on Sharps's DNA because he survives time travel. They all think he's the key to solving all our problems."

It's a lot to take in. "So, fucking complicated," I say, and Anise nods.

"That's Axel for you. Full of crazy ideas. But do you hate me?" she asks. "I know it was a con to start off with, but I really got into you."

I hold her tight. "I don't hate you. It was too weirdly convenient. I knew there had to be a catch, but since you were offering me everything I wanted I went for it. I had nothing left to lose. But what now?"

"We have to get you clean. But c'mon honey, I can't stop smoking, I can't! I can help wean you off the butt dust. AP's a doctor and I can get my hands on meds that will help you. But smoking? I can't stop. The kid will be fine."

"Anise. You're whining. We both know butt dust is way harder to kick than smoking. Plus, there's the nix. I've got a double whammy to deal with."

She looks sulky. "Okay, I'll try." She chews her lip. She runs over to an electrical box and lifts the handset.

"Robbie? You there? Can you get a room ready in detox? Yeah, exactly, AP can't know. Awesome, see you there."

She turns to me. "Thank god for Robbie. We, by the way, have the best detox facility around. The program is two weeks long, but you need it, babe. Trust me."

"Two weeks!" I'm not happy.

"It's for us! You have to if we've got a shot at any kind of relationship."

She's got a point. "Hey, Anise, can I have one last hit? Just one? Please, pretty please." I hate to beg, but the craving's vicious, especially since I know it's going to be my last.

"Sure you can, sweetie. But after that, if you use again, there is no us."

"I promise, I promise!" I lose all my pride and morals when the craving hits.

She looks at me sadly. "Such a junkie. Do your thing, I don't want to watch. I'll turn my back and sing. Any requests?"

"Whatever you like." I am distracted, lining up my snort.

"Ladies and germs, I give you Dionne Warwick, 'Heartbreaker.' Brought to you by our in-house superstar, Anise!"

I attend to my needs and sit back to watch her. She's a superstar alright, and I want to be with her more than anything. Sharps was just a weird obsession. Anise is way over my pay grade, but I'll do anything to keep her. I have to straighten up and fly right. I feel the terror of failure over my high because I know how impossibly hard that's going to be.

Mariangela.

TWO WEEKS HAVE PASSED. I've been hanging out with Axel and helping Fiona in the kitchen. Fiona hasn't exactly warmed to me. I'm pretty sure she knows Axel and I have a thing going, but I get the distinct impression she doesn't really care. I've managed to introduce cereals and fruit to the morning breakfast, sandwiches to the lunch buffet, and vegetables to dinner. The response has been overwhelmingly positive.

I've tried to engage Fiona in conversation, but she's consistently elusive. I wonder what she looked like before she was a Barbie doll. She delights in her face and body, so clearly there are no regrets there.

I've visited Sophie and Baxter. Baxter is still full of fury. Like father like son. Sophie seems mildly annoyed when I visit, as if I'm interrupting her. She has a huge crush on Jinx—and to his credit, he seems genuinely fond of her—so I'm letting that be. Not that I've got any real choice in the matter.

I was content for life to play out for a while, but now Axel has called a War Room Action Meeting. We're all waiting to hear what he has to say. The blinds are drawn, and the overhead projector is ready. Its pointy little square head wobbles slightly.

"We are gathered here today because we face a crisis." He scratches his head and gets distracted for a moment, examining his fingernails. He scratches at his head some more and manages to gather himself.

"A crisis of note!" he shouts.

I look around the triangle-shaped boardroom table. Anise, Jinx, Sister Veronica—the Mother Superior—and an olive-skinned, muscle-bound man in his early thirties who's drop dead gorgeous. I've noticed him hanging out with Anise, but I've never been introduced to him.

He's wearing a white tank top and tiny red shorts. I noticed—who could not—that his ass is a perfect apple, high and round. And those biceps. He's filled out just right. His brown hair is tousled and wild, and he looks like a surfer boy avatar. He gives me an easy smile, and I wave, fluttering my fingers and feeling ridiculous.

"Yeah, he's pretty." Anise is sitting next to me. I flush. "Meet Robbie, the closest thing I've got to a brother. The brains behind all our IT forays. That said, he's a 'roid boy so I do worry about his mental facilities at times."

"Faculties?" I ask, and Axel glares at both of us.

"Calling this meeting to attention," he says pointedly. "Which means no one talks except for me. We are under attack. To recap," he puts a sheet of acetate on the projector, "this is where we stand and what we are going to do about it."

The incomprehensible diagram on the screen makes no sense, and even Axel seems confused by it. He shuts off the machine.

"Back to the drawing board. Robbie, clean the blackboard."

Robbie hops up and takes down the white screen, revealing a large blackboard covered with random scribbles. Robbie attacks the board with two erasers, banging the chalk dust off the black felt and releasing a small white cloud. I can't help but notice that his thighs are pretty damn fine.

"Hot in here," he says, ripping off his tank top. Incredible abs and sharp V-lines above his hip bones. My eyes widen, and I look away. I'm behaving like a dirty old woman.

I fiddle with my pen and try to refrain from doodling anything sexually inappropriate.

"Robbie likes to be admired," Anise hisses at me. "You're hurting his feelings. He's showing off for you."

I give the boy a silent round of applause, and Robbie bows, happiness restored.

"Come on, y'all." Axel is getting impatient. He waves for us to pull our chairs closer to the blackboard.

"ANISE," Axel writes her name in large letters in the centre of the board and circles it viciously, "has brought an INFIDEL into our midst." Anise's eyes widen in horror. "Her name is NOELLE." Axel writes Noelle's name underneath Anise's and connects them with a dotted line and an arrow. He underlines her name a few times, and chalk dust flies.

I swing around to Anise, who nods at me, her eyes still wide.

"Noelle," Axel continues, "paid us to have Anise act as a surrogate for Sharps Barkley's child, using semen she stole during intercourse. Admittedly, it was my genius that put this plan into action."

He adds SHARPS and BABY to the board.

I slam my hand on the table and glare at Anise. "Care to explain yourself?"

She shrugs, and Axel waves me down. "We are gathered here today to join the dots, cross the t's, and get the lay of the land. Noelle is safely in rehab where she will remain for the next two weeks to complete her program. Notice that I am adding a new line linking Sharps to Shasta, who is also here."

"Shasta's here?" I am further incensed. "Why didn't you tell me that?"

"Like I said," Axel reiterates, "this meeting is to bring us all up to speed. A lot has happened." He adds OctoOne's name to the board, along with Ava's, Sting Ray Barb's, and Jazza's. "Let's not forgot that OctoOne is Enemy Number One."

"OctoOne is dying. We don't have to worry about her," Anise says. She sounds eager to make up for her transgression, but Axel just looks at her sadly.

"OctoOne is fine. Ava misjudged the situation, and OctoOne is back in the saddle, so to speak. She is currently rallying her ridiculously named troops—the Brittle Stars, Helmet Heads, Super Sharks, and Bombay Ducks. Ava is still second in command to OctoOne. Which strikes me as odd, but who can understand women? If I was OctoOne, I would have locked Ava up and thrown away the key, but maybe they both need each other for now and will try to kill each other later." He adds the army names to the blackboard.

"The names made sense at the time," I pipe up. "They were oceanic and beautiful. We'd overthrown the Materialistic world and were starting afresh. It was supposed to be a reboot of the garden of Eden."

"Yeah, there were lots of oceanic fish in the garden of Eden. And exactly how did your beautiful world work out for you?" Axel asks kindly. "You fell flat on your faces. However, Mary, I did admire your efforts. You tried to educate your tribe. You created Health and Wellness. In my opinion, you were the only person who didn't just pay lip service to world change. You got out there and worked your gorgeous ass off."

I blush with pleasure.

Anise holds up her hand, and Axel sighs. "Yeah?"

Anise is clearly trying to make up for having brought Noelle in. "You've forgotten the convicts—Dorland, Zayne, and Zuub."

"Gold star for trying, sugar pie, but I did not forget about them. They kicked the bucket. I guess their bodies couldn't handle the strain of being parsed into reality. But I do need to add Mumsy and Niam to the list." He adds them in a bubble to the side.

Anise and Robbie look startled. I've got no idea what's going on. Who's Niam?

Axel grins at me. "This is how it's going to work." He writes his name in at the top of the blackboard. "Notice I am now drawing a straight line from me to Mariangela. She is my new general. You are all to call her the General. Only I can call her Mary."

"What?" A chorus of protest rises around the table. Even Sister Veronica looks perplexed.

"Me?" I stutter.

"Yep, you darlin'. I trust you. You get a lovely solid line," Axel says.

"I thought she was here to be Fiona's assistant," Anise sputters. "Not a key player."

I turn on her. "I have a doctorate in English Literature and Philosophy and a Master's in Political Science."

"Mary has already revolutionized the menu, and Fiona has willingly embraced it. Fiona continues to help me front the makeover program. However," he pauses, "in breaking news, there will be no new admissions to the surgery or spa. Fiona and I will see the current intake to the finish line, and then that's it for a while." He writes FIONA/WIND DOWN SURGERY at the bottom of the board.

"You do recall that your fountain of youth surgeries are our second-most viable world currency and our most important leverage?" Anise is fuming. "And that, as we speak, a dozen world leaders have entrusted their wives to you?"

"Yeah, Anise, I do recall. And, like I said, I will get those ladies to the finish line. Any other questions?" He links FIONA to WIVES with a dotted line.

Robbie puts his hand up. "Robbo my boy, what's up?"

"What about the, um, the other people?" He cocks his head to one side, and Axel looks confused.

"Our other stream of revenue," Robbie reminds him. "Our foremost, extremely lucrative stream of revenue…"

"Oh my god!" Axel slaps his forehead. "I'd completely forgot about them. Well done, boy. I'll add them to the board." He writes SUB REVENUE, whatever that means.

"Who is Niam?" I ask. An uneasy silence falls, and everyone avoids eye contact.

"It's pronounced 'nee-am.'" Axel finally says through gritted teeth. "It stands for 'Now I Am Myself.' My twin was born a woman in a man's body. I do not like to talk about her because she betrayed me. I helped her transition. I created her. She is my finest work, apart from Fiona. And she left me to fight alongside Mumsy. After everything I did for the cause, they both abandoned me."

"Where does she live?" I ask, but no one replies.

Sister Veronica stands up. "I have news. The boy, Baxter, has run away."

"What?" Axel roars. The nun twists her rosary around her hand until her fingers turn white.

"Yes," she says nervously. "We've got no idea how it happened. The hunters are out searching for him."

Baxter going rogue is not a prospect that makes me happy, and I can see that the others agree with me.

Axel scratches his arm, drawing freckles of blood. "Luckily, we've got the sharp ace up our sleevies. Pardon the pun." He adds TIME TRAVEL and a box with GET REINTEGRATION POD next to Ava's name on the board.

Jinx stretches his long legs out in front of him and folds his arms across his chest. "The reintegration pod is *en passant*," he says, and Axel's face turns puce.

"In English, boy?"

"It's a pawn's move in the game." Jinx is dismissive. "The King is St. Drogo's—the only place from which Sharps can time travel. The King is smack bang in Ava's territory, and she's guarding it with all her might. The reintegration pod is the least of your problems. Your game plan is riddled with errors."

"You underestimate me, Jinxie." Axel is surprisingly patient, and his face returns to a normal colour. "Your mission is to find Baxter. You stick to your knitting. I'll keep Sharps and Shasta safely locked up. We will monitor OctoOne, Ava, and their army. I will befriend Mumsy and Niam and win them over to our cause. The Sub Revenue association will continue their important work. And I will take care of the clients." Axel beams and scratches his head. When his hand comes away his fingertips are covered in blood.

Oh dear god. I exchange a glance with Anise, who gives a slight nod as if she understands my concern. "Great meeting, team, great! Off you go, except for my General. Go team!"

***

"Axel," I say gently, after the others have left, "why are you scratching yourself?"

I'm sure he's going to deny it, but he looks exhausted and relieved at the same time.

"It's the aliens," he says. "Oh Mary. It feels so good to tell you. I was so afraid you'd think I was losing my mind. Look."

He leans down and shows me the top of his head. There's a dollar-sized, perfectly neat, perfectly round circle, as if he'd been branded or shaved.

"What happened?" I ask, and Axel rubs the spot.

"It's where the aliens inserted the probe. It was a terrifying experience, utterly terrifying. I can see from your face that you don't believe me, but it's god's own truth. There I was, just a boy, ten or so, looking at the stars through the telescope Mumsy got me. It was my favourite hobby. I saw all kinds of amazing things—meteor showers, you name it. But that night, the stars seemed dim, fuzzy, and pale. I was trying to figure out why, and that's when I saw the sun coming towards me. Of course, I was confused. It was nighttime, and the sun was a blueish white, not yellow. I thought it might be an eclipse I had forgotten about, but the sun kept getting bigger and brighter. I tried to stop looking because I knew I'd burn my eyes, but I couldn't look away. Next thing I knew, there was a spaceship hovering over me. It was just like you see in the movies—a round disk shape with lots of bright white lights streaming everywhere. Like god-rays, only out of a horror movie."

"Hey, hey," I say soothingly, and I hold his hand tight. "I believe you." I didn't but I wanted to. I was hoping the story would make more sense as it unfolded. "Carry on."

"The aliens sent down a narrow green spotlight. It was like a vacuum cleaner, and it sucked me up into the spaceship. I remember travelling up the inside of the green tube. I wanted to scream, but I could hardly breathe. Then I was inside the ship. It was shiny and glittery, just like you'd expect. The aliens looked like giant ants, spindly, with steel claws and red eyes, and I was tiny next to them.

"The light got so bright that I closed my eyes. Next thing I knew, I felt like I was getting a colonoscopy with a cattle prod. They stuck a steel rod up my most private place and jiggled it around. I screamed and screamed." His eyes are shut, and he buries his face in his hands. "Of course, at the time I was a kid, so I had no idea what a colonoscopy was, but I recognized it when I was studying to become a doctor. Oh Mary, it was so many years ago, but I can still feel the pain. There's nothing nice and friendly about aliens, that's for sure. I screamed so much that I lost my voice."

"How did you get back down to earth?"

"Once the aliens were done with me, they released me back down the green column. I didn't see them leave because I passed out. It was sunrise when I woke up. I was so cold, and my insides hurt as if I had been electrocuted. When Niam—her name was Matthew at the time—found me, she just laughed and said I was lying. Mumsy defended me. She said the same thing had happened to Great Aunt Edith. I couldn't really talk, but Mumsy knew everything. I couldn't have a bowel movement for a month. I had to go back on baby formula and wear a diaper. I cried like a baby for weeks. I felt violated, like I'd been raped."

"Did the aliens ever come back?" I ask.

"No, but they put mercury in my blood. Or some kind of shiny poison. I didn't realize it until after I graduated as a surgeon. I felt something under my skin, and I took a scalpel and cut my arm open." He shudders. "It was disgusting. There were hundreds of tiny silver balls mixed in with my blood. Thank god Mumsy helped me. I went to stay in the convent for a while, and Mumsy and the nuns put me on a cleansing diet. Mumsy organized my meds." He scratches his arm again, and I don't know how to make him stop.

"I got better. I became a great surgeon. I helped my twin become Niam, and I took over from my father. Things were going well until they both betrayed me. They didn't approve of my revenue streams, but I made a success of this place, I did. Who are they to judge me?" He's rambling incoherently. "Lately, I can feel the poison moving around under my skin, and I can't get it out."

"I'll help you," I say gently, and he buries his head in my lap. I recoil in shock. His scalp is a mess under his thick hair, matted and oozing. We'd made love only hours before. I should be repulsed but I feel a great wave of love for him. No matter what's really going on, his suffering breaks my heart. It's ridiculous how fast I've fallen for him. He lies still, and I'm not sure if he is dozing. My legs are going numb. Thankfully, Anise arrives with a mug of steaming milk in her hand.

"Hey big guy," she says cheerfully. Axel looks up at her blearily. "I made your fav. Hot milk, just like Mumsy used to."

He smiles like a kid. "Milk from Mumsy," he says dreamily. "Mumsy loves me."

"Mumsy loves you very much," Anise says. "And she'll love you even more if you drink every drop." She gives me a big wink.

Axel sits up and downs the contents of the mug. Anise looks relieved as Axel slumps to the floor.

Robbie comes in and hoists him up like a sack of potatoes. Robbie is a symphony of muscles and anger. "I'll hook him up to his meds. What the fuck, Anise? You dropped the ball, big time. At a time like this? You're in charge of his meds and you know that. Every. Single. Day. That's your main job, and you fucked up."

"I've got my own shit to take care of," she mutters and bites her nails. She's wearing a yellow fringed mini skirt and a tiny yellow leather tank top, and I can't help but notice that she's a goddess of creamy cleavage and long legs. "I'm six and a half months preggers and feeling like hell. Thanks for asking."

"AP *is* your main shit," Robbie hisses. "Not getting into the pants of some junkie from the other side of town. I'm going to get him back on track. Don't you ever do this again, do you hear me? No matter what he's done to us, we owe him. He's family. He took care of us when nobody else did."

"I hear you," she says meekly, but he glares at her and looks at me.

"Brief her," he says tersely, jerking his head in my direction. "Between the two of you, keep him good and dosed. He's a genius when he's firing on all cylinders. He didn't look in control today. His org chart was a fucking mess and Jinx is going to get all kinds of ideas he shouldn't."

"I'm sorry." Anise sounds genuinely contrite. Meanwhile, Axel's hanging off Robbie's shoulder like a carcass.

"And notice that Jinx got all perky at the mention of your gal pal? He's planning something. I'd say we should ice her but she may have intel we need. So we'll carry on getting her clean and sober. But we need to get her out of the rehab centre, it's not secure. I'll utilize one of the sobriety cells, lock her in, get her straight. I'll check on Sharps and Shasta."

Wow. Robbie's intense. I remember Anise's comment about Robbie being a 'roid boy. Axel must have found a way to manufacture anabolic steroids, and my guess is that Robbie's been dipping into the candy jar more than he should have.

"Will Jinx hurt Baxter?" I ask. Robbie shrugs, raising Axel up and down with the motion.

"I couldn't care less. I'm glad his focus is elsewhere so we can get our shit together."

"But what about Niam?" Anise asks. "We don't want her to know that we're in a weak state."

Robbie laughs. "We are not in a weak state. Don't forget, we've got Mr. Time Travel and his offspring. If we really need to, we can send him back to make adjustments. Granted, it's an option I'd rather not use since time travel generally just fucks things up royally. I sampled his DNA when we secured him and results are back. Sting Ray Barb was right. There's something special about him. What with him, his kids, and your unborn fetus, we're locked and loaded for world domination."

World domination. I had heard that phrase way back when. When I was naïve and optimistic.

"What about me?" I ask. "I'm his mother. My DNA counts, too." I figure this will help keep me safe, but they both shake their heads sadly.

"Nice try, Mother Mary," Robbie says. "But you're not his biological mama. You stole him when he was a baby. From No Daddy Street. Remember that? Plucked him from a teenage mother no one cared about. You've got no idea where he came from."

I was hoping they didn't know about that.

"There's still a drought out there." I change tack. "One wellspring can't supply the world with water." Robbie gives the dangling Axel a slight hoist and looks annoyed.

"Niam is meeting with the world leaders," he says shortly. "Negotiating how to reinstate international satellite weather control. And, since we've got the Mainframe under lock and key, Niam can't screw us over. We're holding all the cards." He turns to me. "Don't worry. Jinx won't hurt Baxter. We need all the time-travelling DNA we can get our hands on. And Baxter ticks the boxes of a classic sociopath, just like his father. Therefore, his genes are the most valuable, and Jinx knows that. Now ladies, if I've answered all your questions, how about we get this guy taken care of before he wakes up? He's got the constitution of an ox, and I wouldn't be surprised if he came to at any moment. I honestly don't want to deal with that."

"I want to come with you," I say. "To take care of him." I can't help myself. I'm really into the guy. Besides, I don't want to be in Robbie's bad books or be put in a sobriety cell or whatever they're planning for Noelle. Robbie nods.

"Good thinking. I'm going to brief you on his meds too, so you and Anise can tag team." He flashes that movie star smile at me.

"Funny. Axel always said you were hot, and now here you guys are, having a thing!"

Heat floods my body. All that time, I'd thought I was alone, but Axel was way over yonder, crushing on me! Whatever my life is now, it sure as heck isn't dull!

I smile at Anise as we cart Axel back to his room. It sounds like she really cares for Noelle. I love Noelle, but I'd pretty much given up on her. If Anise can get her to kick butt dust, it will be nothing short of a miracle.

Sharps.

I'M LYING ON A BROWN VELOUR CHAISE LONGUE, reading *The Naked Lunch* by William S. Burroughs. I'm nicely drugged with whatever Shasta's feeding me and I'm feeling no pain. Shasta monitors my meds, and she keeps track of time using a little manual windup clock she found when we arrived. According to her notations, we've been here for two weeks.

Shasta worked out a schedule for us. She said it was crucial to create a sense of normalcy even when the whole world was going to hell in a handbasket.

I've been comfortably numb, happy to not think about anything much at all, snacking, napping, and reading. Hell, after everything I've been through, I deserve some R&R.

I always loved books as a kid, and I had a secret stash as a teenager. My love of real books was one of the few things Mother and I had in common.

"This book is nuts," I say to her. Then I pay attention to her. "What are you doing?"

Her ass is in the air and she's tapping the skirting boards with a bread knife. Her sweet ass, I note with a small degree of guilt, is extremely well-rounded and peachy.

She glares at me. "Having fun?"

Oops. "Apologies." I put my book down. "But you've grown up very nicely."

Ugh. That makes me sound like a pedophile. "What I mean is you, um, well, er—"

"Maybe you should shut up?" she says, but she's smiling. A wave of relief washes over me.

"You could help me," she adds.

"What exactly are you doing?"

"Looking for an escape hatch." Like that should have been perfectly obvious to me, duh.

"It's not so bad here," I retort pathetically. "I've gotten used to the décor."

"It's revolting." She sits back on her heels. "Rule Britannia had a bad acid trip and crawled in here to die, clutching a purple mohair lap rug to her bosom and dragging yellow tea towels."

"I doubt the Queen would have known what a tea towel was," I observe, happy to be talking to her. She'd given me the silent treatment up to this point, pausing to intermittently drop a tablet on my tongue. I don't want to blow the opportunity to impress her with my wit and charm.

"We could make out like teenagers while we wait?" I suggest, and she flinches.

"Oh, sorry." I slap my forehead. "That kind of popped out. You make me nervous."

"You're way too drugged to be nervous," she counters. "And may I remind you that your wife abused me when I was a kid. Kinda ruined any chance of sexual normalcy for me."

She's right. I'm a complete fuckwit. I put my book down. "You know I didn't know about that, right? And I am sorry. She was incredibly fucked up. I had no idea. I wish you'd told me when it happened."

"You would have believed me?"

"I don't know what I would have done." I scratch my head and rub my nose, uncomfortable with how this is going. "Ah yeah, we both know that's not true. I wouldn't have done a thing, would I? In my defence, I was falling apart on so many levels. Not that

that's any kind of excuse. I suspected she was having affairs, but it never crossed my mind that she was abusing teenagers." I clasp my hands together and close my eyes. "You know what? I would have done something. I killed her after I found out, remember?"

"You were going to kill her anyway." Shasta holds her ground. "Don't pretend to take the higher ground when there's no ground to take."

"Okay sure, but I did look after you," I object, sitting up. "We really bonded. At least I thought we did."

"We weren't bonding. We were waiting for time travel to kick in. Again, no effort on your part. I piggybacked a ride and you had to take me back."

"I didn't have to. I wanted to. Taking you back nearly killed me. I could have ditched you, and by all rights, I should have. I tied us together so you wouldn't get lost. And I searched for you in that terrible place when we got separated."

"That's true, you did. It was fun, being on the run like that. Being in the car, together and just talking."

"Exactly." I'm eager to seize the positive moment. "You and me, we're a team!"

"I wouldn't go that far. Now, do you want to help me or not? We've been here for two weeks and all you've done is take drugs, eat rice pudding, and read."

"And your point would be? What do you want me to do? I'm not sure we should do anything that would upset anyone."

She bursts out laughing. "That's so you, Sharps. If we ever get out of here, I'm getting you a t-shirt that says 'Keep Calm and Don't Upset Anyone Unless You're Killing Them.'"

"That won't fit on a t-shirt," I say, and I get up. "When we first got here, you said we'd been taken by the enemy. Alpha Dog. Care to elaborate what else you know?"

She looks at me with head cocked to one side. "Look at you. Finally expressing some interest in the world around you."

I shrug sheepishly. "I'm a man who takes his time," I joke.

"Alpha Plus. Yep. He's nuts. A crazy plastic surgeon who uses butterfly poison as an anaesthetic. He does work on a lot of international high-profile players. Ever since we lost the anti-aging apps, people have been desperately searching for the fountain of youth. That's literally what his place is called, The Fountain of Youth. He's also got an international bank, Alpha Phinance. Phinance with a *ph* instead of an *f*. Stupid name, but everything has to be AP this or that. The bank was started not by him but by his mama. It wasn't called Alpha Finance but Crown Royal Banking. Mama was mad about the monarchy. Mama made money off farming, but when AP came of age and took over, he came up with a better idea. You know what they say—sex sells."

"He runs a brothel?" I'm kidding, but Shasta nods. "Yeah right!" I don't believe her.

"Offers every depravity known to man or woman," she says. "Which is why AP parted ways with his mummy and sister. They weren't into the idea. His operation is called Sextopia. I'm amazed you haven't heard of it."

"In case you've forgotten, I've been stuck in a time warp," I remind her. "When I was banished onto the Mainframe, you guys were in a muddy field thinking you'd saved the world by unplugging it."

She stops and looks at me. "You really don't remember why we had to put you into the Mainframe?"

I shake my head, and she sighs. "Okay. So you were going to go back to be reunited with Mother and your children and live happily ever after. But we knew what you had planned. You hated the new world. Too much filth for you. No AI, no robots cleaning up. Real nature instead of plastic plants. You didn't want to live in it. And you didn't want your children to live in it either. You killed them once before for the same reason—you didn't want them to have to live in a difficult world."

"I killed them because I didn't want them to know I was a fraud!" I protest. She shakes her head.

"You didn't want them to face the hardships of life. You're as easy to read as a book, Sharps. We all saw it. Of course, you'd have done exactly what you did the very first time. You would have killed the kids and then lacked the courage to kill yourself. And we'd all be right back where we started."

I don't know what to say. How can I convince her that there's no way I would do such a terrible thing, when the truth was that that's exactly what I had done to begin with?

"So we trapped you in the Mainframe. And there you had to remain. Except that Noelle wanted to spring you. However, by the time she succeeded, Sophie and Baxter were old enough to have escaped your reach."

"I left them with Celeste the drunk, which completely fucked Baxter up. And I fucked him up by disappearing. And now I can't exactly say, 'hey kiddo, I only disappeared so I couldn't kill you again.'" I let out a sob. "I'm the worst person in the world."

"Yeah, you're not exactly carved out of high moral fibre."

I leap off the sofa. It's a lot to take in. Surely I wouldn't really have killed my kids? Yeah no, I'm one hundred percent sure I would have changed my mind as soon as I saw them. But man, I am one solid clusterfuck of a human being.

I march into the kitchen and sit down on the floor to think.

Shasta's on the other side of the wall, tapping away like some kind of crazy spy. I put my head in my hands. No wonder she won't have anything to do with me. I'm filled with self loathing, but more than that, my heart is broken. I don't deserve anyone's love, least of all Shasta's.

Mariangela.

I LOSE TRACK OF TIME. Between nursing Axel back to health and trying to find my bearings around the compound, the days melt into each other.

I'm in the kitchen with Anise. She's twiddling a cigarette between her fingers like a drum majorette with a small baton, her forehead cut by a Grand Canyon frown.

"I know it's not easy," I tell her, and she glares at me.

"Like you'd know."

"Actually, I do. I was a chain smoker before they banned tobacco. Two packs a day."

She looks mildly impressed. "Therefore, I do know," I continue. "I also know that a couple a day won't hurt the child. Besides, you've got what, two months left?"

A look of relief washes across her face. "Yeah, two long months." She fires up a match and holds it to the cigarette, but she pauses. "I can't. Bloody Noelle. I told her we were in this together. I can't let her down."

"I'm proud of you," I tell her, and she scowls again. I can't win. Granted, she's got a lot on her plate, and her pregnancy has progressed to the uncomfortable stage.

"My ankles are gone," she sighs. "Sorry I've been a bit cranky lately."

A bit? "It's absolutely fine, dear." *Be a bitch to me any time you like,* I want to add, but I hold my tongue.

"At least Noelle's doing well. She'll be joining us soon."

"Great," I say, but my heart sinks. Anise cranky, and Noelle just out of rehab. Fun times.

"How long have the children and I been here?" I ask, more to make conversation than anything.

Anise doesn't answer. She turns and leaves the room. Did I offend her? That girl is so hard to read.

I turn back to the goat's milk cheese I'm making. I, too, am frustrated. Making cheese is a lot harder than I'd thought, and I'd promised Fiona, Barbie queen, that I'd deliver.

Despite my efforts, Fiona still hasn't warmed up to me. Fortunately, my time with her has been lessened by my having to look after Axel and get him back on track.

"You're welcome to him," she'd said to me with a sly smile when I told her I'd be on limited kitchen duties because of Axel's struggles. "He's not what he seems. Prince Charming, ha ha. You can have him, but I'm keeping the ring. I deserve it after all my years of service. I've been where you are, and believe you me, the bloom wears off the rose."

Since Axel has returned to his authoritative, lucid self, I am back in the kitchen. And this time, Fiona has asked me to make goat cheese.

"I don't get why this isn't working. I followed all the instructions to the letter," I mutter.

Anise returns with a handmade paper calendar. "You've been here for a month and three days. I've got two months of this hell left." The calendar had each day marked off with a big black X. "I had just had my six-month check-up with AP when you guys showed up." She points to a circled six. "And honestly, I just want to get to here." She points to a large smiley face two months down the line. "Although if the kid wants to get here sooner, that's fine by me too."

A month and three days. I haven't seen Sharps or Shasta, and not for lack of trying. I keep asking Robbie. But he, equally consistently, keeps brushing me off, saying they are in a different building on the compound, a ways off. The unnerving thing with Axel and Robbie is that they both have a menacing underlying violence and volatility. I don't want to rock any boats and besides, over the years, Sharps has proven to be somewhat indestructible. I hated to admit it, but I feel neither here nor there about Shasta. She was too much in Ava's pocket for my liking and not entirely trustworthy. No, it makes far more sense to keep my head down and attend to the task at hand. Which in this case is trying to make goat's milk cheese and keep Fiona happy.

Speak of the devil, Fiona catwalks in, hips swaying, one foot sashaying in front of the other.

"Life's a runway," Anise comments, and I grin.

"That doesn't look very appetizing." Fiona ignores Anise and peers at my effort. Her nose is so close to the bowl that I wonder if she's short-sighted.

"I'm quite aware of my failure!" I snap at her, and she recoils.

"Well, pardon me, darling. You said you could do it. I never forced you." Her eyes are strangely minimized by surgery. Maybe that's why she can't see properly? She sniffs and forces her trout lips into a smile. "You used oil instead of vinegar," she says.

Damn.

"She did say she couldn't cook," Anise says.

"Look what I found." Jinx pushes through the swinging doors, holding Baxter by the scruff of his neck. Baxter's jaw is bruised, and his lip is cut. Something else is odd about him. His glasses are gone! He looks older, and I'm surprised to see that he's turned into an extremely handsome young man. I rush over to him.

"Baxter! Who hurt you?" He's still my grandson after all. I haul him into a bear hug.

He points at Jinx, who chuckles. "Not my fault. Resisting arrest. Feisty little chap. Reminds me of the first War of Scottish

Independence, when Chillingham was attacked by Sir William Wallace way back when, in 1297." He looks confused. "Wait, I was never in a castle. That's Dorland. Odd. Anyway, the lad is back, and I never laid a hand on him. He punched himself."

"That's a lie!" I spring to Baxter's defence, but then I remember something. A couple of years earlier, Baxter had given himself a black eye and told Shasta it was me. I release him, deflated.

"Oh Baxter." I sigh, and he smiles a twisted smile. I wish he was still hidden behind his steampunk gas mask.

"Yeah, Mary-Ann-gelo, I missed you too. What's this shit?" He peers into the bowl of ruined cheese.

"Goat cheese failure." Fiona sounds annoyed.

Baxter turns to her and his truculent demeanour changes. "Wow," he says, clearly impressed. Fiona curtseys.

"You're so beautiful." Baxter goes right up to her and stares. I wait for Fiona to tell him to back off, but she pats him on the shoulder. Encouraging a crazy teenage boy?

"Thank you, sweetie, thank you. Hey, maybe you can help me out in the kitchen instead of Marylou here?"

Baxter turns around to face us. His erection is a disconcerting baseball bat. "Kitchen," he says vaguely. "Yeah. I'm a good cook."

"It's true that Baxter and I have run into one another in the kitchen," I say pointedly.

"I'm good with knives, among other things." He leers at me, and I make a vow: no more kindness to him. He's a bully. I feel dizzy at the memory of his cruelty, and I lean heavily on the countertop. I've never confronted him about how he has treated me.

"Be careful you don't spill boiling water on Fiona like you did to me," I say. "Or how about when you accidently bumped into me and knocked me off balance, and I burned myself on a hot plate? Or the time you put oil on the floor, and I slipped and blacked out? Among other things."

"It's not my fault if you're clumsy, Marylou," he mocks me. I look to the others for support, but Anise is gazing longingly at her cigarette, Jinx is staring off into space looking confused, and Fiona is stirring my failed goat cheese. I give up.

"I'd love to help you." Baxter takes the bowl from Fiona. "Your wish is my command." He gazes at her adoringly, and I want to throw up.

"A castle," Jinx murmurs. "Bloodshed. I loved it. But that was Dorland. Think, think, think. I can't shoot to save my life. Guns were Zayne's thing. Something's not right."

"Anise!" Noelle rushes into the kitchen, and she and Anise grab each other. Anise's belly is a small planet in between them. "Honey, wow! You're so big," Noelle comments. "Two weeks since I've seen you, and wow, you've ballooned big time."

"Yeah." Anise sounds depressed. "Crazy, right babes?"

"You still look beautiful. Hey, are you smoking? You promised you'd give up." Noelle's body stiffens.

"She's not. Because of you." I stand up for Anise.

Noelle is unconvinced, and she sniffs Anise's hair. "Ah. I believe you. Sorry babes."

Axel and Robbie saunter in after Noelle. Robbie's more muscle-bound than ever, but in a less healthy-looking way. His eyes are glazed, and he looks jumpy.

I notice Noelle stiffen at the sight of Robbie. When we moved her to the sobriety cell, Noelle was adamant that her two weeks of rehab was enough, and she was ready to live sober. But Robbie didn't buy it. Even though Noelle wasn't happy with me, I supported him and so did Anise. We all knew how hard butt dust is to kick. She finally agreed to another two weeks in isolation, with only Robbie for company. If I were in her shoes, I'd be less than happy to see him, too.

I smile at Axel. "I failed at goat cheese," I admit ruefully, and he laughs.

"Fell on her face," Fiona confirms. "But Baxter's back, and he's going to be my right-hand man. Isn't that right, BeeBax?" They've bonded in a ridiculously short time. I'm perplexed. I tried so hard to break through Fiona's shell, with no luck. Yet Baxter strolls in, bloodied and obtuse, and they instantly bond. It's not like there's a maternal side to Fiona. She seems delighted to have a fanboy. And then I realize what's going on. They are two damaged people with an instant understanding of where the other is coming from.

"Your right-hand man," Baxter echoes. I watch his trousers sport a new tent pole.

"Good for you, boy." Axel is cheerful. "Welcome back! Quite the weapon you've got in your shorts, *salut*! I thought I was the Prong King!"

Why am I the only one who thinks discussing Baxter's penis is slightly off colour?

Axel turns to Robbie. "The boy could fit right in."

"My thoughts exactly," Robbie agrees.

"Looks a bit young to me," Fiona says. "How old are you Baxter?"

"Sixteen."

"Not yet, you're not," I say. "He's fifteen."

Fiona puts a protective arm around Baxter, who melts into her. She turns to Axel and Robbie. "Too young," she says. "He can help me in the kitchen."

Too young for what? I've got no idea what they are talking about. I turn to ask Anise, but she's cooing into Noelle's ear.

"I'm losing my mind." Jinx sinks to the floor, clutching his head and groaning. His face twists unrecognizably, and he speaks in a whispery growl. "You see, my mule, she don't like people laughing at her…" He smacks himself on the forehead. "That wasn't me talking. It was Zayne. I thought I was dreaming—having terrible nightmares—but it's real. They're real. Dorland, Zuub, and Zayne are in my head. They take control, and I can't stop them."

"Yeah," Axel says. "An unavoidable side effect. We didn't know how long it would take to kick in. In a perfect world your data would have remained dominant, but the malware is too strong. Never you mind, boy, we've got meds for that. We've got meds for everything!"

"What did you do?" Jinx screams. He's right; he doesn't sound like himself at all.

"We merged you." Robbie's tone is cold. "We took the most useful aspects of Zuub, Zayne, and Dorland and reintegrated them into you. You're a perfectly designed psychopathic sociopath. You have Zuub's chess mastery and computer tech skills, although you'll never come close to my skill level. You've got Zayne's gun expertise, and Dorland's finely tuned methods of torture. And of course, they are all melded with your own unique vile and vicious predilections."

They've created the perfect killing machine. I turn to Axel in horror.

"What? Oh my god." Jinx grabs his head. "No way! Get them out."

"No can do," Robbie says. "You don't feel so good, do you?"

As if on cue, Jinx starts howling. "Argh! I'm on fire! My brain is exploding! What have you done to me?" He curls up like a snail, his hands pressed over his eyes.

Robbie opens one of the freezers and throws jackelope steaks onto the floor. He hauls a small lock box from the back and punches in a code. He whips out a preloaded syringe, skids across the frozen meat, and jabs Jinx in a single flowing move.

"Arghhhh!" Jinx's wails start to wind down.

"Cut it a bit fine." Axel is disapproving. Robbie looks up.

"Nope. A reality check will help him behave."

Jinx slowly unfurls.

"That was only the start of the horrors you'll feel, boyo," Axel warns him. "You need us, remember that. I know you met with Niam and you came back to try to neutralize us. I'm always three steps ahead of you, remember that."

"You're not infallible," Jinx sneers. He's momentarily back to being himself. "I saw you having a meltdown. You're as batshit crazy as everyone else here."

"Casting aspersions on my mental health is unacceptable, boyo. I had a wobble, but now I've got Mary Mary Not Contrary taking care of me. I'm right as rain."

He looks over at me, and my tummy flip-flops. That gorgeous smile! The bloom is still very much on the rose for me.

"What else did Now I Am Myself have to say for herself? She who only is who she is because of me?" Axel asks. Jinx shakes his head.

"Nothing."

Axel hauls Jinx to his feet.

"If thy right eye offends thee, thou shalt pluck it out," he says. "You want to rethink your answer boyo?" He flicks open a small switchblade. "I need to know we're on the same page. Right now, I don't even think we're reading the same book." He holds the knife close to Jinx's eye. "Come on, boyo, get it off your chest. You know you want to." The knife inches closer to Jinx's eye. Baxter and Fiona stop what they are doing and watch.

"Take the eye," Baxter chants, "take the eye!"

Axel pushes Jinx's head against a cabinet. The tip of the knife is a hair's breadth from Jinx's eyeball.

"Niam is joining forces with Ava and OctoOne," Jinx blurts out. Axel chuckles and lowers the knife.

"Nothing I didn't already know. I sent both you and Baxter and neither of you came back with anything I didn't already have."

"You knew where Baxter was all along?" I'm crushed. "Why didn't you tell me?"

Fiona laughs. "Welcome to our world, honey. Need to know, and most of the time we clearly don't need to know shit. I warned you."

"Mary." Axel is gentle, and he pulls me close to him. "Our defence strategies are a work in progress. And anyway, you and I had other things to think about."

"Yeah, you were fucking like rabbits." Fiona sounds disinterested. "I told your new girlfriend that I'm not giving my ring back, Axel. And I'm doing my shows without you."

"You'll get no argument from me." Axel shrugs.

"What shows?" I'm in the dark about so much. "Why won't anybody tell me what's going on?"

"All shall be revealed," Axel says, but I'm beginning to get a bit annoyed when he says that.

"I hate to love and leave you lot when we're having such fun," Robbie says, "but I've got some business to check on." He leaves. I wonder if he's going to check on Sharps and Shasta, but I lack the courage to ask.

"I hate you all," Jinx says. "All of you. I hate you." He glares at Axel and marches off.

Axel watches him go. "He'll be fine. Because really, he's got no choice. Hey Mary, I want to show you something. I know a lot happened here, but everything's going to be just fine. You'll see. You're my girl, and everything's going to be just fine."

* * *

"I'm going to blow your mind!" Axel proclaims and leads me down a hallway into a room with nothing in it. He opens a large empty closet, leans forward, and punches some numbers into what I think is an extremely large safe. The back of the closet slides open, revealing a teal panelled elevator.

There's one button for up, one button for down. I close my eyes. I'm not happy. Sharps and I have that in common: neither of us like enclosed spaces.

It seems like an eternity before the elevator stops with a small ping, and the door opens.

"Out you go, my lady," he gestures with a big sweep of his hand. I step out into a long, narrow hallway lit with blue-green tube lights. It's like being in an underground aquarium.

"Hey Mary, relax my lady," Axel says. "I'm here. Come on, give me a big hug. There, there." I bury my face in his chest. "It's fine, sweetheart. I'll always look after you. People get a bit disorientated when they initially come down here, but don't worry, fresh air is pumped in all the time. Take a nice deep breath in and a nice long breath out. I've got the AC on full blast, so the folks won't sweat while they're on the job. But sometimes, ha ha, to change it up, I turn the AC off. Then the buckets of sweat come off them. The punters do like them all slippery and wet. You need to keep mixing it up, you know, keep them interested."

"Punters?"

"Mary, I don't want you to be offended by what you see. Sometimes a man's got to do what a man's go to do. You know that, right? You're my general and you want to know everything. So I'm going to show you. I need you to be a big brave girl."

I'm getting offended by his tone. What am I? A three-year-old who's scraped her knee? I pull away.

"I'm fine," I say curtly. "What exactly do you do down here?"

"I run the world's greatest sex show!" Axel announces triumphantly. "Every sensuality known to man or woman or those who'd rather remain unlabelled."

"What did you just say?"

"Yes! Amazing, I know! Welcome to Sextopia! Off you go then, explore to your heart's content. Look in all the windows, take your time. No one will bite you. A word of warning, we do satisfy every desire."

I walk over to the first window, and Axel joins me. "Mumsy hates this place." He sounds forlorn. "When I first suggested it, she said I had no moral compass. I love that woman with my heart and soul, but she turned on me. She chose my sister. After everything I did for both of them. But let's not talk about them." He puts his arm around me, and his warmth fills my heart. I know he's got issues, to say the least, but when I'm with him all my worries fall away. It's just our romantic little bubble. Plus, the sex is jaw-droppingly, mind-blowingly incredible.

"I was a star attraction," Axel admits, and my bubble bursts. Oh my god. Axel was a sex worker?

"That woman used to be the cook before Fiona took over," Axel nods at a window. "She was dying to get in on the job, and Fee decided she'd had enough of being down here. Fee was a big star for years. I said fine. Fee's certainly contributed a lot, but I left the caveat that I can call her back for special events. The cook is a bit of a novice, but some of the punters like that. And she's got great enthusiasm, which goes a long way. She's with Reg, who's showing her the ropes. He doesn't like daylight. Most of the crew live down here. There's a lounge area for them, and they love their rooms. They get to decorate them however they like. There's a costume department to help mix things up, and script writers in case anyone wants to do a new act. It's theatre, and they love it! We've even got makeup artists and costume designers. A lot of the crew were actors who lost their gigs in the war of 2055, but the world's their stage right here! They've got their own elevator to ground level. Three hours of sunshine is mandatory. We've also got a lovely stage where they do performances, and we host world famous carnivals and parties. You're going to have such fun!"

"How many actors are there?" My voice sounds weak.

"Three dozen, give or take. They're free to leave or take another job on the compound any time they like, but they love this life. There are queues of people wanting these jobs!"

"How do you broadcast? Via the Mainframe? Is that why you wanted it?"

"You got it darlin'. We kept broadcasting Sextopia even while the Mainframe was asleep. I knew that the meddlesome OctoOne would eventually shut it down forever, and I just couldn't afford that. I didn't have the password or I would have seized control. But, with brilliant foresight, I knew exactly what I had to do. I knew that wingnut Noelle was still hung up on your boy Sharps. I knew he had zero interest in her, and she needed a way to hook him. I also knew that Noelle had stolen his semen and locked it away in the lab in case she wanted to have his kid."

This is all crazy. "I need to sit down," I say faintly.

"Sure, darlin'." He leads me to a cocktail lounge where a dozen mostly naked people are reclining on bean bags and displaying way too much information.

"Do you need a bevvie or a glass of water?" Axel asks me solicitously. I shake my head.

"Great! Okay, so there's Noelle, a weak link in your chain and an in for me. Plus, Noelle's a junkie and I know all the places she goes to score."

"But why did you want Sharps?" I still don't understand the main reason he did all of this.

"A bunch of reasons. His DNA for one. In addition to that, he was valuable to you. He was a way to get me into the Mainframe, which I could then take over." He grins at me with huge white teeth and that shaggy mane of hair. He pushes his black-framed glasses up his nose and continues.

"Bit of a hard sell, telling Anise she'd have to have a baby. But she wanted out of the game, and I told her she could have nine months off. Think about it! Such generosity from me! Nine months of revenue lost! Out of the kindness of my heart, I gave her the whole nine months. She could have worked for at least five. Lots of punters love pregnant women."

I have no retort for that. "And it all went according to plan?"

"Like shooting fish in a barrel. Anise found Noelle at her favourite pub and they got chatting. I mean who wouldn't chat to a looker like Anise? Your girl should have wondered what a rockstar was doing in a shit place like that. But she was lonely, and she's a junkie. Anise told her what she wanted to hear and offered the perfect solution. Ha ha, your girl stole a truckload of money from you lot, and you never even noticed!" Axel is in stitches.

Meanwhile I'm horrified at how we were played. How did I not see this happening? I was the one closest to Noelle.

"And now look. Anise and Noelle are all hot for each other. You and me have got each other. I've got Sharps and the Mainframe, and life is great!"

"Incredible," I say, and I mean it. Incredibly stupid of us and incredibly well played by him. "I think I could do with that glass of water now."

Axel snaps his fingers and a woman appears with a tray. She's wearing little more than a garter belt, fishnet stockings, and platform shoes. Her tasselled pasties nearly bob into my water, and I quickly grab the glass and down the contents.

"Yeah, so anyway, this is a constant live feed," he explains. "The show, I mean." He waves his hand around. "Twenty-four-seven. They're attention junkies. They love being watched all the time."

"How much revenue do you generate annually?"

"Billions of dollars per annum. The human appetite is insatiable. These guys and gals pull in over a thousand dollars an hour. Some of them bill even more." He winks at me, the cat who ate the cream.

I try to think of something positive to say. "Good for them, raking it in while they can."

Axel looks horrified. "Sweetheart, what do you think this is? A charity? They get board and lodging and three squares a day. The money goes towards the cause."

"What cause? Toppling OctoOne?"

Axel gets up and extends a hand. "Mary, you're getting bogged down in the specifics. Have a look around. Get the lay of the land."

"I'd rather not. Honestly, I don't want to know. I want to go back up. I liked your big office with all the windows and the desert view. This is oppressive and sullied."

Axel laughs kindly. "My sweet angel. I get it. Let's go. You wanted the truth, so I showed you. But it's fine. You are pure of heart, and I love that about you. Come on."

We walk back to the elevator. "I can't believe I had no idea about this."

"That's me, baby. I'm full of surprises. Go big or go home. Actually, let's go home and get big. What do you say?"

His face creases into dimples and laugh lines, and he looks so handsome. Bright blue eyes, a hawk nose, and a lion's mane of hair. Despite everything I know about him, I can't resist him.

Sharps.

It's been twelve books and a lot of rice pudding since I realized I'm an irredeemably bad person. Shasta and I haven't talked much. What is there to say?

I get up and grab a can of my beloved dessert. Whoa. Only a dozen cans left. I'd better start pacing myself. Time to do an inventory of what we've got left. Ravioli, creamed corn, spaghetti, alphabet soup, and rice pudding. Rice Krispies squares. Energy bars. And at the back, something fascinating. But first things first.

I open a can of rice pudding and dig in. Oh, the glorious sugary sweetness! I close my eyes and savour the moment. When I'm finished, I rinse the can and clean the spoon. I wash my hands thoroughly. Once a clean freak, always a clean freak.

Then I investigate the thing that caught my eye. I remove the cans, arranging them neatly into categories on the floor with their labels perfectly aligned. I take a moment to admire my work. I've always wanted to work in a grocery store. My aisles would be displays of utter perfection! Then I climb up onto the counter and stick my head inside the empty cupboard. Just as I'd thought!

"The mind boggles," a voice says behind me. I jerk up and hit my head on the top of the cupboard.

"Shit, ow!" I yell. "A little warning would be nice!"

"That was warning," Shasta says. "Really, Sharps? You're tidying? Now?"

"Oh ye of little faith." I rub my head. "I've got a concussion. Is there any ice?"

She shakes her head in disgust and turns to leave.

"Hey!" I yell. "I found a way out."

She swings back. "You asshat. Shouldn't that have been the first thing you said instead of 'ouch, I banged my head?'"

"I was getting to it. Come here, look."

I get down off the counter and help her climb up. "Holy shit," she marvels.

"Yep. I'm a genius! You can thank me later. I saw a tiny gash at the back, and I ripped the paper. Looks like a tunnel." I grin at her. "Cool or what?"

"Cool!" She high-fives me and my life is complete, but just then we hear the unmistakeable sound of footsteps. We freeze and look at each other in horror.

"Put it all back!" Shasta hisses at me. I shove cans at her and she reloads the shelves.

The front door is getting the shit pounded out of it. "What the fuck?" a voice yells.

"I pushed a bunch of furniture against the door," Shasta quickly explains, stacking the last of the cans. "I figured the noise would alert us and it'll take them a while to push through. Sharps, we've got to go lie down and pretend to be asleep. I've got the propping ready. Sleeping meds are next to the bed."

"Fine, I admit it. You're the genius, not me." My heart is pounding. The guy sounds mad. "He's getting in."

"We're nearly done here." She closes the cupboard, shoves the ripped wallpaper under the sink, and grabs my hand. "Come on."

We run to the bedroom and jump on the bed. "Spoon into me," she says.

"I'm kind of sweaty," I whisper. "Sorry. It happens when I get stressed. It's gross."

"Ssh!" She presses against me. "Don't move. We're sleeping, got it? Don't move and do shut up."

The footsteps get closer.

I'm sure my heart's going to leap out of my chest and jump into Shasta's. I can feel her breathing. I bury my face in her neck.

And then the door opens. Is it possible for my heart to explode in my chest? I guess I'm about to find out.

***

I'm stuck to Shasta. Literally stuck. Having a guy breathe murderous sweet nothings into my ear while I pretend to be in a stoned coma is terrifying. Yes, I bury my head into Shasta's neck, which isn't exactly the hardest thing I've ever had to do. Yes, I get a huge boner, but who wouldn't, spooning into that deluxe peach ass? Do I imagine it, or does she press back slightly into me?

She's doing a great job acting like she's off her face, even snoring slightly. Her body is relaxed and pliant. We're both listening for the door to close, but the guy's taking his time.

Shasta's cool as a cucumber, whereas I'm a drenched, sodden, hot prickly pear with a giant hard on. Okay maybe not so giant. In fact, I'm deeply concerned that she's thinking I'm less endowed than she imagined. The thought depresses me. Maybe she hasn't noticed my hard on? Maybe she thinks this is me without a boner? Is that better or worse?

"Sharps," she hisses at me, "he's gone. Let go of me."

I'm so wrapped up in my thoughts that I didn't realize she was trying to wrestle out of my iron clad grip.

"Oh, yeah, uh, sure, sorry." Should I say something about the boner? Should I apologize for having sweated my way through both her and my clothing? She pulls away, and I swear I hear a wet suctioning sound.

"That was terrifying." I sit up. "Weren't you scared? Hey, could you feel, uh, I'm sorry if I was um, inappropriate—"

"We have to leave." She jumps off the bed. "Do you realize we've been in this goddamned retro fucking apartment for over a month? Of course you don't realize. You've been off your face or reading a book or eating puddings while I've been keeping track and trying to find a way out."

I'm taken aback. Clearly she wasn't thinking about my penis at all. "I wish you'd said something to me. I didn't realize I was supposed to be—"

"And then you fucking find a way out in like three seconds flat! Why didn't you apply yourself sooner, Sharps?"

"Yeah, I get that a lot. Actually, I was just running out of rice pudding and doing an inventory and—"

"We need a backpack," she interrupts me. "Supplies. We've got no idea where that tunnel leads. We also need to find a way to put the cans back in place after we leave so he doesn't know how we escaped. I bet he doesn't even know that tunnel is there. Come on, Sharps, get with the program. We need meds, a flashlight, warm clothes. Don't forget weapons. The butterflies are still out there. We might come across ampus. We should see if there's anything of value in case we need currency to barter."

"I'll check out the meds," I offer. I head off, humming nervously under my breath. We've been here for weeks, and the bathroom closet is still stocked for Armageddon. I stare at the stash. What to choose? I smack myself on the forehead. Why can't I do the simplest task? It's time to get my shit together. Be a man, step up, focus. *Focus, Sharps, focus.*

"You'll need a bag." Shasta comes into the washroom and hands me a tote.

"Yeah, I was just—" But she's already left.

So much for impressing her. I must make wise choices with the meds. I have to be discerning. I think about it for a moment and throw them all in the bag. I've got no idea what shit we'll need.

I go to find Shasta. She's rooting around the bedroom closet. She emerges, her hair wild, her eyes darting this way and that. "There has to be a gun. Some kind of weapon. But I've looked everywhere. Are you ready? Come on, let's go."

I follow her to the kitchen and watch her throw energy bars, electrolyte tablets, calcium chewies, and protein yumnuts into a tote.

"I've figured out how to restock the shelf," I offer. "We climb up and lean down to reposition things."

"Sure." She's already emptying the cupboard. "You go first. Then you can hold my legs while I lean down and grab the cans."

"My plan exactly."

"You have to wind up the flashlight." She shows me. "That's how it charges. Keep winding it."

She looks up at me, and my heart melts. Is she going to kiss me? She reaches up and gives me a small pat on the cheek. "Ready? You've got to go into the tunnel backwards so you can grab me. We'll have to go backwards until we can find a space to turn around."

What am I? Some kind of gymnast? "How exactly am I supposed to levitate and float feet first into the tunnel?"

"With this." She hauls the trashcan up onto the counter, and I see what she means. I lean on it and manage to manoeuvre my feet into the tunnel.

That's when it hits me. No way. I can't do this.

"Shazza," I say. My heart is like a wet sock in my throat, and my voice sounds weird. "I can't. You know I've got a phobia about small spaces. You know that. I thought I could do it for you, but I can't. I'm sorry."

She peers up at me. "Sharps, don't make me come up there and feed you drugs."

"I can't," I shoot out of the tunnel and land on the floor, taking a bunch of cans with me. "I've never been an action hero."

She sighs. "This is a problem. Fine. I'll go and do a quick recce of the tunnel. You wait here."

"I'm sorry," I say pathetically. "I really am."

"I know you are, Sharps," she says, and then she's gone. I climb up onto the counter and watch the light getting more and more dim until there's nothing but darkness, and I'm left all alone.

* * *

I'm alone in the kitchen with a mess of cans. My former self would have thrown them at the wall. I would have broken every plate, every glass. And yet here I am, motionless. I feel forlorn, yes. Ashamed of my inability to go with Shasta. But there's no anger. Perhaps the rage has been eradicated by my various jumps through time or has been scoured from my cells?

I shake my head like a dog. None of that matters. I can't just stand here. I have to *do* something. But what? I'm paralyzed. *Sharps*, I tell myself, *just take one step*. In any direction. Just do it, put a foot out. But my foot is stuck. Just an average foot that has forgotten how to move.

What would Shasta do? She'd keep track of things. I rush into the living room and grab her little windup clock. It's kind of cool, with a grinning cowboy on a horse rocking back and forth in time with the second hand. It's three minutes past six. Morning or night? Shasta would have known. I'm going to assume it's the evening because surely the guy wouldn't have shown up at 5 a.m.?

The apartment is quiet and lonely. "It's just you and me, buddy," I tell the cowboy. There's no way I can read or chill out like before. I'm anxious and on edge. I definitely need to self-medicate. Who wouldn't, in my situation? I rush into the washroom before my anxiety can overwhelm me and chew a pill. I go and lie down on the bed with my hands behind my head but that doesn't work either.

I jump up. I've got to wait for her in the kitchen. Maybe she'll come back. Maybe I can try to pluck up the nerve to follow her, although I doubt that.

I peer into the tunnel. Should I call out to her? No, bad idea. Wait, I do hear something. A rustling. Is she coming back? I lean in closer. Yes, there's definitely a noise, and it's getting louder.

"Shazz?" I say tentatively. The next thing I know, something is tickling my nose. I scream and leap backwards, swatting wildly at the air.

I am facing my worst nightmare. A cockroach. It's sitting there at the entrance to the tunnel, looking at me inquisitively.

"Die!" I yell. I grab a can and lunge for the thing, but it just laughs at me, waves its little feelers, and ducks out of my reach. There's a clicking sound, a thousand clicks. The sound of a thousand nightmares. The sound of crickets snapping tiny claws. I know what that means. A tidal wave of cockroaches is flowing through the tunnel towards me.

I gotta get out of here. Who knew I could move that fast? I dive out of the kitchen just in time to see a waterfall of roaches pouring out of the tunnel. I lunge around the door and slam it shut. The tiny beasts scrabble against the wood, their metallic screeches terrifying.

I lean against the door. I swear I can feel it pulse with the weight of the beasts. I've got to wedge the door closed. Oh my god. Is Shasta okay? I can't bear to think about it. Are cockroaches carnivorous? It wouldn't surprise me.

I run to the living room, grab a chair, and wedge it tightly under the handle of the kitchen door. Shit! I feel like I could throw up, but sooner or later I'll be starving, and all the food's in the kitchen.

I leave the angry den of clicking insects and pace around the living room. I'm worried sick about Shasta. Has she been eaten alive? I must escape and find her.

I run down the corridor to the front door and tug on it. No luck. It's locked tight. Claustrophobia fills my lungs and smothers me. I sink to my haunches and bury my head in my arms. I can't breathe.

And yet, through the black blanket of my panic, I see something. An old-fashioned key card slot. The kind retro hotels used to have—white credit cards that never worked. You always ended up going back to the reception desk to ask for another one.

But a key card slide means there's a key card! *Hey buddy,* a voice cautions me, *if someone had used it to enter the apartment, then they would be here,* n'est pas? *And there's nobody, therefore there's no card.* Talk about rain on my parade.

"They would have a spare," I argue with myself. "I'd bet my bottom dollar there's a key card hidden in the apartment. Whoever built it would have planned for this, in case they locked themselves in or were locked in. Don't we all have a spare in a potted plant or under a floor mat?"

I leap to my feet. I've got to find the key, and I've got to be fast. I run past the kitchen. Shit. The insects are gaining ground. Hundreds of tiny feelers are trying to force their way under the bottom of the kitchen door. I run to the bathroom, grab a towel, and shove it against the tide.

I start my search in the bedroom. I empty every drawer and the pocket of every garment. Every shoebox. Every jewellery box, and there are a lot of them. Someone loved diamonds and sapphires. And yet, no key. I search the shoes, the mattress, the pillows, the throws. Nothing.

I go back into the washroom. I search every place I hadn't looked while raiding the meds. Nothing.

I go back into the living room and stop dead. What if the key card is in the kitchen? Dear god. That's unthinkable. Don't think about it. Just carry on searching.

I start with the books, flipping through every one. Then there's the vinyl. I yank every record out of every sleeve. Nothing. I pat the cushions, overturn mats, and dig inside the plastic Ficus plants. There's nowhere left to search. *And you know, buddy*, the voice says, *consider this. Don't you think Shasta would have found this elusive card if indeed it does exist?* Yeah, not helpful.

I'm drenched in sweat, and I flip my hair out of my eyes. I catch sight of myself in a mirror. My hair's really long. Cool, I'm like a young Kurt Russell, even though a lot of people think I look like Jason Bateman. I'm still good-looking, and I give myself a small smile and a wave. Wait! The mirror! A large silver moon with a baroque frame. I rush over to it and try to yank it off the wall. It's locked in place. Shit! I grab a small side table and use a leg to wedge it off the wall. It finally comes loose, and I flip it over. Hallelujah! There it is, a flat, white, get-out-of-jail-free card!

But what if, like the legends of old, it doesn't work? There's no hotel reception desk to ask for a new one. And what about Shasta? What if she comes back? The chair is blocking the kitchen door. I can't leave it like that. I can't take the chance of locking her in the kitchen with the tiny beasts.

I grab a large plastic Ficus plant and run down the hallway. I pause for a moment, hold my breath, and swipe the card. Glory be! The door opens. I wedge the Ficus to keep the front door open, then I run back to the kitchen and ease the chair out from under the doorknob. The creatures are quiet. Have they gone back into their hole? Best not to hang around. I run back down the hallway and out the door, leaving the Ficus holding the door ajar in case Shasta does somehow return.

Then I run for my life. Down a narrow corridor lit by blue-green tubes of light, around a corner, and down a long narrow flight of stairs that leads to a small, well-stocked bar. The bar opens into a low-ceilinged foyer with wood-panelled walls and two washrooms on either side. The foyer walls are lined with daguerreotype photographs of a stern woman with a blonde beehive flanked by two small boys. The foyer is dimly lit and uninviting, with a velvet curtain drawn across the far wall. Where's the exit? I hear a sound and without thinking, I shoot around a corner and dive into the women's washroom.

But wait! I recognize one of the voices. It's that crazy woman, Noelle, the one who came to rescue me. She's with another woman and they're laughing. Then they're gone. Where did they go?

I can't stay in the washroom forever. I belly-crawl across the cool linoleum and spot a flight of stairs across the lobby. I scoot to my feet and sprint up the stairs. Thank god nothing creaks. I scurry into a balcony of seats overlooking a stage. A small film projector room is to the left. A projector! What kind of time warp is this? There's Noelle, naked on the stage, tonguing a heavily pregnant supermodel. They're really getting it on, lit by a puddle of light in an otherwise dark room.

I've got to get out of here. The women must have entered the lobby from behind the red velvet curtain. I've got to go back down. And it's best I do it speedily, before the women run out of steam and decide to leave.

I tiptoe down the stairs and back into the lobby. I tippy-toe across the floor and gingerly pull the curtain aside. More stairs, going down. Fuck. If it wasn't for bad luck, I'd have no luck at all. Is there no end to this underground world?

I've got nowhere to go but down. So down I go, yet again.

Noelle.

"Oh honey." Anise comes up for air. "God, I missed you."

"Tell me about it. Robbie was brutal. But he was effective. He's got me taking some shit so if I ever even try butt dust again, I'll chuck up my intestines."

"How are your cravings?"

"The only thing I crave, sweet pea, is you." I pull her closer, if that's humanly possible. I stroke her stomach. "Man, you are ready to pop." I sit up. "Babes, it's kind of freaky to think that there's an actual kid inside you."

"You've got no idea. I just want it the fuck out of me. Listen, sweetie, I've got to tell you something."

I stare at her in horror. "You're breaking up with me." I sit up and grab a shirt to my chest.

"What? Don't be stupid! Of course not! But you're not going to like what I've got to say."

"Spit it out." My heart is pounding. What can be so terrible?

"I'm a sex worker."

I gape at her. "I beg your pardon?" I wasn't expecting that.

"Yeah. I should have told you, but we barrelled into this thing. You and me, one domino falling after another." She's wide eyed and never more beautiful. She's centre stage, her belly an extravagant beach ball. "Part of AP's operation is a sex show.

It's called Sextopia. He started it years ago to fund his military operations. It makes billions of dollars."

I'm gobsmacked.

"*Every sensual delight known to man, woman, or anyone in between.* That's his motto."

"And you—" I'm at a loss for words. Tears well up inside me. The thought of sharing her, sharing her body, is too much for me. And she knows it.

"I've never loved anyone before, not like I love you. It never mattered. It's just a thing we all do for the cause."

"Axel does it too?"

"For sure! Well he used to, not so much any more. He's called the Prong King. Biggest dick in the universe. Both literally and figuratively speaking."

"It's obviously not in person. How does he stream the shows?" I rub my eyes. "The Mainframe?"

She nods.

"After the baby's born, do you have to go back to work?"

"Yeah. It's funny, you know. I never actually thought about it, but since I've been pregnant, I've had time to think. I realized for the first time that my body is *my* body, not Axel's to barter as he pleases. And I love you. I don't want to do it anymore."

"Will Axel let you stop?" I'm hopeful, and she laughs.

"Not a hope in hell. I'm the star attraction. No one in the world's got a superpower like me!"

"You can say that again," I fervently agree.

"My flower power vag. Viewers love to watch it open up like a peony." She sighs. "But wait, there's more."

"More?" I pull my shirt on.

"Honey, I hope I'm not triggering you into a relapse," she says, and her brow creases adorably. I shake my head.

"As long as you're not breaking up with me, we'll face the rest together." I take her hand.

"My show is with Robbie." She says the last part reluctantly, and I snatch my hand back.

"What?"

"Yeah. Sorry, babes. I mean we're not actually related, but we are like brother and sister. Axel sells the show that way, which is gross."

Gross on many levels. I guess I hadn't actually imagined her with anyone specific.

"I thought maybe you just meant pole dancing or something," I admit pathetically. "Or just you. I don't know. I've never seen a sex show, not even virtually. And my sex was mainly solo, if you catch my drift, at least until Sharps. Man, I was so obsessed with that guy. It feels weird now, how crazy I was. I guess I'm an addict of one kind or another. Drugs, a guy. I don't want to be an addict anymore. I want to be normal and in control."

She strokes my hair. "I don't believe in normal, but in control would be nice for me too. I've been at Axel's beck and call since I can remember."

"I hate him. I want to kill him." I start to get up, but she pulls me down.

"He did rescue Robbie and me when we were kids. We'd be dead long ago if he hadn't taken us in. Which doesn't mean what he did was right, making us sex workers, but he doesn't see life the same way most people do. I'm just saying we have to think before we react. Plan things. I don't want to go back in the game either, but trust me, we can't just go out there with guns blazing. Axel may look reasonable but he's not. He also thinks he's been invaded by aliens who put mercury in his blood to keep tabs on him."

"What the fuck?"

"Yeah. Long story. He's not exactly sane. Then there's his twin, called Niam, and they're archrivals."

"I literally can't keep up."

"Yep. A six-foot-seven amazon woman born in a man's body. Axel helped her transition, which is why there's bad blood between them."

"How so?"

"Have you met Fiona?"

"Yeah. The Barbie doll in the kitchen."

"Yep. Axel's former fiancée and his finest work. All his clients look like her, but Niam wouldn't let him do that to her. She designed her change exactly, and Axel had to do it. She's incredible. She's got an eye condition; she has no irises, and her eyes are the colour of milky blue moonstones. She can see perfectly, but it's kind of freaky-beautiful to look at. She's very striking. Wears her hair in a big, blonde beehive, just like her mother did. Mumsy was a big fan of the 1950s. Mumsy is actually dead, although Axel believes she's alive."

I lie back and groan. "This is too much. Barbies, Axel, Sextopia. You and Robbie."

"Now you understand why I smoke. Can't wait to boot this kid out and fire up a fag. In the meantime, we have to play dead."

"Play dead?"

"Yeah. Like soldiers on a battlefield who don't want to die so they lie down and pretend they're dead."

"Which is another way of saying you've got to go back to work after you've had the kid."

She looks depressed. "I do."

I pull her close to me. "It's incredible that this has been going on all this time. It's like we've been living on a different planet. We genuinely thought we were the centre of the world and that we had it all under control. What a joke. So much for OctoOne being all knowing."

"Oh, I wouldn't underestimate her. She's got Sting Ray Barb, for one thing."

"I've never had much time for Sting Ray Barb. She's ancient, and like, what's she done lately?"

Anise pokes me hard with her finger. "She sprang Sharps. Sting Ray Barb may be in her eighties, but she's a genius. Rumour has it that she's close to finding an antidote for the butterflies by repurposing the venom from African blue blister beetles."

"Honey, you're blowing my mind. African blue blister beetles?"

"Yep. They look so pretty and shiny, but if you touch them, you get terrible blisters. The Africans don't have a problem with butterflies, and everyone thinks that's because they've been harvesting beetle venom."

"Where have I been all this time?"

"Stoned out of your gourd. Anyway, rumour has it that Sting Ray Barb's hard at work manufacturing a cure from the beetle, which she somehow managed to get her hot little hands on. They're still looking into the value of Sharps's DNA. Plus, Sharps is everyone's get-out-of-jail-free card in the highly likely event that this all goes pear-shaped. Just turn back the clock."

"This is a clusterfuck for my brain," I say. "Robbie's got Sharps and Shasta under lock and key?"

"Yep. And don't forget about Jinx, Axel's super killer. Robbie took all the bad stuff he could harvest from the convicts and put it into Jinx. Who, as you saw, is not in great shape. Neither, of course, is Robbie. He's been dipping into the gym-boy-juice a bit too much. If Jinx was smart he'd defect to OctoOne, but he'd need to get his hands on the drug that Robbie gave him. And he's got as much a chance of that as a snowball in hell."

"Once the baby's born, you'll have to go back to work. What about me? What will I do?"

"Axel will put you to work too." She sees my face. "Oh, I don't mean that." Then she reconsiders. "Actually, you'd be so hot, what with your steel legs. You'd be a trender for sure."

"I am NOT doing sex work!" I yell and jump to my feet. I expect her to come to my defence, but she's got a faraway look in her eye. "What?" I yell at her. "What are you thinking?"

She clambers to her feet, and I rush to help her.

"Hear me out," she says, with puppy-dog eyes. "I should have thought of it before. Instead of me and Robbie getting it on, I'll tell Axel that it'll be you and me. He'd fricking love it! It's not so bad! We'd come up with a storyline that you'd feel okay with. You can't see the punters, it'd just be you and me in a room, making out and flashing your legs and my vag."

"I am NOT cool with that! Oh my god. How did I get to this point? What the fuck? No! I've got to get out of here!"

"There is no out." Anise is sad. "If there was, I'd know. Like I said, we have to play dead and play the long game."

"Having sex in front of hundreds of porn watchers is not playing dead," I counter.

"Millions. Not hundreds, millions. All of whom pay big bucks to watch. Sex sells baby, no matter what dystopia we're in."

"Oh my god." I pace around the stage and pause in front of the three giant trees and the red magic mushrooms. "Is this stage part of it?"

She nods. "We hold in-person parties. I do an amazing *Flashdance* re-enactment with the water cascading on me. It's beautiful!"

"You guys are so hung up on the past. You never even got to partake in the whole consumerism fetish that peaked in 2055. Not that you missed much."

"Exactly. It was crazy here, but a different kind of crazy."

"What will happen to the baby?" I gesture to her belly.

"Mariangela will look after it. She looked after Sophie and Baxter, and now she'll look after this kid."

"Sophie's here too? Not that I really care."

"Yeah. She's in the convent."

I burst out laughing. "There's a convent? Why am I not surprised? Got a carnival or two tucked up your sleeve? A midway and a circus with three dancing elephants and a one-trick pony?"

"As a matter of fact, yeah. The Venus Fest. Balloons, soap bubbles, neon lights, cotton candy, a Ferris wheel, and a rollercoaster. And a lot of sex. Naked punters, naked workers. It's a riot."

"I'm just not equipped for this," I say. "Does Mother know?" Anise looks confused. "Mariangela. Sorry, we called her Mother."

Anise claps her hands. "Right, you did! You see! She's perfect to look after a baby! Listen honey, I know it's a lot to process, but let's look on the bright side: we've got each other now! It will be an adventure!"

"I don't like adventures," I say sourly. "Or surprises. And this was a real boatload of surprises. Anything else you need to get off your chest?"

"Nope, that's it." A weird look crosses her face. "I peed myself."

It dawns on me. "Your water broke. But you've got two months to go." I'm suddenly beside myself with worry. "You're going into labour. Let's go and find Mother."

Anise pulls on her tiny aqua leather outfit.

"Come on babes, we've got this. Lean on my arm." I wonder if Mother's got any idea what's in store for her. Most likely nary a clue.

***

I practically carry Anise into the kitchen. The contractions have hit hard and fast.

"Help!" I cry as we stagger through the swinging door. "Help us! Anise is going to have the baby!"

But there's no one there.

"Fuckers." Anise is pale. "Where are they when we need them? I'm going to die. I know I'm going to die."

"You won't die," I say, but I'm terrified. Women do die in childbirth. Where's Axel?

"Press the panic button," Anise says. And then she screams.

"What panic button? Where?" I look around, but I can't see anything. "Come on, let's get you on top of the table." I sweep the dishes to the floor and hoist her up.

"Arghhhh eyyyyyyyy yay yi!"

We're in for a long ride. "Anise, where's the panic button? C'mon honey, tell me."

"Inside the freezer." Anise points. "Take out the jackelopes."

I scramble over to the freezer and pull out the steaks. Those steaks aren't having a good day but then again, neither am I. Where's the button?

"I can't see it!"

"Eyyyyyyyyy!!!"

"Anise!! I can't see it!"

She carries on screaming, and I stick my head inside the freezer. I can't see a button. I feel around with my hand. What's with these people and the freezer? Wait! There's a small switch at the back. I flick it up and down a few times, but nothing happens.

Why is nothing happening? "I need to get hot water and towels, right? I think I found the button. I'm going to boil some water." I'm babbling. I grab a pot, fill it with water, and turn on the stove.

Anise screams again, and I've got no idea if it's an affirmation about the button or an accusation of my ineptitude. I discern all manner of profanities but decide not to take it personally.

I gather a bunch of dish towels and rush back to Anise.

"What the fuck are you doing?" It's Robbie. The panic button must have worked. He slides on a steak and swears. "Pick this shit up," he yells at me. "Why's she here? She should be in the infirmary."

There's an infirmary? "I'm sorry, I didn't know what to do. I was looking for Mother."

He picks Anise up and runs out the kitchen. I run after him. Then I remember I left the stove on. I rush back and turn it off, and when I lurch back into the hallway, he's gone.

"Robbie!" I scream. I run in the direction he went but he's vanished.

I come to a crossroads in the hallway. I stand still, listening. Nothing. Then I hear a bloodcurdling scream to the left, and I run towards it.

The screams get louder. I round a corner and run smack bang into Mother.

"Oh, thank god." I throw my arms around her.

"It's going to be fine, Nellie," she says gently. She pats my shoulder. "Axel's a surgeon. Everything will be fine."

Anise screams again and I bury my head in Mother's chest. "She's going to die!"

"No one's going to die." She leads me to a waiting room that looks oddly traditional, with grey chairs and a coffee table with *GQ* and *Cosmopolitan* magazines from 1998. And a coffee machine. Of course.

"Sit down. Let them do their work. Everything's going to be fine."

"Is it? Really? Did you know that Anise is a sex worker with a vagina that opens like a flower? And that Axel runs a sex empire called Sextopia, and they have massive parties? It's all so sick, and I might have to become a sex worker too." I bury my head in my hands.

Mother rubs my back. "I didn't know about her vagina," she says. I look up at her.

"You knew about all the rest." I am accusing. "You've lost your integrity."

"Baby steps, Nellie." She is gentle. "It's true that we're in a crazy place, but if we let it overwhelm us, we'll drown. Take a breath and try to relax your shoulders."

"Fuck my shoulders! Do you know they want you to look after the baby?" I try to shock her into a reaction I can relate to. "Doesn't that bother you?"

Her face lights up. "They do? I love babies." She jumps to her feet. "I should go and help."

What the fuck? Not the reaction I'd been expecting.

I follow her into the operating theatre.

"Fancy," I say, and it is. State of the art stainless steel, bright lights, and surgical trolleys.

"Gown and gloves," a gowned man yells, and I recognize Robbie's voice. "Think people, think!"

We get gowned up, and Mother rushes towards Anise. "You're doing so well, brave girl," she says. Anise grabs her hand and screams.

Axel peers out from between Anise's legs. "Not so good. We might have to cut her open. Scars are not good."

"No scars!" Anise pops up. "Get this fucker out of me! But no scars! Come on, you little shit, get the fuck out of me!"

Axel buries his head again. "Increased dilation! Keep shouting at the kid! Come on baby, get with the program!"

It goes on for hours. The screaming. Anise and Axel and Robbie yelling at the unborn child while a bunch of nurses in white nun's uniforms look inscrutable and sterilize the equipment. I hadn't expected the surgery to be this large or well equipped. This place is just one surprise after another.

I hunker down in a corner. Mother holds onto Anise and strokes her hair. This is no easy task since Anise is thrashing around like a crazy woman.

"No way around it," Axel finally admits. "We've got to cut it out. Otherwise, your vag will be irreparably damaged. What's worse: your vag being destroyed or having a scar on your belly? Take your pick."

"No scars!" Anise screams. "Don't touch my vag! The little fucker will come out, it will have to!"

I bury my face in my hands. This is not where I thought my life would take me. I look over at Anise howling her face off and I've never loved her more.

I get up, go over to her, and grab her hand. Mother looks relieved to see me.

"I'm here, babes. You've got this."

She crushes my hand and I wonder how long this is going to take.

Sharps.

I CROUCH DOWN AND CRAWL INTO THE BASEMENT. I stop. There's silence. A single lightbulb dangles from a dubious looking electrical cord. I reach up, praying my knees won't crack. I gently tug the gold chain. My knees are fine, but my stomach gurgles. Great. Intruder betrayed by a growling stomach.

The place is filled with antique school desks. Vintage ink wells, sloping, hinged desktops, and wooden seats worn shiny by hundreds of scholastic little bottoms. I've stepped into a sepia time warp. A bunch of blackboards are piled in the corner next to a Jenga stack of black felt erasers that look ready to topple over at any moment.

I sniff the air. Vanilla and a hint of lavender. Odd. I would have expected chalk dust and musty mould.

A rusty rolling clothes rack sports a row of threadbare choir gowns on wire hangers. A mangy old cork board is nailed to the red brick wall. I sneak up and study the faded photographs. There's that tall woman again, the one with the beehive and the two scowling little boys. Another picture shows three tiers of bleachers stacked wall-to-wall with penguin-suited nuns. Then there's the beehive woman being hugged by a grinning penguin. Then there's the woman and the two boys, only they're teenagers and the woman and one boy have large red Xs scratched across their faces. Someone didn't like the family photograph.

A narrow flight of wooden stairs lurks in the far corner. Is that the only way out? How did they get the desks and blackboards down here? Regardless, it looks like my only way out. Shit. Rickety-looking stairs means one thing: creaky noises. I don't want creaky noises. I creep over to the stairs and crawl up on my hands and knees. I've evened out the distribution of my weight, and I can check for creaks along the way. I'm a genius!

Except that when I get to the top, I'm eye level with a pair of shoes. Oh shit! I scramble back down as fast as I can and stare up, breath heaving, ready to face my death.

"You never fail to surprise me, Sharps," Shasta saunters down the stairs, smiling at me.

"What's a girl like you doing in a place like this?" I counter but my heart's hammering like a six-gun salute.

"Why were you crawling?" she asks.

"Because it evens out the weight distribution, and I can check for creaks." It sounds pathetic, and my voice trails off.

"And yet I could have killed you because you weren't looking where you were going." She grins. "You can stand up now."

Why does my every effort to impress this woman fail?

"I left the door open for you," I offer. "Hey, did you bump into like several thousand cockroaches in the tunnel?"

She looks surprised. "You saw the cockroaches? Man, they were scary."

"Tell me about it. How did you get past them?"

"I crawled through the tunnel forever," she explains. "I got to the bottom of a well shaft with a steel ladder. My flashlight was dying. I put it in my mouth and started to climb up. I'm about halfway up and the step broke under my foot. I nearly had a heart attack. There were spikes running up alongside the ladder and I grabbed one of them. Fricking god. It came off in my hand, and I nearly fell off the ladder! A big hole appeared in the wall and an avalanche of cockroaches came pouring out." She looks shaken by the memory. "I screamed and dropped the flashlight. I managed to grab the ladder with both hands, but it was pitch black. I pretty much pulled myself up, hardly stepping on the rungs."

She runs out of breath and sits down next to me. She's shaking. I want to put my arm around her but I don't want to scare her off.

"Then what happened?"

"I got to the top. I could see a light coming through around a latch. I twisted the latch and pushed up. I can't bear to think what would have happened if it hadn't opened. I would have fallen to my death."

"But it did open."

She nods. "And here I am. I wondered if the roaches would find you." She chuckles. "You had my sympathy. Claustrophobic guy gets trapped in an underground apartment with a million disgusting insects. Brutal! But you got out. I'm proud of you, Sharps!"

I flush. "Where are we now?"

"You'll never guess."

"Nor do I even want to try." I'm tired, and my stomach growls again. "I'm starving. Don't mess with me, Shasta. Hangry is an understatement."

She reaches into the bag strapped across her chest and hands me an energy bar and a bottle of water. I chug down the water. The energy bar tastes like old cardboard and is the most delicious thing I've ever eaten. She wordlessly hands me another one and I rip off the wrapping. "You are my angel. So where are we?"

"In the basement of a convent laundry. St. Agnes. There are freshly laundered habits from here to Sunday."

I shudder. "I hoped the new world would be done with saints' names. I did think it smelled good though. The top of the well led here?"

"Nope, to an electrical hut out in the desert. Stocked with food, water, and a bunk bed. It might come in handy for us down the line. I could see the school in the distance. Now here I am, and here you are. Next time you're trying to fly under the radar, don't mutter so loudly to yourself. I could hear you coming from a mile off."

Embarrassing. "I didn't realize I was saying stuff out loud. I came in through a tunnel from a large theatre. Have you used that tunnel too?"

"Nope. Interesting though. There must be more than one exit from there. One to the shed and one here. Good to know."

I'm delighted she's praised me, albeit it for an unintentional snippet of intel. "What's next?" I ask.

"We need to try to find the connection between the school and Axel's operation."

"We could dress up like nuns," I suggest, and she punches me on the shoulder. Ouch. I resist the urge to rub the spot. At least I'll be able to rely on her to protect me in a fight.

"Well done, Sharps. That eluded me." I can't tell if she's being sarcastic or not.

"That's Sister Sharps to you."

We sneak up the stairs and scuttle into the laundry, pulling the unwieldy habits over our clothing.

"Vanilla and lavender," I marvel. "The way to a guy's heart."

"Ha, you're still such a geek!"

"Who doesn't love the smell of fresh laundry? I'm not the neat freak I was before, and I'm not that angry guy, either."

"So you say. You haven't exactly been put to the test yet."

I let that one slide.

Shasta adjusts my coif and veil. "Remember, nuns glide, they do not stride. And they never run."

"You're an expert on nuns?"

"Getting into character. Clasp your hands below your bosom, like so."

"You're hilarious. Hands and bosoms are secure. Let's do this."

She peers around the laundry door. "Good to go. Off we glide." She stops dead, and I smack into the back of her. "What now?" I hiss.

"You're a guy. Don't talk. If they speak to us, bow your head, look downcast and let me do the talking."

I make a zipped-lips motion and wave her into the corridor. I'm getting antsy with all this hanging around. Sooner or later, someone's going to show up.

We glide down the hallway, which is flanked by full classrooms. Where did all these kids come from? Where are their parents? I'm about to say something to Shasta when I remember her caution.

We turn down another hallway. More classrooms. More kids. The polished linoleum stretches like a runway with classrooms on either side.

Shasta stops and grabs my hand. "There's Sophie!" she hisses. I jerk my head towards an arts and crafts classroom. So that's my daughter. She's beautiful. She's beading a necklace and gazing at a man with an expression of adoration on her face. But wait, what the fuck?

Jinx is with her! My mouth falls open, and I'm about to rush into the classroom when Shasta drags me off.

"Why is Jinx with her?" I'm livid.

"I don't know, but shut the fuck up."

I clasp my hands beneath my bosom and zip it.

We turn down another corridor. More magnolia walls and polished linoleum. Where is Shasta taking us? Why was Jinx with Sophie? My heart is insisting we go back and rescue her even though my rational mind knows that isn't an option.

Are we trying to find the offices? All I can see are endless classrooms and closed doors. A piercing bell breaks the silence, and even Shasta jumps and turns towards me, horrified. Pretty soon, the corridor will be filled with kids and nuns.

Shasta recovers first. She bows her head and carries on gliding, her body pushing me towards a door. *Janitorial.* We slide inside and shut the door. Dear god. I can't take much more of this. My habit is soaked with sweat.

Shasta snaps on the light. "I wonder what the time is," she whispers. "Was that end of school day or a lunch break?"

"No idea," I whisper back. "If someone comes in here, we're so screwed."

"Better hope for the best. If they come, we must secure them. At least we've got bleach and brooms, two of your favs!"

I dig deep for some witty repartee, but I've got nothing. I'm struck by exhaustion.

"Best to wait in darkness," Shasta says, turning off the light. "The plan is to stay here 'til school's out. Then we can do some investigating."

I nod. All I want to do is sink to my haunches, cradle my head in my arms, and fall asleep. Instead, I lean against the wall and close my eyes. A little vertical catnap will have to do.

Mariangela.

Axel, Robbie, Noelle, the nurses, and I are all yelling at Anise.

"Shut up!" she screams back. "Fuck! Why isn't this over?"

I understand why she's confused. The room is already filled with the cries of one infant.

"Twins!" Axel is ecstatic. "You're having twins! Good girl! That's my girl! Yeah!" He punches the air with excitement. "Preemies, of course, but we can deal with that. Sister Dymphna, sound the alarm, get the nursery ready for another infant! It's raining children!"

We're caught up in the excitement of the moment. In the end, Anise got her wish. Natural childbirth.

"A boy and a girl," Axel crows, "double trouble! Here, Mary, grab this kiddie!" He shoves a roughly swaddled, sleeping little baby at me. "Gotta get Anise all stitched up."

"Not too tight," Anise snaps at him.

"Honey, your vag is our national treasure. No husband stitching here, believe you me."

"How do you feel?" Noelle asks Anise, stroking her forehead.

"Tired. Annoyed as fuck. I want everyone to leave except you. I want to sleep."

"Nearly there," Axel says, "just wrapping up. Annie my girl, you certainly earned your keep today! We'll have to think of—"

And then the lights go out and the air conditioner shuts off with a shudder. There's silence. Maybe it's just me but I swear I immediately feel the temperature rising.

"Keep calm," Axel says, but he sounds shaky. "Not a great time for this to happen, but it could have been worse. Like when we were in the throes of it. Robbie, go and take care of the generators. They should have kicked in immediately. Be careful."

"On it." Robbie winds up a flashlight and shines it around the room. "Take care of Anise and the babies. I'll keep you updated."

"Good boy." Axel hands a flashlight to Noelle. "Wind it up. Keep it charged. Sister Attracta, you good with the boy? Mary, you got the girl?" We both nod, our faces ghostly. Axel strips out of his scrubs, grabs another flashlight, and winds it up.

"Follow me," he yells as he shoots out the room.

"What about me?" Anise wails from behind us.

"You wanted to be alone!" Axel says over his shoulder. "Okay, Noelle, you stay with her. I'll get the babies settled. Then I'm going after Robbie. Not to be overly dramatic, but this power failure means we're at war."

I clutch my baby to my chest and follow Axel to a nursery where Sister Dymphna is setting up a second cot. A couple of nuns are winding up flashlights. The place is lit up like an illicit graveyard, full of the creepy shadows of scurrying nuns.

"Nasal cannulae for each kiddie," Axel says. "You ladies have got this. Sisters, you answer to Mary here. See you as soon as I can."

The babies are utterly adorable. And utterly tiny. We get them clean, fed, and swaddled. We pop them into their incubators and they fall asleep. I guess the nuns were ready for every contingency because the boy is in blue and the girl in pink. I question the gender stereotyping, but at least it makes it easy to see which baby is which.

I stroke their little heads and my heart bursts with happiness. They've got a surprising amount of hair.

"Welcome to the world, little people," I say softly. These are Sharps's children. My son, a father of four, albeit it two of them unwittingly.

I'll say one thing for Sharps. He was an extremely dedicated and loving father right up until the moment he killed his kids. I move in closer. I'll protect these two innocent little beans from everything, including my own son. In fact, especially from my own son.

Sharps.

I was half asleep when the door opened, but when it did my heart just about stopped. I was pinned against Shasta and we were both trying not to breathe.

"Fee fi fo fum," the voice says. "I smell the blood of the time travelling one. I know you're here my pretties. Come on out, both of you. Two blind mice, two blind mice, nowhere to run."

Shasta clutches me even tighter. We're both hoping he'll just go away.

"Very funny, pretending to be invisible." Light floods the room, and we stare up at Jinx. We're in deep shit now.

"I saw you go past the classroom," he says. "Now come with me, both of you. I'm going to lead you both by the hair on your chinny chin chins. And if you so much as try to get away, I'll snap your feeble little necks. All in agreement, say 'aye.'"

"Aye," I echo. Shasta stays stubbornly silent. Jinx leads us into the principal's office.

"Bad children," he laughs, "have to report to the Mother Superior." He closes the office door and pulls a rug away from the floor. "You're going into a cold hole. There are lots of cold holes scattered around the compound, but I think you'll like this one the best. I'm sure you'll both wish you stayed in the nice and cozy, tidy hidey paisley hippie hole. This doesn't have those creature comforts. Down you go."

I peer down at a step ladder leading into darkness. "I can't go down there," I say.

"Go, or I will push you down," Jinx says.

"I'll go first." Shasta shames me again.

"What do you want with us?" I'm stalling for time.

"The billion-dollar question! I want to get you to St. Drogo's, where you can work your time travelling magic and take me back to when I was me and not some demented ailing convict hybrid. My body and mind are failing. Axel and Robbie are Frankensteins, and I'm their monster. I need you to reset the clock."

"It doesn't work that way," I stammer. "And you know that! Time travel never works the way we think it will. Why don't you just defect to Sting Ray Barb and have her scour the others out of your head? It got you lot out of me."

Jinx gives a snort. "Why would she help me? She wouldn't. Besides, I wouldn't survive a scour. I'm fragile as it is."

"Point taken. But why do you need to jump with me? You can jump solo."

"I can't." Jinx has his eyes closed and I can see he's losing his patience with me. "You're the only one who's survived. Everyone else died. Shasta only lived because she piggybacked with you. And frankly, I don't care where we land as long as it's me, myself, and I, as opposed to me, Dorland, Zuub, and Zayne."

"But I won't be able to come back unless I'm reintegrated. I don't want to be stuck in some other timeline all by myself. Or, god forbid, with you."

"Tough titties, little kitty. You're just my ticket to ride."

Great. I can't think of any other reasons to deflect him or ways to poke holes in his plan.

"St. Drogo's is two days away from here," Shasta says. "Why not go now? Why do we have to go down the hole?"

"I've got to take care of a few matters first," Jinx says. "Down you go, pretty lady. Enough chit-chat."

Shasta climbs down the steel stairs, taking her time. I wonder if I can shove Jinx down the hole and break his neck. He smiles at me with his vampire teeth and neon green eyes. His uneven pupils are unnerving.

"I know what you're thinking. You could try, but you'd end up incapacitated. I wouldn't kill you, but I'd paralyze you. I need you alive, but how alive is up to you." I shudder.

I inch my way down the dimly lit steel ladder, my nun's habit bulky in the small space. I finally reach the bottom.

"It's cold down there. You'll need this for warmth and survival," Jinx throws the rug in, and I'm showered with dust and dander. Don't the nuns believe in vacuuming?

"How long will we be down here?" Shasta yells up at him.

"Hard to say," he replies. "But rest assured, I shall be as swift as possible since I'm the one who's dying. Being a hybrid is killing me."

"We need supplies," Shasta shouts. "Food and water. And tranquilizers for Sharps or I'll have to kill him myself."

Jinx thinks about this for a moment. "True. He's a real sissy boy. Fine, I'll be back in a few days, hang tight."

"Days?" I yell. "What the fuck do you mean, a few days?"

He closes the hatch door, and I try not to panic.

"Look into my eyes and breathe," Shasta says. "Stay with me, Sharps."

"Yeah, that shit never works, but thanks for coming out." I look around. "What the fuck? The nuns had an underground bar?"

"Seems that way."

"Hobbitville meets your friendly neighbourhood pub in Iceland!" I'm momentarily distracted. We're in an underground pub. I try not to focus on the underground part. The place is freezing my tits off and I shiver. A tiny, well-stocked bar curves around the wall, with booze bottles like dusty jewels in the gloom. Red leather bar stools wait for bottoms and the happy chatter of pub life. A red leather sofa hugs the opposite wall.

"Fricking freezing." Shasta swaddles herself in the rug while I investigate the bar.

"These guys," I marvel. "It's like being in an alternative universe." Shasta shivers. "Let's just hope OctoOne got my message."

"Yeah, the cavalry would be nice right about now. Wait. You got a message to OctoOne? How?"

"There was a radio in the desert shed. I've got no idea if the message got through. I tried all the secret codes Jazza gave me, so fingers crossed."

"Back up for a moment. You just 'happened' to have secret codes with you?" I use air quotes and look at her reflection in the mirror. "I get it now. You knew Axel was going to come for me. That's why I was in a less secure environment than the other convicts. You were using me as bait. And you wanted to be there when they came. What if they'd killed you?"

"They wouldn't have. OctoOne had men at the ready. If they so much as touched a hair on my head, they'd all have been toast."

"But how did you know Axel was coming to get me?"

"Axel's twin sister, Niam. She and OctoOne are working together. Niam knows everything Axel does."

I'm hit hard by her revelation. I'm everybody's tool. Everybody's plaything. Hello Mr. Nobody.

I crack open a bottle of Southern Comfort and take a few swigs. "Everybody seems to want a piece of me, but everybody hates me. Jinx wants to time travel with me. Axel wants my DNA. And so on and so forth. You're a spy. For a moment I thought you might be the spy who loved me." I laugh bitterly and drink more.

"Easy there, Sharps. The thought of being down here with a pile of your vomit doesn't appeal to me."

"Good little spy," I mock her and drink more booze. "Not like me. Known far and wide as the village idiot."

She looks up and comes over to me. "Stop being so hard on yourself. You do have good qualities."

"I do? Like what? Name one."

"You're funny. And you care about me. And, in your own fucked up way, you keep trying."

"Great points for my résumé." I've downed a good third of the bottle. I root around the back of the bar. "Hey! Old fashioned tobacco!"

"You're not smoking in here, Sharps! We don't have a lot of air, remember."

Holy shit. I look around. No ventilation. I am locked underground. My brain shrivels like a prune.

"Don't panic!" Shasta rushes over to me and grabs me by the shoulders.

"I'm very calm," I chug another third of the bottle, "very calm. I feel lovely. Very lovely. I'm so cold." I pass out.

When I wake, it's hard to move. I sit up, bound like a mummy. "What happened? Why am I wearing red leather?"

"It was that or die."

Shasta has somehow dismantled the red sofa, and we are both covered in strips of red leather held together by duct tape.

"I found the tape behind the bar," she said. "And a pair of blunt scissors, which are now even more blunt."

"We can use them to stab Jinx when he comes back. Although he seems like a Bond villain. Invincible." I am sobering up, which worries me. I roll over and clamber to my feet and head to the bar. I feel sick to my stomach, but the thought of panicking is worse. "Time to pick my poison. What the fuck, more Southern C, why not? Go with what you know. Isn't that what they say?" I crack it open and take a few swallows. Great, I'm going to end up with alcohol issues on top of everything else.

Shasta regards me calmly. "Have you heard of the story of the mouse and the scorpion?"

"No, that particular bedtime story missed the rounds in my house."

"Okay. So, a mouse and scorpion get trapped in a hole together. The mouse runs behind the scorpion in ever decreasing circles until it's directly behind the tail. Then the mouse runs up the scorpion's tail, hangs on, and starts biting through the tip. In a matter of minutes, the poison sac and stinger get ripped off. The mouse runs down the scorpion's back and bites into the scorpion's head. The mouse stays out of the pincers' way, biting until the scorpion is dead."

I'm silent. "I don't get the moral of the story."

"My mission is not to kill any of the enemy but to infiltrate and provide a way for OctoOne to conquer them and take their spoils. The poison sac, Sharps. What we've done is climb up the tail, and we are in the process of biting off the stinger and the poison sac. You get it?"

"I don't." I'm rude. "We're prisoners. At least I'm not as cold as I was." Shasta did a great job padding the leather strips with the sofa stuffing. I am, however, slightly hungover and drunk at the same time. "I'd kill for a grilled cheese sandwich." I sit down with a thump and raise the bottle to my lips. Fun times, yeah baby.

Mariangela.

A WEEK LATER, I'm studying the little baby girl in her incubator and chatting to Sister Louise.

"Team meeting, pronto!" Axel hustles in. "You need to leave the tots, Mary, and toddle up to the glass room! The good sister will be just fine."

I nod at Louise—she's urged me to drop the "sister"—and she gives me a thumbs up. "Come back with names for them," she shouts as we leave. "This Pink and Blue nonsense needs to stop!"

"It's on the agenda." Axel hurries me along. "But wait." He pulls me to one side and looks at me critically. "When was the last time you had a good night's sleep? Or brushed your hair?" He leans in close. "Did you brush your teeth this morning?"

"Um, I can't remember," I admit. "I've been so focused on the twins."

I've been living in the nursery since the twins were born, sleeping on a camp bed, with the nuns bringing me food. I hardly noticed that Axel was off dealing with the war. I had noticed that neither Anise nor Noelle had come to visit their offspring.

"Hmmm." He doesn't look pleased. "Look, Mary. You're my right-hand woman. Can't have you looking unkempt. Luckily for you, I've got your back. Go and get glammed up, then come up to the conference room."

Unkempt? Is the bloom off the rose so soon, just like Fiona said? Only she said I'd go off Axel, not the other way around. My belly fills with lead, and he hugs me tight. "Darlin', you're my Queen, you know that, right? I just want you to fit the part. Don't worry, someone will take care of you, and they'll bring you up when you're ready."

He vanishes around a corner. I've got no idea where to go or what to do.

"He's quite the character, our fearless leader!" A voice bellows in my ear, and I jump. A woman with white and purple hair and tortoiseshell cat-eyes glasses grins at me. A fuchsia lipstick smear covers her front teeth, and she's wearing red and black plaid dungarees and chunky black army boots. These people! Where do they get their supplies? There we were, living off the land, making rudimentary lip balms with rosemary, lemon, and jackelope oil, and they're jazzed up to the nines.

"I'm Franka." The woman sticks out a bejewelled hand. "Come on, honey, let's get you dolled up."

"Dolled up isn't my style," I retort, but she hasn't let go of my unsuspecting hand. She drags me down the hallway and up a flight of stairs.

"This is your parlour," she says cheerfully. "Your little piece of heaven. Sit down."

I try not to gasp. The room is amazing. It's decked out in cool lilac and pale green, with silk flowers in crystal vases and a sparkling chandelier. The softest cream carpet is underfoot, and gold-framed mirrors make the place look even bigger than it is.

A silver, gold, and pale pink Regency sofa is resplendent with satin striping and carved woodwork. Monet's *Water Lilies* covers an entire wall. I have a view of the desert with the church spires in the distance.

"This is so beautiful," I marvel.

"Just remember that everything comes with a price," Franka says. "C'mon honey, he's keeping the meeting waiting, for you. Trust me, you don't want to get on the wrong side of him. Hair first."

She opens a closet and pulls out a mannequin's head with a tall beehive wig. "I'm going to show you how to put it on because I won't be around much after this. I'll show you the ropes, then you gotta take it from here. There are books on the coffee table—how to create the perfect winged eye and how to blend shadows and blush for the best contouring."

"Wait. What? I've got no idea what you're talking about!"

"Hair and makeup!"

"I'm not wearing wigs and makeup! Axel said he likes me the way I am! He said so."

"He lied, honey. That's what men do. And they want what they want. They revert to type no matter what they say or how hard they try. Here's how you fit the wig." She pulls it on and fastens it with clips.

"It scratches," I object. "I look ridiculous."

Franka ignores me. "The perfect winged eye takes a bit of work; you'll need to practice. Tilt your head back, and I'll do you this time." She takes her glasses off and leans in, so we're nose to nose. "Sorry about being so up close and personal, but my eyes are going and I can't find a pair of specs with the exact prescription. There's a storeroom full of glasses; just fyi in case you need a pair. You're allowed to book an appointment with the optician. Who, by the way, is really just an armed guard to make sure the place doesn't get looted." I wonder if she's a nervous Nellie or generally chatty. Her breath isn't fabulous by any means. "There." She puts her glasses back on and surveys me. "From now on, look at the books I've left you and practice, practice, practice! Here's your lipstick, 'Coral Chorus.' The perfect blend of tangerine and blood orange."

I uncap the lipstick and recoil. Rancid butter and dead fish. "Disgusting!"

"All the cosmetics are old," she says reasonably. "We do what we can with the rapidly diminishing stash. Axel likes his girls pretty, and he doesn't care how we smell. We've got a chemist who makes eyeliner from charcoal and wax, and he can mix up a decent foundation using the desert clay and jackelope fat. It's mainly the lipstick that's the problem."

I feel bad. It wasn't Franka's breath that was foul. It was the lipstick. I want to throw up. The lipstick is thick and rubbery on my mouth.

"Why can't you come by and help me again?"

"Because, sweetie, I've got sixty diva performers who all want me. Besides, you'll learn fast, I can tell that about you. Open your eyes."

I look at myself in the mirror, studying my winged eyes. No way will I be able to do that again. I'm ashamed of myself, subjugating my will for that of a man. I look like a seventy-year-old granny dressed like a *Vogue* starlet from 1960.

I hate to admit it, but a part of me loves it. I may be wrinkled, but I'm glamorous! I grin through the thick lipstick and end up with some of it on my teeth. Oh dear, my teeth. I'd never realized they'd become so yellow over the years.

"We have teeth whitening products," Franka reads my mind and is helpful. "And we can burn off some of those sunspots. Snap on these pearl earrings, add a lovely pearl necklace, and we'll finish you off with a gorgeous housecoat. Then on go the heels, and off we go." She hands me a pair of stilettoes.

"I can't walk in heels," I stammer. "I've never worn heels."

"Heels are for meetings only." She pulls out a pair of flat pumps. "These are for when you're being Nanny."

"I have to wear the rest of this getup when I'm looking after the babies?"

"Consider it your new uniform. It's not so bad? Look around at what you get."

"It's a gilded prison." I'm crushed. "You said it yourself, everything comes with a price."

"Sweetie, be positive! You've got your very own Prince Charming! You're living your own personal fairy tale! You were the damsel in distress. Your knight in shining armour brought you to this faraway land and gave you a castle and a high tower from which you can see the whole wide world! This is your happy ever after."

It's my turn to ignore her. "Is there a lower heel than this? I can't walk!"

She digs in the closet and hands me a pair of pink gabardine slingback kitten heels. "These?"

I try them on. "Doable. Barely, but doable. I'm ready."

I cast a look at the full-length mirror. Goddamn! I'm one hot babe! I'm not sure why Franka had called my outfit a housecoat. It's a pink Chanel Jackie Kennedy–style bouclé suit. The same as the one she wore the day JFK was shot, right down to the navy lapel and gold button. My beehive negates the pink pillbox hat.

I'm a bit worried I look like Margaret Thatcher in drag since I'm not exactly petite. I decide to rock my own version of the Iron Lady and to hell with them!

I straighten my spine and look myself straight in the eye. I'm Mariangela de Pédery-Hunt. Forget Barkley, I'm going back to my maiden name.

Sure, the lipstick stinks, but I'll get used to that, right? I worry that I'm throwing my feminist principles to the wind, but maybe it's more the case that I'm becoming the woman I always wanted to be. Whatever the reason, I'm happy.

"You've got great legs," Franka comments. "See what heels do? Even a low heel. They make you stick your butt out ever so slightly, which works your calves. No flats in the world can match the sexy of high heels."

"I feel like a different woman." I don't tell Franka, but I feel powerful. I can do anything. Move mountains, rule worlds!

"Better hustle or Axel will get antsy." Franka brings me back down to earth. "C'mon, hot stuff."

"I'm ready." Low as the heels are, I'm wobbly as a newborn giraffe. "Can I hang onto your arm?"

"Your wish is my command. Come on, my fair lady, let's get this party started."

She leads me to the boardroom and I enter self-consciously. Axel gives a loud wolf whistle, and Noelle, Anise, and Robbie give me a round of applause.

"Clap, clap, hooray!" Anise and Robbie shout.

"My Queen!" Axel gets up and bows. "I will be your king. We will be heroes."

Even Noelle chortles. "Hot stuff."

I blush.

"Time to get ourselves sorted." Axel takes charge. "My lady, take your seat at the throne beside mine, and let the games commence. We have ourselves a few visitors." He rings a loud town crier's bell, and the door swings open and in come Jinx, Fiona, and Baxter.

"The whole famdambly's here!" Axel cries. "Welcome one, and welcome all. The meeting is now in session!"

I gaze around the boardroom. I'm not one for profanities, but what the heck happened here? Axel wasn't joking about being the King. Has he lost his mind?

Sharps.

I HEAR A NOISE, and I raise my head. I've been drunk for god knows how long. Even Shasta can't keep track of time down here. I'm not sure if being drunk helps or makes the claustrophobia worse, but I can't take a chance on being sober.

"Supplies!" The hatch opens, and an enormous bag crashes to the floor. Jinx is back.

Good thing we weren't standing under the hatch or we'd both have been squashed like bugs. "Plus blankies! Don't die on me! Not even you, Shasta! You've got value, too. Toodle-oo for now!"

"How long have we been here?" Shasta yells. The hatch opens.

"A week!" Jinx yells. "You're doing great! Hang in there!"

The hatch closes again. Man, my life is one shithole after another. Shasta rushes at the bag. "Let's see what we've got." She pulls out a few windup flashlights, dozens of energy bars, and a truckful of meds. Just how fucked up does Jinx think I am? Still, the more the merrier. Oh god. Maybe he's planning for us to be down here for weeks? There are dozens of water canisters.

Shasta sorts our supplies into piles. "I wish there was a way we could track time. That way we'll know how long we are down here."

I raise my head again. "I don't want to know. Is there any cheese? I want cheese. Did he give us a grilled cheese sandwich? I prayed to god for grilled cheese."

"He did not. But I can give you a protein peanut butter energy bar and a bottle of water. Shall we play a game of Scrabble? I found a stack of board games. It's time for you to sober up. I can't give you meds until you're sober."

I sit up slowly. "Scrabble. Sure. I mean why the fuck not? Strip poker would be more fun, but we'd freeze our balls off. Let's give you another opportunity to whip my ass. Bring it on."

"There's even a dictionary. Oxford. No illegal words, Sharps."

"And if I do? You'll punish me how?"

She crawls across to me until her nose is inches away from mine. Her breath is sweet, and my cock instantly swells despite the padded clothing.

"I'll think of a way," she says. Then she blows my whole world apart as she leans in and kisses me, Southern Comfort breath and all.

Mariangela.

A MOTLEY CREW IS GATHERED at the glass boardroom table. Axel wasn't joking about us being King and Queen. He's seated at the head of the table on a gold throne, wearing a white jackelope fur cape and a gold crown studded with rubies. It looks like the real deal. An old British relic? Or perhaps it belonged to a Russian czar? I, too, have a tiara perched on my beehive and a rabbit cape. And I, too, am on a throne, albeit it a smaller one.

The others wait, expectantly. Fiona seems besotted with Baxter in a most unseemly way. She's stroking his hair, and he's practically purring, grinning his weird, twisted smile.

"First order of business." Axel points at Robbie with a jewelled sceptre. "I heard our most valuable asset and his companion have escaped."

Robbie looks shamefaced. "Yeah. Don't worry, we'll hunt them down. Got a team on it as we speak."

"Big fail for you, boy, big fail." Axel is hard on him. "But never mind that, we have to focus on Carnival!"

Do I have Stockholm Syndrome? Axel is clearly out of his mind. But even in his ridiculous get up, or perhaps because of it, I feel inordinately proud to be Queen. This is fun! I'm the Prom Queen! I focus on what Axel's saying.

"Carnival! Our primo money-making event! Princes from around the world will be flying in!"

There's air travel? Axel reads my mind. "Yes darlin'. Oh, you were so in the dark, my sweet lamb! You guys were a tiny hamlet, a speck of sand in my empire."

"Your empire of sandcastles," Robbie says quite rudely. "All of which are about to crumble due to lack of water. Your wellspring is drying up. The water table is dropping like a stone."

"Which is exactly why we need to wine and dine the sheiks! 'Rock the Casbah!' The answer is oil!"

"The answer is satellite regeneration to reactivate control of the global climate," Robbie shoots back. "We need water more than we need oil."

"Boyo, we need both. You're being unnecessarily negative about the water supply. It has not failed us yet, nor will it. But I do agree that a more fully fleshed out plan is essential for world domination. Which is why we need the world leaders in our pocket, and why this year's Carnival is key. The night will be an event of intentional and great debauchery. We will get the contracts signed, sealed, and delivered. And we'll have enough compromising photographic evidence to have every world leader in our pocket for the rest of their natural lives."

"Can't we use Sharps to time travel back and reactivate the satellites without us having to resort to all of this?" Robbie asks, not unreasonably.

"No time travel unless we really have to!" Axel shouts. "It destroys the natural order of things. Besides, you've currently lost him, so it's a moot point. How is the enemy doing with their butterfly antidote and vaccination?"

Robbie looks like he's thrown up in his mouth. "Yeah, about that. They seem to be making real progress. Sting Ray Barb's harvesting the venom from blue blister beetles, and the prognosis is good. Not only is she developing a way to vaccinate people, but she's also developing a drug for anesthesia. Double win. That crazy old witch is quite something. We should have neutralized her years ago."

"I want her science!" Axel yells. "Why didn't you tell me about this? I don't want them to have any advantage over us." He slumps down in his throne, then straightens up with renewed determination. "I will be King of the World. We will colonize OctoOne's sad little republic, but it's not top of the list. First up is Carnival. The world leaders are coming. We'll get our hot little paws on their oil and get them to activate their satellites."

Noelle raises her hand. "What if I can get a hold of Sting Ray Barb's science for you?"

All attention swings to her. "Really?" Axel is skeptical. "Sorry girlie, but you've been a streaky player in the game."

"I'm the only chance you've got." Noelle's voice is shaking, but she holds her ground. "But I'll only do it if you let Anise and me live a free life. No more sex for her. We come and go and do as we please."

"No way José! Anise is my star!"

Noelle shrugs. "And soon she'll be my wife. It's up to you."

"Your wife!" Anise beams.

"Yeah, okay. I guess," Axel concedes. "If you can pull it off. Which I sincerely doubt. How would you do it?"

"I'd break into the lab, neutralize Sting Ray Barb, and bring back whatever's in the lab. But can I trust you? What if I come back with the goods and you don't honour your word?"

"He's a man of his word." Anise grabs Noelle's hand and speaks in a rush of courage. "If he agrees to it, he has to honour it. I won't go back to that life."

"Fine, but one caveat." Axel points at Anise. "You still have to do Carnival."

"I'm staying for that if she does." Noelle is stubborn. "I'm not leaving her in the hands of a bunch of strangers. Will she have to have sex with them?"

"No, honey. It's my *Flashdance* act. Besides," she shoots a look at Axel, "I can't have sex for six weeks after giving birth. It's a medical fact. You can't make me."

Axel looks hurt. "I would never 'make you.' It's always your choice. Sort of. But fine, point taken."

"How are you feeling?" I ask Anise. She looks pretty damn gorgeous. Hard to believe she's just had two babies.

"Sore. And my boobs are leaking like crazy. Fucking gross. I want to go back to bed, where I was happily recovering until this super-urgent meeting was called." She looks extremely pissed off.

"You are in a bad mood," Axel says. "There are meds for that. Anyway, moving on from Ms. Grumpy over there, I've just had a great idea! Fiona's organizing Carnival with Baxter's help. Robbie's hunting down Sharps and Shasta, and boyo, put an urgent sticker on that. Jinx, you're doing whatever you're doing, and that leaves me with a bit of time. Therefore, I propose the following."

He gets off his throne and kneels at my feet. "Mary, my true love, will you marry me?" He takes my hand in his. I'm stunned. "Yes," I say. "Okay."

Fiona bursts out laughing and claps her hands. "Congrats, love birds! But I'm still keeping the ring."

"I'll buy my Queen an even bigger one! Noelle, you put the idea in my head. Double wedding! Time to get planning. Meeting adjourned!"

A wedding? I stand, forget I'm in high heels, and nearly fall over. "Wait," I say. "Before we go, we need to name the twins. They're a week old, and we can't keep calling them Pink and Blue. It's archaic and really stereotypical."

"Right! Yeah. Hmmm. How about Adonis and Aphrodite. Meeting adjourned for real."

Adonis and Aphrodite?

"Go on then, all of you, go and attend to your chores." The others obediently leave, and I'm alone with Axel.

"Darlin', I have to go and take care of secret manly business pertaining to the state of the nation. You good? I'll brief Franka on the wedding dress and the ceremony." He gazes at me with those incredible blue eyes.

"Axel dear, aren't we moving a little fast with all of this?" I'm trying to be tactful, but he grabs me into a hug, and I melt into him. The feel of his large warmth, the way he smells. He's irresistible.

"Darlin', I know it's all very sudden, but you were sitting next to me, the woman of my dreams. And I just thought, why not?" He holds me by the shoulders and gazes into my eyes. "There's so much riding on Carnival and us getting all the sheiks onboard. Our very lives are hanging in the balance. I thought to myself, Axel, if it all goes to hell in a handbasket, what would you want the most? Reach into your inner soul and ask yourself the question. And the answer was you."

"Do you think it will all go to hell in a handbasket? Tell me honestly, Axel."

"Fifty-fifty." He scratches his head, which worries me. I'm giving him his meds, but I wonder if I need to ask Anise about adjusting the dose.

"Are the aliens worrying you?" I ask gently. He looks away.

"I think they're there," he admits. "Mary, can you check for me? Tell me if you can see the mercury."

He bends down and parts his hair, but all I can see are recent scabs.

"Oh Axel, there's nothing there. I promise you."

"I can feel them crawling in my blood." He shudders. "Anyway, I have to go and check in on my patients."

"Maybe we need to increase your meds?" I voice my concerns. "Axel, listen to me, there's no mercury, okay? You're fine. We'll get married and Carnival will go well. We'll get the water and the oil. We'll restore the satellites and live happily ever after, you, me, Adonis, and Aphrodite. Okay?" I hold his face in my hands. "I'm going to make sure of that. But we really need to be here for each other. Let's up your meds. We need you to be on top of your game and get those aliens under control." I surprise myself with my certainty, but I know what I want. Axel might be a bit off kilter, but I want this life with him. I don't want to go back to my previously lonely existence. For the most selfish of reasons, I want this to work out, and I'm determined to make it so.

He leans into me. "This why I want you to be my wife. You take care of me. You're right, we gotta get through this and out to the other side. But," he rubs me appreciatively, "we'll have a darn good time, too!" He catches me up in a waltz, and we swing around the conference chairs while he sings "Moon River." It's one of the sweetest, happiest moments of my life.

Noelle.

I'M PACING UP AND DOWN, THINKING. Anise had a nap and is expressing milk. She's not looking too happy about it.

"Does it hurt?" I ask.

She shrugs. "It's more annoying than anything."

"I should go and get Sting Ray Barb now," I say to Anise. "Why wait? We can get married some other time. This is stupid."

She's inhaling a cigarette with such glee I'm worried she'll scorch her lungs. I wonder if she should be smoking and expressing, but I don't want to risk her wrath. "Ah, what's a week? Good thinking babes, on getting us out of the life. But can you really deliver Sting Ray Barb? She seems pretty well protected to me."

"If it means freeing you and me, then not only can I—I will."

But I'm secretly terrified. Who am I kidding? I've fucked up everything I've touched. "I'll need my car back and in working order. Can you get a hold of Robbie? Plus, I'll need weapons. Oh god, I wish I could go now. I can't relax. I'm going to go. Fuck the wedding. Sorry babes, but I can't wait."

"The perimeter is armed. You got in by sheer luck before. You can't get out until he lets you out." Anise grabs my arm. "I know you look at Axel and think he's just one crazy guy and where's his army, but he rules with an iron fist. The perimeter guards live in underground wells with heat- and motion-sensing radar."

"And they've all got machine guns? And there are bodies littered all over the desert?"

"You're so flippant." She lights a cigarette off the one she has just finished. "If you don't take this seriously, we'll all end up dead. Please babes, I'm begging you."

I hold up my hands in surrender. "Fine. So what do we do for a week?"

"I, for one, am going to find Franka and get my wedding dress sorted!" She gives me that cocky half smile and climbs out of bed. She's so beautiful, she takes my breath away. "Oh my god, though, everything hurts. My poor, beautiful vag. Maybe I should have had a C-section. And fuck this baby fat. Fuck the wedding dress. I'm having another nap. I can't believe Axel dragged me to a stupid fucking meeting. I am done being told what to do by him." She climbs back into bed.

"I think you look fabulous. You bounced back so quickly it's hard to believe you even had a kid."

"I'm hardly bouncing. And it was two kids," she reminds me. "Your offspring."

"Sharps's," I correct her.

"And yours. They only exist because you and Sharps had sex. Therefore, in my mind, they're yours. Well, mine a little bit, too, since I got all fat and out of shape for them. Aren't you curious about them?"

"They don't feel real to me," I admit. "And you?"

"Me neither." She smiles at me. "Maybe we're not good people, but who gives a shit? However," she drags this last word out, "I know what we've got to do. We've got to steal Axel's fuck-you stash."

I stare at her. "His what?"

"His fuck-you stash. It's his backup, so if things go south he can say fuck you to the whole world and go live somewhere nice. I'm pretty sure it's diamonds. He always told me and Robbie that diamonds are a man's best friend."

"And now you tell me! Sure as shit we need to get our hands on them! Where are they?"

"No one knows." She grows alarmed. "I shouldn't have said anything. We can't really steal them, I was daydreaming. If we steal his stash, he'll hunt us down and kill us."

"Not if he can't find us." I'm thinking fast. "This adds a whole new layer to things. If we can find the stash in the next week, we'll run away. I'll tell him I need you to come with me to get Sting Ray Barb. Then we'll leave with the moolah and fuck Sting Ray Barb, and fuck Axel, and fuck the whole world. It'll be just you and me. If we can't find it in the next week, I'll go and get Sting Ray Barb while you keep looking, and we can leave after that. Forget about the wedding dress, babes, focus on the getaway diamonds."

She gnaws at her nails. "I'm sorry I said anything. This is way too much. Too many balls in the air. Too much can go wrong."

"Babe! I've got this. Trust me! Look at me." I lean onto the bed and pull her close. "I love you. I'd never let anything happen to you. You're the best thing that ever happened to me. I'd never put us in jeopardy. Listen. Forget about the diamonds. I'll find them. I'll deal with everything. You go and make your dream dress happen, okay?"

She relaxes. "Yeah. Okay. Thank you." She kisses me. "Don't do anything stupid, okay?"

"Roger that. I'm starving. I'm going to get me a jackelope sandwich. Can I get you anything?"

"No, I'm going to sleep some more. Maybe I'm depressed, but all I want to do is sleep."

"You're healing," I tell her. "Sleep as much as you like."

I leave her and go to the diner. I sit down at a red booth and put my head in my hands. A mouse of doubt gnaws at my stomach. The mouse grows into a weasel, and man, it's got a bite. How the fuck am I going to make any of this happen? I've promised Anise so much. Get my hands on Sting Ray Barb? How the fuck am I going to do that? Big talk sounded great at the time. It even sounded vaguely plausible when I said it.

I rub my forehead. I have a huge fricking headache pounding

behind my eyes. Okay, maybe I can't actually get Sting Ray Barb, but I can, sure as shit, get into her lab and steal the vaccine and drugs. Even if I can't get all of them, I'll be able to get a sample. And surely Axel will be able to replicate it? That should be enough to placate him?

My panic grows. Oh my god. How could I promise them Sting Ray Barb? I was a fucking idiot shouting my mouth off.

Craving hits me like a tidal wave, and I double over. I need a line of nix. Just one line. It'll help me figure out how to get a hold of Sting Ray Barb and solve all my problems. I straighten up. Who will be holding? I've seen lots of shady characters with dealer written all over them lurking around the Emmarentia rose gardens. The gardens are one of Axel's mother's pet projects, filled with sculpted topiaries, plastic rose bushes, lifelike birds, and trickling fountains with plastic koi fish. Anise likes to make out in the silver gazebo.

I pace up and down, gnawing my fingers. Then I swing around and head for the garden. I'll find someone. I'll make sure Anise doesn't find out. It's not like I'm going back on the butt dust. Nix is different. It's more like a super drug for soldiers. It helped us focus during the war, and this is war. I'll do whatever I have to, including a tiny bit of nix. I take a shuddering breath. Everything will be fine. I just need to get my hands on some nix.

Mariangela.

AXEL'S GOT FUCK-YOU DIAMONDS? I overheard everything Anise and Noelle said. I went after Anise to ask her what she thought of Axel's deteriorating state, and I heard them.

I duck out of sight when I hear Noelle leave Anise's room. My heart's going ninety miles an hour.

I'm going to get my hands on his diamonds. Not Noelle. But where can they be? If anyone's got a hope in hell of finding them, it's me. I'm the closest one to him. But where does he sleep? He serenades me in the hotel's penthouse; I've got no idea where his private rooms are. I've got to find a way to be with him twenty-four seven.

In the meantime, I go check on Adonis and Aphrodite. There, shockingly, is Jinx. He's leaning over one of the incubators and humming.

"Where's Sister Louise?" I ask, and he jumps. Why were the twins unattended? Jinx is dangerous.

"She went to get something," he says vaguely. "So cute. I love the way they smell. Tiny fresh little babies, so innocent, so pure."

I have to get rid of him, but I've got no idea how to do it. I wish I could call Axel or someone. To my huge relief, Robbie shows up.

"Ha ha, Aphrodite and Adonis! Poor kids! Hey Jinx, Axel wants you back in the war room. Jinx!" He snaps his fingers. "War room! Pronto!"

Jinx loses his vague look and focuses. "Right."

I exhale after he leaves. "Thank god you came when you did. There's something very wrong with him."

"You think?" Robbie laughs. "He is so fucked up it's not even funny. Don't tell Alpha Dog, but I messed up big time trying to merge the data. He was supposed to be the perfect warrior, but he's just a weirdo. He shouldn't be allowed in here. I'll get a security detail added pronto. Can't have anything happen to this little guy." He's leaning over an incubator, grinning.

"That's Aphrodite."

"Whatever. So cute. Can't believe Anise doesn't want to see her babies."

"They're technically Sharps and Noelle's babies," I remind him.

"Yeah, but she carried them for seven months. You'd think there'd be something there. I love babies."

It sounds normal when he says it, quite unlike Jinx's sinister utterance. Sister Louise returns with a stack of diapers and I turn on her.

"Louise! How could you leave them with that madman?" I raise my voice. "What were you thinking?"

"He was so nice," she stammers. "I'm sorry. I needed to go to the laundry, and he said he'd watch them. I didn't mean to put the twins in danger." She starts crying. I rush over and hug her.

Robbie sniffs the air. "I think someone could use a diaper change. I'll go and organize security and leave you ladies to diaper duty."

"I'm sorry, Louise," I apologize as Robbie leaves. "A lot went on today. It was really crazy, and I just got a fright, that's all."

"Not at all. I'm sorry. I should have been more careful." She studies me. "You look very fancy!"

I smile sheepishly. I've forgotten about my getup. I've even forgotten about the kitten heels. I pat the wig self-consciously. "It's a bit weird, but kind of fun."

"You, uh, do know that the Master's mother wore her hair like that?" She studies the contents of Aphrodite's diaper as if it is the most fascinating thing.

"The Master?"

"Axel Pattersen. Alpha Plus. The nuns have to call him the Master." She looks afraid. "It's a private name. Don't tell him I told you."

"Wow." Just when I thought things couldn't get any weirder.

Louise changes Aphrodite and cuddles her gently. "There you go, baby Pink. Wait, did the babies get names?"

"Yes. Adonis and Aphrodite."

We burst out laughing. "Addie and Effie," I proclaim. "Much easier to say."

"Addie and Effie," she echoes. "Our little treasures."

"Looks like feeding time to me," I rock Effie in my arms and croon at her. My mind is whirring. So many balls in the air. Too many. I've got to figure this out.

Sharps.

OH. MY. GOD. Shasta's tongue. We kiss for hours. We're clad in red leather and strapped into our makeshift thermal wear with duct tape, but our faces are free. We kiss for hours, like teenagers.

"Didn't you have some weird sexual fetish?" she asks me after a while. Talk about a mood breaker. I pull away.

"That's kind of personal."

"We're lying on the remnants of a ripped-up sofa and huddling together for warmth while we're trapped underground. What else are we going to do but get personal?"

"Please don't say trapped." I flail in my padding like a swaddled turtle. "And are you just kissing me to stay warm? Thanks a lot."

"Not what I meant. Come here." She snuggles up to me. How can her hair smell of lilacs and oranges after everything we've been through?

"Nope." I roll onto my side and struggle to my feet. "I'm leaving you. I'm going to the pub. Sayonara baby."

I waddle over to the bar and dig out a fresh bottle of Southern Comfort. "These nuns sure liked SC." I uncap the bottle and take a large swig. "If you must know, I had my issues. I managed just fine with Noelle when she was pretending to be an avatar called Janaelle. But I had to stick my dick through a hole to get it up with my wife. I kiss better than you thought I would, right?"

"You're a great kisser." She comes over to the bar. "I remember hearing stories about your weird hole-in-the-wall activities. Your wife wasn't exactly discreet, but I never knew what she meant. What's the hole in the wall?"

"My dead wife, may she rest in peace. Although she doesn't deserve peace. She deserves to burn in hell."

"Echo that. Listen Sharps, I'm trying to really talk to you. I'm trying to tell you I'm not into sex either."

I raise an eyebrow. "Not at all? What about that guy you were seeing?"

"Knox? The guy you killed? How quickly we forget."

"Yeah, him. What a loser. I thought you were doing the horizontal tango with him for sure."

"Nope."

"Did you kiss him?"

"I did."

"And?"

"You're way better."

Well. I feel cheered. "Glad we cleared that up." I shiver despite being trussed up like a dumpster hermit. "I don't know why, but I'm not feeling horribly claustrophobic right now."

She laughs. "Because I've been steadily feeding you meds."

"For real? How?"

"Your bottled water. I know you too well, Sharps. And despite everything, I take care of you. Take it easy with the SC, okay?"

"You know what, you do take care of me. And because you do, I'll tell you about the hole in the wall, as embarrassing as it is." I sigh. "I struggled to have sex with my wife. But not just with her, with every woman until Janaelle, who we now know was just an avatar. I couldn't get it up even if there was a gun to my head. Forgive me, but it's true."

I really wished I didn't have to talk about this, but I forge on. "But I found this, um, massage parlour, I guess you'd call it. Dim lighting, very anonymous, nice music. I'd stick my dick through a hole in the wall, and then the madam would jerk me off. Not exactly erotic, but it was all I was up to. Pardon the pun."

"But you managed with Janaelle, even though you didn't see her true body."

"I did. Anyway, there you go. Please can we change the subject? How do you plan on us getting out of here?"

"We'll either be rescued, or Jinx will come back and extract us. I'm pretty confident one of those two scenarios will happen. Most likely the latter because Jinx needs us."

She's scrambled up onto a bar stool and has her hands under her armpits. She's shivering, too.

I go over to her. "Hey Shazz. We need to roll ourselves up in the rug and huddle. No sex. The boundaries have been set. Although it would have been interesting to try, wearing these Halloween mattresses."

She giggles. "I'm game. We can tell ghost stories."

We lie down on the ripped-up sofa. I wrap the rug tightly around us and layer the blankets Jinx gave us on top. "No ghost stories," I say. "Fairy tales. Once upon a time there was a beautiful princess, and she took good care of an inept knight she found wandering around in the desert. She took him back to her underground castle and wrapped him in fine linens and lay him down to rest. Then she shared her warm body and her sweet love, and they lived happily ever after."

She smiles. "You're such a nutcase. A knight? I think you're overestimating your standing in life, but it never hurts to dream."

I arrange a piece of ripped foam under our heads. "We'll get out of this Shazz, and you'll see. I'll take care of you."

"Sure you will Sharps." She sounds sleepy. "Sure you will."

"I will," I say, but it's more to me than her. "I will, Shazz, you'll see."

She's breathing softly, fast asleep. I wish I could drift off, but I know that if I close my eyes the only thing that awaits me is a sea of nightmares, a corridor of uncertainty. To sleep perchance to scream. There's no way to escape my thoughts, fears, and memories. My past pushes at me like a tidal wave while my future smothers me like a howling gale. I'm a killer. I was going back to kill my children for a second time, despite all the chances I was given. I'm a disgusting piece of shit, and, even swaddled in foam and meds, I know who I am.

But hey, at least I'm with Shasta.

Mariangela.

"Stop sucking in your belly," Franka says. "You'll have to be able to breathe on your wedding day." She loosens the corset and I exhale with relief.

"You're actually going to do this?" Noelle is in stitches. She's watching me, along with Anise, who's blowing smoke rings.

"Of course I am. I told Axel I would and therefore, I will."

"But why? You can't be in love with the guy. You met him like three seconds ago."

"Around the same time you met Anise," I remind her, and she shakes her head.

"Negatory scotty. I met Anise when I was looking for a baby mama. She and I go way back. We've been through a bunch of real shit together. We know each other inside and out."

"You met her three times. The first was when she hustled you at the dive bar, the second was once again at the dive bar, when you delivered stolen sperm and paid her, and the third time was when you followed me here and found her. Then you instantly fell in love, went into rehab for a month, and have been out in the real world for two weeks. That, in my opinion, does not constitute a deep or lengthy relationship."

"Harsh, so harsh," Noelle comments. "I thought you were in my corner, Mama bear."

"I am in your corner." I don't comment on the old familiar nickname she had for me. Noelle worries me. She's deluded if she thinks she can deliver Sting Ray Barb's science to Axel, and she shouldn't make promises she can't keep.

"I wanted to jump her bones the moment I met her." Anise cuddles into Noelle, rubbing her hand on Noelle's thigh.

"Not in here," Franka complains. "Get a room. You're like dogs in heat, both of you."

"I'm hot for my baby," Anise murmurs, and she licks Noelle's neck and nibbles her ear. The Noelle I'd known would have kicked this woman three ways to Sunday, so maybe they are in love.

Franka swats Anise with a feather boa. "Get off her!"

Anise grins, but she doesn't stop caressing Noelle's leg. "So," she says to me, "you're really going to marry Daddy Gilly." Her eyes widen, and her hand shoots to her mouth. We turn and stare at her.

"Gilly?" I ask. "Who's Gilly?"

"No one. I shouldn't have said anything. My mistake."

"Too late now," Noelle says. "The Gilly is out of the bag. Spit it out."

"Gilbert Alphonse Pattersen. Known to Robbie and me as Daddy Gilly when we were kids. Wee Willy Gilly is what his mother used to call him. A name he didn't particularly like, so he dropped it as soon as she died and changed it to Axel. He said Axel is a powerful name, a name that gets shit done. By the way, if you ask him, Mumsy's still alive, living with Niam and trying to destroy his quest for world domination. But listen," she pauses, "you cannot, cannot, cannot tell him I told you about the Gilly thing. He will flay me or send me to the convent for a retreat, which is what he does when you really fuck up or annoy him. I'll have to say a thousand Hail Marys while crawling along the gravel Path of Sorrow until my hands and knees are bleeding. And then I'll crawl for another thousand Hail Marys."

"I would never betray you." Noelle is sure of herself.

"Baby, don't say that. If you go against him, he'll throw you into a solitary hole in the ground with nothing but earthworms and your worst nightmares for company. I've heard the stories. He drugs people in the hole, so they see demons and claw their way out of their bodies."

"She's not making it up," Franka chimes in, her mouth full of pins. "Mariangela, I take it you don't want the front of your dress cut so high the whole world can see your naked pudenda?"

"Of course not! Why would you even think that?"

"That dress was Fiona's," Anise says.

"What?" I start to yank it off, not caring if I tear it.

"Hey, stop that!" Franka grabs my hands. "A thousand crystals have been hand-sewn into the fabric, it's worth a fortune."

"I don't care! This is disgusting!"

"What's disgusting?" Axel arrives. "Mary! You look beautiful!" He kisses me on the cheek, and I recoil.

"What's the matter?" he asks, his expression hurt and confused.

"This dress was Fiona's!" I shout. "I don't want to wear a second-hand dress that belonged to another woman."

"Darlin'," Axel draws me close, "it's MY dress. It was never Fiona's. She thought she was going to marry me, and I let her believe it. I had this dress made for the love of my life, my bride, the woman I had not yet met at the time. And that time is now, but you can redesign it however you like."

"She was really going to flash her vajayjay to the whole world?" Noelle asks, and Axel nods.

"It's a beauty. One of her finest features, and yes, my work of course. She had perfectly shaped labia when I met her, so it was just a tweak here and there. Darling," he says to me, "yours is very beautiful too, and you can flash it if you like. And might I say that you have magnificent breasts. I couldn't have done better myself."

"I hate the dress." I'm close to tears. "I've been so stupid!"

"Ladies, we need a moment." Axel waves the others out of the room.

"Listen," he says after they leave, "the world's a mess. But I'm going to fix it, and you're going to be right there at my side. You're my queen, and together we'll rule. The dress was never Fiona's, and I'm sorry your feelings were hurt. You don't have to wear it. You can wear anything you like, although it does have to be a wedding dress. You can discuss the specifics with Franka. In fact, hold the phone, I've got an idea." A gleam comes into his eyes, and he yells for Anise. "Anise, get your fanny back in here, I know you're outside the door."

Anise sidles in with a look of fear. Is she worried I told him I knew about Gilly? I shake my head at her, and she looks relieved. Noelle comes in, and she looks at Axel questioningly.

"Anise is going to wear the dress!" Axel declares. "Oh, my freaking lord! The punters will love it! Hey, metal legs, you're in the act, too! You'll be the groom, tuxedo top, bare legs. And yeah, your lady bits will be on full view, too."

"They most certainly will not," Noelle snaps. "Not a hope in hell am I showing my face or vagina on livestream porn." She glares at him.

"Fine, okay. Your legs are your best feature anyway. No one will want to see your face or your ordinary vag. You can wear a lovely, feathered opera mask. I'm thinking black with feathers and sequins."

"Daddy A," Anise says, and she sounds desperate, "I can't flash my lady bits. I gave birth two weeks ago."

"Yeah, but your vag is great! No one will be able to tell!"

"I'm still fucking bleeding! Do you want me to show you?"

Axel pales. "No thank you, I'm good. Hmmm. Look kiddies, I've already put out all the promo work for the wedding. Fortunately, I didn't say whose wedding, I just said wedding. And good thing I did because all you ladies are wearing your little girl panties and none of you are HELPING ME." He yells his last words. "Quiet, all of you, I need to think."

Anise and Noelle send me a desperate look, but I shake my head. I am not wearing Fiona's dress.

Axel scratches his head violently and buries his face in his arms. Then he raises his head. "Franka!"

Franka shoots back into the room. "Yes, boss?"

"Anise is in the dress. Make sure the front rides high enough because she's not as tall as Fiona. Get metal legs here a nice tuxedo top, cropped to show off her legs. She wants panties, so yes to boy shorts, also in black. Very nice against her steel. I'm thinking a phoenix-feathered headdress. Venetian-style with sequins and feathers for her face. You know the drill."

"But," Anise starts.

"We won't show your vag!" Axel yells. "You'll wear panties, okay? I'll have the director swing to footage of your flower unfolding, and god knows we've got tons of that. I'll make it work somehow, no help from you lot."

"I was going to say there's nothing wrong with Noelle's face!" Anise is the colour of a pomegranate. "She will not wear a mask! How dare you insult my fiancée like that?"

Axel looks confused. "I'm not insulting anybody! She didn't want to do it. I was being helpful. Besides, the punters need to pretend it's them marrying her, get it? If they see the real groom's face, they'll lose the fantasy!" He slaps his forehead. "I can't believe I didn't think of this before! It'll be a great preamble to Carnival, and we'll make scads of money ahead of time. Listen." He turns to me. "Trust me darlin', we'll have our day. I still want to marry you, but this needs to be our main focus."

I nod in agreement. The crazy thing is that he seems sexier than ever. What's wrong with me? He so handsome standing there, grinning that wild grin, his hair tousled, and his eyes so blue. I remind myself that he kidnapped me and truly believes there are aliens in his blood. But his smile! And he hasn't actually hurt anyone, has he? In fact, he helped us. Well, kind of. Best I don't go there. I shake my head. I've got to sort myself out. The craziest thing of all is that I'm having fun. It's great to be swept away by him and listen to his extravagant schemes.

"This is great. We'll imply—but not say directly—that the punters, too, will be able to have their way with Anise on the altar of love at Carnival. Blah blah blah. It will be fabulous. Thank god for me! We'll bill it so the climax will be a live in-person event at Carnival. Prolific sexual feasts will be on offer! Don't you love that word, prolific? Carnal prolificity? Is that a word, prolificity?"

"I don't think so," Franka says. I think she's the only one who can speak. The rest of us are trying to process the recent turn of events.

"Yeah, me neither, but it is now. You lot know what you've got to do. I've got to go and prep for an important forthcoming meeting with the world leaders. Bye bye, birdies."

"Should I come with you?" I ask. "I want to be of as much use as I can." The truth is that I want to find out as much as I can about what's going on. He shakes his head, then reconsiders.

"Yeah, why not? It's just going to be a boring meeting with the heads of state about the Mainframe, but I need to get my ducks in a row. God, I get tired of talking about the Mainframe. I thought it would be easy to control, but there are a lot of sticky fingers in this pie. Yeah, come on darlin', good idea, you can help me figure out the ins and outs of what we need to negotiate. You lot, get yourselves ready. I'm moving up the wedding. You've got three days."

"Three days," Franka echoes. "That's not enough time!"

"God, you're exhausting, all of you! Fiona's been planning this for a century. All you've got to do is push play. Ask Fiona if you've got any questions. Kind of weird how quickly she gave it all up." He looks puzzled. "Almost relieved. Anyway, whatever, but ask her. And you, sweetheart," he gallantly gives me his arm, "have a meeting to attend."

I take his arm and head off to meet the world leaders. At the very least, my life isn't boring.

Sharps.

We're freezing to death. The damp cold has wormed its way into the marrow of our bones, and the very marrow is shivering. We're too cold to move.

"I'm so sorry you ended up here," I whisper to Shasta. "I'd do anything for you. I'd die for you."

She manages a small laugh, and a cloud of icy vapour fills the air. "So dramatic." Her icy nose is touching mine. "He's got to come back soon? We're no good to him dead."

"Maybe he doesn't know how cold it is down here."

She starts humming quietly, and it's the saddest sound.

"I love you," I say. "This is not the declaration of a dying man. I know you think I don't know you, but I do. I've loved you since we first met. You know it's true. I don't care what you think of me, I just love you."

"Oh Sharps." She starts to cry. "Now look what you've done. I'll need to blow my nose; I've got nothing to blow it on, and my hands are too cold to leave my sides. I'm going to die covered in a mask of frozen snot, and it will all be your fault."

"Yeah, being with me is deadly," I joke, but my mood is as cold as the rest of my body. "It's true, Shazz. I'm no good to anybody. But I'll tell you this, we need to move. If we lie here, we're going to die. We've got to get up and do jumping jacks or something. You hear me? We are going to move."

"You go first then. If you can."

"Watch me go." I've got to do this. I've got to get us both moving. "The first step is to crawl out of the rug." I wriggle around, but we're stuck. "Shazz, you've got to move too. We wound it around us too tightly, and it's frozen too."

"I can't move."

"Shazz! For fuck's sake!" I start thrashing around. Claustrophobia kicks in, and I go at it like a madman.

"Ow! Sharps! Ow, my god, you're kicking me. Stop it!"

"Help me! Help me! Argh fuck, losing it, arghhhh!" I manage to free myself. I leap to my feet and promptly fall over. "Whoa. That hurt. My feet are frozen." I get up and stagger over to Shasta. "You ARE getting up, Missy!"

"Missy? That's just insulting!"

I grab her and haul her to her feet. "March! Hop on the spot! Spar with me! Do something!"

I start bouncing on my frozen feet and throwing jabs in the air. "Uppercut, hit to the sternum, yeah, baby. I could've been a contender! I could've been somebody instead of a bum. Which is what I am, let's face it!"

"You're no Marlon Brando, but you've got class." Shasta is swaying from side to side. At least she's on her feet.

"Arms away from the body," I instruct her. "Swing the arms. And we will sing."

"Sing? What will we sing? Why are we singing?"

"To warm us up. We will move every body part we can. We just have to think of a song." My teeth are chattering, and my breath is a cloud of steam. "Look Shazz, we're cloud machines. Cool, right? Okay, 'Happy Birthday' it is."

I launch into "Happy Birthday," and on my third go Shasta surprises me by joining in.

"Okay enough of that one," she says after a while. "How about 'If You're Happy and You Know It Clap Your Hands.'"

"Good one. Let's clap too."

We march around the room, singing and clapping and stamping our feet.

"It's working," Shasta says when we run out of being happy and stop clapping our hands. "But I'm getting so tired."

"There is that. Slow it down, Shazz, but keep moving. We cannot lie down again. We'll die if we do."

"But I'm so tired. And I'm so cold." She starts to cry again, and it rips my heart in two.

"Shazz, you're breaking my heart. I've come up with a plan. You can kill me, open up my body, and climb inside. It may be gross, but you'll be warm for a while."

She stops crying. "Sharps, that's the most disgusting thing I've ever heard! What kind of brain do you have?"

"My brain is fine, thank you very much. The warm body thing is an old hunting trick. If a hunter killed a deer or a bear but got stuck in the snow, he'd cut the animal open and climb inside. I'd cut myself open for you, but it would be pretty hard to do. I can kill myself though. I'll down the rest of the meds with Sambuca—which I hate, but there's no Southern Comfort left—then when I'm dead you can cut me open with the blunt scissors and climb inside me. But you've got to promise me you'll do it because I don't want to die for nothing."

"I'm not cutting you open! Stay away from the meds! But thank you for the very kind and generous offer."

"I'm running out of ideas," I say. I'm slowing down too. I'm walking very slowly around Shasta, who's standing still with her eyes closed. "Maybe some poetry? "'He cometh not,' she said; She said, 'I am aweary, aweary, I would that I were dead!'"

Her eyes fly open. "You know Tennyson?"

"'Course I do." I'm blithe. "Mother and I have that in common at least. Back in the day, when Jazza and I were buddies, he got me all the classics. *Mariana* is one of my personal favs."

"Mine too." She's dreamy. "And so apt. 'He cometh not. I am aweary. Oh god that I were dead.'"

"Wrong poem for me to rustle up," I say hastily. "Let me think of a cheerful one. 'I have eaten all the plums…' 'April is the cruelest month…,' um, 'what are the roots that clutch…,' 'we are the hollow men…,' 'indeed there will be time…,' 'I have measured out my life with coffee spoons…,' 'Daddy, I have had to kill you.' No wait, that was me. I was Daddy, and I was the killer. I should rip open my chest and let you crawl inside the warmth of my cracked rib cage. It's the least I can do. I'm going to do it."

I tug at my duct tape, but she opens her eyes and lunges at me. "Don't you dare, you poetry-quoting, crazy fool. You're all I've got, and I'm not going near your gory insides. I wish we could make a fire."

"We'd die of asphyxiation. Besides, there are no matches."

We fall into a moody silence.

"You're not a bad guy," Shasta finally speaks. "And you make me melt when you kiss me. Let's kiss each other until we die."

"Great plan!" I waddle up close to her. "Come here, baby, let's get it on!"

She laughs. "You'll ignore my crusty face?" She tries to wipe her face with her sleeve, but she can't reach.

"I love your crusty face." I lean in, and my lips touch hers. We're both going to die of cold, but at least I'll be going out with a bang, not a whimper.

Noelle.

"FUCKING GILLY IS A FUCKING MADMAN!" I'm pacing the room. The wedding is in two days, and I'm freaking out.

Anise is horrified. "Do NOT say that name! Are you insane? You'll be taken away!"

"Yeah, by who? Where's his army? I've only seen Robbie, crazy-ass Jinx, and Axel himself, aka Mad Daddy Gilly."

"Noelle. Shut the fuck up about the Gilly thing. I said it by mistake, and I thought I could trust you." She stands up. "Fuck you too, if you won't take me seriously. I'm not going to live in fear because you're as immature as fuck. Grow up or get the fuck out. I mean it." She storms out and leaves me alone, my mouth agape.

What's her problem? I was just asking a question.

"Suit yourself," I shout after her, but my heart whimpers and lies down like a kicked dog. But where *is* Axel's army? I just can't see the manpower.

I go into the kitchen to make a sandwich. When in doubt, make a sandwich. I fashion a jackelope and onion on flatbread and stare out the window. I don't feel like eating.

I'm proud of myself for curbing my cravings after the somewhat disastrous meeting with Axel and Co. when I promised them Sting Ray Barb and the world. I did go to the Emmarentia rose gardens, but when I saw the addicts and their sick faces, I knew I didn't want to do that again. I didn't want to be like that again, didn't want to be beholden to a chemical I both loved and hated at the same time.

I made myself watch the addicts, and I ran through the memories of my shame. I self-talked my way out of scoring. I called up Anise's face in my mind and thought about how precious her love was, and I managed to walk away.

But it occurs to me now that I'm going to screw up things with Anise, drugs or not. I just keep fucking up, one stupid comment after another.

"That looks good." Robbie arrives. "I love onion."

"You can have it." I push it towards him and fold my arms.

"Got the blues?" he jokes, his mouth full. "Anise can be a moody bitch, and I say that with all the love in the world."

"I made a bad joke about uncle, I mean Axel, and she got mad." I nearly said the word Gilly, but I caught myself just in time. Thank god for that.

"There're some things you don't joke about." He chews and looks at me, and I squirm. It's the first time we've been alone, just him and me, since he dragged my ass through rehab. He makes me nervous. He's wearing a red headband and a sleeveless vest. He's got arms the size of bulldozers.

"I don't know about you," he says, his head cocked to one side. "Don't get me wrong. You make a great sandwich. But I can't decide if you're a spy sent by OctoOne or if you're just a fucked-up chick who bends whichever way the wind blows."

"You don't pull your punches, do you?" My heart is in my mouth. "Of course I'm not a fucking spy! You guys kidnapped Mother. I thought I could rescue her, so I followed the bus. Then things got weird-crazy in a good way with Anise. I'm sure you know I'm the last person OctoOne or Ava would trust. What I can't figure out is why you guys think you've got the upper hand? That's what pissed Anise off. There's Axel with aliens on the brain and Jinx who's out to lunch. You've got a convent jammed with penguins, a bunch of sex workers in the basement, and a dozen patients who've had facelifts. Oh wait, you've got Fiona the Barbie doll. And that kinda rounds it off, doesn't it?"

He leans back on the counter, folds his massive arms, and lets me continue my stream of consciousness. "You've got a freaky resort in the middle of nowhere and a limited supply of water. You think you've got the upper hand because you've got Sharps and Shasta? But wait, there's more, you lost them. Sayonara to that ace up your sleeve."

"You've got balls, lady, I'll give you that." He smiles in a way that makes my blood run cold. "How about you and me take a little ride?"

"Uh, no, I'm good. I feel a nap coming on. That time of day, etcetera, etcetera."

He walks over to me and grabs me by the elbow. "Let me put it another way. You're coming with me. You need a reality check."

"Going to throw me into a cold hole? Hose me down with boiling water? Sandbag me?"

"I think you mean waterboard you. Not my style. What you need is information, and I shall be the purveyor of said information. Come on. Anise is having a nap, and everybody else is wrapped up in that ridiculous wedding."

He takes me by the arm and leads me behind a warehouse.

"You and Anise having sex. Wasn't that weird?" I ask.

"It was my job. I did what the boss told me." A shadow falls over his face. "I'm, uh, failing to spring to attention these days, and my nether regions are shrinking. But," he flexes his biceps, "I'm willing to do what needs to be done in the name of beauty. Am I right, or am I right?"

"Axel's okay with you not being a rent boy anymore?"

"I was an actor not a rent boy. It was a role, and I played my part."

I don't like the way we're alone, just him and me.

"Anise will never forgive you if you kill me," I say helpfully. "I'm more use to you alive."

He laughs. "I'm many things, but a killer isn't one of them. I can hack my way into anything and fuck the face off anything, but

I'm not a killer. Correction: I used to be able to fuck the face off anything."

"I applaud your high moral standards. Wait, what's that?"

"A helicopter. You like it?"

"It's beautiful! It looks like a mercury bubble with dragonfly wings." I run over to it.

"My design." Robbie's proud. "Thank you. She's my baby. In you go." He opens the door, and I climb in.

Robbie eases into the pilot's seat. "Easy to fly too." He hands me a pair of earphones and flicks a few switches. "Solar powered." He kicks the engines into gear, and a throbbing pulse sounds through my earphones. I check out the back. It's pretty tiny, with one bench seat.

"Up, up, and away!" Robbie yells. We take off. I'm so overcome with joy and exhilaration that I nearly forget how angry Anise is with me. Nearly. My good mood fades, and I wish she was with me. Rising above the world does my spirits a world of good though, and I watch the red earth fall away below us as we take our place among the clouds.

"Man, your compound is far away from civilization," I yell. Robbie adjusts a switch, and the throbbing thrum of the rotors fades.

"You still think your set-up was civilization?" he asks. "We don't have vines. We've got better electricity than you guys. And no butterflies. Our city is a marvel. Look down and be amazed."

I already had, and truth be told I'm inwardly dismayed. It's a huge set-up. How would we ever overcome them? There's the resort. There's the school. What are all those other buildings? The urban planning is extensive, and I'm taken aback.

"Impressive," I admit. "Very orderly."

"You ain't seen nothing yet."

We fly in silence, and I relax and enjoy the ride. The sunshine, the clouds, the purity of the moment. God-rays fill the little silver bubble, and despite all my worries and anxieties, I feel more at peace than I have in years. Who needs drugs? I just need my own helicopter.

"I want one of these," I yell at Robbie before I remember I don't have to shout.

He grins at me. "Get in line, lady. But it's a great feeling, best in the world. I'll tell you a secret. You know Axel's alien fixation? From what I heard, Axel was a bad boy, so Mumsy sent him out into the wilds for a night. He was what, maybe nine? So there he is, poor little tot, in the dark and all by his lonesome. Then, out of nowhere, in flies one of Mumsy's primo clients in a helicopter. Tiny Axel shits himself and loses consciousness, and when he wakes up he thinks he was abducted by aliens."

"Why are you telling me this? I thought you didn't trust me?"

"I don't. I want you to know that the man is traumatized, not insane. Mumsy was a piece of work, make no mistake. Which is why Anise and I are so loyal to him. There's something about Axel that commands not only loyalty but love. Ask your Mariangela. She folded like a cheap tent when he made a pass at her."

"I don't see it." But I'm lying. A part of me wants Axel to acknowledge me and like me too. But all he sees are my steel legs. And he tells me to wear a mask at my own wedding. My face grows red with anger at the memory. "He's got no time for me," I mutter, picking at a thread on my trousers.

"He knows you don't like him. He knows you don't buy what he's selling. I buy it. Anise buys it. Just about everybody buys it. Except for you. Therefore, he doesn't like you."

"I want him to like me." I'm trying to placate Robbie, but I sound pathetic.

"Don't lie, you don't give a shit. At a fundamental level, you don't respect him, and he knows that."

I've got no reply to that.

"Look down," Robbie says, and I force my gaze from the meringue clouds down to earth.

"What the heck?" Large matte-black steel discs dot the earth like mould on an orange.

"Tens of thousands of them, right?"

"Yeah. My god, what are they?"

"Corpuscles. Each one is home to a thousand AI army officers. Those are their storage facilities. You've seen a mosquito, right?"

"Is that a trick question?"

"No. It's a visual image I want you to keep in mind. Imagine a warrior that can fold down to two feet by two feet but expand to be seven feet by two feet. Multiply thousands of them by thousands, and what do you get? Ten million. Ten million AI warriors, all ready to fight for Axel."

"With what weapons?" I'm trying to wrap my head around the idea. "Guns?"

He shakes his head. "They're indestructible and as sharp as knives from a butcher's finest block. They can cut their way through anyone or anything that stands in their way."

"I don't believe it. Who created them?"

He sighs. "Noelle, you're so tiring. I'll show you. Down we go." He lowers the chopper, and the black discs get larger, each of them a matte reservoir, menacing and impenetrable.

We land, and I follow Robbie across the sandy earth. The corpuscle is pretty huge up close. Robbie taps his wrist, and I notice he's wearing a thin black bracelet. A curved black garage door opens, and he bows. "After you."

"Haha. No way."

He smiles. "Okay then."

He walks in and raises his wrist. Hmmm. I need to get one of those bracelets.

Lights flood the arena-sized warehouse. The interior is filled with stacks of black boxes, each the size of a small brick. Robbie has another little chat with his wrist, and one of the boxes at the top of a stack turns a pale luminous green and makes a whirring sound.

One long thin wand extends from the box, followed by another. Out come a few more wands. Then a few more. It's like watching a sea urchin unfold.

The box climbs down off the other boxes and stretches. There's no other way to describe it. The thing gets down and morphs into a creature. A very tall, very spindly, very menacing looking creature.

"Edward Scissorhands minus the Edward," I note. Robbie grins.

"Something like that. But, you Missy, need a demonstration of power. Outside."

We go out, and the spindle monster follows us. I don't really like it being behind me, but I've got no choice.

Robbie goes over to the chopper and hauls a metal crate out from under the back seat. Crafty. I thought the thing had no storage space whatsoever. My head's spinning with ideas. I need to get my hands on Robbie's bracelet and his chopper. Then I need to rescue Anise and fly her away. Destination unknown, but we'll figure it out. I can't believe Robbie's showing me all this shit. Axel must have his loot in a corpuscle. I just have to find out which one. We'll steal the loot, fill our coffers, shove it under the backseat, and fly off into the sunset, hand in hand.

Robbie opens the chest and a dozen jackelopes scatter in various directions. What on earth? Robbie whispers into his wrist, and Edward Scissorlegs leaps into action. I've never seen that many blades work so fast or do so much damage. I'm not an animal lover, but even I feel sorry for the little jacks being turned into mincemeat in a nanosecond.

"Their blood is on your hands," Robbie says when it's over. "Did you see how fast the cutter moved? Did you see that he got every last jack, even though they were running for their lives?"

I did see that. Scissorlegs, definitely less cute minus the Edward aspects, was a blur of chopping and slicing and flying blood clots.

"We've got ten million of those cutting machines." Robbie comes up close to me. "I could get him to mince you up, Missy. How'd you like that?"

Any truculence I had fled. I stand stock still, barely breathing. "I wouldn't like that," I whisper. What an idiot I've been. Here I am, out in the middle of nowhere, completely without recourse or rescue.

"Here's how I see it," Robbie says conversationally. "I love Anise. She's my cousin, but she's more like my sister. We grew up together, and you would not believe the shit we've been through together. She seems to really love you, fuck knows why. So, here's what I'd suggest. You shut the fuck up and behave yourself. No more jokes about Daddy Gilly, and yes, I know about that. No stupid fucking daydreams about taking my chopper and flying away. You're as easy to read as a romance novel, and trust me, I'd rather be reading a romance novel." A dreamy look comes into his eyes. "In fact, I love nothing better than to sit down with a good Harlequin romance novel. I've got dozens of them, and they read just as well on repeat. But," he refocuses on me, and my sphincter clenches, "back to you. There's nowhere for you to go. There's nothing you can do. And," he waves his wrist at me, "if you think stealing this will get you anywhere, think again, Missy. They're password protected, and you'll never get in." He speaks into his wrist and the cutter sprints to one side of the black disc where a nozzle has sprouted from the wall. The cutter stands still while a shower cleans it off. And then the thing conducts a wild sun dance, knives flying in all directions.

"I love watching them dry off," Robbie says. I'm too stunned to say anything. I'm too terrified to say anything.

"I really do love Anise," I manage to whisper, and he nods.

"She's your get out of jail free card. For now, anyway. Let's put this adorable little pet back into its box and head home."

The spindly cutter minces its way back into the black warehouse. It folds down to a few legs and hops up back into its spot on top of the other thousands of lethal slumbering cutters. It pulls in its remaining wands and goes back to sleep. I swear I almost hear the thing give a little sigh as it shuts down.

I run out into the sunshine. I fall to the ground and heave. I've got nothing but spittle to give, but my stomach expels my fear and my despair.

"Enough theatrics," Robbie says kindly. "Up you get. I know what will cheer you up. You can pilot us home. I know you're dying to fly the thing."

"No, I'm good." I'm shaking. "I just want to go home to Anise."

"Too bad. I want you trained in case I need you. And I'm right, you'll do whatever I say, from now on?"

I nod. "Yes."

"Excellent! Let's be off then."

My entire body is shaking like a torn piece of cloth in a gale force wind. I can hardly buckle myself in. I'd been so arrogant. I want to cry, but I won't let Robbie see how he got to me.

"I have one question." I can't help myself. The helicopter is flying steadily, and I can't contain my curiosity.

"Fire away."

"How did you make so many of those creatures? What are they made of? How long have you had them? Who invented them?"

"That's four questions. Axel's father invented them. He wasn't just a surgeon; he was a great mechanical engineer. They're made of black titanium and the robotics are fairly simple. The corpuscles and their contents have been here for decades, but it isn't like we've had scads of visitors nosing around."

"Why didn't you just march on us and conquer us with them?"

"We're civilized people!" Robbie is offended. "The cutters are destroyers. We're not into genocide, just victory. Big difference. I wanted to show you what we've got at our disposal, should we need them. Axel's not a huge fan of the cutters, so they are a last resort."

I fly us home. It isn't hard at all, and Robbie grins at me.

"I knew you'd be a natural!" He gives me a thumbs up.

We get home, and I lower the chopper to the ground.

"Feel free to share any and all of this intel with Mariangela or whomever you choose," Robbie says. "The other side needs to know what they're up against. Grungy hippies, you lot. Quite entertaining though. Sometimes when I can't sleep, I imagine a cutter going at OctoOne. Grilled calamari, here we come!

Hilarious. She thought that turning herself into an octopus would give her the upper tentacle. She's more vulnerable than anyone. You must have wondered why we don't have vines here? Because of the cutters! But now, I must be off, must go to a meeting. By the way, I'm really looking forward to the wedding. Chin-chin!" He salutes and walks away.

It's all too much for me. I sink to the ground and let myself cry.

Then I wipe my eyes and get up. I have to find Anise. And then I have to find Mother. At the very least, she needs to know what's going on.

Mariangela.

Axel, in the meeting with the other world leaders, is magnificent. Gone is his madness, his affectations, his alien fixations. He's focused, decisive and sexy as hell.

We're hooked up online, something else I didn't think was possible anymore. We'd been so shamefully behind.

"Aren't you concerned about OctoPuss?" one of the world leaders asks with a thick accent I can't identify.

Axel laughs and shakes his head. "She's fully under control. Besides, as you know, I've got my backup, and they can make chop suey of her before you can say Bob's your uncle."

The others at the virtual meeting fall about howling. What's so funny?

"Chop chop," chortles another fellow. All men, I noted. No women among the world leaders. I wonder if they can see me on the screen. I doubt it. The camera's up close and personal on Axel, and he works it to the max.

"Carnival will be ready to go as planned, yes?" A tiny little man with frog-eyed glasses leans forward, licking his lips.

"Oh yeah! Gonna be the best ever! Be sure to tune in to the wedding preamble. It'll be live streaming the day after tomorrow, just to give you a taste of how fabulous Carnival will be. And don't forget, Anise is back!"

"Anise!" the men chorus with glee and fill the screens with googly eyes and shiny lips. I look away in disgust.

"Yeah, back from her sabbatical where she learned fabulous new tricks to titillate and tease."

"I would have paid big bucks to marry Anise," one man says.

"My kingdom for Anise!"

Again, the others join in.

"And tomorrow, you can all pretend you're the lucky groom! Gentlemen, that's it for the day. I hope you'll enjoy the wedding tomorrow. I look forward to seeing you in person when we'll party like there's no tomorrow and take over the world once and for all!"

A large cheer fills the audio. Axel punches the air with his fist, smacks his forehead and then his chest, and the men follow suit. "Over and out!" Axel shouts, and the screen goes dead.

"That went well," he grins at me. "You enjoy it?"

"Very impressive." I hide my distaste for the misogyny. "How did you guys all meet?"

"We've known each other for years. Came up through the ranks together, got strong ties that go way back. Best boys club ever!"

Makes sense.

"Darlin', I've got to check on my patients. A lot of those fellows have entrusted me with their wives, and the big reveal will be at Carnival. Fiona's doing a great job taking care of them, but I need to see if any touch-ups are in order. You good?"

"I'm fine. I'm going to check on Addie and Effie."

"Addie and Effie? Who are they?"

"The twins, Axel," I remind him.

"Ah yeah!" He grins and smacks his forehead again. "The tiny tots! I'll see you later, sweetheart." He leaves me all alone in the crystal boardroom. I look around. Could the treasure be here? Dollars to doughnuts, Axel has cameras everywhere. I can't risk looking. But surely I can casually pick up a few ornaments and shake them to see if a few dozen diamonds fall out? I stand up. No harm in just taking a quick look.

"Noelle needs you in the kitchen," Robbie says. I give a little squeal, and I jump.

"You scared me." I give a nervous laugh.

"You must be feeling guilty then," he says. "Go on, I need to lock up here."

I don't need to be told twice. I scuttle off as quickly as my kitten heels will take me and rush into the kitchen, where Noelle's waiting for me.

She looks pale, as if she's been crying. Noelle crying? Impossible. "Nellie, what happened?"

"Oh Mother, everything!" She rushes over and hugs me to her. Which is even more weird.

"Honey, sit down. Tell me everything."

She does, and it's my turn to go pale. "Oh. My. God," I say. "What are we going to do?"

"We can't do anything. We'll die. We'll be sliced and diced and shredded." She shudders. "I will never forget that thing. And he's got ten million of them."

"They must be controlled from a single source," I reason, and she slams her hand against my mouth.

"Do NOT even think that way. Roll over and acquiesce. If you don't, we'll all die, do you understand?"

I nod. "Sorry Nellie. You're quite right. This is our new home, and we'll adjust accordingly. Do you want to come and see the twins? They'll cheer you up. They're your kids after all, and they're just adorable."

She shudders. "Nope, negatory. I've got to go and find Anise."

"Oh, come on." I pull her to her feet. "Don't argue with me."

I haul her along with me, and she must be in a weakened state because she doesn't protest or try to pull away. We reach the nursery and Sister Louise opens the door. "Just about to give them a feed," she says.

I pick up Addie and hand him to Noelle. "Don't argue with me. Hold him."

She takes him from me as if he's a stinking turd and dangles him. "Cradle him, Noelle, come on, get with the program. And cup his head. He can't hold it up by himself yet."

She cups the baby's little head and holds him to her chest. "I'm not a baby person." But her expression softens slightly. "It smells quite sweet. And it's warm. Like a puppy."

"That one is Adonis. Known as Addie." I pass her a bottle, and she handles it like a pro.

"This feels kind of nice," she says dreamily and sinks down into a chair. "Who knew? Hey, little guy, I'm sort of your mommy. Only sort of though, so don't get too attached to me."

I see Louise at the door, and there's Anise peering through the window.

"Anise!" Noelle's face lights up. Louise buzzes her in.

"Honey," Noelle says, "feed the other kid. They're so cool! Like puppies!"

"Yeah, no thanks," Anise says. But I thrust Effie at her, and she's got no choice. "Kinda cute," Anise grunts. "I just don't want anyone to think I'm doing baby duty or anything. Hey creature, you grew in my belly! How freaking crazy is that?"

"Your impossibly tiny belly," I comment. "You don't look like you've had a baby at all." She's wearing a lime green mini skirt and a crop top that doesn't leave anything to the imagination. And thigh-high lime green boots with six-inch heels. If there are aliens on our planet, Anise is one of them. No one should look that good.

"I can sure as heck still feel it," she says and frowns. "And my belly still isn't what it was. I'm not looking forward to the wedding even if there's no sex. I feel so goddamned tired all the time. The thought of being 'on' just kills me. All that fake fucking smiling."

"You probably shouldn't swear in front of the babies. Just tell Axel you can't do it," Noelle says, and Anise laughs.

"The baby doesn't understand shit, and if it did, it would support me. There's no 'telling' Axel, you know that. Hey, I heard Robbie took you out to the desert for an initiation. You're lucky you didn't lose a body part. Probably because you don't have many body parts left to lose. And you told her, right?" She jerks her head at me.

"Yes, 'her' is in the know," I say.

"You got it. Therefore, we do whatever we have to do. Just don't watch. Pretend it's not happening. That's what I do."

I want to object. I want to say that there must be a way for us to stop it from happening. But I know there's nothing we could do. Not a single thing.

"Oh my god! It smiled at me!" Anise is over the moon. "It likes me! Maybe I can do this mom thing!"

I don't want to tell her the smile is most likely from gas.

"Addie's got your eyes," Noelle says. "I love that you're their mom with me." She and Anise look at each other adoringly. I want to tell them there's a lot more to motherhood than one good feed, but I chastise myself for being a grinch. Their enthusiasm is a good thing that I need to run with, not poke holes in.

Sharps.

SOMETHING IS GNAWING AT MY SHIN. "Ow," I murmur. "Stop." I try to move my leg, but the thing with sharp teeth follows me. "Stop," I say again, and I try to jerk my leg away. A searing pain shoots through my leg, and I scream. My eyes are crusty and gritty, sandpapered shut. I force my lids to open, but I can't see anything. The world is a blur.

"I didn't think you guys were this fragile," a voice says. "Come on, up and at 'em, boy. We need to get you and your girlfriend out of here."

Shasta! "Shazz! How are you?" I blink and try to get my eyes going again, but the Vaseline fog blurs my vision.

"She's way ahead of you boy, she's already up the stairs. You're my ace, and I thought I'd blown a tire with you. C'mon, get up."

Jinx. I struggle to my feet. "Why were you biting my leg?"

He waves a cattle prod in front of me. "Had to get you to move somehow. Nothing else worked. Believe me, I tried." He's cut the duct-taped foam off us, and I'm surprised to see we're still wearing the nuns' habits. I'd totally forgotten we had them on.

He steers me to the steel ladder. "Up you go. That's it, one foot in front of the other. Good boy."

I gather my skirt and make it up to the top. I crawl onto the floor next to Shasta, and collapse. "Shazz, how are you?"

She looks at me vacantly. "So cold. I'm never going to warm up." Her face is filthy, covered in layers of muck. "I'd kill for a hot bath," she says. "I wish we'd never left that underground apartment. You could have read books. I could have bathed. Or showered. Or both at the same time. We had a bed. We had clothes. I'm so cold."

"You'll be fine." Jinx is jovial. "And your wish is my command. Back to the apartment you will go. Robbie will never think of looking for you there."

He herds us outside. It's dark, and there's no one around. I want to make a run for it, but I'm too broken. And where would we go?

"Climb in." Jinx gestures to a six-foot by four-foot box on wheels attached to a large tricycle.

"You're going to pedal us back to civilization in a rickshaw?" I ask.

"It's not that far, and besides, it has an engine." I look more closely. So it does.

We get into the box. It's a tight squeeze, and we have to stand. Maybe it's all the horrible situations I've been in, but my claustrophobia's gone. I'm simply resigned to my fate. Besides, at least the box is warm, and the marrow of my bones starts to unclench just slightly.

I want to make a joke of some kind, but for once in my life I'm speechless. I hold Shasta, and she lets me.

Jinx offloads us at what looks to be the back of a hotel. He punches a code into a steel pad, and a door opens to reveal an elevator.

"In you go." Jinx herds us in.

Numbed and stunned, we hum down several floors. The door opens, and there's the old familiar floral carpeted corridor to the retro apartment. Jinx opens the front door. Home, sweet home.

I, like Shasta, am inordinately relieved. Of all the hells in this world, I'll take this one.

"There you are, back, safe and sound. The kitchen wall has been mended, the insects have been removed, and the larder has been restocked. You are both free to recoup and recover."

Thank god for soft cushions and welcoming lamps. I sink into a sofa, and Shasta joins me. She closes her eyes and puts her head on my shoulder. I never want to move again. I look up at Jinx and wait for him to go away, but he stays where he is, his head cocked to one side.

"No," he says, "I'm the one talking here, not you."

He listens and shakes his head. "No, we are not playing the Four Knights Game, nor are we riding the palomino into the O.K. Corral. Shut up, all of you."

He waits and shakes his head again. "I know what I've got to do and I'm trying to do it, but you all need to shut up." He smacks the side of his head with the palm of his hand.

Ah. I get it. Somehow, Zuub, Dorland, and Zayne are wreaking havoc inside his head. I nearly laugh out loud. Yeah, that's not fun.

"Shut the fuck UP!" he yells, and I guess it must have worked because his eyes snap into focus, one pupil tiny, the other nearly the size of his iris.

"In terms of the game plan," he says to us, "here's what's going to happen. Tomorrow there's a fancy wedding so that Axel can entice an ever-bigger crowd to come to Carnival in two weeks' time. You will both remain down here and recover your strength. Why? Because the minute Carnival is in full swing and no one will miss us, we'll take a journey to St. Drogo's so that Sharps, you and I can go back in time to when I was me. Back to before I was caught by the law. I don't give two flying hoots what happens to you or anyone or the world after that. I will get my life back; I will get my health back. And I will be me and only me."

"What wedding? What carnival?" I must know.

"Anise, the woman who carried your babies and who is in love with your warrior goddess Noelle, is getting married. It's really just a front, so Axel can titillate his pre-Carnival crowd."

"Babies? There are more than one? What crowd? Can you possibly be less cryptic?"

"Axel runs an online brothel to fund his cause. The crowd are the millions of followers around the world who pay to watch. Anise is a woman of the night. Her claim to fame is a vagina that opens like the unfolding petals of a flower. But we're losing track here. Axel's holding a massive Carnival to which all the world leaders have been invited. We'll use the chaos of that to slip away and head for St. Drogo's at high speed in one of Robbie's helicopters, which fortunately for you, I can pilot. Until then, you will wait here. Get cleaned up. Eat. Rest. Whatever. And yes, there were twins. Adonis and Aphrodite."

"Adonis and Aphrodite? Did Noelle come up with those names? Listen, how long were we down in the hole?"

"Four weeks and two days! So, all told, you did very well! Gold stars all round! Ta-ta for now, little lovebirds!"

He closes the front door, and there's silence. Shasta starts crying. I feel her tears on my shoulder before I hear her terrible little sobs.

"Listen," I say gently. "I'm going to run you a bath. You'll get all cleaned up, and we'll come up with a plan. We've got intel to work with. Things are not as bleak as they might seem."

But she is inconsolable, and I lay her down on the sofa. She doesn't resist or move but just lies there.

I run a large bath, and don't you know, there's bubble bath. I add a large dollop of rose-scented glop and watch with satisfaction as the white foam swells and rises.

"Come on Shazz," I call out, but there's nothing. "Don't make me come and get you," I joke, but there's still no reply.

I go back to her, and she's in the same position as she was before. Where's my fierce fighter? I've got to fix this.

"Come on." I carry her to the bathroom and sit her down on the toilet. "We'll get these clothes off you and get you into the water." I pull and tear the filthy nun's habit off her. "Here you go. It's not too hot, is it?" No response. I grab a sponge and start to wash her. "Close your eyes, I need to clean your face, okay?" She lets me wash her like a baby. I dry her off and carry her to the bedroom. "What shall we find for you to wear? Oh look, an orange housecoat with red and yellow flowers, perfect! A nice big soft tent to cuddle you." I get her dressed. "Now food. Come on, Shazz, get to your feet. Come on." She's an unmoving mannequin.

"Shazz, I'm going to stick to my guns on this one. You have to buck up." I kneel in front of her. "Come on, please, I'm begging you."

Nothing. "I'm going to have a shower. Lie down and have a sleep. Or go and eat something, but please, please do something."

Nothing. I give up and go to the washroom. I need to regroup and think about what Jinx said. One thing's for sure. I'm never, ever, time travelling again.

Noelle.

It's my wedding day. Man, what I wouldn't give for a hit of butt dust or nix. Yeah, I weakened. I went to the rose garden, and who showed up? Anise. It's like she knew what I was up to.

Who can blame me? This is insane. I'm an introvert. I've been classified as such. In fact, I'm the world's most introverted introvert. I chew my nails and pace up and down. I catch sight of myself in the mirror: Holy mama, I'm one hot tamale. Long shiny silver legs, super-sexy boy shorts, fabulous spotless black tux jacket with a bow tie, and a white shirt so pristine and snowy I never want to take it off. And my mask is a stunner. Cat eyes, and black with silver sequins and black feathers.

My mood improves.

"I look so hot, right?" I ask Anise. I couldn't help preening a bit. She laughs.

"You batshit crazy chick. You look hot as fuck."

She straightens my bow tie. "And me, do you think I look hot?"

"Oh man, you look so incredible—" I lean in and kiss her.

"Hey babes." I pull away from her for a moment. "Can I tell you something weird?"

"You know I love weird." She flicks her tongue along my chin, and I get all hot and wet.

"Seriously, babes. I've been thinking about this, and I'd like to be a mom. Like a real mom. To our twins."

She gives a sharp bark of laughter. "What the fuck?" Then she looks contemplative. "I know what you mean. Those babies are kinda cute. It's like I'm looking forward to seeing them again. I did not expect that."

"Exactly!" I grab her. "I had no interest in them at all, but me too. I want to change diapers and teach them to say mama and shit like that."

"Let's get through this," Anise says, "and we'll tell Mariangela we want to be more involved."

"She'll be pleased as fuck," I grin. "Now come here, you, and give me more of that superb tongue."

"You both clean up good." Axel arrives. "Enough of this love fest. Let's get this show on the road. Anise, change of plan, just slightly. As soon as you've said your vows, I'll cut the camera to old insets of your awesome cootch. You'll get out of the dress and a body double will step in. She'll lie on the altar. The Lost Boys will perform cunnilingus. Everybody will think it's you, but there'll be no vag closeups. You two are hot though, so feel free to make out after you say your vows. Lots of visible tongue."

"*The Lost Boys?*" Why do I always sound like a vapid parrot around Axel? "Like the movie? They're vampires?"

"Don't be stupid, Noelle. Of course they're not vampires. They're rent boys. We just call them the Lost Boys because it sounds cool. Noelle, you're with me. Anise, you know what to do."

She nods and blows me a kiss.

I follow Axel through the theatre foyer and into the large ballroom. The set is transformed. We're in a cathedral with sunlight streaming through the stained-glass windows.

"Super wow," I say to Axel. "Your set designer's amazing." I'm trying to forget that he called me stupid.

"The best!" Axel swells with pride. "Been with me for decades." We walk up to the red-carpeted aisle, and the place is packed. Where did all these people come from? The crowd is glammed to the max, wearing shimmering ballgowns and luxe black tuxedos. Every head cranes back to look at me.

Axel is resplendent in a purple damask Regency tailcoat with canary yellow satin lining. The sweeping lapels of his jacket are accentuated by a high-collared white ruffled shirt that cascades down his broad chest. The man even has an antique silver cane. And a top hat to boot. He looks like a circus ringmaster.

"There are too many people," I hiss as soon as we reach the start of the six-mile red carpet. I'd thought I'd be okay with this, but I hadn't bargained on this big of a crowd.

"Relax sweetheart, no one can see you. You're wearing a mask, remember? And if people are staring, it's because of your legs. You're hot, remember? So chill. Listen, I know you like to party, do you need a hit of this or that?"

What? He's offering me drugs? No way! But... ah yes... but no, no way! But maybe just this once... I'm so torn.

"Maybe just this one time. These are unusual circumstances. I can clean up later. Just once won't hurt. Maybe just a hit of nix." I turn to Axel and lean into him. "Yeah, give me a snort of nix."

He digs in his coat pocket. But just at that moment, Mother arrives and barrels into him. "Oops," she says, "did I interrupt something?"

My cravings are so bad it's hard to breathe. I reach for Axel's pocket. "Actually," I sputter, "Axel was just going to help me out, nothing serious."

Mother grins at me. "You don't need drugs. You've got this. Axel, my sweet, please don't encourage her to fall off the wagon. She's the mother of two children. She's a good woman. She needs our help and support."

Axel sighs. "Yeah, good point."

I want to scream. So close.

"Nearly show time anyway." Axel points towards the stage where an orchestra is tuning up.

As if to emphasize his point, three jumbo teletron screens spring to life. One's on the stage and two more are on either side of the room. The main camera pans around the glamorous crowd and zooms into the piano pit, where a handful of white-suited tux wearers are getting their instruments ready for the big occasion. The orchestra looks like any other except that the cellist is naked. So is the stunning violinist, whose large breasts and extravagant pubic bush make a fetching picture against the red velvet curtains of the stage. The camera lingers on the violinist, who seems unaware we can see the details of her dimpled areolas.

"Oh my." Mother presses a hand to her mouth.

"No holds barred." Axel grins. "Mary, my Queen, you're upfront with me. Noelle, you wait until we reach the front. As soon as 'November Rain' starts, you walk up the aisle. You know the song?"

"Yes," I manage to squeak. "But Axel, I need the—" but he's gone, walking Mother up the aisle. Whoever thought Mother would be in a situation like this? They reach the altar and turn to face me.

Holy shit. The altar. It had somehow escaped my attention. But there it is, the loving focus of the camera's attention, a white satin meringue-fest of swirls and curvy softness. It's unmistakeably an altar, but it's also a fairy-tale princess bed, high off the floor with steps leading to its pinnacle, a confection on a white platform with red rose petals scattered around its base.

The first strain of "November Rain" starts. My cue. But I can't move. I can't.

"Move along, little lamb." Robbie appears at my side. "Or I'll have a cutter come in and help walk you down the aisle. Would you like that?"

No, I would not like that. I find it within me to walk. I head for Mother, my gaze locked on hers. She gets it, and she offers me her strength. We're in this insane situation together, but we will get out. The only way out is through. And through, we will go.

Is that canned applause? Or does the crowd really love me this much? The clapping and hoots are deafening as soon as I hit the big screen. Who needs drugs when you have the adoration of a thousand beautiful strangers? I relax into it and take my place at the front. Axel and Mother move aside to let me through. Mother gives me an approving nod, but I don't need her anymore. I'm loved! I'm powerful, and this is my moment in the sun!

"November Rain" begins its crescendo. Anise makes her entrance. If I thought I was well received, it was nothing compared to the crowd's wild adulation for Anise.

She stops on the edge of the red carpet and flashes her rock star smile. She gives a queenly wave and starts a slow catwalk strut down the aisle, her dress a vision of glittering layers, the lights sparkling and flaring off a thousand faceted crystals. The skirt is cropped high in the front to show off her famous vagina, although she's wearing delicate lacy underwear. It looks incredibly sensual. She pauses for a moment with one leg thrust to the front and side.

As she passes, the audience in her wake shed their clothes. Clearly, this isn't their first kick at the can. They are sensual, silent, and graceful, and their movements are orchestrated like a corps de ballet.

Anise reaches out and takes my hand. I pull her close. We turn to the priest, who has ascended on a small platform with a Bible in hand.

I'm trying not to show it, but the priest cracks me up. Elvis is in the building! He's decked out in a teal suit with a high-cocked collar paved with rhinestones and a wide white leather belt. He looks like a glitter-spangled crustacean.

"Dearly Beloved, we are gathered here today to join these two in holy coitus and matrimonial bond. Together we shall celebrate their love and, more importantly, their lust."

He pauses to flick back his hair and roll his hips. He sweeps around and points at us. "Let's cut to the chase. Do you take one another to love, cherish, fuck, and adore from now until death do you part?"

The crowd claps and roars. Mother and Axel are—thankfully—still fully clothed. As are Robbie and Jinx, who are off to the side, watching.

"Yes," Anise and I chorus. "Yes! We will!"

The spotlight swings to the entrance of the ballroom where Fiona's waiting, bearing a pink satin pillow with two ring boxes.

She too is clearly loved by the crowd. I feel the tiniest bit hurt. I swear she gets more applause than I did. I remind myself that she has a following. This isn't my wheelhouse.

Fiona is dressed in dominatrix leather, taking minimalism to a new level. The straps, buckles, and sharp studs are designed to show off her zipper tattoo to maximum effect. Thigh-high shiny latex boots with six-inch stiletto heels with enormous platform fronts complete the outfit. She's at least six feet tall. She sashays up the aisle, and the naked crowd waves as she passes, a perfect show of hands that carries her forward. Was this something these guys did often? Have crazy naked weddings?

Fiona reaches us and smiles her trout-pout smile, her complexion a thick paste. Long, newly applied cosmetic eyelashes are hawks' wings on her lids. Is blinking actually possible?

Someone grabs my hand and thrusts a ring onto my finger. Right. I must do the same to Anise.

"You may now kiss one another and do what God created you to do! Join in love and carnality! Celebrate your physical form and revel in your God-given beauty! Thanks be to God!"

The orchestra swings into "Hound Dog," which seems incongruous and perfect at the same time.

"Thanks be to God!" the crowd yells. Anise and I lock lips and tongues. Axel told us we have to go at it for at least two minutes. Kissing on the clock doesn't feel the same, and I didn't realize two minutes was that long.

"Cut!" Axel yells. "Anise, out of the gown."

Anise is wrestled out of the gown. I'm pushed to the side. A body double, whose face looks nothing like Anise, is hustled into the dress and carried up to the altar.

"And, action!" Axel yells.

Half a dozen ab-clad boy models march down the aisle. The Lost Boys are here, in leather jackets, with killer sunglasses and spiked hair. And erections like batons. They head for the altar and chow down without hesitation.

"But surely they'll see it's not your vag?" I ask Anise. She shakes her head.

"Axel's director will splice in footage of me. He's totally amazing at shit like that. Come on, honey, our work here is done. Let's go visit our little chickadees!"

"Good thinking. Man, I'm so tired."

"You're a movie star now, honey! It's hard work!"

"It was a one-off," I mutter. "Never again." Then I stop. "Hey, we forgot something." I pull her close. "Happy Wedding Day, Wife!"

She grins. "Happy Wedding Day, Wife, to you, too!"

We kiss, and this time it's for real. The whole thing was worth it just for this.

Mariangela.

ENOUGH OF THIS SHIT. It isn't ladylike to think in those terms, but I'm done with being ladylike. Besides, ladylike was never my style. I admit that I enjoy the fancy clothes and getting dolled up. I can look good and still want to rule the world. That's what I want. It's time to come clean to myself about my ambitions.

I suffered through Ava and OctoOne's rule because they had the power. I ended up with no choice, but bowing and kowtowing to them wasn't what I'd had in mind when I fought so hard for independence. Let's face it, OctoOne is a weird freak. Sure, she was the mastermind behind all our planning and the one who brought us together. And Ava, well, no one could stand up to her. Sting Ray Barb was treated like a queen, but I got dumped. I worked my ass off and got rewarded with a big fat dose of nothing, despite being one of the most influential leaders in the revolution.

No wonder I fell for Axel so fast. It didn't hurt that he's highly charismatic, funny, charming, generous, super handsome, and fun to be with. I genuinely like the guy. I also genuinely believe the guy is nuts and must be overthrown, but that's a different issue. Heart versus state.

With Carnival coming, I've got the perfect opportunity to seize the reins of power. And who better to help me than Noelle?

I've hauled her off to take a walk with me. It's been three days since the crazy wedding, but there's no rest for the wicked. We're gearing up for Carnival, which is in eleven days, as Axel keeps reminding us.

We can't risk talking indoors. Noelle suggests we scout the perimeter in a golf buggy, but I tell her that Axel probably had the carts bugged. "He's probably watching us right now, but we're just two old friends out for a walk."

She snorts then shrugs. "Not strictly untrue. Although I do think of you more as my mother than my friend."

We bring each other up to speed. This mainly involves Noelle ranting about how Axel called her stupid and offered her drugs at her weakest moment. When she finally winds down, I've got one thing left to tell her, something I saved until I was sure we wouldn't be overheard.

"Sophie saw Sharps," I say. Noelle stops dead.

"Saw him? Where? When?"

"Over a month ago, from what I can tell. Kids don't have the same sense of time as we do. She saw him with Shasta. She said they were both dressed as nuns and they were right outside her classroom."

"She's sure? She's just a little kid."

"Who knows her dad," I remind her.

"Who was stuck in a virtual prison for most of her life," she counters.

"But she does know Shasta. And she was certain. But there's more," I continue. "Jinx knows where they are."

"And you know this how?"

"Sophie told me. He visits her often. I'm really not good with it, but who can I complain to? The nuns can do no wrong in Axel's eyes, and he won't hear a word against Jinx."

"Yeah, Jinx is pretty scary," Noelle agrees. "We've got to get Sophie out of that school."

"And take her where? Besides, she loves it. We've got to plan this properly, Noelle. We can't go off half-cocked. Sophie said Jinx told her that he's keeping her daddy safe until he can get him to a place where they can make a difference to the whole world. Jinx told her he's going to save the world by taking it to a better time. Time travel, from the sounds of it. He said he's not really himself in this world, but he's going to come and find her when he is who he's meant to be. And he said he'll build her a castle made of diamonds."

"Diamonds?" Noelle snaps to attention. "Why do you mention diamonds, of all things? What do you know about diamonds?"

I sigh. "I heard you and Anise. I'd assume that's what Jinx was referring to, wouldn't you? How many diamond stashes can Axel have hidden away? I asked Sophie to ask Jinx if he can take her to see her daddy. But I also told Sophie not to tell Jinx I'd said anything, and to make sure he didn't know she told me. She said, 'don't worry Nana. He's weird, I'll be careful.'"

Noelle puts her arm around me. "You look happy around the Prong King. You're happier in this life."

"Don't call him that! I am happy, but at what cost and to how many? Here's a thought. If Jinx is going to change the world by going back in time, he'll have to go back to St. Drogo's. I wonder how he's going to open the time portal? It has to be activated by the Mainframe."

"He'll need access to the Mainframe, and he'll need to set a scheduled event. Either we stop him from accessing it, or we access it too. Then we can trap him."

"We don't even know where Axel's server room is. Robbie knows. And Anise will know. Noelle, you've got to find a way to get Anise to spill the beans."

"She's pretty terrified right now," Noelle says. "She's convinced that Axel will cut us off from the twins if we put a foot wrong. Let me get this straight: we need to find out where the diamonds are, find out where Sharps is, find out where the server is, get our hands on said diamonds, free Shasta and Sharps, and then, last but not least, get our hands on the server so we can control it, disable the cutting army, and stop Jinx from going back in time."

"Sounds rather overwhelming when you put it like that. And there's one more thing. We need to wait until the world leaders have given their access codes to Axel. If we don't, we won't be able to control the satellites, the weather, and the oil."

"And the password exchange is only going to happen at Carnival!"

"Correct."

"Let's say we manage to get all of this impossibly crazy stuff done. What do we do with Axel and Robbie? Neither of them will go down without a fight."

I cross my arms. "I don't know. We'll have to incapacitate Robbie, at the very least."

"But you love Axel, you foxy old hen! What will you do about him?"

"No idea. War is war." I pick up the pace. "I could never kill him. I couldn't even entertain the idea."

"How do you feel about Ava and OctoOne?" Noelle asks carefully. I laugh.

"I've had it with both of them. Jazza's a good guy, and he's just been reunited with his mother. But Ava and OctoOne… Ava would never concede. OctoOne would be easy to control—we can just put her in a tank and put an armed guard at the door."

We walk in silence for a while.

"Now that we've sorted out who will live and who will die and made our grocery list of who's doing what, I guess we need to get back to Carnival preparations," I say. "Have a chat with Anise. I'll go visit Sophie and see if Jinx has been back."

"Robbie's helicopter is leaving," Noelle cuts me off and points up. "That, by the way, is the alien that Axel thinks abducted him."

"A helicopter?"

"No less. Okay, Mama bear, let's head back. Listen." She grabs me and swings me to face her. "Don't do anything stupid, okay? I love you. If we don't nail this at Carnival, we'll do what we have to in order to survive, and then we'll try again. No unnecessary risks."

"You're my voice of reason?" I tease her. "Didn't it used to be the other way around?"

"It did." She hugs me. "You took good care of me. Now, I'll look out for you."

"I do hear you, Nellie. No stupid risks. Good luck with your end of things."

"Luck?" She chuckles. "I'm a seasoned warrior. Who needs luck?"

"Nellie." I stop. She looks at me enquiringly. "I'm proud of you," I say.

"Aw! Don't be. Not yet, anyway."

She turns to head home, but I stop and grab her by the arm. "Let's run through the plan one more time. Tell me every single thing you know. I'll do the same. We need to make sure we've left nothing out, okay?"

"Mama bear, I've got nothing but time. Let's take it from the top."

Sharps.

I felt way better after my gloriously hot, post cold-hole shower. I went the whole hog, shaving and playing with all the man products in the cabinet. Nice of Jinx or whoever to make sure I had aftershave. I've had three showers a day since then. By my count, we've been here four days, and my girl Shasta is still in a funk.

I slap my face and turn to look at my gut in the mirror. A little flabby around the edges. I suck my belly in and flex my arms. I need to do some push-ups or something.

"Admiring yourself?" a voice laughs, and I spin around, red as a beetroot.

"Ah, um, oops, well—"

"You look pretty good to me." Shasta pats my backside. I realize I'm naked. And that my body is pretty happy to see her.

"Oops-a-daisy." I reach for a towel, and she grabs it out of my hands.

"No, you don't," she says. "It's a nice view. I'd like to admire for a while, if you don't mind."

"Which will instantly deflate him," I say. "He's not good under pressure."

"He's holding up just fine." She runs her hands over my chest. "Very nice."

"I was thinking I should do some push-ups."

"I was thinking you should stop talking."

"I can do that." I'm about to add more, but she kisses me. And then we take her clothes off. To my great joy, my guy doesn't deflate whatsoever. It all works out just fine. At least I think it does.

"Was that, uh, good for you?" I ask as we lie on the floor.

"You couldn't tell?" She chuckles. "Yes Sharps, that was very good for me, thank you for asking."

"Phew, nice to know. I wasn't expecting that. I was expecting you to still be in your coma when I came out."

"Sorry about that. I ran out of steam. Thank you for taking such good care of me."

"Anytime." I stroke her hair.

"In return, I made you dinner."

"You did? Now that you mention it, I'm pretty hungry."

She gets up and holds out her hand. "Follow me."

She leads me to the living room. She's laid out the coffee table with napkins, plates, and glasses, with a cushion on each side for us to sit on. The plates hold a delectable selection of energy bars, protein bars, and tiny packets of dehydrated food.

"Cool!" I sit down. "Candles, too!"

"Or we could have cans?"

I look down at my plate. "I could go for some alphabet spaghetti." I get up and come back with a selection of cans and a can opener. She unwraps a protein bar.

"Do we have a plan?" I ask. She cocks her head.

"I say sit tight and don't rock any boats." She makes a slicing motion across her throat and gestures around the room. Right, there might be mics and cameras.

"I agree, we just stay put. At least we're warm and dry and fed." I want to say more, but she's right. Who knows who's listening? There's nothing to do but wait it out and do the best we can when the moment comes.

I'm staring into the empty spaghetti can as if it can tell my future when she crawls over and kisses my cheek. "You wanna play a game to pass the time?"

I grin. "Have anything specific in mind?"

"Actually," she runs her hands over my chest again, "I just might."

I want to ask her about her being a spy. Is she just playing me? Is she just passing the time, or do I actually mean something to her? I want to ask her, but I'm in too deep. If heartbreak hotel is the next stop on my travel itinerary, I'll just have to face it, like everything else.

Mariangela.

"I'm a genius!" Axel announces. "It's all coming together, Mary, my Queen. Every single piece. Nine days to Carnival! How are you, darlin' girl?"

"I'm good. Excited! Do you like my dress?"

"It's great, but I prefer it when it's on the floor next to my bed," he jokes and gathers me in his arms. "I'm wound up. Nothing to do now but wait. Come on, let's take a ride!"

"It's the middle of the night!"

"Yeah, but like I said, I'm wound up. Come on, let's grab a golf cart and go make out under the stars."

I grab a coat and follow him. It's a stunning night. "I'm going to show you my favourite place in the whole world."

We drive past the school, which is closed and quiet for the night. The Virgin Mary's grotto glows with fairy lights. "So pretty," I say. "Fairy lights make me feel carefree, like a teenager at a party with the handsomest fella asking me to dance."

"You're my best date ever," Axel declares. "I love those twinkly lights too. That big statue is my fav. Belonged to my dad. If the whole world ended, I'd take the statue with me over everything." He looks over at me. "And you. I'd take you."

I reach out and take his hand. We drive for a long time, and there's no sound except for the wheels of our buggy crunching over the desert sand.

"We're here." Axel finally pulls up next to a wooden door set deep in a round adobe dwelling.

I gasp in wonder. We're standing at the base of an enormous tree with a trunk the size of a house. Branches spread in every direction. The whole thing is covered in fairy lights.

"Welcome to The Fairy Tree! Concrete, obviously. But realistic, no? Even the leaves are concrete. It will last forever. Come on in, darlin', and welcome to my great escape! No one's allowed here, not even Robbie or Anise. And, before you ask, Fiona's never been either. Not her cup of tea." He unlocks the door with a large, old-fashioned key. I feel like I've stepped into a five-star French hotel. A double staircase winds around gold elevator doors, and the floor is a black and white checkered mosaic. A lobby chandelier glitters and sparkles, reflected by twin gold-framed mirrors. Axel leads me inside the gleaming elevator. The walls are mirrored, and there are several floors.

"This is amazing!" I'm utterly delighted. "How long did it take you to build this? Such luxury! How many floors are there?"

"Four floors plus a deck, darlin'. My father built it. I wish I could take the credit for it. We're going to the penthouse nestled among the topmost branches, where we can strip off our clothes and make love under the night sky." He draws me close. "I have a cask of ancient Egyptian herbal wine and as many snacks as your heart desires. We'll have so much fun!"

This crazy man! No wonder I'm having the time of my life. He makes it so easy to forgive all his transgressions.

The penthouse deck doesn't disappoint. It's a Moroccan expanse of exotic rugs, pillows, and throws, and the stars are inches from my face. We're on top of the world.

"Beautiful, isn't it? You've got way too many clothes on, darlin'. Let's fix that."

I still feel self-conscious when I'm naked with Axel. I'm happier when we make love in the dark, but the man loves light and mirrors. He loves to watch us, and while I simply can't bring myself to watch two old people getting it on, he has no such inhibitions.

"I revel in your every inch," he exclaims, planting butterfly kisses, which just melt me, on my knees. "Every single inch. You are a delight to me, Mary, my Queen."

I can't stop thinking about Carnival, but I decide to have one night of sheer pleasure. I let the feeling of silk and satin caress me and the cool night air kiss my skin. Axel does the same. Heaven is the feeling of his body against mine. Once again, his stamina outdoes mine.

"I think it's time for a small nap," he finally murmurs. We spoon into one another. "Don't let me sleep too long, okay? I've got to be up and at 'em early."

"I promise." Before I say the words, he's asleep.

I sit up and pull on my clothes. I've got to explore the place, get a lay of the land, and see if I can casually stumble across a fabulous stash of diamonds. The Mainframe could be here. But what if Axel catches me? I've got to take the chance. Surely anyone would want to explore? I'm already thinking of excuses.

I tiptoe to the elevator and go to the first floor. I'll start at the bottom. My heart is beating like a drum. The elevator doors open, and I peer out. The place is a shrine to Henry Moore. How has Axel amassed these treasures? Or his father, I remind myself. A quick scout around reassures me that there are no diamonds hidden in the curves of Moore's polished lines.

The second floor is dedicated to classic 1980s movies. Oh my god! He loves the same movies I do! Posters line the walls—*Dirty Dancing*, *Flashdance*, *Footloose*, *Pretty in Pink*, and *St. Elmo's Fire*. All the movies I know off by heart. No diamonds. I pat down the cushions and give the stacks of VHSes a quick check.

I'm running out of time, and I break out in a sweat.

The third floor is a deluxe hotel suite, pristine and neat, decorated in charcoal and black with lime green accents. There are too many places to search here. I have to wrap this up; this is too dangerous. I've still got to check out the fourth floor. I run to the elevator and punch the button.

And there, Eureka, is Axel's link to the Mainframe! The entire fourth floor is home to a vast array of computers! I haven't found the diamonds, but I have found the most important piece of the puzzle. I punch my fist in the air and run back to the elevator.

Maybe the diamonds are on the deck, among the cushions. But wherever they are, I have to admit defeat.

I go back up to the deck and stand looking out into the darkness. The night is starting to show signs of dawn, with fuzzy peach edges nudging the navy-blue velvet. The stars are fading, as if leaving me to my own devices, and I feel horribly alone.

"Darlin'?" Axel is awake. "Did you sleep well?"

"I did." I smile and slide down beside him. I'm concerned that Axel will smell the panicked sweat resulting from my search. "I'm afraid I don't feel very fresh." I sniff at my armpits. "Apologies my love."

"None needed." Axel is gallant. "We should start getting back. The world leaders will be coming soon, and I, too, need to freshen up. Let us away!"

He's sitting among the cushions, his hair sticking out in every direction. He looks a bit like Kevin Bacon in *Footloose*, albeit fifty years older. It's amazing how clearly I can see the younger man in him. I hope he can see the younger woman in me.

"One for the road?" I ask him suggestively. He draws me to him.

"Why not?" He kisses my neck.

I fall back into his arms. I even suggest a couple of new things that raise his eyebrows. I feel quite proud of myself.

"I could stay here forever," he says dreamily, once we're done. "I love it here so much."

"Me too," I agree. "It's like a fairy tale."

"My father was an architectural genius. That reminds me." He brushes the hair away from my eyes, and I'm glad he's become quite relaxed with me, abandoning the beehive in our private moments together. "He had an underground bunker done up like a pub. Quite cold, as I recall, but charming in its own way. A round well, deep in the earth. And he had another underground apartment perfectly kitted out like a retro '60s London apartment, including details right down to a lava lamp and a corduroy sofa. Very interesting fellow, my father. Time to get dressed, my lady."

"I'd love to see the apartment." I pull on a shoe, trying not to sound too keen. Perhaps that's where they've stashed Shasta and Sharps.

"I'd quite forgotten about it, 'til our chat reminded me," Axel says, yawning. "Sure, I'll show you. We'll get Carnival over and done with, and then I'll show you everything. We'll come back here and have our own wedding and honeymoon."

"I can't wait. How can I help with Carnival?"

"Just be at my side. I'm warning you, darlin', it's going to be a wild ride."

"When will you meet with the world leaders?" I slip the question in, aiming to sound casual, but feeling cramps of worry seize my gut.

"Before all the revelry gets going. In other words, while they're still sober. Then they'll be happily reunited with their wives and the real debauchery will begin. I'm the first to admit that it even gets a bit much for me sometimes."

"I feel really stupid," I say. "There we were, impotently fighting vines and killer butterflies and subsisting off jackelopes and onions, with no real educational system to speak of, while you were living in the lap of luxury, with schools, an underground wellspring, and not a care in the world. Why didn't we try to explore? We had no idea there was any kind of life other than ours. We ventured out, but only slightly. We were afraid."

"Fear, darlin', wasn't your and OctoPussy's mistake. It was that you didn't nail down your one true goal, your most important dream. You had abstract ideas about society, and general notions about how you'd like the world to be, but those weren't *your* dreams. True dreams call for blueprints, bloodshed, heartache, and sacrifices."

He takes my face in his hands. "The one true dream is our individual destiny. I call it the Dream of Congruence. The Dream of Congruence is when your dream and reality become one, and everything you dream is real. Most people don't follow their own dreams. They follow the dream laid out for them by their parents, their schools, their societies, their religions."

He's not making much sense. "How do you find out what your true dream is?" I ask.

"You strip away internal lies. You have to be honest about what you really want. And IF you're willing to make sacrifices—and for each of us, those sacrifices differ—THEN your dream WILL become reality."

He sounds like a slightly unhinged motivational speaker. I'm waiting for the aliens to make an appearance in his diatribe but it's not to be.

"The caveat," he continues, "is that you must read the fine print. You not only have to sacrifice everyone you love, but you have to sacrifice your soul. Your morality will be eroded by ambition, and that ambition will be stained by greed and dirty deals. Love will be worth no more than political currency. Even worse, by the time your dream is real, you'll find you won't care about it with the same fanaticism as when you started."

He leads us to the elevator. "I knew my dream of becoming world leader would be real one day. You've got no idea how much work I put into planning this. The cost was enormous." He looks haggard, and I've got no doubt he means every word he says. I'm wondering if he knows what I'm up to? Does he suspect me? Is this a kind of warning?

I watch Axel lock the door, and we hop into the golf cart. I try to spot landmarks and clues as to where we are, but it's still dark and Axel takes a bunch of twists and turns on the way home. I despair. I'll never find my way back. I know where his computers are stored, but I've got no idea how to get back to them. I also don't have the key to the front door. I'm utterly worn out from searching for the diamonds all night.

But then we pass the school and the inscrutable army of Virgin Marys, and it hits me. The diamonds are in the big statue that Axel loves so much! They must be! Axel's fixated on the statues, and I've looked everywhere else. They have to be there! I can't wait to tell Noelle! She can do some investigating.

Noelle.

I glance around the Emmarentia rose gardens. "Thanks a bunch, hun," I say to the dealer. I pocket the butt dust, grinning to myself. Score!

I know Mother's worried about me holding, but I've got this. I think about all the things Mother updated me on when she got back from visiting The Fairy Tree. At least we know where Axel's connection to the Mainframe is. I'll say this for Mother, she's got balls of steel, sleuthing around like that.

Eight days to Carnival, and I feel ready but not cocky. Mother's visit filled in a bunch of gaps for us. We've adjusted our plans, but who knows what might pop up next?

The Fairy Tree sounds kinda cool. I'm musing about asking Mother if Anise and I could spend a honeymoon there once Carnival is over when I turn around and run smack bang into Anise. Oh no! Did she see the exchange? Of course she did.

"It's not what you think," I stutter. She slaps me across the face, turns, and runs away.

"Anise!" I rush after her. "Seriously, wait!"

But she's gone. Shit, shit, shit. I run to the kitchen, hoping she'll be there, but all I find is Fiona, hysterical. Baxter is trying to comfort her. They're surrounded by a thousand terrible Jell-o desserts.

"He's going to kill me!" Fiona sobs. She sinks down to the floor with Baxter at her side.

"I'm afraid to even ask," I say.

"The Jell-o desserts are a signature part of Carnival," Baxter explains. "Mom was in charge of them, and they're all fucked up."

"Language," I chide him. I look at the offending desserts—melted yellow and green Jell-o puddles with lumps of canned meat floating like sewage. "Yeah, they look pretty bad…Wait, did you just call Fiona 'mom'?"

"I did." He's defiant. "I love her. I never had a real mom."

I can't fault him there. "Well that much is true, and I'm sorry Baxter."

"I love you too, sweetie," Fiona says. Her makeup is streaked down her face. "Axel is going to kill me."

Robbie rushes in, takes one look at the desserts and howls. "Oh, my fuck."

"I ruined them!" Fiona sobs. "I'm so sorry."

Robbie whips out a two-way radio and yells into it. "Jell-os are yours!" He turns back to Fiona. "The Mother Superior's on it. I thought you'd screw it up, so I had her prep too. This was so important and you fucked it UP!" he yells at Fiona who cowers with her arms over her head.

Baxter hugs her tight. "Leave her alone!" he growls at Robbie.

I'm not necessarily a big fan of Fiona, but I feel for her. Robbie's becoming a Class A dickwad. I picture a cutter running after him and I feel slightly more cheerful.

"Where's Anise?" he barks at me.

"No idea." I shrug. "I'm trying to find her, too."

"It's all going to shit!" Robbie is puce. "Why am I the only one making things happen? Fiona, sort yourself out and get the wives ready. We've got so much to take care of and look at you." His two-way radio springs to life. He sprints out of the kitchen.

"He never used to be such a prick." Fiona is helped to her feet by Baxter. "The power's going to his head. Axel told him he's going to be in charge of everything after Carnival."

"You can't be serious?" I'm stunned. Robbie's been off his rocker lately. Why would Axel do that? I must find Mother and let her know. But first I've got to get a hold of Anise and set things straight.

She isn't in the nursery. She isn't in our bedroom. I rush into the theatre. Huge mistake. It's full of builders and technicians yelling about the sound and lighting. Electrical cords are looped around like streamers, and it doesn't look safe. The nuns are yelling their heads off about god knows what, and it's a crazy circus. I check for a ringmaster in a top hat, flying monkeys, and sequin-bedazzled elephants because they're the only things missing.

I fight my way backstage. No Anise. The makeup room is home to another flurry of fragranced chaos.

I run down into the piano pit and make my way through a crowd of scowling musicians. Nothing. I've run out of places to look. I fight my back through jugglers tossing flaming swords in the air. If this is practice, what will the actual Carnival be like?

I've got no idea where to find Anise. I've looked everywhere. One of the hostesses—a pole dancer who practices acrobatic feats that blow my mind—goes by. I grab her.

"Hey! Have you seen Anise?" Oops I forgot. The woman doesn't like to be touched.

She glares at me and shrugs. "Have you tried sick bay?" She looks pointedly at my hand, and I remove it.

"Sick bay? Where's sick bay?"

"In the convent, of course." She looks at me like I'm a prize idiot for not knowing.

"Great, thank you!" I run outside and jump in a golf cart. Anise had given me a tour of the convent, so I know where I'm going. I head over as fast as I can.

I pull up outside the convent like a drag racer. "Where's sick bay?" I shout at a nun carrying a stack of linen.

She points down the hall. "Three rooms to your right."

I run down the hall. Sick bay? There's no sick bay. I'm about to sob and pound the wall with my fists when I see a small sign on a door next to me. *The Wellness Room.* Close enough. I yank the door open.

The room is spartan. Linoleum floors are waxed to a sheen, and a sombre statue of the Virgin Mary stands guard alongside a lone wooden crucifix. One old-fashioned wrought iron hospital bed is home to a curled-up figure. Anise, with just the tip of her head peeking out from the blue and white chenille blanket, is curled up like a small child napping.

I rush over and yank the blanket aside. "Thank god," I say. "I've been looking for you everywhere. The butt dust isn't for me. Mother and I need to drug Robbie to get the bracelet off him. We have to stop him. In breaking news, which I still have to tell Mother, Axel's putting Robbie in charge of everything after Carnival. Mother is going to be SO pissed off. Come on, sweetie, please believe me. I'm telling you the truth."

She lies still, like a small kitten, with her eyes closed.

"I promise you, Anise, the drugs are not for me. Do you think I'd put you or our family in jeopardy? You think I'd choose drugs over you? You're my drug, my love drug, you and our babies." I'm babbling fiercely. She opens one eye.

"I promise." I crawl onto the bed with her. It's a tiny, single bed, so this is no mean feat. "Whoa. This bed is hard as rock. Come on, honey, please trust me." I spoon into her. "Robbie's got an army of knife machines, and they're very scary, believe me."

"I know about them," she whispers. "I've got a bracelet too."

"You have? Oh, sweetie. Will you help me? We've got to stop him. Mother will get Axel's off him. Where is yours? Do you know Robbie's password?" I'm firing too many questions at her. I'm worried she'll retreat back into her shell, but she sits up. I sit up with her and rub her back.

"Axel doesn't wear his. He keeps it locked up in his tree house."

"You know about the tree house?"

"Of course I do!"

"Why didn't you tell me?" This isn't going well. We're arguing, when all I'm trying to do is tell her that I love her. And get her to help me save the world from Robbie and the cutters and Axel, the madman.

She shrugs. "It never came up." She nestles into me, which is a relief.

A clock chimes in the distance. "It's noon," she says. "Time to say the Angelus." I've got no idea what she's talking about. I'm about to ask her when she continues.

"Honey, do you really think you can take on Axel and Robbie? It was bad before, having to do everything they said, but it's going to get much worse. I can't bear the thought."

"I know we can beat them," I say, with a confidence I don't feel. "Trust me. And trust Mother. Mariangela. Whatever. She's really good at running things. I've trusted her my entire life. She's never been given the credit she deserves."

"I don't want to do Carnival." Anise says. She starts crying. "Look at me. All my sass is gone. I'm sass-less."

"You've got the sassiest sass of anyone I know," I say. "It's been tough. Come here, honey." I hold her close. "You'll have to do Carnival dance, but you won't have to have sex with anyone. But I need you to tell me where the treehouse is. I need the bracelet and the passcodes. You've got to bring me up to speed."

She wipes her eyes. "Hell yeah. Let's do this!" She grins through her tears, and I kiss her hard.

"C'mon, let's get this show on the road."

"Wait," she says. "You know Axel's fuck-you diamonds?"

I stare at her. "Yeah?"

"We'd better take the Virgin Mary with us."

I stare at the sombre statue and my jaw drops. "Holy Mary, Mother of God! Mother got it half right!"

Anise punches me. "Don't blaspheme. And don't drop her either. Actually, let me carry her." She gives me a peck on the cheek and hops off the bed. "I love you, but you're prone to irreverence."

"Hang on a moment, Anise!" My face is turning purple. "You told me you didn't know where the diamonds were."

"And you never told me that Mariangela thought they were hidden in a statue, did you? Anyhoo, you don't exactly keep things to yourself, do you? If I'd have told you, you'd have rushed off and told Mariangela. Stop bitching at me. We're here now, so let's take her and go."

"Does Robbie know where the diamonds are?"

"Of course. Him, Axel, and me. But Robbie's only interested in his cutter army. Have you finished interrogating me yet?"

"Sorry, honey. It's just that I asked you about them, and you said you had no idea where they were. And now you're like 'oh hey, they're in this statue I just happen to be lying next to.'"

"I'm sorry! Okay? Sorry for all of it. Please, Noelle, let's not argue. Please?"

Her chin is set, and her lip is pouting.

"You do realize you're super adorable when you're angry?" I move in close, and she softens.

"Noelle?"

"Yeah?"

"Please don't take the drugs."

"I won't honey. I promise you with all my heart."

A promise I hope I can keep.

Sharps.

A WEEK HAS PASSED, according to Shasta, and it's two days before Carnival. Surely Jinx will come to get us soon? He told us it will take two days to get to St. Drogo's, and we'll need to be there when Carnival peaks.

I'm super stressed out by the waiting. I jump every time I hear sounds, most of which are imaginary.

"I have to tell you something," Shasta whispers. "Come close."

I have a feeling of foreboding. She leans in and speaks so quietly I can hardly hear her. "Once we're on the road, I'll get a signal to Ava."

"Have you been snorting nix in secret?" I ask her. "Or do you have a homing pigeon tucked under your wing? No wait, you can send a smoke signal in morse code by the power of your very breath?"

"Ha ha, very funny. Seriously, I've got one shot to let Ava know I need her help." She opens her mouth wide and shows me her tonsils.

"Cool. But what's your point?"

"Lower left molar, tooth number thirty-seven. I pull it out and there's a tiny GPS. When I crush it, an alarm will sound over on Ava's end."

"You're fucking with me, right?" I can't believe what I'm hearing. "You've had this the whole time? You could have called the cavalry at any point, but you didn't? Why didn't you?"

"Because it wasn't the right time," she says calmly.

"The right time? We nearly froze to death in that hellhole for a whole fucking MONTH. You could have called for help, but you didn't." I jump up and throw my can across the room. It hits the wall. It's a flimsy gesture, but it makes me feel better.

"Wait." I look at her pointedly. "I thought you said you sent a signal to Ava in the electrical hut?"

She nods. "I did. It was just to say I was making progress but I needed more time before she and the others could attack."

Great. Another lie by omission.

"Besides," she looks away, "I don't really trust Ava. I was trying to find a way we could resolve this ourselves. I was hoping we'd connect with your mother, and that she and I would figure it out."

"My mother? What in hell's name are you talking about?"

"Your mother was a key player during the war. When the new regime took over, they didn't treat her well. Ava and OctoOne shunted her to the side. Besides, OctoOne is nuts, and she's dying. She's not the future, that's for sure."

"You could have told me all of this." I'm gutted. "Seriously, you should have told me. I thought you, me, us, I thought we were a thing."

"We are a thing. I'm not playing you. You mean a lot to me."

I mean a lot to her? "Cheese means a lot to some people," I retort.

"You mean a lot more to me than cheese!" She pulls my shirt off and runs her hands over my chest.

What's interesting is that the former me would have rushed over and tidied up the can I'd thrown, but I don't care. I'm a new man. Whatever they did while reintegrating me, worked. I prefer being this way. I've lost my rage and my compulsions to clean. What's more, I'm perfectly capable of having sex like a normal man. I thank the universe for this unexpected turn in my life and turn my attention to the woman who loves me. At least, I hope she does.

Mariangela.

It's four hours until Carnival kicks off. The past week has been interminable. Noelle and I have taken several walks and gone over the plans repeatedly but there will be so many uncontrollable variations.

Axel and I are in the glass boardroom, going over the plans for the night.

"I think we've got everything covered." Axel looks exhausted, and he scratches at his head.

"Are you okay?" I ask him. He shakes his head.

"Not so much," he admits. "It gets worse when I'm stressed. Which is why I'm handing the reins over to Robbie. This is my last hurrah, Mary, my Queen. I'll get the world back into good shape, and then that's it."

Robbie? Noelle had briefed me, but I'd been hoping she was wrong. "But Axel, you and me, we could do it together."

He shakes his head. "I'm going to level with you Mary." He sinks down on the triangle-backed sofa and takes my hand. The sun is setting, and the sky is awash with wild streaks of yellow, orange, and red.

"I was hoping, as a last resort, that your son would take me back to a better time. Remember those sacrifices I mentioned? All the years of wheeling and dealing, of juggling, of doing surgeries, of trying to do Mumsy proud, and of trying to outdo Niam with my empire-building. All the years of fighting the aliens in my blood. It's destroyed me. After Robbie lost Sharps, I realized that going back in time wouldn't work. When would I go back to? To when I was a child, before I was abducted? I'm too tired to do it all again."

"But you'd be renewed, you'd have a fresh start," I object. He shakes his head.

"I don't even have the energy to go to St. Drogo's. You know what I do want?"

He swings around and kneels in front of me. "I want to live in my treehouse with you. Will you come with me and take care of me? And make sure the aliens don't take me away?"

He looks so sad and vulnerable. I stroke his head. "Of course I will."

"The truth is, I don't want to go back in time because of you," he says. "If I came back, I might not have you. I love you Mary, I really do."

"I love you too, Axel." He's so damaged and broken. I know I should despise him for the things he's done, but I love him. He brings me joy. He delights in me. And yes, I will look after him.

"Do you need more meds to get through this?"

"Yeah, another dose wouldn't hurt."

I dig out a tablet, and he chews it with relief. "Maybe I should carry a few with me tonight?"

"Sure." I hand him a pill bottle. "Just don't go overboard, okay?"

"What, me?" He grins his super wattage smile. "Nah." He shakes his head like he's trying to get water out of his ears. "Let's run through this one more time. First off, we bring the world leaders here and sign the agreement. Then we go to the ballroom and show the world leaders a great time. Their wives will be presented, then Anise will do her show. And then the wish fulfillers will do whatever it is that the guests want. Nothing is off the table. We're prepared for any eventuality."

"Got it," I say.

He looks at me. "It might get nuts out there. If I lose you, I'll meet you at the treehouse, okay?"

"I don't know how to get there."

"Oh, it's easy darlin'. All the golf carts are programmed. There's a blue button under the steering column. Just one touch, then sit back and enjoy the ride. Did I mention that you look very beautiful?"

"You did not, but thank you, kind sir, for saying so." I curtsey.

"Come with me, my Queen." He offers me his arm. "Let's go find Franka. I want to have some fun with my hair and makeup tonight!"

Noelle.

WHAT THE FUCK IS WITH AXEL'S HAIR? He's got a beehive! Dear god. He and Mother have matching hairdos. I look at Mother with raised eyebrows, and she shakes her head: *don't go there.*

Okay. But his winged eyeliner and crimson lipstick are distracting. Axel grins at me, flashing lipstick-stained teeth. Mother is a vision in shimmering silver and teal. It occurs to me that I've never shown her the respect I should have. Mother is as regal as fuck, and I'm going to help her rule the world if it's the last thing I do. It probably will be the last thing I do. They wave at me and disappear into the throng.

Carnival is in full swing. The atmosphere is electric. The ballroom has been transformed into the Palace of Versailles. Who knew there was that much gold paint left in the world? The ballroom is full of gold- and chocolate-marbled pillars, arched windows, statues, sconces, swirls, velvet, and cherubs.

The nuns are an odd touch. They're gliding through the crowds with silver trays, offering sparkling yellow beverages and Jell-o snacks.

The guests—displaying mountains of cleavage, their buttressed buttocks perky as hell—are as ornate as the décor. The gentlemen sport Victorian top hat attire, rich with ruffled collars, pointy black shoes, and white knee-high stockings.

And the music! A bipolar DJ has taken the wheel and is veering across a freeway at rush hour. Bob Marley is interspersed with the Bee Gees, Soft Cell, Gordon Lightfoot, New Order, and a crazy extended remix of a song whose lyrics seem to be primarily "chirpy-chirpy cheep-cheep." The guests love it. Some are waltzing, others are breakdancing, and a few are doing the chicken dance. Chirpy-cheep switches to "Oops Upside Your Head" and I shudder.

I push through the crowd, trying to find Anise. Maybe she's near the stage. So many people. Am I going in circles?

I stop dead. Is that a buffet of drugs? I stare at the table, mesmerized. How had I not seen this before? It's a druggie's delight, piled high with bowls of nix and butt dust, booze and barbiturates. I wasn't prepared for this. All my resolve washes away, just like that.

Before I can stop myself, my hand shoots out and I grab a fistful of nix and butt dust baggies, along with an assortment of pills. I shove the stash deep inside my pocket. I force my mind away from the thoughts of the relief and the release they will bring, and I finally make it to the stage. There's no sign of Anise.

I'm starving. I help myself to a serving of wobbly green jackelope Jell-o. It's pretty good, and I grab a tray from a passing nun. "Gotta keep my strength up." She bows, whispers namaste, and glides away. Do the nuns have rollerblades under their long skirts?

The crowd is definitely feeling the delights of the chemical buffet, and things are getting wild. The lights have dimmed, and with them the crowd's inhibitions.

Mother appears at my side, and I jump. "How did you find me?" I ask. "Where's Anise?"

"No idea. But good news, the satellites are a go. We've got to reset the password tonight, while the world leaders are partying. You need to get to the treehouse. Here." She shoves a piece of paper in my hand. "That's the current password. It will ask you for the current password before you can change it to a new one."

"What must I change it to?"

"*#FuckAva!*" She grins at me. "Don't forget the hashtag and the exclamation point. It's all written down. Now I've got to find Robbie and get his bracelet off him."

"Will you be able to find him in this mess?" I ask. She nods.

"Don't worry about me. Hurry! If you leave now, you'll get to the treehouse while Anise is doing her show. I'll zap Robbie while he's watching her. It's the only time he'll stand still for a moment. Off you go."

"Look after Anise," I shout as I back away. It isn't easy pushing through all the bodies, and the revellers scowl at me as I barrel through them.

I follow Mother's instructions and find the blue button to activate the golf cart. *Go to treehouse. Change the password.*

I've got this.

* * *

I make it to the treehouse. I get the front door open and head for the elevator. So far, so good. I check the time. Anise will be doing her dance just about now. I find the computers and rush towards the central console. I grab the piece of paper that Mother gave me. Holy shit. One of the pills has leached blue onto the paper. All I can see is a sprawl of letters. What's the existing password? Why hadn't Mother told me what it was? She just handed me the piece of paper. I know *#FuckAva!* is the new password, but what was the old one?

I smooth out the piece of paper with trembling fingers. Don't smudge it more. Oh fuck. What does that say? *PartyGirlz? SmartyFrilz?* I'm so fucked.

Then I hear the unmistakeable sound of the helicopter.

Robbie's on his way to find me. Mother failed to contain Robbie. I must fix this. I have to change the password.

But first I have to figure out what the existing password is.

Sharps.

WHERE THE FUCK ARE WE NOW? The last thing I remember, Shazz and I were gnawing our fingernails waiting for that fucker Jinx to show up. But a full day passed, and there was no sign of the elegantly evil psycho. We discussed all the possibilities of what might have happened at length, but whatever it was, he missed the window to get us to St. Drogo's. For which I was inordinately grateful. No more time travel.

So what happened? He must have grabbed us while we were sleeping.

I hear a throbbing, pulsing sound: *whoop, whoop*. I'm lurching around in the darkness. My hands are tied, and my wrists are screaming with agony. Where's Shasta? My head is a throbbing abscess, ablaze with pain.

I try to call out to Shasta, but my tongue is thick in my mouth. My knees are pulled tight into my chest. Where are we? And the noise, oh dear god, the noise.

The volume increases, as does the shuddering and shaking. I get it: we're in a tumble dryer in an earthquake. But then great silence descends upon the land. I lie as still as I can, ears pricked like a Doberman, trying to make out what's going on.

Nothing. Then I hear a familiar clicking, snapping sound. A seat belt is unbuckled, followed by a terrible groan.

"I can't," a voice says, and he sounds in pain. Whose voice is that? I can't place it. A strange click is followed by a relieved sigh. A door opens, feet hit the ground, and the door slams shut. Silence. I'm going to assume that the groaning man is Jinx, and that he's stepped out from wherever we are.

I hear a muffled cough that I immediately recognize. Shasta. Thank heavens. At least she's with me.

"Shazz?" I manage to whisper.

"Urgh," she replies.

"Shazz?" I try again.

"You said that already," she replies thickly. Okay, she's her feisty little self, and all is well with the world. Kind of.

"What happened?" I ask.

"Jinx drugged us. I think we're in a helicopter. Look up."

A helicopter?

I struggle to roll onto my back. It isn't easy since I'm trussed up like a turkey. Yep, there's Shasta, equally bound and on the bench seat above me. I'm squeezed into the floor space below her. And yes, we're in a helicopter.

"Who knew these even still existed?" I aim for casual banter to demonstrate that I'm not as terrified as I feel. "This place is the gift that keeps on giving," I add. "As least he didn't gag us."

"Agreed. But my wrists are killing me. Are we at St. Drogo's?" Her voice is hoarse. "He's going to kill me and time travel back with you."

"If he so much as harms a hair on your head, I will refuse to jump."

"You're such a romantic. Wait, shh, did you hear a noise? Something banging?"

We both listen. "Nope," I say. "Probably just the helicopter settling."

"There it is again." We both listen, but there's nothing.

"What now?" I ask. "Eye spy with my little eye?"

"It's not like we can manage rock, paper, scissors. Ah, jokes aside. Sharps, my wrists are on fire, and my entire body feels broken."

"Yeah, I get you, Shazza."

"Pretty shitty of him to shoot us full of drugs while we were sleeping. I should have thought of one of us staying awake to keep watch. We relaxed into the situation, Sharps. We should have been more vigilant."

"Yep. My bad."

"Our bad."

We hear a loud crash and I jump. "Is that a window breaking?" I ask. "I wish we could see what was happening."

Another crash, and a high-pitched scream.

"Oh my god, I swear that was Noelle," Shasta says.

"You've heard her scream before?"

"Mostly in rage, but yes. Oh shit. Sharps, this isn't good."

"Hey, you, don't steal my lines. 'Oh shit' is my mantra. But ditto that, we're in deep shit."

The helicopter door opens, and we both freeze.

Jinx fires up the bird, but not before I hear a noise. Something or someone is inside the holdall of the bucket seat next to me. I wait until the helicopter has taken off, so I won't be heard, then I turn my body towards the bucket seat as much as I can. I can't reach it with my hands, so I headbutt it slightly three times, *tap, tap, tap*. And there's a reply, *tap, tap, tap*. I repeat it twice, and the double tap is returned. And then there isn't much more I can do except wonder who the heck is inside, and how it will affect things to come.

Mariangela.

It's time for the big reveal. The world leaders will see their wives in all their new fabulousness, then they'll watch Anise do her famous *Flashdance* act, eat Jell-o, and party like there's no tomorrow, while I quietly take control.

"And now," Axel announces into the mic, "the moment you've all been waiting for. My friends, my dear friends, you entrusted me with your most valuable possessions, your wives. You gave me the jewels of your heart to use as clay to sculpt into the finest works known to man. Each of these women have been treated like the queens they are. They have not seen each other. Like pieces of fine artwork, they have been sequestered in isolated vaults of luxury while they put themselves through a series of painful procedures in the name of love. They put themselves in my hands, my loving hands!" He holds up his hands into the spotlight. His hands, which bring me such pleasure.

I look over at the stage. A dozen red velvet drop cloths are artfully arched over a dozen hidden wives.

A drumroll sounds. "Are you ready?" Axel asks the row of world leaders, who have clustered at the base of the stage like eager groupies. They had been brought around to stand in front of the orchestra, and they're lined up, their faces red and sweaty with anticipation.

"Here they are!" Axel turns with a flourish, and, in a single motion, the red velvet curtains are yanked up.

There, in a row, modelling tiny bikinis and giftwrapped in colourful satin banners proclaiming their countries, topped with tinsel tiaras, and hoisting cocked legs, are a dozen Fionas, a dozen Barbie dolls. All identically trout-mouthed and double-D breasted, with cat eyes pulled tight and with high beaver-butt cheekbones.

There's silence. My hand flies to my mouth. Axel's blown it. Who in their right minds wants a Barbie doll for a wife? And the women? What do they think? I'm ready for carnage and outrage, but there's just silence.

The first strains of "November Rain" start, and the world leaders scramble up onto the stage to claim their wives. I was wrong. The world leaders are ecstatic. The wives look drugged, anesthetized, and robotic. Maybe they've been given lobotomies too.

"I did good!" Axel has leapt off the stage and is standing next to me, flushed with joy. "We'll let them enjoy this moment, and then we'll welcome Anise onto the stage. We're on track, Mary, my Queen!" He grins, scratching at his head. I study him closely. A thin snake of blood trickles down his forehead and around his mouth. He's lost his beehive, and he looks like a half-plucked chicken with scabby, bloody patches on his face, neck, and arms.

"Oh Axel," I say. "Come here." I tug him to me and grab a napkin from a passing nun carrying a silver platter with an enormous lime Jell-o mould topped with candied cherries. I dab at him. "Do you need another pill?"

"No, I'm good!" He's manic. He's far from good. I pat him down and find his pill bottle. "Take one more," I say. "Just for me, okay?"

He nods, and his face is oily with sweat. I hope he's not heading for a heart attack. Perhaps I shouldn't have suggested more meds, but it's too late now.

I need to find Robbie. "They're clearing the way for Anise's show," Axel shouts. "The rest of the show is choreographed, so I'm going to have a lie down. You've got this, Mary, my Queen!"

"Yeah honey, I've got this. Where are you going to lie down?"

He shouts something, but I can't hear what he says. He's trying to push through the crowd, but it's too thick. He drops to his knees and disappears. I squat down and see him scrum-crawling through the forest of legs. I'm worried about him. I want to go after him, but he vanishes. And besides, I have to find Robbie and deactivate his bracelet.

A runway is being assembled through the ballroom. I know Anise is going to perform the chair scene from *Flashdance*, only she'll end up flashing her flower vagina. The punters who paid a premium think they will have free access to her, but the plan is for security to carry her off the minute the song ends. She's still in no shape to have sex, something even Axel acknowledges. I'm pretty sure Robbie will be close to the runway, ready to keep an eye on Anise.

I'm right. I see him. I grab my skirts in a bunch and follow Axel's lead, dropping and going low. It works like a charm. I crawl like a bug through a cornfield, pop up next to Robbie, and smooth down my skirt.

"Having a good time?" I ask him, and he glares at me.

"I love Anise," he shouts, his eyes red and his pupils the size of pin pricks. "I hate that she has do this shit. I hate that I had to do this shit. Fuck Axel, fuck all of it. But I'll be in charge after tonight, and then he'll see!"

He's clearly high. Has he been at the butt dust? I was concerned when I saw Noelle pause at the table of chemical delights, but she seemed to move on okay. But Robbie? He's whacked out of his skull.

"I do know," I say comfortingly. I grab two glasses of crimson punch and reach into my pocket for the butt dust that Noelle scored. If I'd known that drugs would be a dime a dozen at the party, I wouldn't have asked Noelle to meet up with the dealer.

I drop a couple of pills into a glass. Dear god. Which glass? I didn't pay attention, I was too busy worrying that Robbie would see me.

"Here." I pass him a glass, praying it's the right one. He downs it in a gulp. Great. Well, great if it was the right one.

The nuns continue to set up the stage. They're dragging out all kinds of lights and electrical cables. Some of their equipment looks a bit dodgy. Out comes the chair, with a brown square seat and steel legs. Next, they hook up an elaborate water device that will shower Anise in a glittering splashy arch.

And Robbie's still standing there. I must have given him the wrong glass.

"You look thirsty." I thrust the other glass at him. He downs it, crushing the empty one underfoot. Note to self, no more crawling on the floor. Robbie probably isn't the only one crushing glasses as the revelry increases.

And then there's Anise. She looks spectacular. Her costume is *Flashdance* to a *T*. Big, black, man's suit. Bow-tied stiletto shoes, big '80s hair. The orchestra fires up "He's a Dream," and the audience howls. I just hope my plan works out.

Noelle.

MOTHER GAVE ME TWO JOBS. One, to change the password, so the world leaders no longer have access to the Mainframe, and two, to activate the satellites. I can't do two until I've done one, and I can't do one because I can't read what the password was. And now Robbie's in the elevator. I can hear him. My hands are shaking so much I can hardly read the paper. I've already tried every combination I can think of that even vaguely resembles the melted scribbles on the scrap of paper. I'm not only letting Mother down. I'm letting Anise down. I wonder how her act is going. She's holding up her end while I'm screwing up here. Wait! The smeared writing makes sense. *Flashdance1234!* I punch it in. Yeah baby! I fist pump the air. Success! Okay, now change it. And type carefully.

Do you really want to change this password?

Fuck yeah I do!

The elevator slowly hums towards me. The computer asks me again if I really want to change the password. I want to scream. Yes motherfucker, I really, really do want to change the password. There! Done with not a nanosecond to spare! But I also need to find the satellite activation software. Mother told me it would be as easy as pie, that'd I see the icon on the desktop and all I had to do was double click on it. However, she hadn't factored in that Axel's desktop is a fucking mess, with thousands of folders jumbled on top of each other. I am so fucked.

Hands shaking, I aim the mouse for the search icon. I've barely typed in "sat" when the folder obligingly appears at the top of the list. Yes! Double click to open! Double click the installer. Even I know how to do that, thank god.

The elevator pings.

Confirm satellite activation.

Hell yeah. Who knew the world's weather and so much more came down to a simple double click? Well, it also took a world war and a bunch of other shit, but still, in the end, it's a double click. And voila, it's done!

Satellite activation in progress.

That fucker had better not have some kind of system error, or fail to load, or we are all fucked. The scroll bar starts to dawdle across the screen. I want to punch the computer to make it go faster, but the elevator doors open. I turn to face Robbie. Too late, mofo, ha ha!

But wait. Holy shit. It's not Robbie. It's Jinx. This is not good.

"What are you doing here?" he asks. His voice is quiet and calm in a way that terrifies me. He also has a weird British accent.

"Just chilling out." I try for nonchalance. "You know. The party was out of control. Too much for me. I'm an introvert really. I heard about this place, so here I am, just laying low, taking it easy."

He dives towards me, but I see him coming and shoot out of the way, crashing over the desk and bringing a monitor with me.

"Don't break anything!" he yells at me. "It has to work so I can fix my fucked-up life. Now come here so I can secure you. I won't hurt you. I just need to know you are secure."

"Secure, my ass." I crawl under the desk and lunge for his ankles. "Take this you crazy weirdo." I hug his calves, trying to bring him down, and he falls on me. Bad move on my part.

"Not nice to call people names," he snaps. "You fucked-up junkie."

"That's just rude. You know I'm sober these days."

He swats me and catches me hard, and it feels like a thousand bees sting the inside of my nose. Blood spurts like a geyser.

I grab my face. Tough guys in movies and stories break their noses and carry on, but I fall to the floor, clutching my face and howling. Maybe now that I'm clearly incapacitated he'll leave me alone. But no, he kicks me in the ribs, and I'm devastated by pain. I can't breathe.

"I need to set the time code for my jump," Jinx hisses at me. "I want my old life back. Are you going to stay down?"

I mewl something affirmative. I'm broken in a hundred places. He steps over me and pulls a chair up to the computer. The screen is still active, and he doesn't need the password.

I wonder if he will notice the satellite software activation or if the window closed.

"Satellite successfully activated," he mutters. "Like who gives a flying fuck? It won't matter soon, anyway. God, this desktop is bloody heinous. Yeah, yeah, I know, I'm trying to find it. Got it."

I assume he's found the time travel software. "Stupid shitty outdated coding. Crazy that they're still using this. Good for us. Yes, I know how to set a time code, Zuub, leave me alone. I know what I'm doing. Yeah? Okay, good thinking." He carries on muttering to himself and punching in numbers and codes. Who knows what else he's resetting? I've got to stop him. I wipe the blood away from my eyes and look around. There must be something I can attack him with. Nope, nothing, not even a dust bunny. Wait! I've still got my legs. My beautiful, powerful, shiny legs. I'll kick him. I'll muster all my strength, and I'll roundhouse that motherfucker the minute he stands up. All I have to do is shimmy around so I'm in a good position.

"Nearly there," he mutters, tapping the keyboard. "Have we covered every base?" he asks. There's silence. I guess he's listening to the voices inside his head.

The pain is overwhelming. I'm going to pass out before I get the chance to have a go at him.

"Yes, yes, I believe everything is in order. Good to go, boys, good to go! We'll soon be free of each other. I'll be me again, and you can happily go back to lording over the rest of the data on the Mainframe."

He's done. Thank god. He gets up and turns around, and I let my roundhouse fly.

But he swats me with one hand, and I go flying. *So much for that*, I think as I pass out.

* * *

When I wake up, Jinx is gone. Every part of me feels hacked by swords. I can't catch my breath, let alone move. But I remember that there's a way to heal the pain! I've got a stash of drugs in my pocket. *You can't take them*, I tell myself. *You'll be letting Anise down. You'll be letting the twins down.* But I've also got to be able to carry on. I'm no use to anyone if I'm incapacitated. I'm not making excuses, right? It's medication, that's all there is to it.

I dig in my pocket and go straight for the butt dust. Nix winds me up, it isn't a pain reliever. Robbie told me he gave me something that will make me throw up if I take dust, but I decide to take the chance. Anything to ease this pain. Robbie lied. Release instantly fills my body, and I'm engulfed in a sensual wave of cozy warm delight. Hello old friend. Pain? What pain? The world's a beautiful place, filled with love and peace.

But I can't enjoy this high. I haul myself up and sit down in front of the computer. I need to find out what Jinx did, and I have to fix things. He's on his way to St. Drogo's, I know that much. But truth be told, I don't know my way around a computer. We are fucked because of me.

I sit back and let my drug-addled mind soak in the horrible realization that I've failed. Sure, I reset the satellites, but Jinx is going back in time. The whole world is fucked. My life with Anise is fucked. I let my little babies down. They probably won't exist in the world he'll take us back to. I'll probably find myself back on my shitter, wearing rhinestone dungarees, and working for Ava and OctoOne.

I stare at the screen for what feels like hours. There must be something I can do. But no, there's nothing. The icons mean nothing to me. I can't contact Mother. She told me she'd come and get me. There is nothing to do but wait. I get down off the chair and lie on the floor. I'm not enjoying this high at all. I just want it out of my body.

I must have dozed off, but I wake up with a start when I hear the elevator ping. It can't be Mother yet. Carnival will still be in full swing.

I swing around in terror and watch the elevator doors open. "Who's there?" I sound pitiful and small.

"Hey Noelle, long time no see."

What the fuck? The cavalry's here! It's Sting Ray Barb, Jazza, and Ava. The band's back together!

"Hey guys!" I'm stoned out of my tree and thrilled to see them. "You're here! Oh my god! Yay! Never been so glad to see you! You've got to stop Jinx, he's going to jump back and change everything."

"Way ahead of you. Of course we know that." Ava is calm. She's also still a bitch, and my joy diminishes. "Shasta pinged me. We've got this."

"Shasta? Pinged you?" I get out of the chair and sink down against a wall.

"She's with Jinx and Sharps. They're heading for St. Drogo's and are probably close to arriving. The plan is to let them jump, and when they do, Jazza will trap them in lost time. We don't have much time. We need to hurry."

"Shasta sent you the intel?" My fuzzy rush is starting to wear off. There's nothing like Ava to sober a person up.

"Not just her. Remember Fiona?"

"Fiona?" I'm flabbergasted.

"I love your parrot impersonation," Ava says. "Yeah. Apparently, she was pretty pissed off when Axel dumped her. Our dear little Baxter orchestrated a way for her to feed us info. Such a sweet boy. It seems he hates his Nana. Hates everybody except for Fiona.

So, thanks to Bax and Fiona, we've been in the know from the start. But Shasta did ping us, which was nice of her. She's been generally silent throughout all of this, went dark. Too busy fucking that loser Sharps."

Baxter. I'm not surprised. That little shit. It's getting hard to breathe. I'm regretting betraying Anise by taking the butt dust, but I'm also wondering whether I should take another hit. My ribs and face are fucking killing me. I've already fallen off the wagon.

"You look like shit," Jazza comments. He's poised at the keyboard, studying the scrolling data on the screen, but he turns to look at me. "You're high. I thought you'd cleaned yourself up."

"I was trying to save the world, and I was in so much pain." I sound pathetic. I dig into my pocket. "Take this. I fucked everything up by taking a dose." Tears fill my eyes and splash down my cheeks. "I've fucking ruined everything."

"Oh Noelle, don't be such a crybaby." Ava is brusque. "Everyone falls off the wagon. At least you were justified. You were attacked by an assassin. Your intentions were good. You got clean once. Just see it as a dose of medicine and move on."

Who knew she had such a kind and loving side? "I can do that." I'm cheered. "But if you trap Jinx in lost time, won't you trap Sharps too?"

"Collateral damage," Ava says. Just like that, I hate her again.

"That's not fair to him," I protest.

"There's no other way. If we want to get rid of Jinx, we have to get rid of Sharps."

"Not entirely true," Sting Ray Barb pipes up. "If Sharps pushes him into the jump zone and we activate the code, then only Jinx will go. If Sharps leads the way, which would be so stupid he'd deserve to die, then yes, it will be unavoidable."

"They're there now!" Jazza's nose is pressed to the screen. "Oh my god, no!" He claps his hand to his mouth.

"What?" We cluster around the screen.

"Sophie!" Sting Ray Barb shouts. "Sharps is carrying Sophie. Why is our sweet little Sophie there?"

"To give Sharps added incentive, I'd imagine." Ava sounds cold.

"He's putting her down. They're all having a good old chat. I wish we had audio."

"Concentrate, Jazza!" Sting Ray Barb snaps. "You must be ready to activate if Jinx goes first for any reason."

"I'm three thousand percent focused," Jazza mutters. "I'm here, Sharps. I'm here, buddy."

Sharps.

He's got my little girl. I've never hated anyone as much as I hate Jinx when he takes her out of the bucket seat at St. Drogo's.

"Daddy!" She runs to me, and I grab her to me, looping my bound hands over her head and hugging her close.

"I won't let anything happen to you, sweetie. I promise."

"Why did you bring her?" I yell over her shoulder at Jinx.

"Just in case your girlfriend here wasn't enough incentive for you to jump. I had to sweeten the pot a little."

"I thought you were my friend." Sophie looks at Jinx with wide, hurt eyes. Prince Charming has turned into Little Red Riding Hood's evil wolf. Jinx is deteriorating. His eyes are blood red, and he's snarling, fangs bared.

"I am your friend, Sophie," he says. "We're best friends." Then he slaps himself across the face. "No, we're not, you stupid little twat."

"That's a guy called Dorland," I explain quickly to Sophie. "Jinx is your friend, sweetheart, there are other people inside his head. You're all in there aren't you?" I ask Jinx. "I wish I had some sympathy for you, having had the experience myself, but you deserve each other."

"We're dying," says a voice I recognize as Zuub. "We have to fix it, or we'll all die."

"I do love you Sophie." Jinx is back, and he's sorrowful.

"Tick tock, tick tock. Shut the fuck up, and let's get this show on the road." Zuub takes control. "Into the station! Now!"

"I can't walk," Sophie says in a small voice. "My legs hurt too much from being squashed in that box."

"It's a miracle you didn't suffocate in there. Hook your legs around my waist, honey. Come on, Jinx, come on, Shasta." I'm going to save Sophie and Shasta if it kills me. I'm a dead man walking anyway, and besides, I got lucky—I got to come back and see my kids and fall in love with Shasta and have her fall in love with me. It was way more than I deserved.

The last time I was in St. Drogo's, the place was full of dead people, and the stench from their rotting bodies was overwhelming.

Eleven years have passed, eleven years of drought. There will be no mush, no rot. I'm expecting a web of tangled vines to impede our progress, but the place is a dusty cavern. The stairs are covered in three inches of dirt, but otherwise the path is clear.

I carry Sophie down, and she clings to me. "When we get down there, honey, you'll have to let go of me," I whisper. "I have to go with Jinx, okay? And you can't come with me."

"Will you come back, Daddy?"

"Maybe. I came back this time, right? But if I don't, you must promise me you'll look after Shasta, okay? Promise me, baby."

"I promise."

"Honey, I'm so sorry I was a bad dad. I never meant to hurt you. I did the worst thing, but it was because of how much I love you. You know that, right?"

She buries her head in my shoulder. "I know, Daddy. I love you."

My throat closes with tears. "Love you too, honey. Okay, we're here. I'm going to have to put you down. Stay away from the gates no matter what, okay?"

"Okay Daddy." She kisses me on the cheek, and I put her down.

"You have to uncuff us," I say to Jinx. He grins, and I recoil. He's lost a few teeth.

"I don't have to do fuck all," he says.

"Untie them, or I won't jump." I sit my ass on the ground. Not the sexiest move, but one I hope will work. "You're not strong enough to carry me, so untie them or I'll sit here until your body falls apart just like your teeth."

Jinx looks annoyed, but he fishes out a pocketknife and snips off Shasta's cuffs. "Don't try any heroic shit," he tells her. "Hang onto the kid and hope for the best."

"Look after each other," I tell Shasta and Sophie. "I love you guys."

"Aw, so sweet," Jinx sneers. "Enough treacle honey pots for one day. Time to get a move on."

He snips off my cuffs, and I rub my wrists. "Dorland sure has got a hold on you," I say to Jinx. "All those quaint little phrases peppering your utterances. So cute. You get how this works, right? Stand in front of me, I'll put my arms around your waist, and off we'll go, magic carpet ride."

"Liar, liar, pants on fire. No dear boy, I hold onto you. In fact, I literally piggyback a ride. I'm very light, you see. I've lost a ton of weight as a result of all my ailments. I'll be hopping on very shortly."

Oh shit. I'd hoped he'd fall for it. To borrow a phrase from the old chap, my goose is well and truly cooked.

"Bye bye, ladies." I try to sound chipper as I face my fate. "Come on then, Jinx, get up and at 'em."

I hoist him onto my waist, and he wraps his skinny arms around my neck. I take a tentative step towards the old gates. They're rusted and dangling, but their appearance is deceiving. This innocuous place has the weakest temporal structure in the northern hemisphere, and it will work no matter how ramshackle it looks. Once I go through the gates, there will be no turning back. I'll be sent to another time and another place. Or, even worse, to lost time.

"Do it," Jinx screams, and he tightens his legs around my waist. "Do it! Go now!"

Oh god. I'm not ready to die. I'm wracking my brain trying to figure out how to buy more time and how not to go through those gates. Jinx starts kicking me like he's riding a horse. "Stop that," I yell. "I'll do it." I hoist him up and resign myself to my fate. There's no way out of this.

Mariangela.

Anise starts to strut her stuff, and Robbie's head dips. About time! The guy's got the constitution of a mule. Must be all those steroids.

I see a commotion in the corner of my eye, and I turn around. The Barbie wives are attacking their husbands! The fur is flying. The drugs must have worn off, and clearly, they aren't delighted to meet their cookie-cutter counterparts. I chuckle out loud. Fake toupees are tossed like graduation caps. The world leaders are screaming as their wives lay into them tooth and nail.

"What the fuck is going on there?" Robbie slurs. "I have to go and—" But he forgets what comes next as he slowly sinks to the ground. Thankfully no one notices because all eyes are on Anise. No one's even watching the world leaders being pulled apart limb by limb. Who knew the wives were that strong?

Anise is oblivious to all of it. She sheds her clothes slowly, and the crowd cheers her on.

The minute Robbie is horizontal, I lunge for him and grab his wrist. The trick is to hold the side of the bracelet, press a button, and talk into it, but it's so loud in the ballroom that I'm worried the device won't hear the command.

"Shuttle logic!" I yell with all my might. Nothing. I pull Robbie's arm over his body and lie on him, hauling my large ballgown skirt over my head to create a soundproof cave. I pull his wrist close, press the button as hard as I can, and scream. The sounds of the crowd are muffled, and bingo, the bracelet snaps open!

I snap it onto my wrist. "Power down," I instruct it. The bracelet glows neon green and fades to black. I did it! I roll off Robbie and straighten my gown. I wonder what to do. If I let him live, I'll be faced with a lifelong enemy I had the chance to neutralize. But he was also just a kid who was used by Axel, and it isn't his fault all of this happened. Yes, he let the power go to his head, but that's human nature—and drugs. I haven't met a single person who hasn't fallen in love with their own egos while they're surfing the Napoleonic wave.

I can't kill him myself, but I need him out of the picture until this is all sorted out. I look up. If I leave him, he's in danger of being trampled. I'm eye level with Anise's runway. Maybe I can drag him under it? He's so heavy, a fallen monster, but for how long? I have to make sure he stays out for the count. I reach into my pocket for another tab of butt dust. "Sorry," I mutter, "but better safe than sorry." I force the pill inside his mouth and roll him onto his side as close to the runway as I can.

I stagger to my feet. There's Anise, naked on the chair, her legs wide and the spotlight shining on her glory. She's so stunning! But then I spot something.

"Anise!" I yell. "Stop!" I wave my hands frantically. On the far side of the runway, out of my reach, a frayed cord snakes in the direct path of the waterfall. Right near Anise's left foot.

She reaches up for the hanging cord. "No!" I scream, "don't do it!" but she gives it a good tug. A glittering waterfall cascades down on her, and she arches her back perfectly. But then she keeps arching and jerking as if her body is being yanked by an invisible cord.

Anise is being electrocuted.

And then the lights go out. Utter blackness falls. A power surge fried the circuit.

The room erupts with screams. I drop down onto Robbie. I grab him by the arm and pull him onto me, flattening my back against the runway. I'm not going to die. I use his body as a shield while the world goes to hell in a handbasket and the frantic crowd bolts over us.

Noelle.

Sharps hoists Jinx up on his back again, and Jinx kicks him hard, horseback style. We're glued to the screen.

"Sharps," Jazza yells and pounds the table, "grow a pair, you stupid bastard. Throw him to the ground and drop-kick him in front of you. Push him through the gates so he leads the way. Sting Ray's right. C'mon buddy, you've got this!"

"Why do you even care about the guy?" Ava comments as she picks up a crystal triangle paperweight and studies it in the light of the screen. "Cool souvenir."

I glare at Ava. "Come on, Sharps," I shout.

The group on screen seem to be arguing about something. Sharps is waving his hands around, and Jinx uncuffs him.

"My, my, haven't you lot made yourselves at home," a voice comments.

It's Axel. Looking like the walking dead, mangy as all hell, with blood pouring down his face.

"Jazza!" Sting Ray Barb and I both yell, "watch the screen!"

"It won't work." Axel sinks down into a chair.

"You don't even know what we're trying to do," I say. He grins at me with gross, blood-smeared teeth. He scratches his head, and more blood dribbles down his cheek.

"Jinx wants to go back in time," he says. "I know what's what. I know Anise gave you her and my cutter bracelets, along with the passwords. I know that Mary's going to rule the world when Carnival's over and Robbie's most likely dead. I know that I ruined the world leaders' wives. But hey, credit where credit's due, I set up things so we could get control of the satellites, thereby saving us from eternal drought. But this time, the time-travel garbage won't work."

"Of course it will work," Sting Ray Barb says. "I made sure we always had it at the ready. It's my life's work. There's no way I was going to let anyone destroy it. However, that said, we don't want it to work, not this time."

"They're still standing at the gate." Jazza gnaws at his fingers. "Buddy. It's now or never, come on, do something."

His finger is poised to click, and we all stare at the screen. Even Axel gets up out of his chair, comes over, and peers closely. Sharps hoists Jinx onto his back again and lunges for the gate.

And then the lights go out.

Sharps.

Just as I rush forward through the rusty old gates, the world turns black. I hit a wall. Literally. I must have run through the gates and hit the wall on the other side. Holy fuck! I'm still here, in St. Drogo's! A power failure interrupted the jump! I drop to the ground. Jinx falls off me and I hear him crawling away, groaning.

"Sharps, come back!" Shasta is frantic. "Come back!" She's right. I need to get back to her side of the gates asap if there's any chance of me surviving. If I stay where I am, the time travel will kick in as soon as the power comes back on and I'll be transported to god knows where.

"Where the heck is back?" I yell. "I can't see my hand in front of my face. Keep talking to me. I don't know where I am." I crawl as fast as I can, hopefully towards Shasta. "Shasta! Where are you?"

"I'm here! Come on, Sharps, we're over here!"

I barrel into something soft and warm, and we both roll over.

"Oomph," a voice says. I guess I knocked the wind out of Shasta, but at least I found her.

"Daddy?" It's Sophie. "Are you okay?"

"I think so, baby." I've got no idea what to do next. Shasta is still groaning. Where's Jinx? I turn and see a faint glow coming from the top of the stairs. "We've got to leave. Hurry! Shasta, get up."

I scramble to my feet, and at that moment, light floods our little cave.

Jinx is lying on the time travel side of the gates. He's a curled up, broken mess. His legs are twisted away from his body in a way that makes me want to throw up, with one knee at a horrible, unnatural angle.

"Come on, Sharps." Shasta jolts my focus back to her. "Let's go." She picks up Sophie.

"I'm not a baby! I can walk now," Sophie protests and wriggles out of Shasta's grip.

"Shazz, look!" I point.

Jinx is disintegrating into tiny, pixelated mosaic pieces. The pixels twist upwards in a spiralling vortex, spinning faster and faster. And then he's gone.

"What happened?" Sophie asks, her voice tiny. "Where did he go?"

I brush the hair out of her eyes. "It was just a dream, honey, a bad dream. We'll get you home safe and sound. All of this will feel like a bad dream."

"This dream was real," Sophie insists. "Can we leave now?" she asks, and Shasta and I nod.

"Oh yes honey." I grab her hand and we head for the stairs. "Now would be a really great time to leave."

Mariangela.

Two weeks later, in the aftermath of Carnival, I survey my kingdom. It's taken a while to get all the pieces sorted out. We're seated in the glass boardroom, and I face the team.

"That was quite the adventure," I say evenly. "We've been a bit scattered, cleaning up the mess. I figured it was time to get us all on the same page.

"In case anyone's wondering, I'm the captain of this ship, for reasons that will become clear as the meeting unfolds. I ask you to bear with me. To start, let's share our insights of what went down. Shall we go around the room? Noelle, you kick things off."

Noelle looks around. "The faulty electrical cord on the runway was to blame for the power outage. It electrocuted Anise and caused a short circuit from here to St. Drogo's. That Anise is alive is thanks to the quick-thinking medical team. They had a defibrillator at the ready in case any of the world leaders keeled over. Given their drug and alcohol consumption, it wasn't unlikely. Luckily, the power failure interrupted the time travel, and Sharps got back to the other side before the power came back. Otherwise he'd be toast, just like Jinx. Honey," she turns to Anise and grabs her hand, "I can't believe I nearly lost you."

"Yeah, I'd like for that to never happen again. My head is still killing me, and my foot is badly burned, with permanent nerve damage. But I don't care about that. My Robbie got trampled to death." Tears run down Anise's cheeks. She left her hospital bed to come to the meeting, insisting that she needed to know what happened.

"I know you loved Robbie," I say gently to Anise. "But the steroids destroyed his mind. There was no saving him. He was going to use the cutters to control the world, something we'll never do. I have, however, tasked Noelle with one so she can address the vines in our hometown."

"Yeah." Ava lounges in her chair. "Your generosity and faith are astounding. Trusting a junkie over us."

"I've no reason whatsoever to trust you." I smile at her. "And Noelle is clean. Your use was a one-off, right Nellie?"

She nods, and I can see she means it. "I'm sorry I used," she says to Anise.

"Oh sweetie, it's all good. Don't even think about it."

"I've developed a vaccination against the butterflies," Sting Ray Barb says. "But we won't lose the anaesthetic power of the butt dust for surgeries."

I smile at her. "You're a marvel, my dear."

"A tired marvel. A marvel ready to retire. A marvel ready to admit my brain doesn't quite have the firepower it once did."

"And you shall retire in the finest way, with your every need attended to."

"Mother, are you always going to dress like that?" Sharps raises an eyebrow. I've kept my look: the winged eyeliner, the crimson lipstick. I never want to see another beehive wig in my life, and my hair is twisted into a fabulous chignon. Franka and I are fast friends, and I'm her primo client.

"I am. I like it, dear. Any objections?"

"None whatsoever." Sharps grins.

"Where's Daddy Axel?" Anise asks.

"Ah yes." It's hard for me to talk about him. "He, uh—"

"He's dead, sweetie." Noelle draws Anise close. "I went back to check on him after I was sure you were okay, and he was gone."

She doesn't mention that I had gone with her. I can't get the memory out of my mind. In the end, my poor love clawed his way out of his skin, fighting his demon aliens. His crumpled, sad body was more than I could bear. Noelle and I buried him at the base of his Fairy Tree.

"I'm glad he's dead," Anise says. "He was a terrible man. You didn't suffer because of him like I did. Yeah, so he adopted Robbie and me, but that doesn't excuse what he did to us for all these years." She looks at me defiantly, and I nod.

"You're right, dear." I can't tell her that part of me misses him so much. I miss his wild grin, his infectious enthusiasm. But Anise is right. It's better that he's gone.

"Where's Fiona?" Anise asks. "I heard she and Baxter were feeding intel to the enemy."

"They were, but we're not going to hold that against them. Baxter was an angry young man acting out, and Fiona had her reasons. There'll be no repercussions, and we will welcome them into the fold moving forward." My tone brokered no argument.

It turns out that Fiona was gutted when Axel ditched her for me. She just didn't want to show it. It was a sad scene, finding Fiona and Baxter in the kitchen after Carnival, both of them sitting on the floor, thinking they would be banished to the backend of nowhere or jailed. Baxter was hostile; Fiona, in tears.

"This is all your fault, Nana." Baxter leapt up when he saw me. "That fucking old man broke mom's heart when you arrived on the scene. You never care what you do as long as you get your own way."

I sat down next to Fiona. "I'm so sorry. I thought you didn't care." I took her hand. I was surprised when she leaned her head on my shoulder. Baxter sat down and took her other hand.

"What did you expect? Tears in front of everybody? Not my style. Fuck you is more my style." She's still crying. "I wanted to hurt you, hurt him. Hurt everybody. Except for Bax. Thank god Bax came along when he did."

"Oh mom. I'm the lucky one. I wanted to punch Axel so many times," he told me, "but mom said I had to be cool."

"I'm sorry we did what we did." Fiona extracted her hand and wiped her eyes.

"It's okay," I told her. "I'm so sorry. I really mean it."

"What are you going to do with us?" Baxter was belligerent.

"Nothing at all. I hope you'll stay with us and put all this behind us."

"On one condition," Fiona says. "No more Jell-o!"

"No more Jell-o!"

But the team doesn't need to know all the details, and I'm glad they don't ask anything else.

"What's going to happen with the sex workers?" Anise asks.

"That revenue stream has been discontinued. They've all been offered alternate careers in the arts or pensioned off."

"Whoa! It was a pretty huge source of income." Anise is incredulous. "You're shutting it down? Crazy! Still, there's a fortune in the bank. I guess we can live off that for a while."

"There is no money," I announce, and the group around the glass table leans forward, shocked. I've been dreading sharing this news.

"What do you mean?" Anise sputters. "We all worked so hard!"

"Axel and the world leaders made a bunch of bad investments," I admit. "In all fairness, he hadn't been thinking straight for quite some time. However, we can't forget that he orchestrated the satellite reactivation and saved us." I wave a hand at the glass windows. Outside, a beautiful rain is falling. We watch for a few moments, revelling in the good it will bring.

"Things will get back on track," I say. "International currency is another area that the new world leaders and I will pour a lot of energy into."

"Fabulous. The world will be run by a bunch of deformed Barbie dolls." Ava folds her arms.

"The wives and I are politically aligned, and nothing short of world peace is acceptable. We are going to share resources and find a way to heal our world. Besides," I remind her, "never judge a book by its cover. Books, by the way, will be making a large comeback, and education will be another high-profile portfolio. We're going to start a printing press!" I can't contain my happiness.

I hear voices in the corridor, and I get up, smoothing down my dress.

"I've been meaning to ask, what's the status on Niam?" Noelle asks as I head for the door. I turn and smile at her.

"As a matter of fact, there's someone I'd like to introduce you to." I open the door and lead my guest inside.

"Ladies and gentlemen, I have the great pleasure of introducing you to our good friend, Niam."

There's a collective gasp and I understand why. Niam is magnificent. She's six-foot-three and statuesque. She's got all of Axel's good looks but is unmistakably a woman. She wears her hair Cleopatra-style, with eyeliner and aqua eye shadow to match. Her eyes are a strange moonstone colour, and she doesn't have any irises. She's clad in a gold tunic and Egyptian sandals, and two manservants with polished skin and white linen waist-to-knee kilts follow in her wake.

I guide Niam to a seat, and she lowers herself with careful grace.

There's silence, and I let things sit like that for a moment.

"I have a question." Anise sticks her hand up likes she's in grade school. "Where the fuck have you been all these years?"

We are all taken aback by Anise's rudeness, but Niam is unfazed.

"As you know, I left the Fountain of Youth to Gilbert and forged a new life for myself. Mumsy came with me and was very happy for many years."

"And you were funded by what?" Anise is rigid with fury. "And you used our water?"

"We shared the underwater spring, yes. And we mine palladium, which makes us rather popular."

"Palladium?" Sharps asks.

"Essential for catalytic converters in cars and planes. It took a hit when the world went electric, but after the war, it became essential. Axel didn't care about the mine. He figured he had the upper hand, what with his surgical charms, his army of cutters, and his crew of sex workers. And he was right, particularly when it came to the cutters." She looks at me. "Kudos to you, my dear, for disabling that mechanical menace."

"I couldn't have done it without Noelle," I say, and she blushes.

"We all came together at the right time," Niam continues. "But Anise, I do owe you an apology."

Anise leans forward glowering, her fists on the table.

"I realize I let you down. I should have come and rescued you and Robbie from Gilbert, isn't that so?"

Anise's face crumples. "Well, fuck yeah. We're family. Adopted or not, you are our aunt. And where the fuck were you? Nowhere. Busy being fucking Cleopatra and living a life of luxury."

"I couldn't, dear," Niam says. "I was powerless until Mariangela came along. Don't you see that?"

Anise chews her lip and refuses to look at Niam.

"Time will heal all wounds," I say. "We will work together and move forward."

"Well, I'm not going to roll over that easily." Ava gets up and leans on the table, palms down. "Come on, Jazza. We're going home. I'm still the leader of my zone and don't you ever forget that, any of you."

"Have you ever seen a cutter in action?" Noelle asks idly, studying her fingernails. "Mincemeat. That's all I'm saying. Mincemeat. But whatever floats your boat."

Ava sits back down.

"Good doggie," Noelle says, and Ava snarls.

"Ladies, we will all get along," I say. "However, Ava, you will work with Noelle and you'll do whatever she says. I know that OctoOne shrivelled up and died and you have no other allies. Jazza, you and your mother and kids are welcome here anytime."

Jazza looks over at Ava. "I loved you so much, but I haven't liked you for a long time. So yeah, I'd like to set up home base here."

"The kids are mine!" Ava hisses.

Jazza sighs. "Really, Ava? How old are they? Do you even know when their birthdays are?"

We wait.

"I've been busy taking care of shit!" she yells. "So that's it? You're all kicking me to the curb?"

"I was one of your biggest fans," I remind her. "I had so much faith in you when we started the war on Materialism. Don't you remember? I do. You were simply marvellous, but you let the power go to your head. You lost focus of what really matters. If you really want to be a part of the new world, there will always be a place for you. But you have to prove yourself first."

"And I loved you so much they had to scour me to get intel on you," Jazza says. "You know the pain I went through for you. And when we got together for real, I thought my heart would break because it couldn't handle being that happy. But you slowly chipped away at me with your sarcasm and your scorn."

He leans towards her. "You will always be the love of my life. There can be no other. But you have to find your way back to me and the kids, if you can. I hope that, deep down, you're still that woman I fell in love with."

Ava stands up. "What the fuck is this? An intervention for poor fucked-up Ava? Screw you all. You know where to find me if you need me."

"Likewise," I call out to her as she leaves, slamming the door behind her, and the air in the room feels lighter.

"Sorry Jazza," I say. "I know it must be hard."

"She'll figure it out. Or she won't. We'll just have to wait and see."

Jazza and Sting Ray Barb get up. "I'll fly Barb to get her stuff," Jazza says. "We'll pack up the lab and bring it here. Then I'll come back with Mom and the kids." He turns to Sharps. "Man, those 'copters are way cool!"

"Yeah buddy, so easy to fly," Sharps agrees. "I wasn't sure I could fly me, Shasta, and Sophie back, but it was a piece of cake!"

Shasta giggles. "You were slightly more stressed than that, but you did pretty good, all things considered."

I can just imagine Sharps sweating bullets and being panic stricken but doing it anyway, and I'm happy to see that they're still together.

"I'm going to catch up with Franka." Niam rises gracefully to her feet. "See you for dinner, Mare?"

I nod, and she smiles. "Promise me one thing," she says. "No Jell-o."

I chuckle. "I think there's a universal consensus on that! No more Jell-o! See you in a few."

Niam and her manservants leave, and I wait until only Anise, Noelle, Shasta, and Sharps are left.

"So," I ask Anise, "where is the Blessed Virgin?"

Anise digs out a tote bag out from under the table. "Here." She places the statue on the table. We all look at it.

"What's going on?" Sharps asks.

"Are you getting all religious on me?" Shasta's not happy. "You know how I feel about the Catholic church."

"Hang on." I hold up a hand. "It's not what you think. The statue holds Axel's stash of fuck-you diamonds. If you like, you can have the honours of smashing the statue."

Anise shrieks and grabs the statue to her breast. "Don't even think about smashing her!"

"How else will we get the loot out?" Shasta asks. Noelle lays a hammer on the table.

"Are you sure the diamonds are in there?" Shasta asks, and Anise shakes it. There's the distinct sound of something rattling around inside.

"We have to get Sister Colmcille in to deconsecrate the statue first," Anise insists. "You've no idea what this means to me. Robbie and I used to hide in sick bay when Axel was losing his shit, and the statue looked after us."

"Fuck-you diamonds!" Sharps is cracking up. "No wonder you called a halt to the sex trade, Mother. You had a backup plan."

"I have no idea if there really are diamonds in there. I'd like to think I would have ended it regardless." I hope that's the truth. I speak into a two-way radio, calling for Sister Colmcille.

"And now we wait," I say.

"I hear there are still a lot of Jell-o snacks in the fridges," Noelle offers. We all shudder. Noelle is the only one who seems to like the dreadful stuff.

"No Jell-o!" we chorus.

"I wonder if things will start to grow again?" Shasta asks. "Are there dormant seeds in the soil, or will we have to replant? Do we have samples?"

"I'm sure Sting Ray Barb's team will come up with a plan," I say. "And, like I said, I'll be working with the world leaders to exchange resources. Planet Earth has a way of bouncing back, we've just got to make sure we're along for the ride." I look out the window and try not to look as anxious as I feel. What if there aren't any diamonds in the Virgin Mary? I try not to think about it, but the noise of the others chatting is getting on my nerves. I get up and pace around the room. Why can't we just smash the damn statue?

"Where is she?" I finally snap. Just then Sister Colmcille pokes her head around the door. She's a tiny wizened old woman with a bunch of scraggly whiskers on her chin.

"Please deconsecrate the statue so we can break it open." I'm brusque, and she looks horrified.

"Just DO it!" I say. I don't care if I sound rude.

"I'll pray a rosary, and I'm sure it will be fine."

"A whole rosary? No, just say a decade. Actually, just say a Hail Mary. And make it fast."

She nods. The nun bends her head in prayer, and Anise murmurs along with her.

And finally, it's done. I grab the hammer and lay the statue down. I give it a sharp tap around the ankles and the base falls off.

And a lovely pile of glittering diamonds flows onto the glass table.

Thank god! I exhale with relief. If the statue was empty or just full of dust, we'd be in deep trouble.

"But diamonds?" Sharps is baffled. "Because we all need tiaras in a time of crisis?"

"They're not just a pretty face," I tell him. "They're old-fashioned currency and they're semiconductors, essential for maintaining the Mainframe."

Anise gives a cheer and gathers up the pieces of the statue. "We'll get this mended. Time to go and visit our babies. Unless there's anything else?"

I shake my head. "Off you go. Give my love to Addie and Effie. Tell them Nana will see them soon."

"I'm coming to meet the babies too," Shasta says. They leave, with Anise leaning heavily on Noelle and limping. It's just Sharps and I left at the table.

"How are things?" I ask him carefully. Meaning where on Earth do we go from here, he and I? Our past is so complex, so horrifying, and so tangled. I want to believe in him. I trust Shasta, so if she has faith in him, so can I.

"I want to help you," he says. "However you'd like me to. I mean it. I can clean toilets, feed the jackelopes, whatever. I'm not fussy. I'd like to live out my days with Shasta, if she'll have me, and I'd like to have a kid with her if it's not too late. I'd like to be a better son to you. You rescued me when I was an abandoned baby on No Daddy Street. I never thanked you for that. I behaved like a primo a-hole instead. Worse than that, even. Whatever you want, Mother. Just know that whatever you decide you want me to do, I'll respect that one hundred percent."

"I've always loved you, Sharps. I always knew you had great potential." I chuckle wryly. "And I wasn't wrong. You certainly set the world on fire. Imagine what you could do if you put all that energy into good?"

"I don't feel super energized, to be honest. I'm trying to muster up the energy to face Baxter and help out with the twins. But like I said, I'll do anything you ask of me."

"Come here, Sharps." I get up, and he walks towards me with clear trepidation. I grab him and hug him.

"All I ask of you is that you be happy," I say. "It's all I've ever wanted."

"Well, this time, I may just be able to do it," he says. "Man, I sure took the long way home, didn't I?"

I know that he's apologizing for everything that's come before.

"But you got here in the end." I kiss his cheeks. "That's all that matters. You made it home, and we're in this together for the long haul."

He grabs me close and hugs me with all his might. If he says something, I don't hear it. We're both too busy crying, while outside, the beautiful rain continues to fall.

ACKNOWLEDGEMENTS

Grateful thanks to my wonderful publisher, Inanna Publications, for always having faith in my books. To Brenda Cranney, Ashley Rayner, Renée Knapp, and everyone in my Inanna family. I can never thank you enough.

To Luciana Ricciutelli, our fearless warrior, sister and friend. You are missed daily.

Recently the writing community lost another dear friend, Mayank Bhatt. A talented writer and strong supporter of the arts, Mayank is missed by us all.

Many thanks to my lovely Bradford Dunlop—your patience knows no bounds. To my family, particularly my niece and nephew, Tully and Grayson Sloot. I hope your lives end up being better than anything we could dream or imagine!

Many thanks to Jen Hale for wonderful substantive editing and to Jane Kirby for detailed and careful copy editing.

Huge thanks to early readers for all your support: Wendy Barrows, Lynn Crosbie, Rich Ehisen, Darcia Helle, Ionna Kormouli, Mark Sampson, Daniel Scott Tysdal, Terri Favro, Shirley McDaniel, and Melissa Yi.

Thanks to the Crime Writers of Canada and the Mesdames of Mayhem and everyone in the writing community, in real life and online. Without your friendship and support, this would be impossible.

And, most importantly of all, to you, Dear Reader, I truly hope you enjoyed the book!

Credit: Bradford Dunlop

Lisa de Nikolits has been hailed as "the Queen of Canadian speculative fiction" (All Lit Up) and is the international award-winning author of eleven novels. Her short fiction and poetry have been published in various international anthologies and journals.

Lisa has appeared on recommended reading lists for both Open Book Toronto and the 49th Shelf, as well as being chosen as a *Chatelaine* Editor's Pick and a *Canadian Living* Must Read. Her novel *The Occult Persuasion and the Anarchist's Solution* was longlisted for a Sunburst Award for Excellence in Canadian Literature of the Fantastic. Her most recent book, *The Rage Room*, was a finalist in the International Book Awards.

She has lived in Canada since 2000. She has a Bachelor of Arts in English Literature and Philosophy and has lived in the U.S.A., Australia, and Britain.